RAVEN REBEL

ALY HOLLIS

Edited by Ilea Pavel, Karina Simler-Graham, and Anandi de Jong, and proofread by Kathy Huizingh.

Map designed in Inkarnate and painted by Aly Hollis.
Cover artwork by Hannah Sternjakob @hannahsternjakob.
Alternative paperback cover by Bronwynn Gooch @bgooch.art.
Character guide artwork by Bamboo @Bamboo_.
Landscape artwork by Olesia Bazuhla @suselok.
Chapter headers by Art by Tori @_arttori.
Illustrated faerie guide by Yuma Yukino @yuki_ono.
Additional character artwork by Aly Hollis.
Backgrounds are classic paintings by Victor Westerholm, Albert Bierstadt, Alexander Helwig Wyant, Frederic Edwin Church, Jacob van Ruisdael, and William Trost Richards.

First Edition
Paperback ISBN: 978-1-966611-06-6
Deluxe Paperback ISBN: 978-1-966611-07-3
Hardcover ISBN: 978-1-966611-05-9

Come away, O, human child!
To the woods and waters wild,
With a faerie hand in hand,
For the world's more full of weeping
than you can understand.

—W.B. Yeats

A GUIDE TO THE FAE COURTS AND THE HUMAN KINGDOMS

Queendom of Liosliath
Brenna
Nursemaid
Meara
Herbalist

Court of Autumn Harvest
Ayala
Spymaster
Seda
Captain
Tayen
Ambassador
Cerne
Autumn Lord

Kingdom of Dornadan
Rydan
Prince
Emeric
Crown Prince
Eladin
Prince

Court of Summer Light

Luce
Heir

High Court Tara
Emrys
Advisor

When the Vernal Heirs come of age,
one shall wield the light, the other the darkness,
the land will quake with the marching of armies,
one led by the just, one by the damned.
The fate of all rests upon their shoulders,
For they will determine the destiny of the Otherworld.

Prophecy of Seren, Oracle of The Court of Snow and Shadow
To Lord Daryan and Lady Lakiya of The Court of Spring Renewal
Upon the birth of their twin daughters

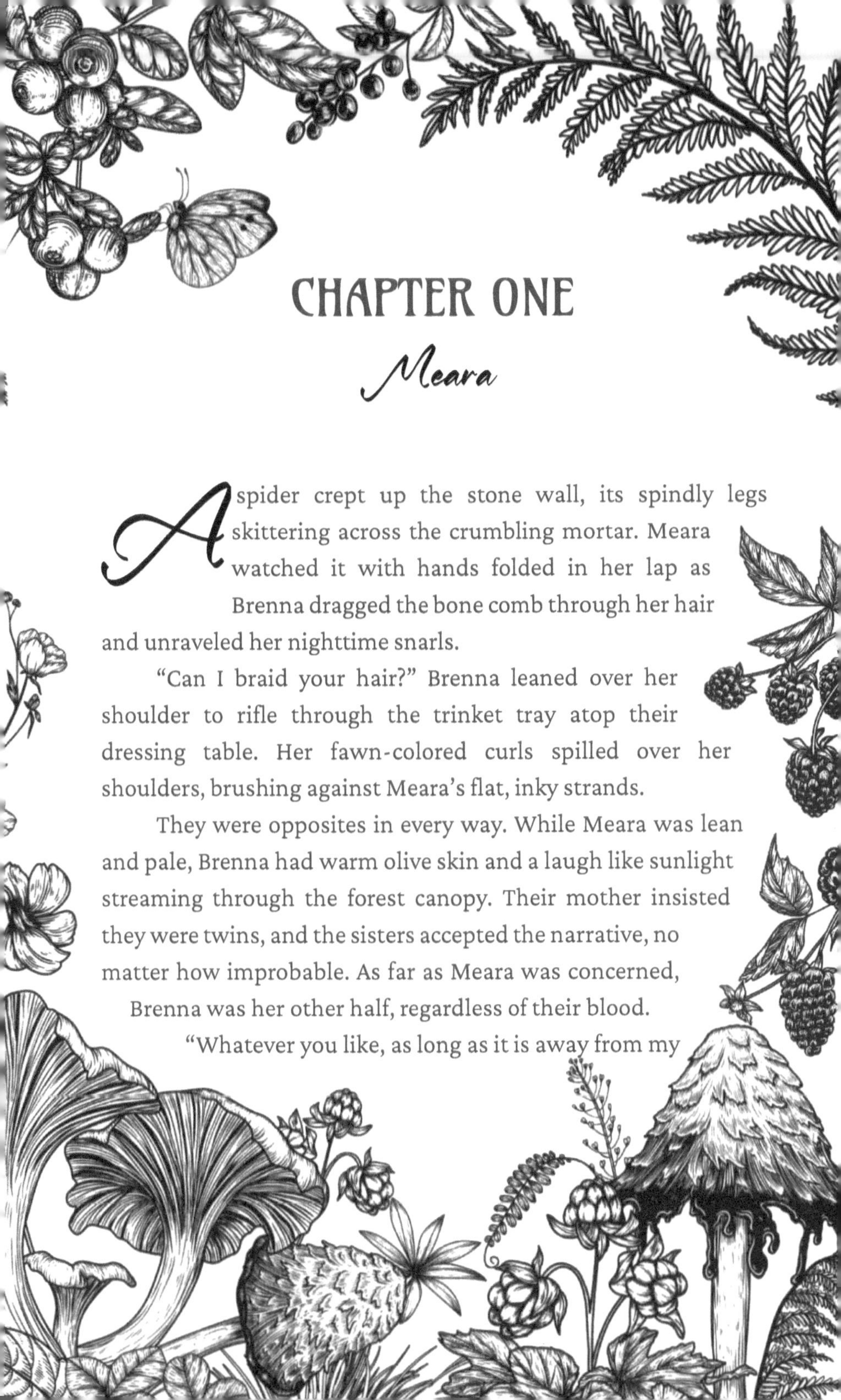

CHAPTER ONE
Meara

Aspider crept up the stone wall, its spindly legs skittering across the crumbling mortar. Meara watched it with hands folded in her lap as Brenna dragged the bone comb through her hair and unraveled her nighttime snarls.

"Can I braid your hair?" Brenna leaned over her shoulder to rifle through the trinket tray atop their dressing table. Her fawn-colored curls spilled over her shoulders, brushing against Meara's flat, inky strands.

They were opposites in every way. While Meara was lean and pale, Brenna had warm olive skin and a laugh like sunlight streaming through the forest canopy. Their mother insisted they were twins, and the sisters accepted the narrative, no matter how improbable. As far as Meara was concerned, Brenna was her other half, regardless of their blood.

"Whatever you like, as long as it is away from my

face. A pretty hairstyle isn't worth falling from a tree."

With a flourish, Brenna drew out a woad-dyed ribbon the color of the blackberry brambles clawing their way up the cottage's exterior walls. Her tongue pressed against her full top lip as her fingers threaded into Meara's hair to tease apart sections to braid. Meara's eyes drifted closed at the pleasant tug. Brenna adored playing with her hair and she loved indulging her.

"I think that will do." Stepping back, she propped her hands on her hips.

"Thank you." Meara ran calloused fingers over the tidy plaits encircling her head. "Lovely."

The sisters traded places, the floorboards creaking under their feet. Meara deftly gathered up her sister's wild hair and twisted it into the proper bun expected of a nursemaid.

They fell into a familiar routine with movements as precise and practiced as a dance. Meara fastened the buttons of Brenna's petticoats over her linen chemise and hand-me-down stays. Brenna slipped into a chaste cotton gown while Meara tugged on her worn woolen dress that always smelled faintly of loam and pine resin even after laundering.

Brenna knotted the ties of Meara's apron, the deep pockets discolored with the blood of herbs and wild berries, before securing her own ruffled apron with a looping bow. Meara was ready with pins to secure Brenna's dainty white cap.

"How do I look?" Framing her face with her hands, Brenna fluttered her lashes.

"Pretty as a daffodil."

A beaming Brenna tucked a pair of thick goatskin gloves into her sister's apron. "Make sure to use these! We don't need you coming home with stained fingers."

Meara scowled. "It was one time."

"One unforgettable time," Brenna said ruefully. "Your fingers were stained black as midnight from those walnuts you love so much, and it took Mum three days to realize you were hiding your hands."

"The neighbors called me Walnut Witch for months," Meara grumbled as she reached for her boots.

"You had plenty of creative nicknames for them as well, as I recall." Brenna clicked her tongue as she rolled her stockings up her calves.

Damp morning light cast a pallid glow over their garden as the sisters stepped out of their cottage. The autumn weather brought dreary clouds and colder mornings, but it would be weeks until frost threatened the rows of vegetables radiating out from their home.

"Looking forward to your day?" Meara asked as Brenna bounced between rows of carrots and beetroot.

"It is the end of the week so I will receive my first salary." Her hands clasped over her skirts as she turned, the sunlight illuminating her irises into glowing amber. Seeing Meara's hesitation, Brenna continued, "The children are sweet, and the pay is excellent. I'm lucky to have received the position."

Even the additional income and her sister's reassurances couldn't stop the prickling dread Meara felt when she thought of Brenna's employer, the esteemed Mr. Lyndhurst. She had no evidence, merely her intuition, but the nobleman made her nervous.

Forcing an appeasing smile, Meara followed her across the yard. The straw mulch rustled under the swaying leeks, causing the sisters to pause.

Brenna crouched and held the alliums aside to reveal a teeny hedgehog blinking up at them with shiny ink drop eyes. "Good morning, my little urchin," she cooed. "Did you have a nice night eating all the beetles?" The beastie wiggled its pointed nose at them before burrowing deeper into the straw.

Brushing off her hands, Brenna rose with a furrow in her brow. "Do you think you could bring back a treat for him?"

Meara scrunched her nose. "I'm not sure what hedgies like to eat aside from slugs and caterpillars."

"I won't ask you to gather those," Brenna replied with a laugh that lightened the dreary morning.

"Is there anything you would like?" The gate's hinges groaned as Meara pushed it open. Brenna scurried through before it swung shut.

"I would love wild strawberries."

"I'll do my best, but they're out of season. Blueberries are more likely."

"Those would be nice too."

Meara shoved her hands into her pockets, fiddling with the dried remnants of figwort leaves. "How about some hazelnuts?"

"Yes, please."

They passed the neighbor's elderly milk cows and a potato field freshly harvested. Meara's stomach knotted as they approached the road that stretched through the center of their borough.

The sisters paused at the edge of the lane. The morning's chill subdued the stink of manure and piss, but it would be unbearable by the afternoon.

"Have a nice day," Brenna said brightly, a wisp of her hair catching the light as she turned.

Meara wavered, her soft gray eyes studying her sister. "Please be careful."

"I should be saying that to you." Her plump lips pressed together in chagrin. "You're the one out in the wilderness." With an elegant arch to her eyebrow, Brenna took her sister's hand and traced the ragged scar that ran down her index finger and across her wrist.

"Please, I have a bad feeling," Meara said in a quiet plea.

Brenna sighed dramatically as she pressed her hand to her generous chest. "I am always cautious. All will be well." She winked before spinning on her heel and setting off.

Meara watched her sister's careful steps along the edge of the muddy carriage tracks. Her breathing was tight as anxiety clawed at her ribs. She trusted Brenna, but many would prey on her sister's kind heart if given the chance.

Shoving her worries back into the tidy bundle she kept buried in her chest, Meara turned the other way toward her mother's shop. Her path passed the bakery and the scent of roasting flour filled the air. Two girls gossiped through the open door as one washed the display window and the other arranged tidy rows of barley loaves and wheaten bread.

A theatrical cough had Meara rolling her eyes and slowing. "Good morning, Luella." When the woman's sister leaned out the door and waved, Meara added, "And Orla."

"Meara, what brings you to town?" Luella's smile was like holly berries, a beautiful and toxic crimson.

"I'm going to our apothecary, like I do most days." She kept her voice level and light.

Luella raised a hand to her mouth in faux surprise. "I didn't realize you were still working there. I thought you had become a wild thing and ran off into the woods to be with those nasty faeries. Your temperament suits them, after all."

Orla's giggles wafted out the door, souring Meara's mood further.

"What an appealing thought," she said dryly, snapping her fingers dramatically. "Oh, please mention to your mother, we restocked the balm she likes for her swollen joints. You should visit the shop too." She drew her pointed finger in a circle toward

Luella's sneering face. "We might have something to help the unfortunate situation of your face."

Luella let out a squawk like an angry goose. Gathering up her skirts, she marched to Meara and pushed into her personal space. Her voice was low and nasally. "If you ever hope to catch a husband for you or your sister, you should start respecting your betters. Men don't like girls with smart mouths."

"No, thank you. I wouldn't want to marry someone like Sandon or his greasy friends." Meara's lip curled, revealing canine teeth slightly too long, much like most of her body - a little too angular and thin. She couldn't help her disdainful reaction, but the thought of damaging her sister's prospects was ice sliding through her veins. She may have no interest in a husband, but Brenna was a romantic.

Smoothing her features, she stepped away from Luella. "This was such a nice visit, ladies. I hope you have a day worthy of your character." Stubbornness kept her head high as she stalked toward the apothecary. She wouldn't reveal how hard her pulse beat or how sick the exchange made her.

The familiar arched door with flaking green paint felt like a sanctuary. She stepped in, breathing in the poignant smell of medicinal herbs like chamomile and lavender, layered over softer scents like beeswax and myrtle oil.

Her mother balanced on a step stool in the workroom, reaching for the jars holding their infrequently used ingredients on the highest shelves. Meara rushed forward and stepped on the stool beside her, snatching the jar of dried nettles her mother couldn't quite reach and presenting it to her.

"Thank you, love," her mother said. Laugh lines marred her tanned face, framed with wavy hair the color of cinnamon. Brenna inherited her cheery nature from their mother, while Meara gained her affinity for plants. If only she was decent at speaking with patients and devising their treatments, she could take over the apothecary like her mother had from their grandfather. Unfortunately, Meara was useless at the duties involving people. She was far more comfortable roaming the forest, foraging for the coveted botanicals that gave their shop's tinctures and balms their potency.

Her mother set the jar aside and crossed to the counter where a pencil rested atop a scrap of paper. She added one more item to the list before handing it to Meara. "I am hoping you can find some elderflowers before the frost kills them off."

"I'll do my best," Meara promised. She stooped slightly to allow her mother to press a kiss to her forehead. "Have a good morning, Mum."

With the list tucked safely in her apron pocket, Meara slipped out the back door, heading toward the shadowy edges of Sablewood that felt like home.

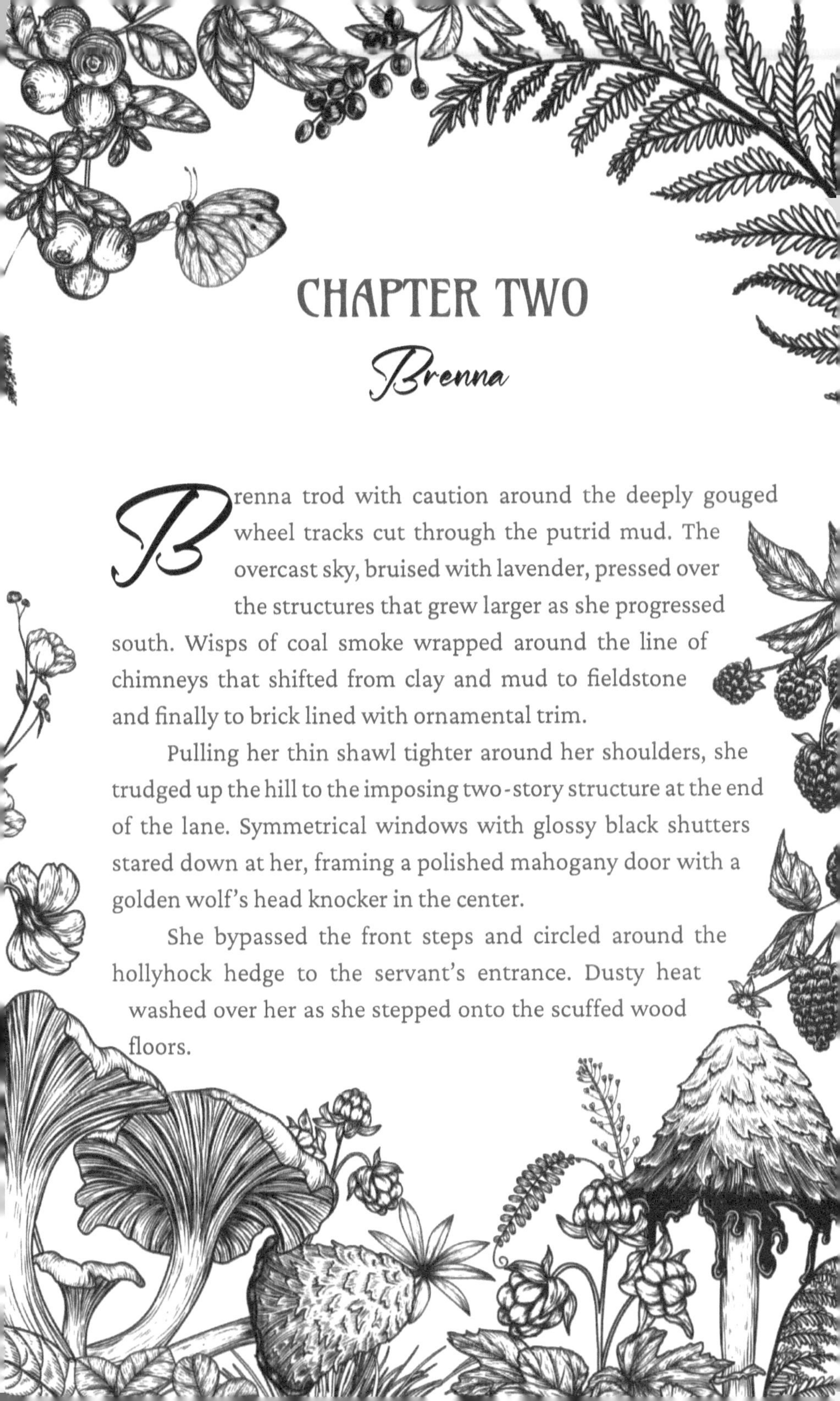

CHAPTER TWO
Brenna

Brenna trod with caution around the deeply gouged wheel tracks cut through the putrid mud. The overcast sky, bruised with lavender, pressed over the structures that grew larger as she progressed south. Wisps of coal smoke wrapped around the line of chimneys that shifted from clay and mud to fieldstone and finally to brick lined with ornamental trim.

Pulling her thin shawl tighter around her shoulders, she trudged up the hill to the imposing two-story structure at the end of the lane. Symmetrical windows with glossy black shutters stared down at her, framing a polished mahogany door with a golden wolf's head knocker in the center.

She bypassed the front steps and circled around the hollyhock hedge to the servant's entrance. Dusty heat washed over her as she stepped onto the scuffed wood floors.

"Brenna," a worn-out voice greeted her. The graying housekeeper eyed her from the kitchen, her mouth pinched into a displeased line. "Come in. I have the children's breakfast ready."

Scones surrounded petite pots of jam and cream on a platter, awaiting her. As she reached for it, the old woman grabbed her arm. Her rough fingers scraped the delicate skin of her wrist. "Master Lyndhurst is in a foul mood today, so make sure the children do not disturb him."

"Yes, Mrs. Fisher. Thank you." Brenna's curtsy was stilted, the housekeeper's grip restrictive and her face stern. Finally, she released her and watched suspiciously as Brenna carefully lifted the dish and walked to the family's dining room.

Brenna's shoulders relaxed as she stepped into the bright space. Thick, wavy glass filled the windows, diluting the morning light that fell across purple, fluted blooms of wolfsbane drooping in a crystal vase at the center of the heavy table. A sleepy girl slumped in a high-backed chair, her rosy cheek pressed against the damask tablecloth. Her brother sat straight as a sapling beside her, a book laid open on the table before him. From the floor, their younger brother whinnied and waved his stuffed horse in the air.

"Good morning, my loves." She brushed the girl's tousled hair off her forehead. Lottie sat up when she noticed the pastries, already reaching for them.

The platter clinked as Brenna set it down and began slicing the scones in half. She set one on a plate and slid it beside Herman's book. "Hermie, what are you reading there?"

The boy scrunched his face, torn between the desire to share about his book and wanting to be obtuse. His excitement won out. "It's about history! About the par-par-parli-mans where Uncle works, and how the queen makes the rules."

"How grown up," Brenna said, enjoying the proud smile on Herman's face as she slathered jam and cream onto Lottie's scone.

"It sounds awfully boring to me!" Lottie chimed in, doing her best to take small lady-like bites, though more of her pastry crumbled to the table than made it into her mouth.

The youngest, Clarence, scrambled into his chair beside his sister. Without hesitation, he shoved his breakfast into his mouth, leaving a glob of red jam on the edge of his lips.

Napkin in hand, Breanna reached for the youngest Lyndhurst child. The moment the linen touched his face, he jerked away, smearing the jam so it looked like a streak of blood across his cheek.

"Clarence, you're an absolute mess now. It's time to wash up." He whined and pushed back from the table to escape her, but she was faster, gathering up the squirming boy and carrying him to the washroom to rinse his hands and face.

When they returned, Lottie announced, "I dreamed about bunnies in the forest."

Brenna sank down beside her, dressing a scone for herself. "Really, what happened?"

Crumbs sprung from her lips as Lottie continued, "The bunnies were having races. And I got to give flowers to the winner and then they ate them!"

"That sounds lovely," Brenna murmured, scraping the excess jam off the remainder of Clarence's scone to prevent a second mess. "So the bunnies ate the flowers?"

Lottie laughed. "No, the foxes ate the bunnies."

"Oh, of course. You know, girl bunnies are called does." The two older children weren't listening but had started arguing about which forest creatures they could beat in a race.

Brenna rolled her eyes and took a bite of her scone. The buttery pastry melted in her mouth, the warm tang of rhubarb and ginger jam cutting through the richness.

After breakfast was tidied, the children curled up around Brenna as she read from their newest storybook. A brave prince battled vicious faeries to rescue a fair princess. Despite Brenna's animated storytelling, soon they grew restless. Remembering Mrs. Fisher's warning, she herded the children outside.

They ran through the garden with joyful shrieks and squeals. Brenna perched on a garden chair, letting the sunlight caress her skin and warm her from the inside out. She wished they could stay outside all day, but eventually Herman and Lottie began to quarrel, and the housekeeper called them in for a luncheon.

After a cold meal of cheese sandwiches and sugared pears, they retired to their nursery. Herman settled by the window with his book in his lap while Brenna knelt between the younger children's low beds. She traced circles on their backs with the tips of her fingernails. Clarence was asleep within seconds, his lashes thick on his chubby cheeks.

Lottie rolled over, sniffling dramatically. "Miss Brenna, Hermie said since I was bad, the faeries are going to take me away."

"Sweetheart, nothing like that will happen." She wiped away the girl's tears and smoothed her hair. "The fae don't take humans. They have their own girls and boys. And Queen Malacia protects us, remember? So any time you feel afraid…"

Lottie let out a snuffly snore, stopping Brenna's speech. She wanted to tell her that most faeries were normal folk, albeit with a few inhuman features and according to some, the ability to wield magic. The traveling merchants that supplied her mother's shop often spoke of the fae, some good and some bad.

But if Lottie repeated any of that, her father would dismiss Brenna. It was inadvisable to speak of faeries as anything but monsters in Liosliath. Sighing, she straightened her apron. With one last glance at Herman, who resolutely ignored her and turned a page in his book, she headed to the door. It was best that she clean up while the children rested.

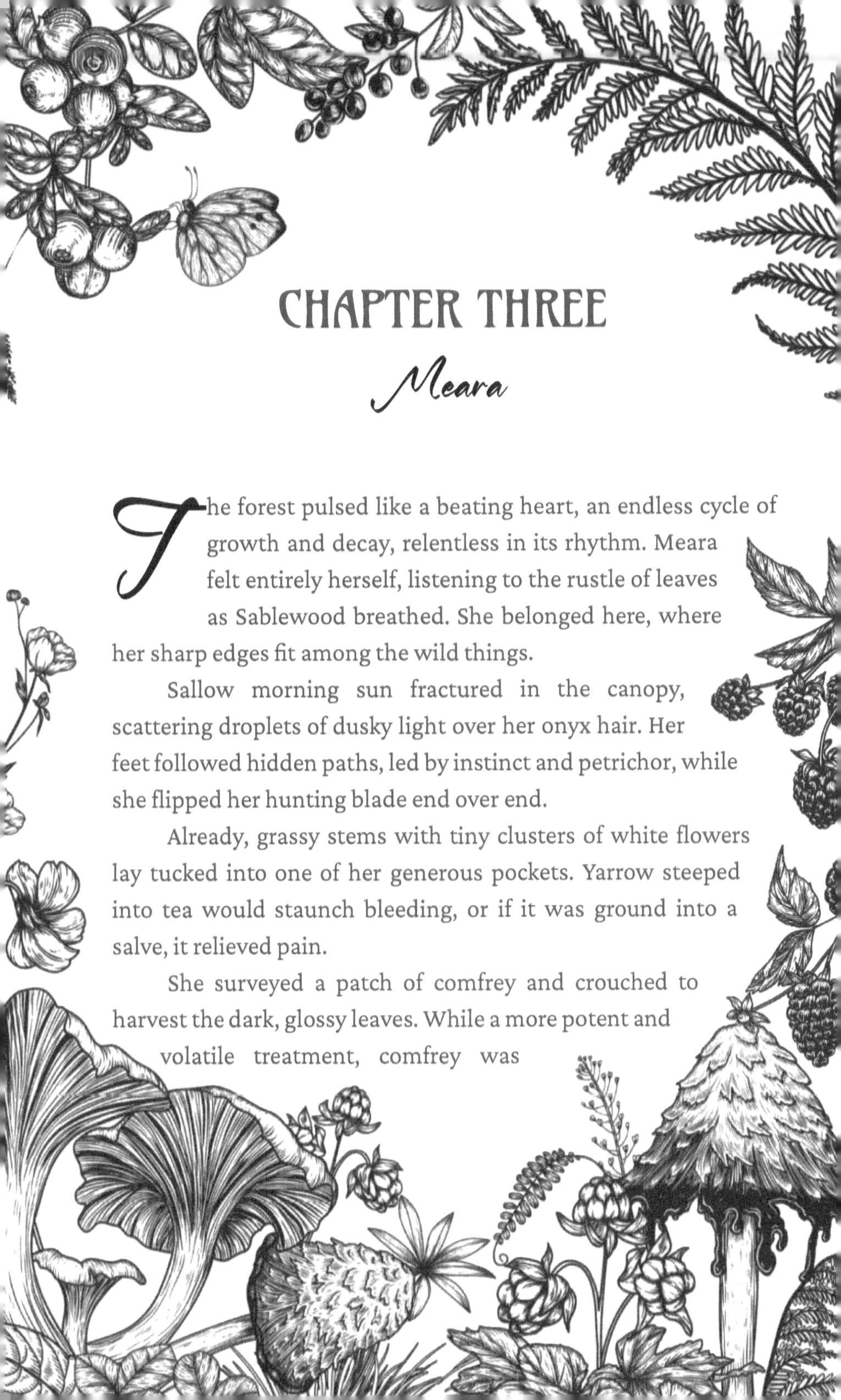

CHAPTER THREE
Meara

The forest pulsed like a beating heart, an endless cycle of growth and decay, relentless in its rhythm. Meara felt entirely herself, listening to the rustle of leaves as Sablewood breathed. She belonged here, where her sharp edges fit among the wild things.

Sallow morning sun fractured in the canopy, scattering droplets of dusky light over her onyx hair. Her feet followed hidden paths, led by instinct and petrichor, while she flipped her hunting blade end over end.

Already, grassy stems with tiny clusters of white flowers lay tucked into one of her generous pockets. Yarrow steeped into tea would staunch bleeding, or if it was ground into a salve, it relieved pain.

She surveyed a patch of comfrey and crouched to harvest the dark, glossy leaves. While a more potent and volatile treatment, comfrey was invaluable for easing the gout crippling local farmers. After years of practice, she knew exactly how to hold the stems and slice while keeping her hands free of the harsh sap. Her fingers stacked, rolled, and bundled the leaves in a ritual that needed no thought. Their bittersweet scent perfumed the air as she rose.

Hedge sparrows flitted overhead, their discordant melodies floating over the thick underbrush. Once Meara was satisfied with her haul of medicinal herbs, she looked to the sun to gauge the passage of time before plunging deeper into the woods in search of chanterelles that would fetch a good profit.

The fog of morning lingered in the shadowy depths of the forest. It swirled around her feet and coated her skin with dew. The path narrowed and gnarled roots snagged at her skirts as she walked. Ignoring the claws of the underbrush, she hunted for the ferns that curtained deteriorating fallen tree trunks. The logs' decay created the perfect conditions for the curly golden mushrooms. They glowed in the murky dim. Her long fingers pinched off bunches at the spongy stems, careful to avoid crushing the delicate caps.

Brushing off her hands, Meara rose and stretched her neck and shoulders to relieve the tension. She should turn back toward the wild orchard of hazel and walnut trees that edged the forest, but her sister's request for strawberries drew her further into Sablewood.

She moved cautiously northward, her heartbeat a moth fluttering against her ribs. The edge of their queendom lay ahead, where Liosliath met with the kingdom of Dornadan - a people who traded freely with and even welcomed faeries into their townships.

The forest reluctantly released her into a meadow, the stillness a void that unsettled her after the trees' tangled embrace. It was carpeted with alabaster wood anemones and curved foxglove swaying in a silent symphony of amethyst bells. She crouched and swept back the greenery to reveal low-growing wild strawberries. A few ruby berries clung to the stems, but they made up a meager handful.

Hawthorn berries glinted along their thorny cane in the border between sun and shade. Maybe Brenna could make a mixed berry pie with them and some of the blackberries ripening in their garden. With her sister's warning echoing in her mind, she slid her gloves on before she set about harvesting the tiny red fruit.

A gleam of burnished bronze caught her eye. A looming stag materialized from the shadows, gliding through the trees with eerie grace.

Her breath caught and every muscle tensed in a primal wariness. White ghosted the creature's snout, fading to a rich coppery brown crowned in dozens of gilded tines. Intelligent, soulful eyes met hers. Entranced, her body moved on instinct, but the hawthorn vine caught her wrist, slicing into her skin just above her glove. With a gasp, she pulled back and glanced down at the jagged line welling with blood. When her eyes rose, the stag was gone.

The ache of disappointment stung worse than her injury. Hissing, she pressed the corner of her apron over the cut until the bleeding stopped. Meara stared into the shadows for a moment more before slowly exhaling and straightening. Her fingers flexed inside of her gloves, hands aching for something ineffable. A wildness seethed under her skin as if the forest had slipped into her veins.

The brittle silence shattered as chittering squirrels raced through the boughs overhead. With a set to her jaw, she turned southeast toward home.

The forest thinned and the air warmed, afternoon sunlight tinting the waving hairgrass a vivid chartreuse.

The copse of young hazel trees in the edge of the forest's shadow drooped with low branches, inviting her to climb. Their pantry supply had grown thin, so Meara reached for a low branch and heaved herself up and onto the bough. Anchoring herself, she gave the thinner branches a vigorous shake. Ripe hazelnuts shed from the branches and tumbled to the ground, landing among the empty hulls strewn about.

Her gathered skirts fell around her ankles as she landed heavily, her breath escaping with the impact. Stooping, she gathered hazelnuts when something moved through the leaf litter toward her. She jolted, leaping back and dropping the nuts in her hands. A rat scurried over a root and past her. Exhaling in a huff, Meara resumed gathering hazelnuts.

The afternoon matured and her stomach rumbled, leaving a hollow feeling in her gut. Pockets bulging with her harvest, she trudged back down the path away from the woods and into the rural village. Her mother always kept food for her in their shop, and having two sets of hands would make sorting and cleaning the ingredients go quickly.

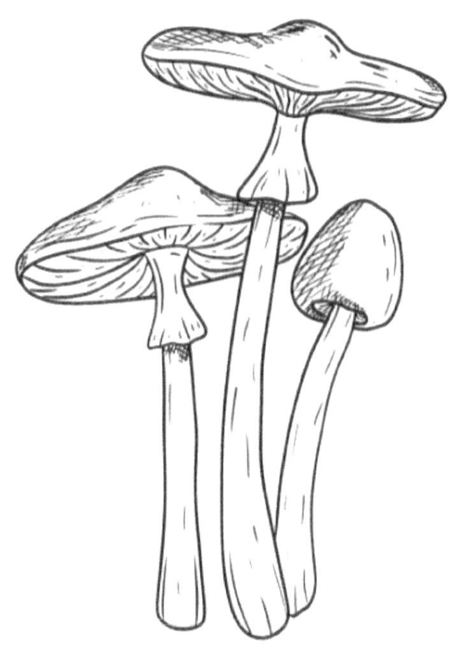

CHAPTER FOUR

Brenna

In the sitting room, a maid polished the florid mantle. Her petite hands shook as she ran a rag over the spring-powered clock. The house grew stuffy with afternoon heat, and Mrs. Fisher did not allow the windows to be opened until sundown when Brenna would be leaving for the day.

Brenna gathered the children's belongings and straightened the decorative pillows perched on the settee, glancing at the girl but too nervous to ask her name.

Heavy footfalls thudded on the landing above. The maid stiffened, her eyes going wide. Mr. Lyndhurst must have been pacing in his office. Brenna let out her breath audibly, aiming to soothe herself and the skittish maid.

As if her thoughts summoned him, Mr. Johnathon Lyndhurst descended the grand staircase, his heeled boots clicking on the stone steps. He looked smart in his tailored day suit, but his face was sour as if the entire world had failed his precise standards.

"Miss Aldridge, please join me in my office."

"Yes, sir," she answered. His chin jerked and he turned to ascend the steps without looking back at her. She couldn't help the way her stomach churned, though she knew it was most likely a discussion of her first week in his employ or perhaps details around her salary. She shouldn't be afraid of her employer, and she had no real reason to be aside from unsubstantiated rumors. He had never been one of the men leering at her in the market.

Regardless, she wished Mrs. Fisher was in the home instead of out shopping. The maid wouldn't meet her eyes as she passed, and Brenna felt utterly isolated. The only noise was the ticking clock and her tentative footsteps as she climbed the stairs, her heartbeat pulsing in her throat.

A burgundy carpet ran the center of the narrow hallway, warming the upstairs. Flickering gas lamps cast an orange glow over the paneling. The singular open door beckoned her forward and she dutifully went through.

Oak paneling was replaced by dark stained wood lit only by a brass lamp on an overbearing glass-topped desk. Heavy drapes smothered any natural light that might have illuminated the oppressive space.

Lyndhurst leaned against his desk, ankles crossed and weak blue eyes appraising her. Documents splayed across the surface behind him, but his focus was solely on her.

Clasping her hands behind her, Brenna dipped into a whisper of a curtsy. Words lodged in her throat, the fear of offending him strangling her. Safer to let him speak first. As if relishing his authority, he let the suffocating silence stretch. Slowly, her eyes traveled from the carpet to his face. A serpentine smile twisted his thin mouth.

"I've appreciated how efficiently you've managed your duties. It's rare to find a woman as dedicated as you." Her stomach flipped again, hope that he was pleased mingling with her unease.

"Thank you, Mr. Lyndhurst." Her voice was small.

"Remind me what you were doing before my employment," he commanded. His fingers tugged at his cuffs, rolling them back.

"Washing and mending, sir. For Miss Hughes' laundry house."

"You are much better suited for my household, don't you agree?"

There was a tightness to his mouth and a narrowness to his eyes that she could not read. Her voice wavered. "I appreciate the opportunity. Your children are lovely."

"Of course." He pushed off the desk and stepped forward, closing the gap between them. She tensed, instincts urging her to get out of the dim room, but she simply adjusted her shawl over her arms and stood her ground with a forced, docile smile. Making an irrational dash for the hall would only lose her employment.

"You see, I feel that I am responsible for the wellbeing of all my staff," he continued, "and I take that seriously."

"You are a generous employer."

His height was apparent as he leaned over her, smelling of stale tobacco and bitter juniper liquor. "You've had a difficult path, haven't you? Growing up without a father and your mother running a business on her own."

She bristled at his condescension, but averted her eyes. "No more so than many people in our community," she deflected.

"I'd like to do more for you."

Shattering any sense of propriety, he reached up and twined an escaped curl around his finger.

She should have stepped back, apologized, and redirected

him, but she was frozen in place like prey before a hunter. Chest constricted and stomach roiling, she could barely pull air into her lungs.

If her sister was here, Meara would verbally cut him down and rescue her, but she was alone.

Her voice scraped as she said, "Sir, I'm not sure your meaning."

His reaction was immediate, his voice lowering into a casual threat. "It would be a shame if I was forced to dismiss you from my household." His free hand moved to her shoulder, skimming over the fabric of her dress. "But that won't be necessary, will it? We understand each other, I believe. I enjoy being generous, as you said."

Repulsion rose in her throat. How could she have let this happen? She recalled nothing in her actions that could be considered provocative. This conversation was the longest they had ever spoken. She struggled to keep her frenzied thoughts from dissolving into panic. There had to be a way out of this situation without losing her position or her reputation. Another appointment would be impossible if she lasted a mere six days in this household.

Her feet edged backward as she took a shallow breath. "Sir, are there shortcomings in my work that would lead to a dismissal? I'm confident I can fulfill whatever tasks *pertaining to your children* that are required."

Another cold smile spread across his face. "I'm confident you could fulfill whatever duties I set for you." He stepped closer, herding her away from the door.

Her shoulders rounded, just shy of cowering as her vision tunneled. She couldn't get enough air. Prickles of pain ran up and down her arms, as if blood was returning to muscles formerly numb and cut off.

Undeterred, Lyndhurst's hand trailed down over the sleeve of her dress to touch the bare sliver of skin above her shawl. "You're so beautiful, despite your complexion." His fingers encircled her upper arm possessively.

The pain of his tightening grip shocked her, sparking a flame that burned away the foggy panic, leaving something akin to vengeful rage for all the times she was considered a pretty commodity.

With a strangled shout, he released his hold. The acrid scent of burning flesh filled the air. She stumbled backward into the door frame and a jolt of pain lanced through her hip.

Light sparked off her skin, across her palms and running up her arms in streaks of lightning. There was no time for the shock of watching power rushing over her skin.

"Witch!" Lyndhurst choked out, cradling a hand with jagged burns like blackened tree roots feathering out from his charred palm. "Faerie demon!"

Reeling, Brenna tumbled into the hall. Sparks fell from her fingers to the carpet. She clenched her hands into fists, attempting to stop the burning magic and protect the sleeping children.

Lyndhurst slumped across his desk, his unmarred hand wrenching open a drawer. He withdrew a knife, one used to open correspondence, but sharp enough to cut her all the same. His arm flailed, the blade slicing through the air as he lumbered toward her. Brenna shoved off the wall, sending herself hurtling down the hallway. She took the stairs as fast as she dared while her employer grunted behind her like an aggressive hog.

The young maid gawked, her cleaning rag dropping from her hand to plop onto the rug. Brenna darted past and seized the ornate handle of the front door. For a terrifying moment, it did not budge, but then the hinges twisted and ground together with a metallic groan as she dragged it open wide enough to slip through and escape. As her hand released the knob, the metal glowed orange.

She had mere seconds until Lyndhurst resumed his pursuit. He may have been hesitant to touch her again, but she knew that he would gladly stab her with his knife.

An inferno crackled in her veins. She lurched forward, running faster than ever before.

The door slammed behind her as enraged yelling echoed between stone buildings. Doors opened and neighbors peered out. She frantically searched their faces for sympathy, hoping someone would intervene on her behalf. Their expressions melted from confusion to fear as his shouts reached them. Men shoved past their wives, ready to answer the call to arms.

Brenna realized with sickening clarity that no one would help her. Not when a nobleman screamed, "Faerie magic," over and over. Her neighbors poured from open doors, joining Lyndhurst in his hunt.

Mud coated her ankles and the hem of her dress, squelching and sucking her boots down. Her lungs splintered, layering needling pain over the ache of her hip and the burn of her legs. She gasped, tasting blood in her throat as she pushed herself harder, rounding the bend in the road.

Passersby scrambled out of her way. Her pulse pounded in her ears, drowning out the yells of the growing mob. One more row of shops to her mother's apothecary. She had no thought past reaching the familiar door and barricading herself inside until her mother and sister could make this nightmare end.

Ahead, her mother's cinnamon hair caught the light as she leaned out of the shop's arched doorway. Brenna let out a breathless cry. She stepped back, allowing Brenna to throw herself inside before her mother slammed the door shut and slid the bolt into place.

Meara emerged from the workroom, drying her hands on a

rag. Her mother shook her head, expression drawn tight. "She was being chased!"

"What in the hell is happening, Brenna?" Meara braced her, gripping her shoulders. Sparks danced across her hands where they touched, but the strange magic did not burn her.

Brenna drew in a breath, struggling to find the words to explain. Angry fists pounded against the door, causing the bell to jingle. Voices filtered through the shutters: demands, accusations, threats. Brenna's lips parted, fear rising again as she searched her sister's face for reassurance. Meara narrowed her eyes and looked from their mother to the door, the hard line of her mouth promising violence to any who dared harm her family.

CHAPTER FIVE
Brenna

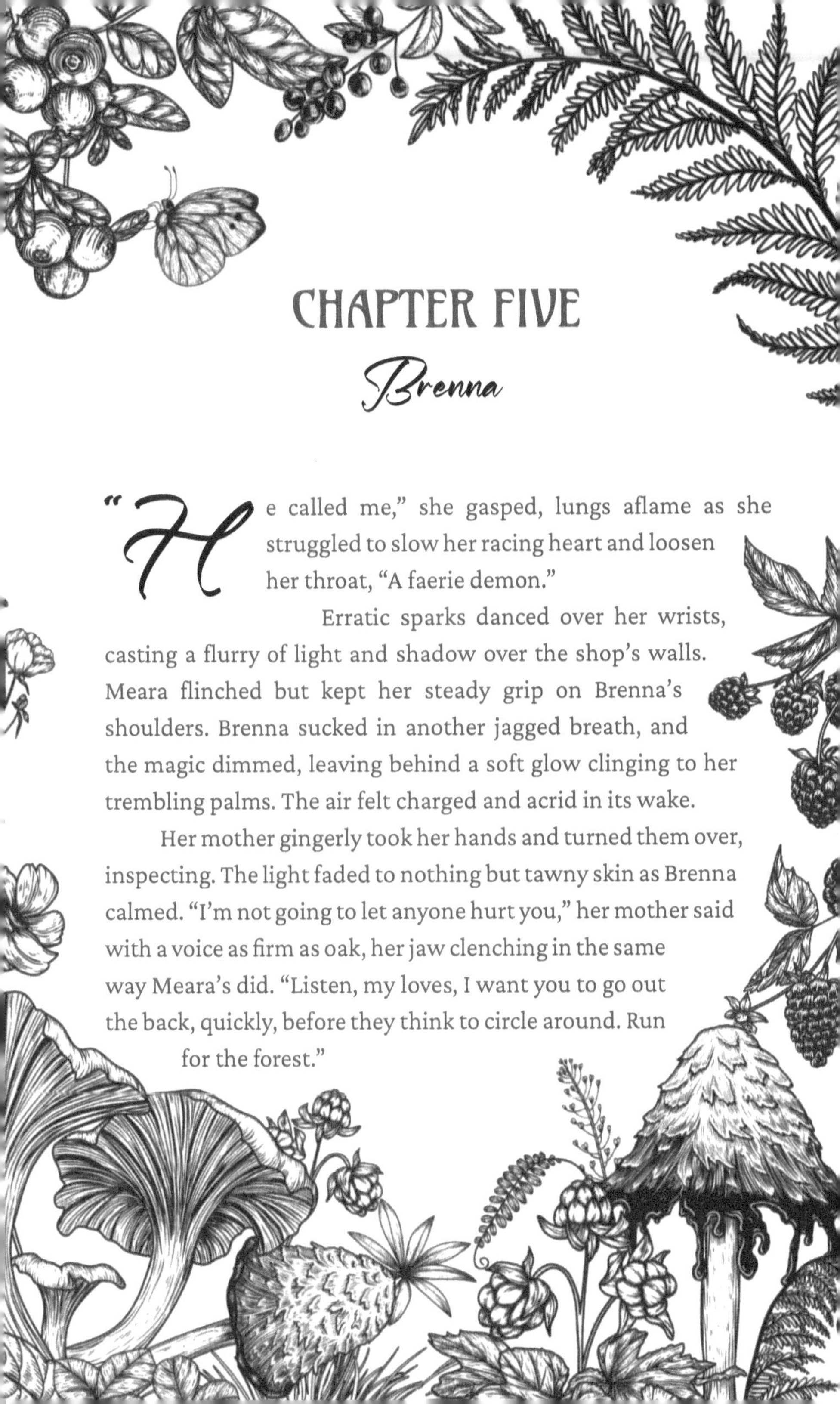

"He called me," she gasped, lungs aflame as she struggled to slow her racing heart and loosen her throat, "A faerie demon."

Erratic sparks danced over her wrists, casting a flurry of light and shadow over the shop's walls. Meara flinched but kept her steady grip on Brenna's shoulders. Brenna sucked in another jagged breath, and the magic dimmed, leaving behind a soft glow clinging to her trembling palms. The air felt charged and acrid in its wake.

Her mother gingerly took her hands and turned them over, inspecting. The light faded to nothing but tawny skin as Brenna calmed. "I'm not going to let anyone hurt you," her mother said with a voice as firm as oak, her jaw clenching in the same way Meara's did. "Listen, my loves, I want you to go out the back, quickly, before they think to circle around. Run for the forest."

"No!" Meara argued, her voice raw. "We can't leave you here alone to face them."

Their mother withdrew her monies purse from her skirts and pressed it into Meara's hand. "I want you to travel onward to Dornadan. There's an inn on the edge of the woods called The Silver Spectre. Any merchant or local should be able to send you in the right direction. It's well known and easy to find. I'll meet you there when it's safe, within a day or two."

"Mother," Brenna protested, wiping wetness from her eyes with the back of her hand.

"I'll be fine. Enough of these brutes rely on me for their health and comfort. If you are gone, their anger will cool quick enough without a target."

Meara nodded, her expression hardening. She tucked the pouch of silver chips into her skirt pocket and withdrew her hunting knife. The dim shop light reflected off the blade like the early morning's fog swallowing up sunrise.

Their mother cradled Meara's cheek for a moment and then placed a kiss on Brenna's damp forehead. "Meara, Brenna, be wise, stay together, and I'll see you soon."

Brenna wanted so badly to believe her. Meara tugged Brenna toward the back room, but she twisted to see their mother select a long chopping knife from their work table. Whispered prayers for her safety spilled from Brenna's trembling lips as the woman who raised her turned and resolutely faced the rattling door. She would never forgive herself if she was the cause of her mother's death.

The sisters slipped through the smaller back door, facing an alley where the backs of connected shops faced rows of narrow homes. Wildflowers and weeds tangled on the edges of the cobblestone walkways. Overhead, the shouts of angry villagers echoed over the rooftops like distant thunder.

Meara guided Brenna forward, the hold on her hand unyielding. Otherwise it would be shaking, and Brenna was grateful for the point of contact. She squinted in the daylight, her entire being feeling wrung out.

"There she is!" a grating voice rang out, the volume increasing as it neared. "I wonder what we'll get when we drag her before the constabulary."

Meara whirled, knife at a vicious angle, ready to strike. Her hold never wavered as she pulled Brenna behind her and faced the threat.

A squat young man with a patchy beard sneered at them as he slowed his jog and halted. His ruddy cheeks puffed as he regained his breath. Behind him, his gangly companion guffawed as if he couldn't believe their luck.

"Sandon, if you take one step closer, I'll gut you like a deer," Meara spat.

His sneer faltered and his face drained of color as his beady eyes took in her blade and her ready stance. There was nothing but violent determination in the set of Meara's jaw and the tension coiled in her lithe frame.

"I'll happily do so," she continued, her gaze flicking to the taller boy. "You know all about slicing an animal open, don't you, Kipp? You've seen how they bleed."

The butcher's son's pocked skin paled to ash. He raised his hands in a gesture of peace. Unfortunately, Sandon ignored his slightly-more-sensible friend. Stubby fingers withdrew a short knife from his belt as he lurched forward.

Meara stepped diagonally to meet him, holding her longer blade low in a lethal warning. Sandon faltered and stumbled back as survival instinct overrode his arrogance. She bared her teeth at him, her voice as dark as shadows. "Do not follow us or I will kill you."

The boys' courage wilted as they took a step back. Meara adjusted her grip on her blade, her knuckles white against the hilt, and tugged Brenna forward with her other hand. They darted through Miss Hughes' yard, where lines of laundry hung drying. Brenna wove through them carefully, afraid a stray spark of her magic might ignite the drying linens.

"They went that way!" Sandon's shrill voice echoed behind them.

Brenna sucked in a sharp breath and broke into a run. The cacophony of angry shouts crescendoed, and she could pick out Lyndhurst's furious commands as he drove them forward. Words like "Faerie" and "Magic" stood out from the din.

Meara was relentless, pulling her forward. They passed the sprawl of farmsteads, plunging into fields of damp grain. Ahead, the trees stood waiting, beckoning them into their shadowy sanctuary.

Once they reached Sablewood, they would be safe. Their neighbors would not dare to venture further than the tree line. The forest led to the enemy kingdom of Dornadan, the faerie-lovers.

Legend said the forest was brimming with fae like the Wild Hunt, though Brenna was fairly certain that was not the case. In her experience, it was full of nothing but flora and fauna. Brenna didn't crave the forest like her sister, but she did not fear it either.

The canopy closed in, wrapping them in a murky dim. Her steps faltered as the ground grew uneven, dipping into hollows and rising up into tangles of roots and rock. Brambles ripped at her skirts and caught her stockings.

"Careful." Meara gripped her wrist and steadied her.

Calves burning, Brenna stumbled to a stop. Shock and fear bled into a cold nausea. Bracing her hands on her knees, she bent double, gasping for air and trying to slow her breathing and quell the jagged pain in her lungs.

"I think we're safe for now," Meara said, pacing forward a few yards and then circling back, her arms wrapped around her waist. Ferns swayed as she passed, their fronds brushing her skirts. Her keen gray eyes locked on Brenna. "What exactly happened?"

She exhaled harshly. "I don't know. A curse, maybe?" The forest seemed to await her answer, even the buzz of insects and the trill of birdsong stilling. "It happened after I put the children down for a nap and Mr. Lyndhurst asked to speak to me." She hesitated, the memory vividly raw. "He grabbed my arm."

"He *what?*" Meara's posture stiffened and her voice dropped into a dangerous register. Brenna opened her mouth but no words formed. Her throat swelled, silencing her as hot tears dripped down her cheeks. Adrenaline spent, she was left with nothing but crude emotions. She swayed, and Meara lurched forward to catch her. Brenna sagged against her, letting her sister hold her upright.

Her whisper was scratchy and choked. "He said…" Her courage failed and shame heated her face. It sounded innocuous when repeated. "He wanted to help me, and he didn't want to dismiss me." Her words tangled together. "He said I was beautiful and he touched my hair and my arm."

Brenna rested her temple against Meara's shoulder and matched the tempo of her breathing until the icy shame subsided in her sister's stable presence.

"I wish you had turned him to ash," Meara whispered, low and fierce. Her anger was oppressive like storm clouds, but Brenna was safe in the eye of the hurricane. She breathed in Meara's scent of wild mallow and dandelions. Her sister smelled like home.

"I'm sorry. I'm afraid I've ruined our lives."

"Don't apologize. You do not bear any blame, and I'm proud you defended yourself. Mum will sort everything out." Meara's hand stroked over Brenna's tangle of curls that came loose during their escape. After a long moment, she spoke again. "I'd like to see that magic again if you can."

She didn't want to, but after everything Meara had done for her, Brenna couldn't refuse. With a slow exhale, Brenna sank to the forest floor, her sister settling beside her. Thick moss cradled her hip, the coolness easing the tender bruise from striking the door frame.

Closing her eyes, she laid her palms open on her knees, her breathing slowing as she sought out the feverish crackling energy within her. She could feel something, but it evaded her, slipping away like smoke. Her hands remained cold and empty. Frustrated, she stole a glance at her sister.

Meara wasn't watching her. She was half-risen, every muscle coiled as she stared over her shoulder. Brenna's breath hitched, her stomach dropping. She twisted, following Meara's line of sight.

A magnificent stag emerged from the underbrush with an uncanny, spectral grace. Dual crowning antlers branched into a dozen deadly tines that could gore a man with one swipe. Muscles shifted under a gleaming coat of burnished bronze as the beast drew closer. Intelligent, dark eyes seemed to pierce through her.

Brenna grabbed Meara's hand and she squeezed back, her lips parting as she whispered, "Don't move."

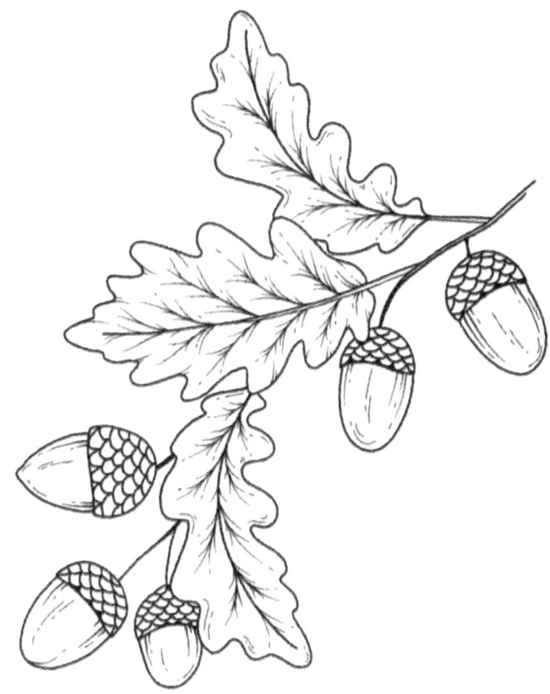

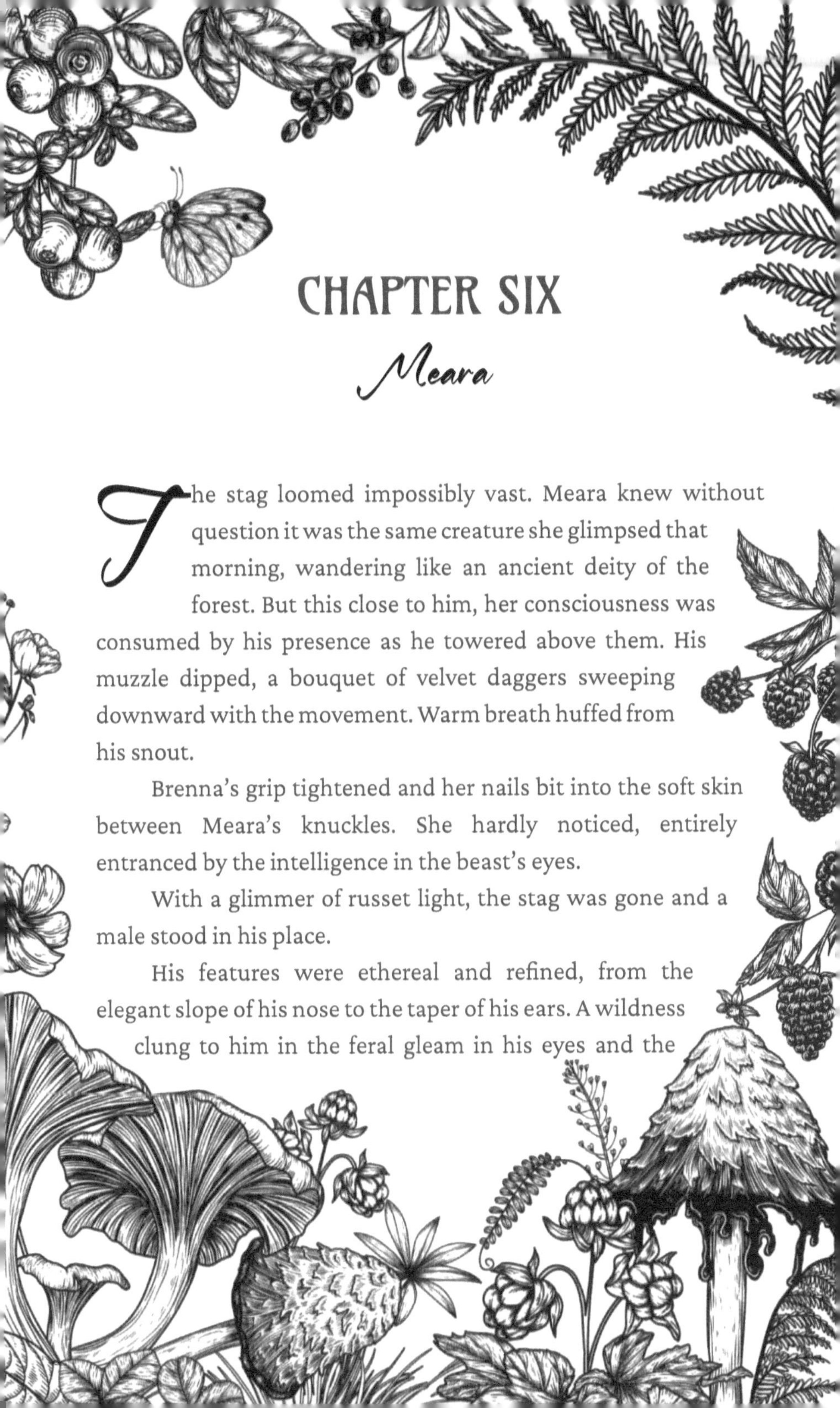

CHAPTER SIX

Meara

The stag loomed impossibly vast. Meara knew without question it was the same creature she glimpsed that morning, wandering like an ancient deity of the forest. But this close to him, her consciousness was consumed by his presence as he towered above them. His muzzle dipped, a bouquet of velvet daggers sweeping downward with the movement. Warm breath huffed from his snout.

Brenna's grip tightened and her nails bit into the soft skin between Meara's knuckles. She hardly noticed, entirely entranced by the intelligence in the beast's eyes.

With a glimmer of russet light, the stag was gone and a male stood in his place.

His features were ethereal and refined, from the elegant slope of his nose to the taper of his ears. A wildness clung to him in the feral gleam in his eyes and the slender antlers rising from his shaggy chestnut hair.

Meara scrambled fully to her feet and jolted back a step, dragging Brenna with her. Leaves crackled under their feet, the sound jarring in the shocked silence. Her fingers closed over the hilt of her blade, drawing it from her pocket but holding it low, concealed within the folds of her skirt.

"That," Brenna muttered, "is not a deer."

Meara would have laughed, but fear strangled the air in her throat.

The faerie's sensuous mouth curved into a sly smile, revealing a subtle point to his teeth. Umber eyes flicked from their faces down to their boots and back. Meara's breath faltered as their gazes connected. What must they look like to him? Disheveled, dirt-streaked, and wrapped in layers of restrictive clothing - nothing like the figure before them.

Breeches the color of oats hugged his waist and thighs. His chest was bare save for a garnet cloak draped over his shoulders, framing an expanse of sun-bronzed skin taut over sinew and muscle. As beautiful as he was, Meara couldn't take her eyes off the antlers rising from his hair. Her lips parted as her eyes traced the elegant arch of each wicked tine, sharp enough to kill. The blade in her hand felt flimsy facing this living, breathing weapon.

"My ladies, are you in need of assistance?" His voice brushed over Meara's skin like fine leather, smooth and warm.

Brenna moved beside her and cautiously lowered into a shallow curtsy, her face raised and eyes never leaving the faerie. "My lord, we are simply traveling to Dornadan."

Behind him, two horses materialized through the foliage. They were not the sturdy workhorses from Liosliath farms, but sleek equines with shimmering coats. Both bore riders dressed in light, flowing clothing.

A fae female slid from her silver dapple horse. She wore a gray dress without a chemise, exposing her toned arms and an expanse of her chest. Warm, dark hair slipped over her bare shoulders as she walked to the fae male's side. Dark eyes assessed them as she delicately pressed a hand to her chest.

"They are the ones I sensed," the female murmured. Tilting her head, she raised her voice to address them. "You are fleeing some danger. I could feel your distress."

Chest aching, Meara inhaled slowly, pushing down her panic and trying to keep her voice steady. "How can you know that?"

"It is my magic." The fae female said simply.

"Xurey is a puca," the male explained, a fondness in his tone. "You are lucky she was in the area."

Meara studied Xurey. Her soft expression seemed genuine, and there was a gentleness to her that whispered of safety. It was not enough to calm Meara's racing heart, but she felt her panic ebb. She cleared her throat. "Thank you for your concern, but we must continue to meet our kin at Dornadan."

"Why are you disguised?" The third figure dismounted and drew closer. Hair the color of sunlit nasturtium flowers curled over his ears, concealing their shape, but there was no doubt about his heritage. He was as fae as the first two with a delicate nose, dagger-sharp cheekbones, and a smattering of freckles over his creamy skin.

The antlered faerie frowned, a deep crease forming between his brows. "What do you mean?"

The flame-haired male folded his arms, squinting at the sisters. "I am fairly sure they are faeries with an illusion over them. Well, they may be only half-fae. I can't tell for sure unless we strip away the enchantment."

Sparks danced from Brenna's wrists and down her hands, warming Meara's fingers and betraying them both. Three sets of eyes honed in on the display of magic.

"See?" The second male held out a hand as if to say *I told you so*.

Meara raised her chin and stepped protectively in front of her sister. "We do not know where this magic comes from, but we are humans with a human mother." She tasted the lie on her tongue, bitter and caustic. "Perhaps it is a curse."

"Not a curse." The newcomer tilted his head, his clever golden eyes glinting. "The spellcraft over your sister is already breaking. I see the same magic over you. I can remove it before it fractures completely and causes any backlash."

Her mind stumbled over the idea. They had an illusion over them? That couldn't be possible. There was nothing to hide. She took a step back, herding Brenna behind her. "I apologize, but we should continue on our way. Thank you for your concern, but we can handle it."

"Wait," the first fae male commanded, stepping forward. Broken sunlight shone across his antlers, illuminating them into polished ivory.

"Please, excuse us," Meara said. Instincts urged her to flee to safety and protect her sister, but Brenna pressed back against her, wanting to stay.

"You are frightening them," Xurey said, pushing past the males. She opened her hands and spoke softly as if she was soothing a wild creature. "We mean you no harm. My name is Xurey. I help travelers like you."

"And I'm Tayen," the second male said, giving them a charming smile, "and I happen to like humans."

Meara measured their words. The fae were supposedly incapable of lying. Tales of their monstrous nature were woven into every bedtime story in Liosliath, but not so in Dornadan. She knew they lived beside humans, so perhaps these fae were of that sort.

"I'm Brenna, and this is Meara," Brenna offered, breaking the tension.

"Brenna, why were you running?" Xurey asked.

Her sister drew in an audible breath. "The magic. It's never happened before," she began, nibbling at her bottom lip as she picked her words. "We live in Liosliath. I was protecting myself, and when my employer saw… this." She held up their connected hands. "They called me fae and chased me."

The antlered faerie stiffened, his eyes darkening as he met Meara's gaze. "Then it is wise that you are traveling to Dornadan. No one there will attack you for being fae."

"We can't be faeries," Meara protested.

"But you are," Tayen said.

"I suggest you learn to control your magic, though. Even Dornadan will not be safe if you set things aflame," the first male warned. Meara watched the curve of his cupid's bow as his lips moved. Perhaps this was how faeries lured in prey. They were painfully beautiful and it made it difficult to think. Meara's hand squeezed Brenna's, trying to clear her mind of his beguiling influence.

"Like I said, we have someone we are meeting," Meara insisted.

Brenna looked between Meara and Xurey, concern lining her eyes. "Our mother is back in Liosliath holding them off while we escape. She said she would meet us in Dornadan, but the villagers were so angry, I fear for her."

Silence stretched, the faeries exchanging meaningful looks. The leader nodded. "Tayen will go to Liosliath and assist your mother. Did you have a meeting place planned?"

"The Silver Spectre Tavern," Brenna answered before Meara could interject.

"Good."

"You can't go to Liosliath. They will kill you," Meara said, turning to Tayen.

"Are you worried for me?" He chuckled. "They could try, but I assure you they cannot harm me. Besides, I will conceal that I am fae." Meara frowned at his obviously inhuman eyes, too bright and unsettling, like molten gold.

"Bring her to the Silver Spectre so they may deliberate what to do," the leader instructed. Tayen nodded.

"We will take you there," Xurey said, "and then we can discuss your untrained magic craft."

"No," Meara blurted. "We aren't going anywhere with you. We will be going on our own."

The antlered fae male narrowed his eyes. "Why are you so unwilling to accept our help?"

Her hands clenched, her blade still tight in her fist. "Because you are strangers and fae. You could be stealing us away to be slaves or trick us into our deaths."

With a startling grace, he stepped nearer. Meara held her position, her thoughts whirling as she assessed the distance, the angle, and where her blade would land if she struck, if he became aggressive. They would not be taken by the fae, not after escaping Liosliath.

His voice dropped, the tone rich and dark, sending a shiver down her spine. "When a fae lord gives you his word that you will not be harmed, then you are safe. And that is what I am offering you. You are within the Autumn Court so it is within my power to do so. If, after you discuss the matter further tonight at the tavern, you wish to part ways, then so be it. But it would be a mistake to walk away now."

Brenna bowed her head in submission. "Forgive us, my lord. We were taught to fear faeries, but I know you are telling the truth, and we would be grateful for your help."

Meara grit her teeth. They should be running the opposite

direction, not accepting help from faeries. "What do you want in exchange for your help?"

She waited for the fae lord's anger to blossom again, but instead his voice gentled. "If you are faeries raised by humans, then our realm owes you a debt. Consider this a partial repayment."

Xurey watched him with a slight tilt to her head.

"Thank you. May we know your name?" Brenna asked.

"Cerne," he answered simply.

Meara caught the faint echo of Brenna conversing, but the words were overwhelmed by the rushing of her heartbeat in her ears. Cerne, as in Lord Cerne. Leader of the Wild Hunt. One of the most well-known and feared monsters from their village's faerie lore. The Wraith of Sablewood.

The only thing worse than having to ride with the Wraith of Sablewood was allowing her sister to ride with him, so Meara found herself sitting atop the white mare with a fae lord of legend settled behind her. A masculine forearm wrapped across her middle, pressing her back against a firm chest.

"You don't need to hold me," she said, trying to ignore the taut muscle against her shoulder blades and the way his thighs brushed against her backside as she shifted. His arm fell away, skimming her hip as if he wasn't sure she'd stay upright without his assistance. She tensed, determined to stay balanced as his body heat soaked into her back, scorching her. As the horses navigated the trees, he leaned one way and another, directing the horse with either his weight or his legs, she wasn't sure, but each movement brushed his chest against her back, the touch maddening her.

The horse took a rocky step and she slid sideways a handbreadth. Cerne's arm looped across her stomach again, anchoring her. Even if she had briefly considered throwing herself from the mare to escape his nearness, she hadn't intended to actually do so.

"I can ride!" she hissed.

"Humans ride with saddles and stirrups. We do not." His tone could have been considered haughty until he conceded. "But you are doing very well considering your lack of experience."

Huffing, Meara looked to the side where Brenna sat behind Xurey on her silver mount. The two spoke quietly and wore matching small smiles.

"Why couldn't I sit behind you?" she complained.

Cerne tsked. "And stab me in the back with your little blade? I think not."

"I don't have to be sitting behind you to stab you," she muttered, her eyes drawn back to her sister. Cerne followed her gaze.

"I promise, your sister is safe with Xurey. She is the best rider I know, and Airgid is a gentle and sure-footed stallion." His voice was warm against her ear. Her focus narrowed to his touch.

"And what of your mare?" she asked.

"Eirlys may not be the brightest, but she won't cause any trouble if you ride with me." His dark chuckle rolled over her skin, and she fought off another shiver. She had to get away from this fae male before she fell entirely under his spell. His warmth and charming words chipped away at her misgivings, and that was dangerous.

They rode in silence and Meara got lost in her anxious thoughts. Her fingers snared in Eirlys' snowy mane. The silken strands slipped over her knuckles as she brooded on all the ways this could end in disaster. That was safer than dwelling on the heat of the Autumn Lord behind her.

The forest thinned and buttery light filtered in, limning the trees in electrum. Eirlys slowed and ambled to a stop. Cerne slid from his seat. His dark hair curled around his shoulders as he looked up at her and offered his hand. Stubbornly, she swung her leg over and dropped to the ground without accepting his assistance. The landing jolted through her spine, but she clamped her teeth together and refused to wince.

The suggestion of a smile curved his lips as he turned toward a sprawling tavern. Smoke drifted from a multitude of chimneys, scenting the air with roasting meat and charred bread.

Meara stared up at the expanse of weathered wooden siding broken up by windows in various mismatched shapes. Spiraling calligraphy painted above the doorway declared it The Silver Spectre, Alehouse and Lodging. Cerne paid the stable boy and urged Eirlys forward with a murmur to behave. A docile Airgid followed, head bobbing with each step.

"Well, we reached Dornadan," Brenna said as she stepped up beside Meara with her hands on her hips, "and picked up some faeries along the way."

Together, they passed through the open doorway. The dim interior coated her skin in humid warmth and the lingering smog of alcohol and woodsmoke. A few curious humans watched Cerne, though none stood or displayed any hostility. It seemed that faeries entering this tavern was a common occurrence, and as she scanned the crowd, she spotted a few tapered ears among the crowd. The patrons' attention returned to their own tables quickly.

It was early for supper, but many people sat with plates of food in front of them. Steak pies, roasted carrots, parsnips, and potatoes, all covered in gravy. Meara's stomach gurgled. It had been hours since breakfast. Cerne spoke with the bar matron, his antlers dipping as he inclined his head and grinned at her. With a crooked smile, she provided four dishes of the evening's provisions. Meara thanked her and offered a few silver chips, but she waved them off. The fae lord had paid for their meal. Her stomach clenched, hating this feeling of indebtedness. The two sisters selected a small table along the sloping wall. It provided a sense of privacy as Xurey and Cerne sat at the polished bar top and chatted with the staff amiably.

Meara settled into her seat and took a deep, slow breath. For now, they were safe. She peeled her attention off the faeries and focused on her sister. Brenna's eyes glittered with emotion, her breathing shallow. Meara studied her sister for a moment. "Are you well?"

Brenna's smile was brittle as she tore away some of the pastry crust from her pie. "Of course. We were lucky to meet Lord Cerne, though I suppose they were looking for us. A puca's magic being what it is."

"And that is?" Meara knew Brenna was well read on the topic, while she knew almost nothing.

Taking a sip of ale, Brenna glanced up at the faeries. "Pucas are shape shifters who aid travelers, either in goodwill or for mischief. But she said she wouldn't harm us."

Meara's brows furrowed. "We can't know their intentions. Words can be deceiving. They have no reason to help us."

"We are faeries like them, like they said. And besides, it is difficult for the fae to lie."

"We cannot be faeries." She trailed off, her eyes on Brenna's hands. They looked the same as always as they slid forward and tapped the edge of Meara's plate in a silent command. Sighing, Meara gave in and cut into her meal. It was overly seasoned so she took a draught of honey mead to cut the saltiness.

"It makes sense to me," Brenna said softly. "Faeries care about both fairness and hospitality. So if we were abandoned as babies, it makes sense we missed whatever education they provide their children, and therefore we are owed some aid." She shrugged, turning over a chunk of potato with her fork. Lines crossed her forehead as she glanced up.

Meara sat back in her chair and scowled. "I still don't see how that is possible."

"I don't see how I can produce fire or light with my hands, but it happened," Brenna snapped, her jaw tight. Her agitated fingers tapped against the rough wooden tabletop.

"What are we going to do?" Meara's words trailed off.

"See what Mother thinks, I suppose." Brenna paused. "I hope that Tayen can help her."

The sisters' gazes met, agreement passing between them. Around them, the room hummed with dozens of conversations, all melding together like the thrum of a beehive.

Meara pinched the bridge of her nose. "I cannot fathom relocating our family and also having magic or not even being human." Brenna flinched, and guilt twisted in Meara's chest. "I'm sorry, I'm overwhelmed. But your safety is the most important thing. I am not upset to leave our neighbors behind." She rambled, hoping to bring light back into her sister's eyes.

Brenna looked away. "We need rest and time. I think we should get a room."

"Alright."

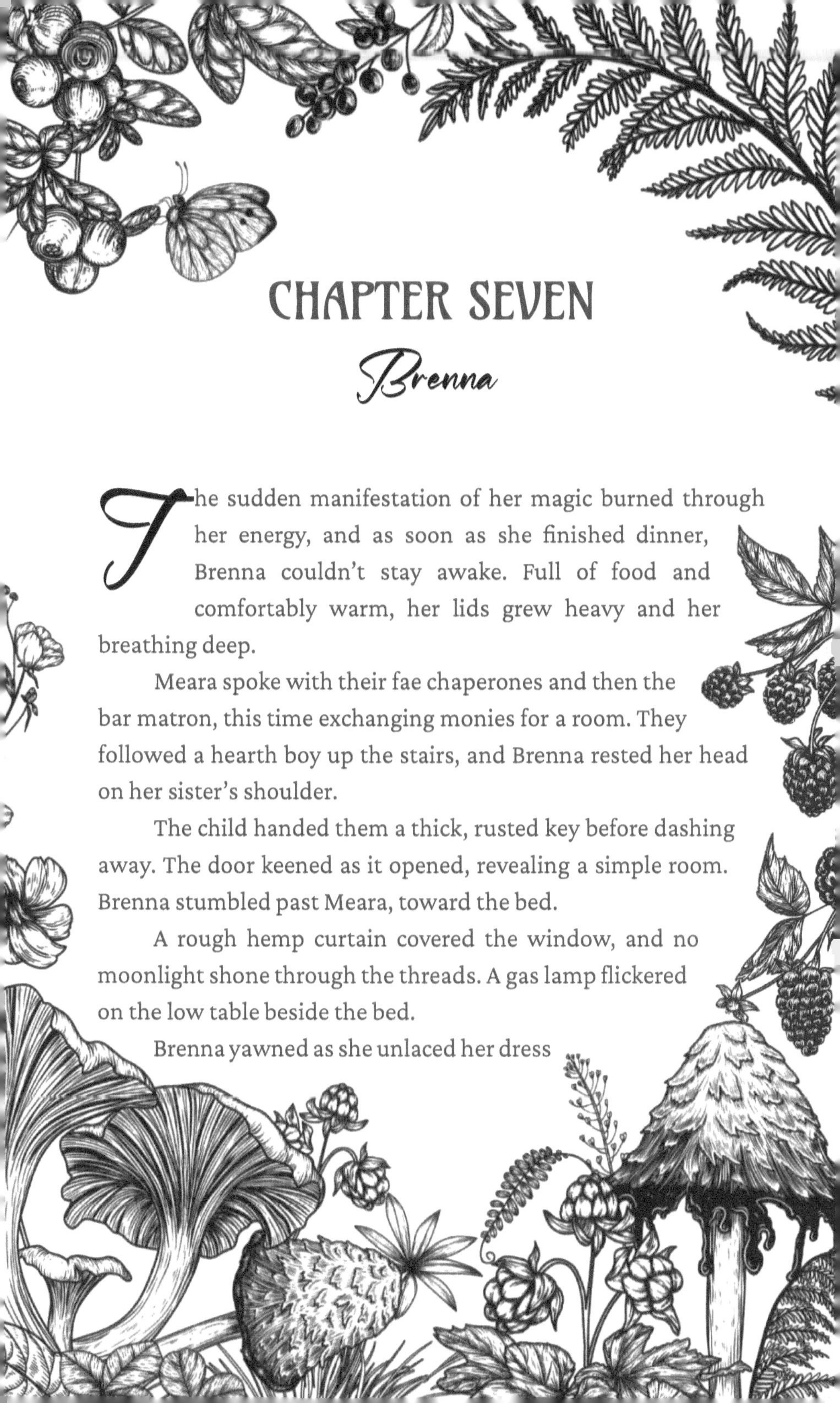

CHAPTER SEVEN
Brenna

The sudden manifestation of her magic burned through her energy, and as soon as she finished dinner, Brenna couldn't stay awake. Full of food and comfortably warm, her lids grew heavy and her breathing deep.

Meara spoke with their fae chaperones and then the bar matron, this time exchanging monies for a room. They followed a hearth boy up the stairs, and Brenna rested her head on her sister's shoulder.

The child handed them a thick, rusted key before dashing away. The door keened as it opened, revealing a simple room. Brenna stumbled past Meara, toward the bed.

A rough hemp curtain covered the window, and no moonlight shone through the threads. A gas lamp flickered on the low table beside the bed.

Brenna yawned as she unlaced her dress

and tugged it off. Exhaustion dragged her down, and she fell into the bed. The linens smelled clean with a hint of woodsmoke as her face pressed into the thin pillow. Sleep claimed her before her sister returned from the washroom.

There was only darkness when Brenna awoke. Something touched her shoulder, and she could make out a figure standing beside the bed from the sliver of light peeking from under the door. Brenna pitched backward, waking Meara. Her sister drew her hunting knife in a fluid movement, ready to defend them.

The intruder moved to the window and yanked the curtains aside, allowing ashen moonlight to illuminate a heart-shaped face, warm brown eyes, and wavy cinnamon hair. Recognition melted away Brenna's panic, but Meara let out a startled shout.

Their mother lunged forward, grabbing the coverlet from the foot of the bed and smothering the flames licking along the blanket pooled around Brenna's hips. Panicked, Brenna flung herself back, away from the flames. She tumbled over her sister's lap and toppled to the floor. Hands waving, she chanted, "Stop, stop stop," as she willed the spark dancing around her fingers to fade.

"You're safe," her mother said, kneeling to steady her. She grabbed Brenna's wrists, holding them still and squeezing until Brenna could focus. She sucked in a deep breath and then another, and slowly the magic faded.

"Well done, love," their mother said.

Brenna grabbed her around the waist in a crushing hug, pressing her face against her soft stomach. Euphoric relief flooded her body. "Mum!" Brenna sniffled. "I was so frightened we wouldn't see you again!"

"Everything is fine." Nimble fingers smoothed her daughter's hair. "We are safe now. And you've had an adventure, meeting a faerie lord."

"They said we were," Brenna began, but her mother gently drew her away, nodding.

"Tayen explained. I knew you were special when you arrived on my doorstep."

"What do you remember?"

"Just your beautiful faces. There was nothing else, my dears."

Meara cleared her throat and frowned at them as she tucked her blade away. "We have a lot to discuss, but it's still night. We should rest while we can."

"Yes, go back to sleep, girls. Everything will look brighter in the morning."

Untangling from her mother's arms, Brenna crawled back into the bed. Her muscles trembled, the exhaustion of too little sleep edging her mess of regret and concern.

Exhaling, she eased back down, tucking against her mother's side with Meara curled around her back. Sleep felt less like being taken against her will and more like a soothing embrace, safe with her family again.

The bustle of the inn woke Brenna. Meara slumbered beside her, but their mother was already gone. For a moment, she wondered if it had been a dream, but the scorched blanket sat crumpled in the chair in the corner. Seeing the results of her loss of control was sobering. What if next time it was an entire building that went up in flames?

After using the washroom, Brenna gently woke her sister. Meara sat up, glossy black hair escaping its braids and tumbling in waves over her cheeks as her eyes darted around the room. Her wild expression hardened as memories returned to her.

Guilt clung to Brenna, making her movements sluggish. She was the reason her family was displaced and her mother lost the apothecary opened by her great grandfather. She sank onto the foot of the bed, head dipped and fingers threading into her hair, tugging roughly at the roots.

Meara's hand landed on her shoulder, pressing into the nerves and pulling her from her spiraling thoughts. She tipped her head to the side, resting her cheek against her sister's arm.

"Let's go talk to Mum." Meara released her and slid off the bed.

While she was washing up, Brenna finger combed her hair and twisted it into a loose spiral, securing it against her scalp with the few pins that survived their flight. She couldn't leave her hair loose like her sister. It felt improper and exposed. But then again, Xurey wore her hair sweeping over her naked shoulders. Brenna nibbled at her bottom lip, and then removed the pins and let her hair unravel down her back.

"Ready?" Meara asked, framed in the open doorway. Brenna nodded and followed her down the stairs. Meara leaned back and scrunched up her nose. "Do you think she's down there giving health advice to the lodgers?"

A giggle worked its way up Brenna's throat and for a few seconds she felt normal. Her levity shattered as they rounded the curve of the staircase. Their mother sat at one of the larger tables, sipping a cup of coffee and chatting with two ethereal faeries.

The bar matron was replaced with a broad man sporting a salt and pepper beard. Without being asked, he placed plates of egg, ham, and tomato in front of both sisters. A coffee pot was offered, but Brenna declined. It was a luxury they rarely had at home and she'd never developed a taste for the bitter drink.

"Good morning, Meara, Brenna," Tayen said, his full lips stretched into a wide smile. Those amber eyes danced in the mix of flickering lamplight and muffled daylight coming in the windows tucked beneath the eaves. "Feeling rested, I hope?"

"Fine, thank you." Meara said, suspicion a sharp edge to her words. "Where is the Lord?"

"Cerne had to return to our court. Hopefully we will join him today." His tone was light, as if discussing the weather.

Brenna ground her teeth, guilt burning in her gut. Her words spilled forth, the confession clawing its way from her throat. "I was startled when our mother arrived, and I accidentally set a blanket on fire." Hands shaking, she set her fork down on the table and laced her fingers together in her lap.

Xurey and Tayen traded glances, before Xurey leaned forward in her seat. "We've all had a few mishaps with our magic craft. A little fire is nothing to be ashamed of."

"I'm afraid that next time, I will destroy our home or hurt someone," Brenna whispered, her throat going dry. She reached for a flagon of watered mead and drank deeply.

Their mother set her coffee mug down with a resolute clink. "That is why I think you should allow the Autumn Court to train you so that doesn't happen."

Meara's eyes narrowed as she watched the two faeries. "How would that work exactly?"

"My magic is a shield that can contain her fire. She can practice safely," Tayen explained, "and we have others with elemental crafts, such as my sister. I'm confident we can help you learn to access and control your abilities."

"It's not only Brenna. You are fae as well, Meara," Xurey said softly. Her wide, dark eyes were sincere, and warm gratitude ignited in Brenna's chest.

Meara's gaze shadowed. "We couldn't impose upon your court like that."

"We have an obligation. You should have grown up learning your magic craft. I don't know why you were left in Liosliath, but it should never have happened," Tayen said.

Meara's scowl deepened, clearly disliking the idea of

obligation and being a burden. "When does that obligation end and we are in your debt?"

"When you no longer need our help, you can go home," Tayen said.

"That's generous," Brenna said, smiling at him. Something about the male put her at ease. Perhaps his bright eyes or his relaxed demeanor.

"You can't be considering this," Meara whispered. "Going with them to the faerie court?"

"Why not?"

"Meara," Xurey said. "I know you've heard stories about all faeries being dangerous. But I assure you, the Autumn Court is not like you are imaging. The monsters of your stories live in the further kingdoms like the Court of Snow and Shadow or the Court of Darkness, and they aren't so bad. Usually."

Tayen folded his arms across his chest. "The Autumn Court is close allies with Dornadan. Eldric would not let us into their keep if we were abducting and exploiting his people."

"I think we can trust them," Brenna said softly.

"I was speaking with your mother," Tayen continued, "and I believe the king would appreciate having an apothecary in his court. I would like to accompany her to an audience with him."

Brenna covered her smile. "That's incredible, thank you."

"We should go with her," Meara said stubbornly. "She will need our help opening a new shop."

Wrinkling her nose, Brenna sniped, "It won't be helpful if I burn it down."

Shoulders drooping, Meara sat back in her seat. Her jaw ticked, but she withheld her reply, the shadows across her face darkening her eyes and the hollows of her cheeks.

"Love," their mother said, grasping Meara's hand, "perhaps it would be wise to learn this side of yourself and harness whatever abilities you have. It's certainly safer than trying to manage it on our own. And you can come back to me when you're ready."

Meara opened her mouth to argue but their mother silenced her with an arch of one brow.

"I'll be occupied arranging everything and gathering materials. I am quite capable of handling these tasks. I supplied the shop on my own before you came into my life."

Meara grumbled her agreement.

"I'm so sorry I ruined everything in Liosliath," Brenna said, a flush rising in her cheeks, "And lost you the shop."

Their mother shook her head. "Don't apologize. You've done nothing wrong. You are worth so much more than a shop, and I can't wait to see what you can do with your magic."

Bolstered by her mother's warm smile, Brenna raised her chin. "I accept your offer to train in the Autumn Court."

Meara stiffened, brows pinched and shoulders tight. Brenna knew Meara would never agree to go, but she also wouldn't let Brenna go alone. She was forcing her hand, but it had to be done for her own good.

"Meara," she said gently. "Are you joining me?"

Despite the set of her jaw, she answered immediately. "Of course. I would never let my sister go into the fae lands alone."

"They will need clothing and toiletries," their mother said. "We took nothing with us when we left."

"That is not an issue. We will take care of their needs, I promise," Xurey said.

"Thank you. We are grateful," Brenna said.

"Are we ready to go? I will get the horses," Xurey said. Tayen rose as well and walked to the counter to speak with the barkeep.

"Are you sure it is safe to go with them?" Meara asked, barely more than a whisper. Her wide, gray eyes were bright with concern as her hands clenched in her skirts.

Their mother held their gazes, a softness coming over her features. "I should have spoken up more often when you were children. Our neighbors were fearful and superstitious. The fae are not so different from us. Are *you* monsters hiding in human disguises?" Meara let her breath go audibly and nodded as if making up her mind. "You will be safe. They have been nothing but honorable and kind. And you'll have each other."

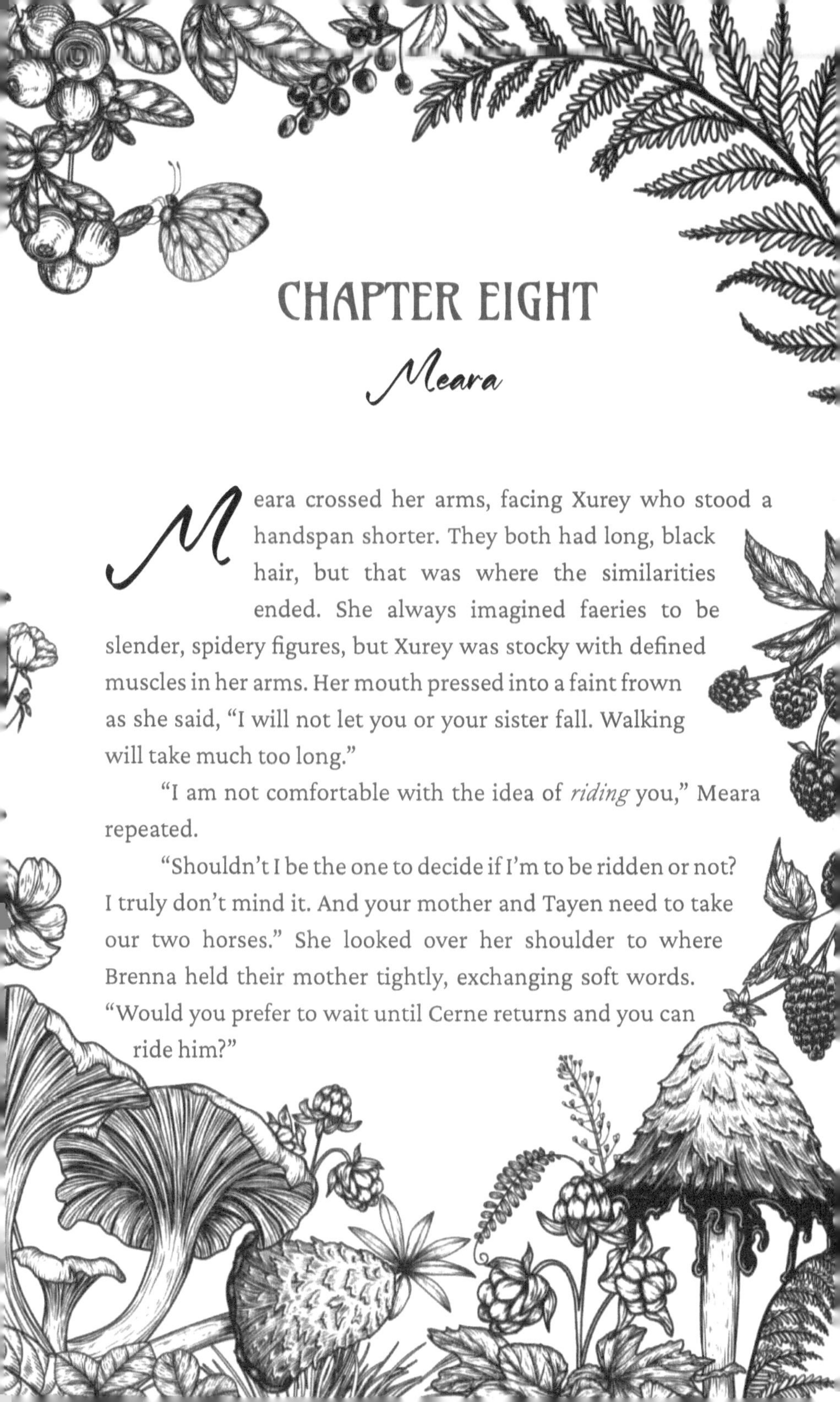

CHAPTER EIGHT
Meara

eara crossed her arms, facing Xurey who stood a handspan shorter. They both had long, black hair, but that was where the similarities ended. She always imagined faeries to be slender, spidery figures, but Xurey was stocky with defined muscles in her arms. Her mouth pressed into a faint frown as she said, "I will not let you or your sister fall. Walking will take much too long."

"I am not comfortable with the idea of *riding* you," Meara repeated.

"Shouldn't I be the one to decide if I'm to be ridden or not? I truly don't mind it. And your mother and Tayen need to take our two horses." She looked over her shoulder to where Brenna held their mother tightly, exchanging soft words. "Would you prefer to wait until Cerne returns and you can ride him?"

Nose wrinkling, Meara took a step back and dropped her hands in defeat.

"Go say goodbye to your mother. It may be a few weeks or even months until you see her again." The words were gentle, more of a loving suggestion than a command.

Brenna opened her arms and welcomed Meara into their embrace. The three women - one human and two lost faeries - huddled together with their foreheads touching and breath mingling. "My daughters, remember that you have every right to be among the fae. You are one of them," their mother murmured, "and if you desire, you can stay among them forever and we can visit each other often."

"We would never abandon you," Meara insisted.

Their mother stroked over her hair and down her spine. "Stay close and listen to each other. You'll be fine as long as you're together."

"Yes, Mum," they said in chorus, sounding more six than twenty-six.

With one last kiss to their foreheads, she released her daughters and accepted Tayen's hand. Brenna wiped at her eyes and sniffled, so Meara wrapped an arm over her shoulders as they watched their mother clamber up to sit astride Airgid. The patient white stallion stood perfectly still.

Beside them, Tayen leapt onto Eirlys with a preternatural grace. Meara blinked. She would have to get used to these faeries if they were to live among them. Be one of them.

"Ready?" Xurey asked. No sooner had the girls nodded, silver magic shimmered over her and she was replaced with a slate gray mare. Meara resisted the impulse to touch her black mane. Instead, she hoisted Brenna up onto her back and then allowed her sister to tug her up to sit behind her. With a toss of her head, Xurey set out.

Her gait was smooth, and without Cerne's imposing

presence, Meara could almost enjoy the ride. Conversation was stilted, knowing the equine beneath them was listening as well. The sisters watched the forest change as they cut through the edge of Dornadan and continued northwest to the fae lands.

The change was gradual and Meara didn't notice until they were well into the territory of the Court of Autumn Harvest. Green leaves turned to gold and then shades of burnt orange and crimson. The trees rose, the forest older here than by their forsaken home. The air felt heavy, ancient. Tales of faeries living for hundreds or thousands of years trickled through her mind. In this place, it was easy to believe.

Birdsong rang out around them, quiet at first, but building until the trees were teeming with life. A bright red squirrel leapt across branches in front of them, chirping as it darted away.

"Oh, how cute!" Brenna gasped. Meara covered her smile with her hand, feeling like a child again walking the forest with their mother and learning of the herbs that supplied their apothecary, Brenna squealing every time they encountered a new animal.

Through the trees, Meara glimpsed a cottage. It was difficult to spot with its gray-brown stones covered in vines heavy with orange and red flowers that blended into the surrounding trees beautifully. The roof was a slope of mossy shingles above a door painted a rich earthy hue.

A faerie opened the door and stepped out. Her eyes caught Meara's, and her mouth formed an "O" before she darted away. Her hair caught the light, flashing a deep shade of evergreen. Within seconds, she evaporated into the forest.

Meara's eyes lingered on the cottage until it faded from view. It didn't fit with the stories told in Liosliath about monsters living off the blood of maidens.

Soon, more homes emerged from the trees, grouping together

until they formed loose rows flanking their pathway. As the forest floor melted into a cobblestone path, Xurey stopped and dipped her head. Meara slipped off her back and helped Brenna down.

In a glimmer of silver magic, Xurey transformed and stood beside them. With an audible sigh, she stretched her shoulders and shook out her hair.

"Meara, Brenna, it's only a short way now. Welcome to the Autumn Court." Holding out her hand, Xurey ushered them into the township.

It was shockingly clean. No piles of refuse or puddles of piss marred the street. The air smelled of roasting nuts and spices blended with the musty pine scent of the forest. Meara wanted to soak it in, absorb it into her soul.

Little shops and businesses popped up between the houses, making it feel like a proper village. The buildings grew closer and taller. They passed a bakeshop, a tinker, and a tavern all within a few steps of each other.

Brenna beamed, squeezing Meara's arm. Her wide, amber eyes searched the shops, greedily taking everything in.

The faeries on the street waved or nodded in greeting to Xurey. They looked happy and well-fed with faces unblemished and bright, wearing loose dresses or tunics and trousers in the same earthen shades as the charming structures they walked between.

The path rose and they rounded a curve. Orange and red leaves overtook the cobblestone as the buildings dropped off. Ahead, the trees framed a sprawling manor house. It was fashioned much the same as the rest of the court with large stones, wooden beams, and shingles, but at a grander scale. Polished wood trim surrounded a multitude of windows spreading out from a set of gilded front doors thrown wide open.

This was not a house, it was a palace. Meara's anxiety rushed back and she clenched her hands in her skirts near her hunting blade to reassure herself.

Xurey ascended the shallow stone steps and greeted an older faerie. He stood tall and broad with a tangle of leaves poking through his braided beard and thick hair. His skin was the rough brown of tree bark. Brenna took Meara's arm and eased her forward until they stood before the dryad.

"Welcome to The Autumn Estate." He stepped aside and ushered them into an expansive parlor.

The last dregs of sunset streamed through arched windows and fell upon a mural of an autumn forest. Dark wainscoting covered the bottom of the wall and warm cherrywood pillars broke the artwork into sections, framing scenes of leaping deer and dashing foxes. The millwork continued onto the ceiling in an array of beams and carved corbels. The entire room glowed from a trio of massive wooden chandeliers studded with hundreds of candles.

"This is Ryles." Xurey tilted her head toward the dryad. "Ryles, this is Meara and Brenna. They will be staying with Cerne for a few weeks, perhaps longer."

"Honored to meet you," Ryles said with a formal bow.

"Ryles cares for the household. He will take care of anything you need," Xurey explained.

"Thank you," Brenna said as she dipped into a curtsy. Meara attempted to copy her, but her movements were awkward and she refused to take her eyes off Ryles.

"I'm sure we will all gather for breakfast in the morning, but for tonight you can get settled and rest." Xurey tapped her chin. "We can find some comfortable clothing for you as well."

"This way," Ryles said, his long coat rustling as he moved.

"I'll see you soon," Xurey said with a reassuring smile. Meara wanted to call after her to stay for she was the only faerie she felt reasonably safe with. Now they were alone in a strange palace with a dryad who looked less than pleased by their appearances. Her thumb smoothed over the handle of her blade, reassuring herself.

The dryad led the girls past the mural and down a hallway covered with the same intricate paneling and plush carpet so thick it felt like walking on overgrown, springy moss.

With a sweep of his hand, Ryles opened a door to reveal a suite of rooms larger than their family's cottage.

"These rooms will be yours as long as you stay with us. There is a bathing room there." He motioned to the middle of the three doors along the back wall.

"This is too much," Meara blurted. "We aren't visiting royalty."

Ryles canted his head. "These are our guest rooms. Not for royalty."

"It's wonderful, thank you," Brenna said, squeezing Meara's arm to stop her protests.

Bowing again, he stepped away. "I will send an attendant along shortly. You can make any requests with her, unless you need anything before I leave you?"

"No, thank you, Ryles," Brenna said with a winning smile. The dryad steward nodded and closed the door behind him.

The sisters stood in the sitting room, taking a moment to adjust to their new surroundings. It had been a whirlwind of change in the last twenty-four hours and Meara could never have imagined it would end here.

Calling the rooms comfortable was an understatement. An ornate table and chairs stood to one side, while a pair of plush armchairs sat facing a fireplace mantle of gleaming dark walnut. A low fire burned within, lighting the lucent green stones of the hearth into opalescent emeralds. The extravagance soured her stomach. She did not belong in a place like this.

Meara warily moved to the first of the doors, pausing on the threshold. Glass covered the back wall of the bedroom, revealing swaying branches mottled purple in night. A bench stretched the length of the windows, piled with pillows and cushions. Another fireplace stood opposite an oversized canopy bed surrounded by shelves and shelves of books wallpapering the entire room.

Brenna surged past her, entranced by the library. She ran her delicate fingers over the spines, a smile spreading across her face. The titles covered a litany of subjects: botany, mythology, history, poetry. Brenna smiled blissfully, the weight of the day forgotten. Meara watched her sister relax, and she knew she would do anything to keep her this happy.

"My ladies?" A soft voice called from the sitting room. Meara spun, her hand going to the knife in her skirts. A girl with skin like tree bark stood by the hearth with a tray on her hip.

"Hello," Brenna said.

"I am Kirrily, and I'm here to help you." Her voice was light, like wind rather than earth. "I thought you might be hungry."

"Why, thank you. I'm Brenna and this is Meara."

Raising a hand in greeting, Meara met the dryad's leaf green eyes. Her sharp ears poked through the long tendrils of brown and green hair cascading down her back. Vines and leaves threaded through the curls.

Meara accepted a mug and breathed in the steam. It smelled familiar, like the lavender tea her mother drank.

Kirrily's smile was sweet as honey. "Ryles mentioned you would need some clothing, as you were unable to bring any personal possessions. You'll find soaps, lotions, and combs in the bathing room. Is there anything else I can get you?"

"Thank you. I can't think of anything else," Meara said, ignoring the sudden urge to scrub the grit from her skin accumulated from two days journeying through the forest.

Brenna sipped her tea. "We really appreciate everything."

"Of course," Kirrily said, setting the tray on the table. "Good evening. If you need anything, I'll be close by." Her footfalls were silent as she crossed the room and disappeared, the door closing behind her.

Eyeing the set of earthenware dishes on the tray, Meara slid into a seat. The scent of the fae food was unfamiliar but enticing as she eased the lid off a shallow bowl. Dark fruit sat over stewed grains.

Brenna picked up a bundle of silverware and handed her a spoon. Together, they tucked into their supper. Warmth curled through her as she savored the sweetness of plums and cloves.

"Oh, no," Brenna groaned, slapping her hand over her eyes.

"What?" Meara asked, looking up from her dish.

"This is delicious. I am ruined for our own cooking." Brenna took another bite and slowly pulled the spoon out of her mouth, her lips stretched in a pleasured grimace. Meara's exhale blended into a chuckle. As she finished the porridge and moved onto a meat-filled pastry, she had to agree.

Stomachs full, the sisters moved to the bathing room. A copper tub stood on a stone platform at the end of the room. Intricate stained glass depicting falling leaves filled the arched windows surrounding it. The black patina crisscrossing over the gemstone glasswork gave a sense of privacy from the outside world.

A polished faucet curved over the edge like the neck of a swan. Brenna twisted knobs at its side and water poured from the tap. "We should bathe," she said. "Do you want to go first?"

"No, go ahead." Meara shrugged, looking over the stretch of wooden counter with a rough edge like the tree had been sliced vertically and left with its natural curves and notches. A basin sat buried in the counter with only the rim sticking up. Another shiny faucet arched over it.

Brenna gasped. "The water is warm!" Frowning, Meara swished her fingers through the stream. It felt like water warmed over a fire. "They must have a hot spring," Brenna mused.

"Or magic." Meara flicked her fingers to fling droplets at her sister. Brenna huffed in response, though the sound was tired and hollow. She turned her back to Meara and held aside her hair, a silent request that Meara fulfilled, undoing the laces of the calico dress. As Brenna shrugged her chemise over her head, Meara stepped out of the room and closed the door. Through the crack, she said, "I'll be right here if you need anything."

"You sound like Kirrily," Brenna chimed. Water splashed and she let out a dramatic sigh. With an exhausted smile, Meara wandered to the third room.

This bedroom mirrored the first, but instead of books, the walls were covered in glass shadow boxes. Flowers, moths, and beetles filled the frames, all pinned in place for eternity. Meara had seen plenty of insects in her days roaming the forest, but seeing them laid out was astonishing. She walked slowly, taking in the variety of shapes and colors. Brenna would hate this room, but Meara found it fascinating.

The bathing room opened and Brenna's voice drifted through the ajar door. "It's all yours."

Meara emerged, taking in the fresh, white chemise hugging Brenna's curves. The stitching was so delicate, it was almost invisible. Her damp hair was already curling over her shoulders even as water soaked into the linen.

"Kirrily left us clothes already." Brenna held up a matching shift for Meara to take.

"That was expedient," Meara muttered. Garment in hand, she poured a fresh bath and slipped out of her dress and dirty chemise. As she stepped into the deepening pool of heated bathwater, she sucked in a breath at the sensation. It was far warmer than a summer bath at home, stinging her skin at first contact. Sinking down, she pulled her knees up against her chest and leaned back against the edge of the tub. The warmth unraveled the tension that lived in her back and shoulders, ebbing away fear and stress until she took a full, deep breath. Steam filled her lungs.

Finding a bar of soap that smelled like pine, Meara scrubbed at her skin and hair until all the dirt and grit was washed away and her scalp tingled. Reluctantly, she pulled the stopper in the tub and watched all the evidence of her filth drain away.

Clay colored towels filled an alcove beside the tub and Meara used one to wipe away the droplets from her skin. She wrapped it around her hair and squeezed out what moisture she could. The room's humidity warmed her skin as she dressed. The new chemise felt heavenly against her skin, finer than anything she had at home.

Brenna sat perched at the table beside a set of mugs. Kirrily must have taken their supper dishes away when she delivered the clothing. Meara joined her, picking up the comb and working to untangle her hair.

"Try this," Brenna pressed, pushing the second mug to her. Meara obeyed and tart cider washed over her tongue. Her eyes closed as she savored the spices softened by the apple's sweetness.

Bodies warmed from bath and drink, the sisters tumbled into bed. It was never a question that they would share a bed, and the insect room remained empty.

The bedding was soft like rabbit fur, and Meara couldn't help running her hands over the cool, smooth fabric. Brenna let out a contented sigh as she nuzzled into the pillow.

"How are you doing?" Meara whispered. The fire burned down to a mere glow of embers, dancing across Brenna's tawny skin and goldenrod curls.

She pressed her lips together, conflict etched into the lines of her face. "This feels like a nightmare that has turned into a fantasy."

"I know we agreed to come here, but we do not know their laws or traditions." Meara's cheeks hollowed as she ruminated.

"It's going to be fine. Mum felt it was safe. And they've gone through a lot of trouble to help us if their aim is to harm. And besides, I have magic that can defend us, remember?"

Meara searched the canopy above. "I still can't fathom that I might have magic too."

"I feel the same way, and I've seen mine." Brenna's brows furrowed but a smile warmed her face. "What do you think your magic will be? Fire like me?"

Sighing, Meara drew the coverlet over her shoulders and sank deeper into the mattress. "I don't know."

Silence stretched, and Meara let sleep pull her deeper, but before she lost consciousness, Brenna spoke. "So do you think it's always autumn here? Or is it merely the name?"

Without opening her eyes, Meara replied, "I guess we will find out."

"We have a lot to learn," Brenna whispered.

As the firelight faded, the soft bluish moonlight spilled in the wide windows painted the room the darkest lavender. Outside, the crickets sang their chorus, bats squeaked as they swooped over the treetops, and an owl cooed from a high branch. The glass tempered these noises into a soothing lullaby as the sisters fell into peaceful sleep.

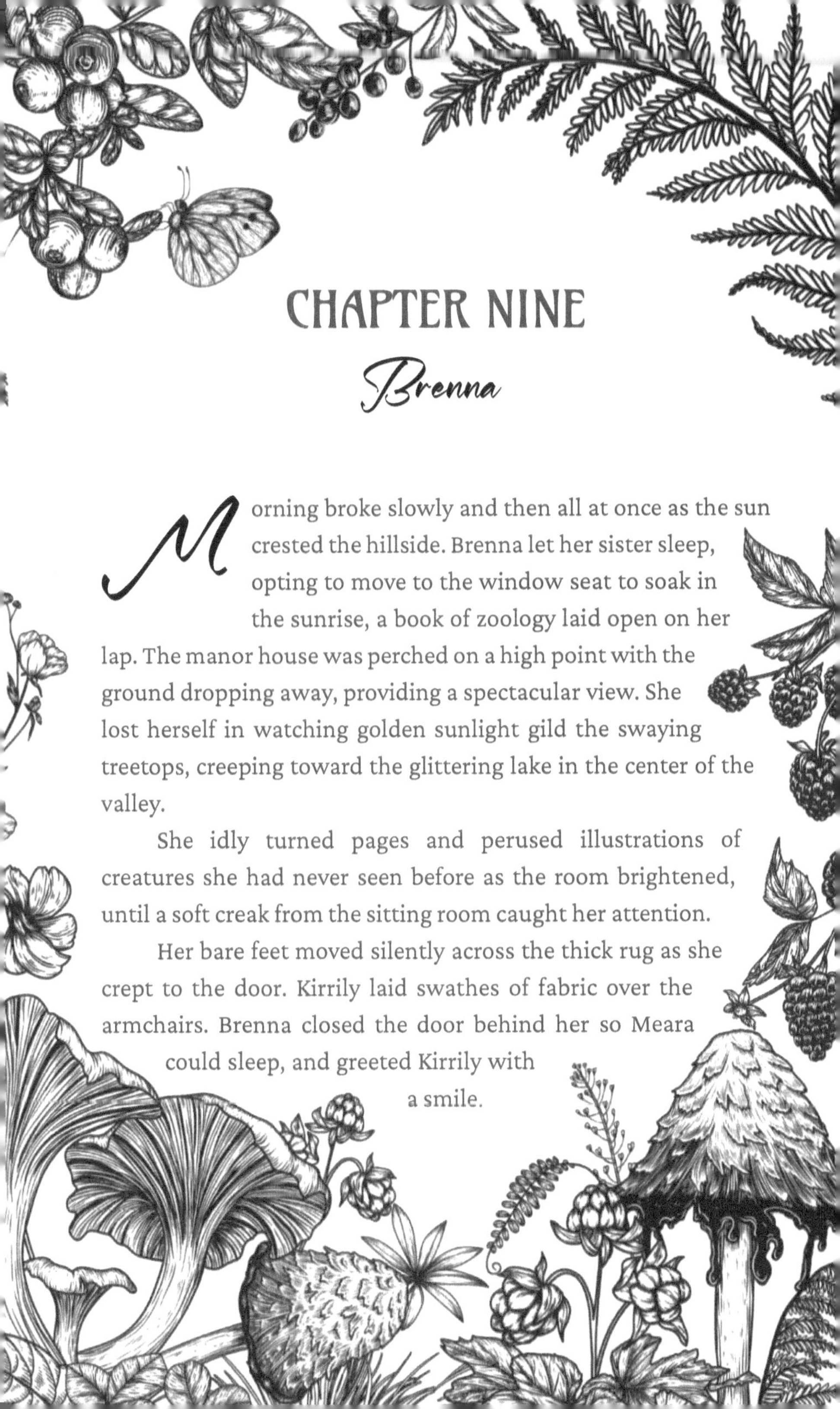

CHAPTER NINE
Brenna

Morning broke slowly and then all at once as the sun crested the hillside. Brenna let her sister sleep, opting to move to the window seat to soak in the sunrise, a book of zoology laid open on her lap. The manor house was perched on a high point with the ground dropping away, providing a spectacular view. She lost herself in watching golden sunlight gild the swaying treetops, creeping toward the glittering lake in the center of the valley.

She idly turned pages and perused illustrations of creatures she had never seen before as the room brightened, until a soft creak from the sitting room caught her attention.

Her bare feet moved silently across the thick rug as she crept to the door. Kirrily laid swathes of fabric over the armchairs. Brenna closed the door behind her so Meara could sleep, and greeted Kirrily with a smile.

"Good morning, my lady." Kirrily dipped into an elegant but brief curtsy. Her limbs stayed close, her movement precise and restrained. It was beautiful, but different than what Brenna knew, and she found herself attempting to capture the memory so she could adjust her own curtsy to match.

"Hello, Kirrily. Are those dresses?" She couldn't help the excited rise to her voice. The beauty and novelty of this world kept the doubt and sorrow pushed to the back of her mind. No time to be sad when one had beautiful dresses to try on.

Kirrily's polite smile widened into a true grin as she held up a gown. Silk the color of green pears flowed from the hanger. The neckline sparkled with beading a shade darker. "Would you like to wear this to breakfast?"

"Is it common to wear ball gowns to breakfast?" Her fingers ran over the dress as she drew closer, unable to help herself.

Kirrily crinkled her nose, her smile becoming lopsided. "This isn't a formal dress. It's too loose for that. I promise it's acceptable for breakfast with the Autumn Lord, but I can bring other attire if you prefer."

"Oh, I don't want to cause any additional work for you. It's only that I am accustomed to simpler clothing. Fae fashions are strange to me, but this dress is stunning and I would love to wear it."

"I will pick up additional undergarments from the seamstress today, but you'll need to get measured if she's to make you dresses. These were borrowed from Lady Seda and Lady Xurey," Kirrily explained, laying the dress down reverently.

"Who?" Brenna asked before she could think better.

"You've met Lady Xurey, and this green dress is hers," the dryad answered. Brenna nodded along. "And Lady Seda is the Master of the Autumn Guard."

"A female is the head of the guard?" The questions continued to spill out of her. She pressed her fingers over her cheeks, a flush crawling up her neck.

"Yes. She comes from a family line that has always served Lord Cerne's family." Kirrily drew herself up, her verdant eyes analyzing Brenna's appearance. "May I style your hair for you?"

"I would appreciate that."

She settled in a dining chair as Kirrily located a comb and hair pins. Humming to herself, she untangled Brenna's wild waves, murmuring about how beautiful their rich amber color was.

A tight type of joy twined in Brenna's heart. Only her mother and Meara had styled her hair for her, and Kirrily's efficient motions felt like a luxury.

"Morning," Meara muttered, pushing the bedroom door open. Her cool gray eyes surveyed the room. "Good morning, Kirrily."

"Good morning, Lady Meara. I brought you some dresses to wear, and I'd be happy to style your hair for breakfast." The servant delicately threaded another pin into Brenna's hair and stepped back, declaring it complete.

Brenna ran her fingers lightly over it, trying to discern the style. Most of her hair was left loose and down her back, but the hair from her temples back to the crown of her head was gathered up into a loose braid that was pinned into a spiral. "Thank you!"

As Kirrily brushed out Meara's hair, Brenna slipped into the borrowed dress. Xurey was taller than she was, and lacked Brenna's soft curves, but the flowing style suited both builds.

Brenna turned to admire herself in the full length mirror on the far wall. The verdant shade brought out the gold in her hair and skin. She wondered if she looked anything like the fae parents who left them. It was possible they were residents of the Autumn Court, or perhaps they had passed away or suffered some other tragedy that led to abandoning their children.

"So who will be at this breakfast?" she asked.

Kirrily pursed her lips as she brushed Meara's hair smooth. "Lord Cerne, Ladies Seda and Xurey, and I believe Lord Tayen has returned. And his sister Lady Ayala as well."

"Is there anything we should know to do or say, or not say?" Brenna asked.

"Oh no, my lady. It is a gathering of friends, not a formal court dinner. You will do fine."

Kirrily presented Meara with a dress of plum lace over matching silk. Brenna peered closely, admiring the lace's pattern of leaping foxes and crescent moons. Lace was uncommon in their village, but she was fairly sure it was typically a floral pattern, not vines, animals, and celestial designs.

It fit Meara well enough, and once Kirrily was satisfied with her hair and they had rejected her offer to apply cosmetics, it was time for breakfast.

The sisters stood hand in hand. Meara hesitated, and Brenna paused, pushing up onto her tiptoes to speak into her sister's ear. "Are you well?"

Meara shook her head and the tremor moved down her sheet of silken hair. "We aren't prepared for a semi-formal breakfast with a faerie lord."

"Oh, so it's the faerie lord that is bothering you?" Brenna inferred. A smirk warmed her face, but Meara did not return it. "Are you worried about seeing him or speaking with him?"

"No, it's fine." She shrugged off Brenna's teasing.

Brenna wanted to see and taste everything, drown in the colors and feel of it, and she hoped her sister would overcome her doubts and join her in this experience.

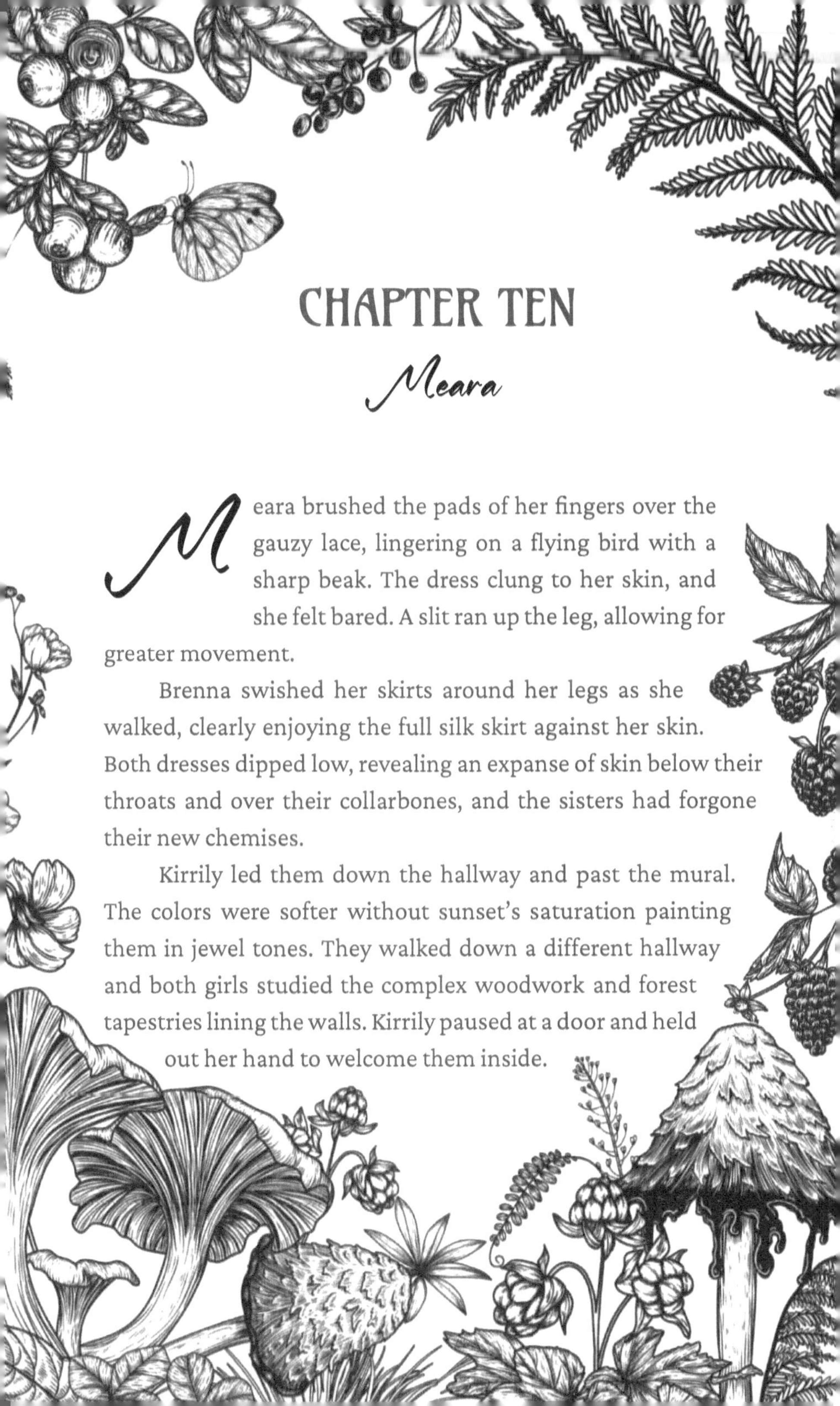

CHAPTER TEN
Meara

Meara brushed the pads of her fingers over the gauzy lace, lingering on a flying bird with a sharp beak. The dress clung to her skin, and she felt bared. A slit ran up the leg, allowing for greater movement.

Brenna swished her skirts around her legs as she walked, clearly enjoying the full silk skirt against her skin. Both dresses dipped low, revealing an expanse of skin below their throats and over their collarbones, and the sisters had forgone their new chemises.

Kirrily led them down the hallway and past the mural. The colors were softer without sunset's saturation painting them in jewel tones. They walked down a different hallway and both girls studied the complex woodwork and forest tapestries lining the walls. Kirrily paused at a door and held out her hand to welcome them inside.

The antechamber was relatively small, though still bigger than the main room of their cottage. The entire back wall seemed to be missing, and only a low bench piled with pillows separated the guests from the open hillside and a descent into the valley. Meara's eyes widened as she took in the view. This part of the house was further out over the edge of the hillside, and it seemed a sheer drop down to the lake below.

Two women rose from faded ruby velvet cushions. Xurey had replaced her riding clothes with a simple gray dress cut like a vest across her chest. "Good morning. How was your first night in the Autumn Court?"

"Very nice. Thank you for lending us dresses," Brenna replied.

Xurey's gaze flickered up and down Brenna's body. "I'm afraid it looks better on you than it does on me. You should keep it."

Brenna beamed. "I couldn't, but thank you for the offer."

"Meara, Brenna, this is Seda, the Master of the Autumn Guard and a good friend."

Seda stood taller than Xurey and Brenna, with a warm, dark complexion and hair shorn close to her head, making her wide nose and full lips all the more dramatic. Meara envied the way her lithe frame was graceful instead of spindly.

"Thank you for letting me borrow this," Meara said, her arms curling around her middle. She felt entirely out of place draped in fine fabrics and standing with such beautiful women.

Seda's dark eyes studied her, and she leaned closer. "You're welcome to borrow any of my dresses. It is not my preferred attire. I will spend the rest of the day in fighting leathers." Meara felt her mouth tug into a genuine unbidden smile for the first time since leaving their home.

"So what do you think of the Court of Autumn Harvest?" Seda asked, looking from Meara to Brenna.

"We haven't seen much of it yet, but it seems pleasant." She folded her arms over the glittering bodice of her dress. "Have you always lived here?"

Seda nodded, and even that movement was regal. "My mother was the Master of the Autumn Guard under Lord Cerne's mother."

"Is it typical to take up your mother's position in court?" Meara asked.

"For some."

"I was born in the Court of Learning," Xurey supplied, "but I have not lived there since I was a child. I only visit the Observatory once every few years. I prefer to stay with friends in the Autumn Court when I am not traveling."

"Few faeries reside in the Court of Learning. It is attended by scholars and musicians from all courts. Those that are born there tend to wander," Seda explained, correctly interpreting Brenna's slight frown of confusion.

"I have never heard of the Court of Learning," Brenna said.

"I imagine it's not discussed among humans," Xurey mused.

"Perhaps you can tell me about it?"

The puca nodded, smiling. "I am sure we will find some time."

An unmistakably masculine presence filled the doorway. Meara's lungs seized as her breath halted. Cerne's cloak was replaced with an emerald day coat. An ivory shirt hung loose over his shoulders and tucked into tailored trousers. Damp hair curled over his tapered ears, skimming his shoulders. He looked every bit the Autumn Lord, as untamed as he was refined.

He greeted Seda with a grasped hand and a curt nod. As he turned to Brenna, his smile widened. "I hope you are enjoying your time with us."

"Ryles and Kirrily have taken good care of us," Brenna responded politely.

Meara stubbornly kept her eyes above his neck and away

from the vee of exposed chest as Cerne closed the distance between them. She should be grateful he was finally wearing a shirt, but the billow of semi translucent fabric only served to highlight the line of his body.

He took her hand and brushed the lightest kiss over her knuckles, his eyes rising to meet hers through thick lashes. They were not the earthen brown she originally thought, but a weave of moss and chestnut rimmed in gold. Eyes that could never belong to a human.

Her inhale was shaky, and the scent of woodsmoke and wild chamomile soaked into her lungs. The day apart had done nothing to lessen the effect he had on her.

"Lady Meara." His voice brushed over her, warm and gentle.

"Good morning," she said, her voice sticking in her throat.

A smirk that felt illicit ghosted across his lips. "Everyone ready to break their fast?" He led them through the wide door on the side of the antechamber and into a long dining room.

Cathedral ceilings soared over an expansive table of gleaming cherry covered in a rainbow of platters and bowls. Sparkling crystalline carafes held teas ranging from deep violet to pale honey. Tiny quail eggs sat stacked between baked apples and cranberry scones.

Beyond the head of the table stood a massive obsidian hearth. The flames lit up Brenna's golden curls as she settled to Cerne's left. Meara slid into the seat beside her, her fingers gliding over the high gloss finish of the chair's ornate arms.

Seda sat to Cerne's right and began updating him on new recruits for the guard. The Autumn Lord reached for a little cake studded with blackberries as he listened. Meara looked between him and the food, unsure of proper decorum. Across the table, Xurey added food to her plate and nodded encouragingly when she noticed the sisters' hesitation.

There were so many options, it was overwhelming. Brenna placed a mushroom and wild onion tartlet on her own plate and then added one to Meara's. Her reservations tamed, Meara began selecting a little of everything to her plate - slices of salted boar, roasted and sugared acorns, and dark molasses bread with glazed persimmons.

The door opened, the breeze drawing the delicate ringlets framing Brenna's face across her cheeks. Tayen strode in, his ivory coat contrasting with the vibrant tone of his curls and the warmth of his freckled skin.

Beside him, a willowy faerie walked with her arm linked through his. The upturn of her nose and the curve of her cupid's bow echoed his features, but her beauty was chilled by the curl of her lip as she surveyed the table. Meara's shoulders straightened and her chin rose in defense.

"I apologize for our tardiness. It was a late night." Tayen sank into the seat beside Xurey and reached for a sliver of egg custard tart topped with sprigs of fresh dill. "Brenna, Meara, this is my sister, Ayala."

Ayala's fingers brushed the back of Seda's chair as she sauntered past. She perched herself on the arm of Cerne's chair and draped her arm along the back of it. "Good morning." Her voice was clear and musical.

Cerne ignored her and leaned forward, focused on Tayen. "How did everything go?"

"Eldric was delighted to have an apothecary nearby, and he gave her apartments and promised to provide the resources for her to set up a new shop."

Brenna's hand went to her mouth and her eyes crinkled. "Thank you so much."

Tayen nodded, smiling.

"By Eldric," Meara asked, canting her head, "do you mean?"

"King Eldric of Dornadan," Ayala drawled, a laugh in her words. The gauzy dress dripping off of her lean frame was the color of peaches. She leaned forward and plucked an apple pastry off of Cerne's plate, displaying her breasts with the movement.

Looking away, Meara took a long drink of the pear blossom tea in her glass. Across from her, Xurey's lips thinned and she shifted in her seat, looking as uncomfortable as Meara felt.

"So, Tayen, were you so late because of time with the human King, or were you visiting Eladin." Seda smirked and raised an eyebrow at him.

From beside her, Brenna frowned, and Meara pressed her lips into a line. *Prince Eladin,* Xurey mouthed.

"He is doing well, if you must know. And I bring an official invitation," Tayen said with a lazy confidence. He produced a thick, ivory envelope and passed it to Cerne with a flourish.

The wax seal broke with a pop and Cerne scanned the letter with his lips slightly parted. "We are invited to a betrothal celebration."

"Who is marrying?" Seda asked.

"King Eldric is finally remarrying." He paused, an unhappy tilt to his mouth. "The princess of Liosliath."

Xurey set her glass down, her brows pinching. "I was not aware Liosliath had a princess."

"She is a recent addition," Brenna said, clearing her throat. "A year or so ago, Queen Malacia married King Barrach and Liosliath gained control of Tuar."

Tayen nodded. "Small kingdom, coastal and mostly trade-based."

Frowning, Seda sat back in her seat and crossed her arms. "Like that witch needed more power."

Brenna drew in a slow breath, looking between the sober faces at the table. "Well, Princess Elysia is his daughter from his first wife. Queen Malacia was keeping her quiet, but the girls in the washhouse were gossiping. Supposedly, she's quite lovely."

"She's barely eighteen," Meara added.

A sour silence stretched between them. Finally, Cerne sighed and took a long drink of his cider. The flagon thudded on the table. "We will have to go and support our friend."

"Perhaps this will work in our favor and we can gain access to Liosliath's famed metalwork." Tayen's hopeful words and half smile brought warmth to the table. "It's in Dornadan. Brenna, Meara, you'll have to join us. You can see your mother."

"I'd appreciate that," Brenna said softly.

"There will be time to worry about trade later. For now, we have guests with magic to unlock." Cerne's sincere smile was ruined by the way his hand skimmed across Ayala's thigh. "Tayen, can you join us this afternoon to attempt stripping away the remaining enchantment?"

"It will be the highlight of my week." His charming smile relaxed Meara. "We will need to find suitable mentors once we know their magic craft."

"Don't we already know mine?" Brenna asked innocently, holding up her hands though no sparks appeared.

"You could have fire craft or light craft, or something else. They can look similar. Once you discover the range of your abilities, it will be easier to train you." Tayen's answer was patient.

"What kind of magic do you all have?" Meara asked, stiffening when she realized her question might be considered rude.

Unbothered, Tayen answered, "I am a shield, so I can block other's magic. This allows me to undo a lot of magic as well. I can also divert physical objects, but that is especially draining." As if to prove his point, Tayen tossed a roasted acorn into the air and changed its path in the air with a simple flick of his wrist. It sailed across the table and bounced into Xurey's goblet. She scowled at him and he grinned boyishly and shrugged.

Ayala let out a scoff and adjusted herself. Her arm had moved from the back of the chair to Cerne's shoulders. "So what is her craft?" Her gaze rested on Meara for the first time.

No one spoke. Meara's cheeks flushed. "I don't know. Nothing, I suppose."

"She looks human to me. How do we know she is fae?" Ayala flipped her vibrant hair over her shoulder.

Cerne pulled away from her hold and narrowed his eyes as he said, "Your brother."

Tayen's light laugh softened the tension. "We will find out soon enough, I am sure." Ayala rolled her eyes at him, looking more like a petulant teen than fae nobility.

"I'd like you to see my court today, if you're agreeable," Cerne said.

"Yes, please," Brenna answered, seemingly unphased by the skepticism coming from Ayala.

Face flushing, Meara picked up her spoon and nudged a scrap of food left on her plate. A fierce desire welled up in her chest to manifest magic that eclipsed anything the red-headed fae female possessed.

CHAPTER ELEVEN

Brenna

After breakfast, Brenna found solace in the cushioned window seat in their bedroom. She selected a stack of books this time, and another volume of botany sat unopened on her lap while she stared at the mesmerizing shimmer of leaves in the breeze. The forest was a patchwork of verdant evergreens and flame-kissed canopies.

As beautiful as this place was, the guilt and grief of losing their home gnawed at her, hollowing her chest and clogging her throat. She could only keep up her cheerful positivity for so long before memories crept in. Eyes stinging, she rested her temple against the cool glass while she counted out her breaths. Behind her lids, the flash of Johnathon Lyndhurst's knife, mud flying as she ran, and the shouts of their neighbors surged uncontrollably.

"Brenna," Meara asked, "do you want to

change?" Her lithe figure stood in the doorway, concern etched into the lines on her face. Meara always sensed when Brenna's emotions were spiraling.

"Good idea." Her voice was falsely bright, but her sister wasn't fooled. Meara crossed the room and sank to her knees beside the bench. Her arms snaked around her hips as she pressed her face into Brenna's waist.

Meara peered up, weighing her words. "Please tell me how to help."

"All is well, I swear. I'm no worse for wear." Exhaling, Brenna released the tension in her face, and then her shoulders, and finally her hands.

"Brenna," Meara pressed.

"Help me figure out an outfit that won't have my knockers escaping if the walk is rocky."

Meara barked a laugh and rocked back on her heels to stand, propping her hands on her hips. "Can I convince you to wear trousers?"

"I'd prefer a dress if there are any suitable. But not the ones we came in. I don't want to stand out." Brenna allowed herself to be pulled to her feet as Meara set about picking out clothing items for her to try on. Their selection of garments had expanded yet again to include a handful of embroidered tunics, billowing shirts, and fitted pants. Brenna made a note to thank Kirrily when they saw her again.

Her sister happily donned trousers and a smokey gray shirt she tucked into the waistband and secured with a simple belt. Her normally cynical expression relaxed into a pleased smile. Perhaps living as a faerie suited her. She fit in better here than she ever had in Liosliath.

Unsure of herself, Brenna vacillated between a few options and finally pulled on the chemise from the night before and an ivory day dress that covered her upper arms. It dipped low in the chest, showing a sliver of her chemise, but Brenna liked the contrast. It reminded her of the layered dresses she saw the noble women wear when they rode through their rural village on holiday.

"Should we go find something to do with ourselves?" Brenna suggested, smoothing her hands over the cotton bodice.

Meara bit the inside of her cheek, carving out the hollow of her face as she deliberated.

A knock on the door caused Brenna to turn. Meara opened the door to reveal Lord Cerne. He leaned against the door frame, one half of his mouth pulled up in a charismatic smile. "Can I tempt you to join me on a tour?"

Meara regarded him, that suspicious glint back in her eyes. The way her hand rested on her hip, Brenna knew she was unhappy with the faerie, but her voice was neutral when she spoke. "I did not expect you to be our guide. We wouldn't want to take you away from your important work."

"Nonsense, this is the perfect excuse to spend the day enjoying my court." Cerne held out his hand and Meara eyed it like a snake. "Shall we?"

When she didn't take his offered arm, Cerne swept his hand out to usher them into the hall. Meara strode past him, her shoulders and back stiff. Something about the fae lord unbalanced her. Unable to help her smile at Meara's turmoil, Brenna followed the pair out. She doubted Cerne would be able to charm her stubborn sister, but it would be entertaining to see him try.

The trio strode down the hall and through the grand entry. Brenna turned, motioning to the expansive mural. "This is incredible."

Cerne slowed. "Yes, we have many artists here. This was painted by my great grandmother."

"Was she the Lady of Autumn?" Meara asked.

His chin rose as he examined the artwork, as if it was new and not something he had looked at for his entire life. "Yes, she was. We are one of the longest ruling bloodlines. Seven generations."

"Are other courts less stable?"

His hazel eyes drifted to Meara's face. "Rulership is based on magic here. It's not inherited like the human kingdoms. But if your parents are strong in their craft, it is likely you are as well."

"So if someone more powerful came along, they could unseat you?"

"No," Cerne said with a laugh. "I have earned my place serving my court. But when I pass rulership on to my heir some day, they will have to prove themselves, or another could take their place."

"And do you have an heir?" Meara asked, her eyes widening slightly as if she was surprised at her own brashness. Brenna covered a smile.

"Not yet," he said, moving away from the mural. Meara's lips pressed together as she followed his lengthy stride, glancing over her shoulder to check on Brenna.

Ryles stood by the front door, holding it open as the Autumn Lord crossed the threshold with a nod of thanks. It was the first genuine smile Brenna had seen on the dryad. Cerne's people adored him. It was undeniable as they descended the hill into the court.

Cerne led them to the left, down a different road than the one they took when arriving. A few faeries tended to shops while others walked down the cobblestone. They all smiled and greeted their lord with relaxed bows or friendly waves.

Structures lined the right side of the road, while the left opened to the river running alongside their path. A low masonry wall ran the length of the road, protecting careless pedestrians from tumbling down the hill and into the water.

One of the first buildings was dark with a brick arch and a cold forge inside. "An old blacksmithy?" Brenna asked.

Cerne nodded, slowing his steps as he turned toward the empty space. "Never used, unfortunately. I built it for a friend years ago and he was never able to take up residence."

"Oh, that's a pity." Her gaze lingered on the space, understanding why it looked so clean. No soot stained the forge. No ash clung to the corners. And Cerne hadn't offered the space to another, as if he held out hope his friend would come.

His shoulders rose and fell in a resigned shrug, his serious expression melting away to a charming smile. With a tilt of his head, Cerne led them onward. "We have a book maker up here you might find of interest."

"Brenna loves books," Meara said, looping her arm through Brenna's.

"The rooms we are staying in have so many books on the shelves. I imagine it's like the libraries in the Queen's city," Brenna followed the Autumn Lord, curiosity bubbling up in her chest.

"I suppose the fae produce more books per capita than humans do, though I've never thought much about it," he mused, stopping at a bright yellow door with stained glass in the center depicting an open book with a golden swirl coming from its center. "This bookshop has been printing periodicals and books for generations. I always enjoy watching them work."

Brenna tentatively stepped into the space, taking in slate floors and rows of standing bookshelves in mismatched wood tones. Her hand pressed to her chest as she took in hundreds of books lined up neatly all around her.

An imposing desk stood to the side with a clerk taking notes on paper. Past the display area, a low dividing wall separated the workers and machines from visitors.

"So nice to have you here, my lord," a young faerie said, smiling through her lashes at Cerne. At first, Brenna thought she was a child because the top of her head was level with Brenna's shoulder. Pink hair streamed over her shoulders, dotted with tiny white blossoms - a nymph.

"Would you like to see some of our recent work?" She held out a book in delicate hands the same pale pink as campion flowers.

Cerne accepted the book and turned over the cover, running his hand over black leather gilded with ornamented words. Brenna drifted closer, making out the title: *Wildflowers of Roven*.

"Roven?"

"That's what we call our city. Not widely known among humans, least of all Liosliath, I expect," Cerne muttered, thumbing through the pages. "These illustrations are beautiful."

"Thank you, my lord. Please keep it. The Autumn Lord should have a first edition of a book written about your land, should you not?"

Meara watched the machines work with her head cocked. Brenna joined her, mesmerized by the sheets of paper moving in and out of the printing press. She recognized the machine from the technology books that the little boy Herman loved to read, though these were intricate, petite versions. Along the wall, a row of faeries sat stitching paper into books. Each movement was graceful and practiced, and Brenna could have watched them for hours.

"We should leave them to their work," Cerne said. With great effort, Brenna peeled her attention away from the workshop. She trailed after the Autumn Lord with Meara on her heels. He paused at the desk to leave coins despite the worker's protests.

Once outside, Brenna spun to face her sister. "Can you believe it? They were creating books right before our eyes!"

"You can come back anytime you like. And if you ask nicely, they might even let you learn to operate the machinery." Cerne said as he began to walk away from the bookshop. With one last peek through the display window, Brenna followed.

"How many people live in the Autumn Court?" Meara asked, stepping up beside him.

"Seven hundred or so? But many live away from Roven." His brows furrowed in thought. "A few families split their time between courts."

"That's very few compared to the human kingdoms," Meara said.

Cerne scrubbed his hand across his short beard. "Faeries live longer, but we rarely have children. Though we can die from illness or injury as easily as humans." He shrugged.

Slowing, Brenna squinted through the picture window of the next shop. "Meara, it's an apothecary!"

Shelves lined the walls, covered in jars and wooden boxes. Bundles of herbs hung from the rafters in the dim light.

"Do you want to go in?" Cerne asked. "Our herbalist isn't the friendliest faerie, but his shop is well stocked."

"Perhaps another time," Brenna said, noting the way Meara took a step back and turned her head.

Cerne didn't question her, but led them around a bend in the road where it diverged from the river and shops sprouted on the other side of the road, hemming them in.

Their next stop was a bakery. Cerne procured flakey pastries filled with hazelnut cream. They strolled and ate, and Brenna was pleased to see Meara relaxing.

As morning melted into midday, some shops closed for a meal and more faeries appeared on the street. Everyone smiled and seemed genuinely happy. Something ached in Brenna's chest. She didn't know a town could be like this.

"Is Roven similar to where you grew up in Liosliath?" Cerne asked, leaning against a wall beside a tavern that had yet to open for the day.

"Not at all," she answered honestly. "I doubt any part of Liosliath is as lovely as your court." He was pleased with her answer, a charming grin spreading across his face.

"Well, we have an upcoming appointment to keep, so we had better keep going." Cerne pushed off the smooth stones at his back and led them across the road.

"What is it?" Meara asked, her steps slowing.

Cerne turned, now walking backwards as he raised an eyebrow. "Don't you trust me?"

"Absolutely not," Meara muttered. Her eyes narrowed, but Cerne just laughed. Brenna didn't miss the faint blush staining Meara's pale cheeks.

"Don't worry. It's a seamstress. Since you were forced to leave your home without your wardrobes, I thought you might need some replacements. Especially if you're joining me for the betrothal feast."

The dressmaker's shop stood nestled between a candlemaker's chandlery and a carpenter's showroom. A lace curtain blocked much of the view of the interior from where they stood.

"We can't," Meara argued, her voice dropping.

Cerne stopped one step from the door, his hand reaching behind his back for the handle. "You can and you should. Borrowing dresses from Seda and Xurey is not a sustainable option. Both of them deplore dresses and I promise you will deplete their selection rather quickly."

Meara opened her mouth to respond, but paused and looked to Brenna, who clutched her hands together and tried to not look too eager.

"Is there a concern other than the expense?" Cerne asked quietly. "I have already placed it onto my accounts. You don't need to worry about the cost."

"That's too generous," Meara said.

"My dear, the cost of a few dresses will not hurt my court's budget, I promise. Besides, it's important that my guests are well dressed." He pushed the door open and stepped inside before she could argue again.

With a reluctant smile, Brenna grabbed her sister's hand and towed her into the shop. As she passed Cerne, Brenna said, "Thank you. I appreciate this."

"My pleasure."

CHAPTER TWELVE

Brenna

A rainbow of fabrics covered one wall. Mirrors stood along another wall, with a trio of low platforms placed before them. Wooden forms stood opposite the fabric rolls, already dressed in an array of dresses with colors ranging from blazing oranges to deep reds to the softest brown. They shared similar flowing cuts and featured delicate accents such as embroidery, beading, or even feathers.

A small faerie stepped from the back room. A rich walnut brown dress hugged her abundant curves, matching the shade of her wide, dark eyes. White freckles covered her chestnut cheeks and velvet doe ears stuck out from her multitude of caramel braids.

"Dyani, I hope you are well," Cerne said, leaning down to kiss her cheek. Her warm skin flushed raspberry.

"These are my guests that Ryles spoke with you about.

Please outfit them with a wardrobe fit for our court. At least two weeks worth of garments, both formal and day wear, please."

"Of course, my lord." Her cheeks dimpled as she smiled.

"Hold on, that's far more than a couple of dresses," Meara objected. Cerne shrugged and slipped out of the shop, pausing at the door to wink at them. Meara spun to face Dyani.

The fawnling sighed and held up her hand. "There's no use arguing. Lord Cerne does as he pleases. We might as well enjoy ourselves."

"If we must," Brenna said with a grin. Meara's exhale was rough, but she didn't argue. "It's lovely to meet you. I am Brenna and this is Meara."

Dyani raised a hand to her mouth, tapping a manicured finger over her lips. "It takes time to sew new dresses, so I think it's best if you both pick at least one gown from my stock so I can quickly alter it to fit. Then you will have something to wear while I work on custom pieces for you." She fluttered her hands, herding them toward the dress forms. "Anything catch your eye? I have more in the back if nothing suits. Come, explore."

Brenna's gaze snagged on an apricot dress with sparkles raining down from the rounded neckline. She stepped closer and reached out to touch the layers of chiffon.

"Lovely choice. That will highlight the warmth in your hair beautifully," Dyani said, coming to stand beside her.

"Thank you."

Meara passed over a multitude of colorful options and finally selected an evergreen dress with a metallic sheen. As the fabric flowed over the hips and trailed to the floor, it darkened into shadowy black.

"Please try them on so I can pin them, and I will take your measurements as well." Dyani held back a curtain to reveal a dressing room behind the mirrors. The girls ducked into the space.

A moment later, Dyani passed them the dresses now removed from their forms. Brenna's breath caught as the silky fabric slid over her fingers.

As soon as Meara finished lacing her up, Brenna eagerly stepped onto the platform. The dress was snug across her stomach, but only a touch. Dyani reassured her it was an easy fix as she flitted back and forth with a measuring tape, noting everything about Brenna's figure.

Meara watched apprehensively, her arms folded over the low cut of her dress. When she dropped her hands to her sides, Brenna inhaled with a soft, audible gasp. "Meara, you look incredible!"

"I look like a phantom," she muttered. As Dyani measured her and pinned the dress, Meara eyed herself in the mirror.

"I can have these tailored by tomorrow and I'll send them up to the estate along with some basics. And I will send additional items as they're completed." Dyani's smile was crooked.

When the sisters returned from changing back into their prior outfits, Cerne stood by the shop entrance, leaning against the door frame with his arms crossed and a rogue grin on his face.

"You can't have them back yet. I need to know their fabric preferences," Dyani warned. Warm friendship glowed between them, and Brenna wondered how many of his subjects Cerne knew with this level of kinship. They clearly adored him.

Dyani held out various silks and laces, murmuring to herself. Occasionally she asked their opinions, but mostly she noted how the fabric suited the girls. As Brenna admired a creamy satin, the fawnling's lips twitched and she jotted down a note.

"I believe I have everything necessary to create you enough clothing for a fortnight. If you need more, you just have to ask." Her furred ears flicked as she smiled politely at them.

"I can't begin to express my gratitude," Brenna said.

"Dressing you is honor enough," Dyani said as she shooed

them out of her shop.

Cerne did not ask how the appointment went, but observed their contented faces and smirked, leading them away. They passed a potter's studio, a gallery, and a small restaurant. The Autumn Lord shared snippets of information, like "That painting was done by the oldest artist in residence at the Autumn Court," or "That chef makes the most incredible venison roasts."

"Your court is called the Court of Autumn Harvest, so do you have farming?" Brenna asked. Meara watched, her dark mood slowly creeping back.

"Not really, we are better known for our artisans," Cerne said with a laugh. "Our northern border is shared with the Summer Court. Most of the realm's crops are grown there. Unfortunately, it's a cooperative process."

"What do you mean?" Meara asked, squinting.

"The Court of Summer Light is *challenging* to work with." Each word flowed with disdain. Seeing Brenna's worried expression, he conceded, "Nothing to worry about. Our mutual dislike stretches back decades and isn't likely to reach a breaking point any time soon."

They reached the end of the road. Cottages stretched out before them in a rough grouping, becoming further spaced apart until they faded into the trees entirely. Brenna couldn't help but study the small gardens around many of them, curious what vegetables they were able to grow under the forest's cover.

A strange crowing noise startled her. She grabbed Meara's arm and her sister tensed, searching for the source. Brenna let out a surprised laugh as a small flock of chickens toddled toward them. They sported feather top-knots that flopped back and forth as they walked. "Oh, hello! Aren't you darling?" Brenna said, sinking down to take a closer look.

Cerne crouched beside her, sweeping his coat out behind

him. "Would you like to pet one?"

"I doubt they'd let me." Her hand reached out anyway, though they were still a stretch away. Cerne wiggled his fingers and clicked his tongue. The entire flock rushed forward and surrounded them, bumping into his knees and hips. He brushed his hand over the birds and they purred.

"Animals tend to like me," Cerne explained, seeing Meara's raised eyebrows. In response, the little flock clucked happily.

"That makes sense. You turn into an animal," Meara said coolly.

Cerne stood, allowing the chickens to swarm his shins. Brenna stroked the backs of the hens nearest to her and almost missed the way Cerne sought out Meara's attention before saying, "I've been told this form is far more charming. Wouldn't you agree?"

"Debatable." She crossed her arms.

"Can you turn into *any* animal?" Brenna asked, breaking the tension.

He shook his head. "Only my stag."

Sighing, Meara looked him over. "Pity. I think you'd be more charming if you could transform into a cock like these. They certainly like you enough."

Brenna's exhale turned into a snort of laughter, which she covered with her hand, warmth stinging her cheeks. Cerne threw his head back and laughed heartily. "That's quite the suggestion."

Meara's facade broke and her lips curved, her eyes alight. Hope flooded Brenna's chest, seeing her sister relax and jest. Cerne wiped at his eyes and cleared his throat. "As delightful as this has been, I think it's time we return home to meet Tayen. I am looking forward to seeing you without this enchantment suppressing your magic." Brenna stood, anxiety sparking under her skin as they followed Cerne back.

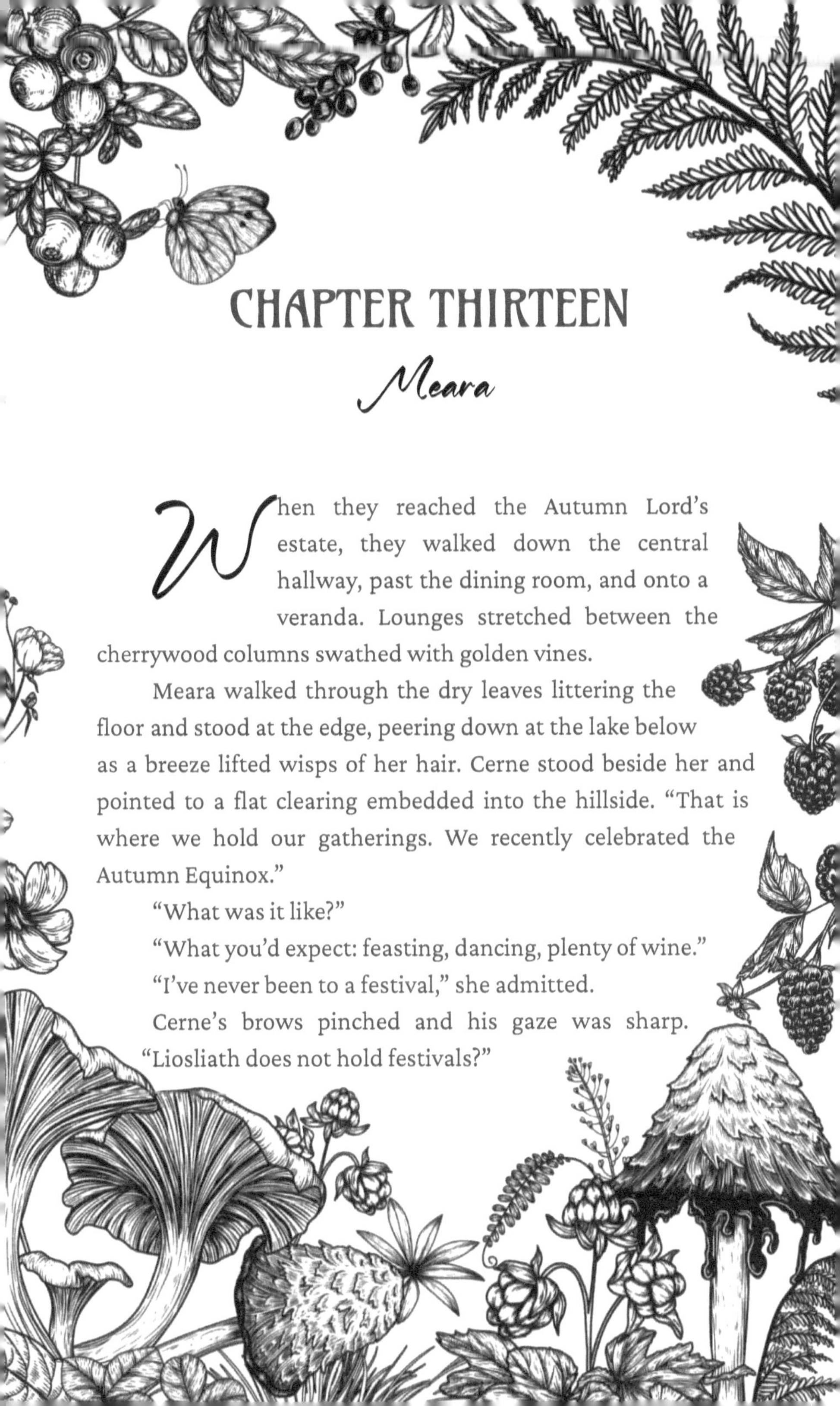

CHAPTER THIRTEEN
Meara

When they reached the Autumn Lord's estate, they walked down the central hallway, past the dining room, and onto a veranda. Lounges stretched between the cherrywood columns swathed with golden vines.

Meara walked through the dry leaves littering the floor and stood at the edge, peering down at the lake below as a breeze lifted wisps of her hair. Cerne stood beside her and pointed to a flat clearing embedded into the hillside. "That is where we hold our gatherings. We recently celebrated the Autumn Equinox."

"What was it like?"

"What you'd expect: feasting, dancing, plenty of wine."

"I've never been to a festival," she admitted.

Cerne's brows pinched and his gaze was sharp. "Liosliath does not hold festivals?"

Brenna shook her head, looping her arm through Meara's as she drew closer. "Not in the rural villages."

"Then perhaps you'd like to join me for the next one?"

Meara studied him. His forest eyes were steady as he met her gaze, and his full lips turned up in a sincere and hopeful expression. It would be so nice to trust him. "I suppose we could be persuaded, but I'm afraid we won't be here in a year's time."

The Autumn Lord looked over the treetops. "Our next celebration is Samhain, but we will travel to the Summer Court for it. It's not the first experience I would hope for you."

"Why?"

A dark lock of hair fell over Cerne's brow as he cocked his head. "Maybe I don't want anyone from the Summer Court trying to steal you away from me." Meara's lips parted, but she could think of nothing to say to this male with his soulful eyes the color of the forest and those audacious smirks.

"I think I've got it." Tayen breezed into the room, smile wide and golden eyes bright.

"Got what?" Brenna asked.

"I was thinking about the enchantment all morning, and I believe I know how to remove it." He had shed his morning coat, and his cream shirt billowed over breeches the color of burnt sugar. Copper buttons caught the light.

"How?" Brenna asked.

"My magic can disrupt what was left on you, and once that hold is broken, it should dissolve. Well, there is more to it than that, but you get the idea."

"What do we need to do?"

"Nothing. Just allow me to work my craft. If you're ready, we can do it now." Tayen rolled his shoulders and raised his hands.

"That quickly?" Holding up her hand, Meara looked between the two fae males. "Could this potentially harm us?"

Shaking his head, Cerne explained, "Tayen's magic cannot harm. It's protective in nature."

Brenna turned her sweet smile on Meara. "It'll be okay."

Nodding, Tayen rested a hand on each of their shoulders. "If it works, it will be immediate. Otherwise, it's back to the drafting table." Meara swallowed the lump in her throat and nodded.

With a long exhale, Tayen closed his eyes. For a moment, nothing happened. His brows knit and his mouth thinned. Brenna's hand tightened over hers, and Meara tensed. A fizzing, buzzing feeling hummed under her skin, starting to gradually feel as if it had always been there.

Tayen shifted his weight, his hands flexing on their shoulders. A feeling of tightness spread over Meara's skin. Her lungs constricted, chest tight.

With a pop, a sudden rush of sensation overwhelmed her. The light breeze felt like a physical caress. The smell of musty rotting leaves and sharp pine resin filled her lungs and made her eyes water. Brenna's sharp intake of breath matched her own.

Tayen stepped back, and Meara blinked up at him, seeing a bleary but satisfied expression on his face as her vision swam and finally came into focus.

"How do you feel?" Cerne asked. The tone far richer and textured than a moment before.

Brenna jerked back and her fingers untangled from Meara's. As she moved, the light caught her curls. Meara blinked, hesitant to believe what she was seeing. Her sister's hair was closer to spun gold and her warm skin was almost glowing. As their gazes connected, her lips parted in surprise. Brenna's warm, light brown eyes were filled with flecks of gold.

"Meara, you look so beautiful!" Her voice fluttered like music. "Your eyes are mesmerizing."

Frowning, Meara held out her pale arms. The tan she

developed each summer was gone, leaving an expanse of unmarred cream. The muscles felt fluid as she rotated them. She felt strong.

As she stepped closer, Brenna cocked her head. "Your eyes aren't gray anymore. More like, I don't know, lilac or lavender."

"Your eyes have gold in them now," Meara replied. The sisters stared at each other for a long moment. Brenna's fingers traced the edge of her ear, and Meara copied her, shivering as she felt the tapered end. It felt disconnected, like the sharp tips of her ears were not yet a part of her, yet the skin was so sensitive.

She dragged her fingers down through her hair and held it out. The black gloss of her hair shone with a rainbow of colors, like the feathers of a raven. Purple, blue, and green reflected on the strands as they moved.

"How do you feel?" Brenna whispered.

"Good, I think. Strong," Meara replied, rising onto her tip toes and back down. The soft ache of soreness from their morning walk over cobblestones was gone from Meara's feet. It was replaced with an awareness of everything around them, the unevenness of the floor through her boots, the way her hair brushed her neck. Slowly, she let her breath go and focused on her sister.

Brenna smiled and the radiance felt like sunshine hitting Meara's face. "Tayen, thank you."

Cerne drew closer, and Meara tracked every precise movement of his muscles and the animalistic tilt of his head. His dark hair gleamed with red where the sun hit it. She saw every detail. He reached out and hooked a finger under her chin, lifting it to stare into her eyes. "I thought you were perhaps half-fae, but you are clearly full-blooded faeries."

Tension coiled in her muscles, pulled taut as he held her attention, that point of contact consuming her senses. Finally, he dropped his hand, allowing her to take in a breath.

"That enchantment was self-sustaining and complex," Tayen

said. His galaxy of freckles shone like bronze.

Her heightened vision caught the way Cerne's eyes widened a fraction. "Now there's the question of who set this enchantment. After hearing your mother's account, I think it is likely whoever left you on her doorstep is also the one who set the magic. And quite possibly your kin."

"Does it matter?" Meara asked, her jaw clenching. It was hard to think straight with Cerne's soft scent invading her brain and filling her stomach full of fluttering moths.

Tayen rubbed the back of his neck. "It was magic few could accomplish. Only the most powerful of ancient faeries can leave their magic craft working in their absence. They are the ones that fade away from the world and the ones who shaped it."

"I'd like to know," Brenna said.

"We have a mother in Dornadan awaiting our return," Meara snapped. It felt disloyal to look for a second family among the faerie. "Why would you want to find someone who took away our magic and left us?"

Scowling, Brenna crossed her arms. "Don't you want to know why? That's not an answer we will find in Dornadan."

Meara pressed her lips together and exhaled slowly, counting in her head. This wasn't a discussion she wanted to have in front of their hosts.

With all of the intense sounds and smells overwhelming her senses, Meara's emotions were spiraling and it was impossible to stay calm. Exhaling, Meara nodded, and Brenna's eyes flashed triumphantly.

"Can you feel your magic craft?" Cerne asked, breaking the tension between the sisters.

Warmth radiated from Brenna's body, and Meara was unsure if it was her increased fae senses or if her sister was creating heat. Smiling, Brenna raised her fingers and sparks danced between them.

"Very impressive," Tayen murmured. "Meara, can you sense anything?"

It took great effort to block out the abundance of sensation and turn her attention inward, looking for any foreign feeling, any spark. Nothing.

Opening her eyes, she looked between the males. "No, not really."

"I'm sure it'll come with time," Tayen said. "Brenna, we should test your range and see if we can determine your type of craft."

"It's definitely elemental," Cerne said. "Most likely Ayala or Seda is the closest match."

"So Seda will train her?" Tayen asked, his eyes crinkling with mirth. Meara didn't miss how he excluded his sister, though it was a relief. She didn't want either of them to have to spend more time with the faerie.

The sounds of the forest beyond the veranda welled up, and Meara pressed her palms to her eyes, trying to block out light and color.

"Why don't we go inside and leave Tayen to work with Brenna?" Cerne asked. Meara could only nod weakly and follow. His hand brushed her elbow and guided her through the door. Once it closed, the sensory onslaught faded to a manageable level. "Better?"

"I'm sorry, I don't know what is wrong with me," Meara muttered.

"You aren't used to having fae senses," Cerne said simply. "I should have realized. But it will get better with time."

"Thank you for helping us." Meara paused, looking up into those swirling eyes. Verdant earth. Soil and moss. His pupils expanded, eating up the color.

His voice was rough. "You were in my territory." She bit her lip, trying to determine the meaning under those words. He continued, "You are one of us, and I will protect you until you decide your allegiance is to another." The fierce loyalty in his voice sent her heart racing.

Each breath was thick as she took in his wild chamomile scent. Cerne was the one to break the connection as he glanced away. "Do you remember the way to your rooms?"

Meara turned, her eyes sweeping over the familiar mural and lingering on the noble stag near the center. "Yes, I think so."

"Until dinner," Cerne said, dipping his head. She nodded and wrapped her arms around her middle. As she walked, she felt clumsy like a foal learning to walk, though her gait stayed smooth and she never lost her footing.

In their rooms, she found a tray of afternoon tea and a low fire burning in the hearth. Kirrily spoiled them. But even these rooms seemed to hum. Her sensitive faerie hearing picked up every rustle of the curtains in the bedrooms and the soft slide of the carpet under her feet, even distant noises of other house occupants. She dropped onto the bed and threw her arm over her eyes, enduring the thrum until it began to dull. Only then did she rise and return to the sitting room for a cup of tea. It was floral and delicious. She curled up in the armchair and sipped the cooled drink. The concern of being ruined for their own cooking was becoming a valid fear.

Meara set her cup down on the tray and leaned her head back against the plush armchair. Eyes closing, she attempted to sense any magic within herself. She could feel energy running through her veins, warmth in her stomach, heat in her skin. But nothing that felt like the buzz of magic radiating from Brenna. Sighing, she sank deeper into the cushions. She felt nothing but darkness, however, it was only the first day. There was nothing to do but wait and try again.

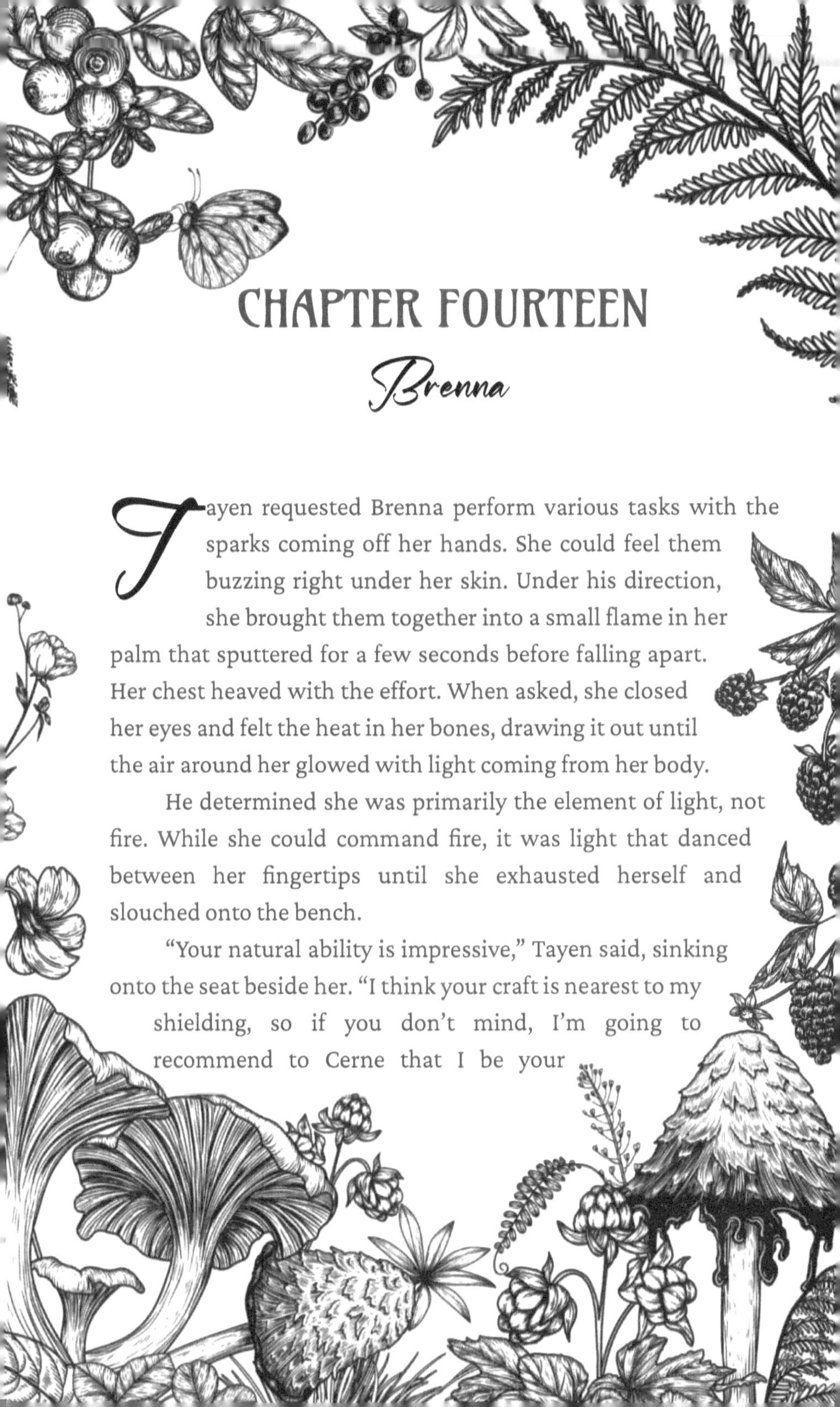

Tayen requested Brenna perform various tasks with the sparks coming off her hands. She could feel them buzzing right under her skin. Under his direction, she brought them together into a small flame in her palm that sputtered for a few seconds before falling apart. Her chest heaved with the effort. When asked, she closed her eyes and felt the heat in her bones, drawing it out until the air around her glowed with light coming from her body.

He determined she was primarily the element of light, not fire. While she could command fire, it was light that danced between her fingertips until she exhausted herself and slouched onto the bench.

"Your natural ability is impressive," Tayen said, sinking onto the seat beside her. "I think your craft is nearest to my shielding, so if you don't mind, I'm going to recommend to Cerne that I be your primary trainer. There are some aspects you'll need to learn from Seda, but much of how your light functions will be nearer to how my shielding operates."

"I appreciate any help I can get," Brenna said, tipping her head back to rest against the nearest column.

"Of course," Tayen murmured, raking his fingers through tousled orange curls. "I'd have to be there anyway, to keep you from committing incendiarism." Brenna scrunched up her face, and he chuckled. They fell into a companionable silence for a moment.

"Will it be possible to identify our parents? Truly?" she asked, the question escaping her. Worries battered her mind, but she chewed the inside of her cheek and waited.

Slow to consider, Tayen stared across the treetops and exhaled audibly. "Like I said, there are few faeries that could have left such an enchantment on you. That is how we will identify them. And then, we *may* discover they are your parents, or that they placed the magic at the request of another. We will see."

The possibility hadn't occurred to Brenna and a strange, hollow pang grew beneath her sternum. She never expected she'd know her true parents. But here, it felt possible, or even likely.

Anxiety and excitement warred within Brenna when Kirrily informed them dinner would be a formal event and include leaders from the court.

Brenna slipped into the apricot dress Dyani had altered and sent up, admiring the sparkle of the delicate beading in the dying afternoon light. Kirrily tutted it was not formal enough, but it would have to do. She redid her hair, keeping it loose but adding jeweled pins.

Holding her hand out to her sister, Brenna said, "Ready for a fae dinner party?" Meara looked sick, her skin taking on a greenish tint that had nothing to do with her evergreen dress. Brenna bumped their shoulders together. "It's going to be fine. Relax."

Tayen met them in the hall, looking aristocratic in a nutmeg jacket that matched his freckles. She happily took his arm, and prodded Meara until she took his other side, and together they entered the gathering.

The scent of roasted meats and spices fill the air. A myriad of auburn, ivory, and pumpkin satin swirled through the dining room. Every seat would be occupied when the residents settled. Males in doublets escorted females with golden rings hanging from their tapered ears. Brenna admired the style and made a note to ask Kirrily about earrings later.

As eyes turned to appraise them, Brenna tightened her hold on Tayen's arm. His answering grin chased away her anxieties. They were not stranded in this crowd. She leaned closer and murmured, "How often do these dinners happen? Is it a special occasion?"

"No, this is merely the leaders that Cerne keeps close. He holds court dinners every few weeks or so."

At the head of the table, Cerne held court with an array of faeries, many with silver threaded through their hair. Advisors or elders, perhaps. Seda sat stoic beside a fae female with graying braids and white fox ears. Even the lines on her face were elegant.

In the middle of the table, Ayala laughed with a tall male faerie with elegant rams horns arching over his mahogany curls. Her flame-colored hair draped over her bare shoulders and covered her naked back. The blood red dress hanging from her neck gathered at the waist, showing a swath of ribs. Such a dress would never have been worn in the queendom, except for perhaps as a negligee. Brenna bit her lip, feeling a hypocrite as her dress hugged her curves, revealing skin she was growing comfortable baring.

Tayen pulled out a chair for Meara and then one for Brenna on the other side of his seat. Easing in, she folded her hands in her lap and looked up to meet the curious gaze of the dinner companion sitting across from her. He was a small, stout male with warm skin darker than hers. From his short, stocky stature and sparkling smile, she suspected he was a brownie, a woodland faerie with helpful magic. She wondered what he could do.

Around them, the guests took their seats. Cerne cleared his throat and the room fell silent. The jeweled buttons on his dinner jacket glinted as he pushed his chair back and stood. His hair was pulled back to reveal his graceful cheekbones, and charcoal accented under his lower lashes.

"Thank you for joining me tonight. I trust all of your families and people are well. Our court is in its predominant season, so let us enjoy the bounty of the land we tend." He raised a glass of vermilion liquid, and everyone lifted their own goblets. Brenna watched the bright drink swirl as she clinked it against Tayen's glass and her sister's.

"Here, here!" the brownie across from them called out in an earthy tenor. Around them, the faeries drank deeply and called for refills.

The first sip of the sweet liquid warmed her. It tasted of apples and cranberries and something she couldn't identify. Tayen's head dipped toward her and he murmured, "Take it easy on the wine. You aren't used to it." Eyes wide, she nodded and set her glass down. Already, a bubbling lightness filled her veins.

The scent of roasted meat filled the room. Kirrily and a selection of women who appeared to be her sisters set about placing plates before each guest. Brenna caught her gaze, and the dryad winked at her.

The first plate held slivers of braised rabbit over root vegetables and drizzled with an oil that tasted of walnuts. Brenna lifted her fork and took a bite, her eyes closing at the succulent flavors. Using her magic that afternoon left her hungry, and the lightness of the fae wine meant her inhibitions were falling away. The plate was soon replaced with a bowl of velvety butternut soup swirled with cream. Sugared flowers floated on the top, and Brenna smiled as she scooped one up. The delicate, floral flavor crunched in her mouth as the sweetness exploded on her tongue.

"Are you enjoying the Autumn Court?" A musical voice asked. She glanced up to see Meara nod at a tall, wraith-like faerie. Her ears ended in a longer, sharper point, and her dark eyes were framed in long lashes. Everything about her seemed daggerlike.

"Lord Cerne has been so generous to host us," Meara said, her voice softer than usual. Brenna could sense her anxiety. She let out a trilling laugh, pulling attention from her sister.

"I never realized how remarkable the cuisine was. If I had known how delicious everything here was, I would have come sooner," she joked. Tayen laughed politely, and the female sniffed and turned her attention elsewhere.

The soup was replaced with rounds of pheasant surrounded by mushrooms and wrapped in a flakey pastry. Knives glinted down the table as each guest sliced into their dish. Brenna lost herself in the buttery flavor and the way the meat melted on her tongue. Pungent herbs laced the mushrooms and the effect was like tasting the forest. It reminded her of her mother's workshop. Her stomach protested the rich meal, and Brenna took a deep breath and straightened her posture. Tayen's eyes flicked to her, and she quirked her mouth into a small smile, silently communicating her wellbeing. Past him, Meara watched the table warily as she picked at the scrap of pastry crust left on her plate. Dessert was wine-poached pears set into a dark molasses cake. Brenna dared a few more sips of the sweet fae wine, rolling it over her tongue.

The guests grew raucous as the faeries finished their meals and leaned back with glasses in hand. Tayen handled most of the conversation, and Brenna smiled and commented when she could.

The wine filled her head with spun sugar, leaving her feeling light and sweet.

Cerne rose at the head of the table, holding his goblet aloft. "Thank you, dear friends, for joining me tonight. May your houses grow strong and be filled with warmth. I look forward to the next time we gather."

Around them, the faeries voiced their agreement. Brenna smiled, leaning back in her seat and listening to Tayen's discussion with the friendly brownie, named Perran, across from them.

Meara rose from her seat. "I'd like to return to our rooms. Join me, Brenna?"

"I think I'll stay a bit. Will you be okay?" Brenna asked.

Nodding, Meara left the room with the last of the guests that chose not to stay. Down the table, a small faerie with rough skin like hewn rock sat and conversed with another dryad.

The fire kept the room warm, and Brenna sipped her wine. Perran spoke with his hands, gesturing with short, expressive motions. Tayen laughed, his curls falling over his face. Brenna found herself laughing along, even if she didn't understand their discussion. The brownie seemed pleased and gave her a radiant smile. He leaned forward and drew her into the conversation.

Time slipped away, and Brenna felt as if she was home.

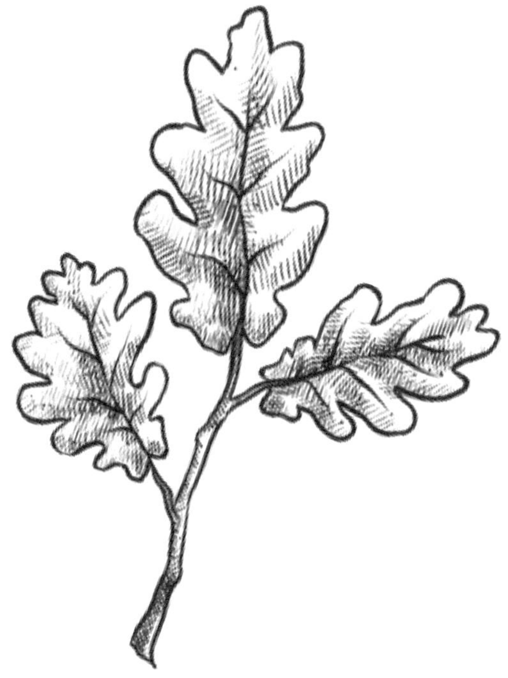

CHAPTER FIFTEEN
Meara

Meara felt entirely out of place. She knew that her features were now fae, her skin flawless and her hair shimmering with a rainbow of colors in its inky strands, but she didn't belong here. The conversations buzzing around her made her anxious, so she cautiously sipped the fae wine, letting the pleasant bubble relax her.

By the time dinner ended, she felt lighter. As everyone scattered to continue their conversations, she drifted down the hall. Her fingers trailed over the millwork absently. Once she was on her feet, she felt too restless to return to their rooms.

Her sister wasn't with her, and something in the back of her head worried for her, but Tayen had proven himself trustworthy. Brenna was enjoying herself and there was no reason to worry.

Meara wandered onto the veranda at the end of the hall.

Head blissfully empty and calm, she drifted toward the edge and rested her shoulder against an ornate post. The lake stretched below them, an expanse of navy and silver, fringed in ruddy foliage. A great crescent moon hung low with its shining reflection rippling in the breeze that swept from the valley up to tease at Meara's hair. She took it into her lungs, enjoying the scents of frost and forest.

"Meara, I was hoping to see you." The tall faerie from dinner glided across the space. Meara tensed. She had not heard her approach.

The stranger was sharper in the moonlight. Her black hair billowed around her, seeming to absorb all light. Wickedly curved nails glinted as she folded her hands across her stomach.

"I apologize, I am not up for a conversation," Meara said, edging back.

Cold, onyx eyes met hers, and a slick of fear ran down her spine. There was no reason for her to fear this faerie. She was under Cerne's protection and this was one of his subjects.

"Excuse me, I need to get back to my sister."

The woman's head tilted, the movement reminding her of a predator. Without her fae senses, she wouldn't have noticed the bunching of the woman's muscles, the forewarning of movement. Meara's hand went to her skirts, but there was no place to hide a dagger in this flimsy dress.

The woman's hand closed over her throat, pushing her back into the wooden pillar. "Just a taste. Your blood smelled so sweet," she hissed. "So powerful."

Meara's hands scrambled to shove her away or claw at her, but the faerie used her other hand to grab her wrist and wrench it aside.

She had felt the bite of thorns before, even the slice of a knife in her skin, but fangs pricking the delicate skin of her neck was like being burned by ice. Sharp, fiery, arresting her muscles. A metallic scent bloomed. Her eyes looked past the woman's flowing black hair and found no help.

The faerie pulled at her blood, and nausea gripped her, churning her stomach. Her vision blurred, stars spinning.

After a moment, she released her, and Meara slumped against the railing. A shriek echoed in her ears and a fierce, feminine voice shouted. She swayed, the voice screamed, and Meara fell.

Her back hit dirt, twigs and branches digging into her shoulders as her ass tumbled over her head, her jaw snapping shut with a jolt of pain. Knees hit the dirt, and she slipped down the hillside. The darkness threatened to swallow her entirely as she fought against her descent. Her hands found a sapling she wrapped her arms around and halted her progress.

"Meara!" Brenna screamed. Light shone from the veranda, and Meara blinked up to see the silhouette of her sister climbing over the railing. A flash of copper hair grabbed her sister, hauling her away from the edge. Brenna's hands waved, desperate in her attempt to reach her.

A figure with antlers rising from his head leapt past Brenna and landed in the brush with knees bent. He balanced precariously as he slid through the fallen leaves and stopped a short ways above her. One of Cerne's hands held firm to a young oak tree as he stretched out the other and snagged Meara's forearm. With inhuman strength, he lifted her upward until she could grasp his shoulders and his arm snaked around her waist. She clung to him, burying her face into his fine woolen coat. Her knees came up to bracket his hips, and he held her so tight against his side that she could feel his chest rising with steady breaths as he clamored up the embankment.

A few faeries watched as the Autumn Lord climbed over the railing and delivered Meara to her feet beside her sister. Brenna wiped at tears, her tawny skin pale.

Cerne ran a hand through his ruffled hair. "Are you hurt?"

"I'm uninjured," Meara said, her voice a hoarse whisper. Her eyes scanned for danger and caught on the faerie who had attacked her. She stood by the door, glaring at them. The black dress she wore was smoking and one strap was burned away entirely. "Did you...?"

Brenna followed her gaze and nodded. Shame heated Meara's cheeks. She was the protector, and yet her sweet sister had to use her volatile magic to defend her.

"You scared me," Brenna murmured. Turning to Cerne who warily watched Meara, she snapped, "Why is that creature not under arrest?"

Cerne rubbed a hand over his face, exhaling slowly. "It is not unlawful for a dearg due to take blood. But you are under my protection. Therefore, she owes me penance." He met Brenna's outraged glare. "Which I will exact per our laws."

"So she can attack anyone she likes except anyone who is your special pet?" Meara said, her shock flowing into a cold anger. She wiped at her neck, her hand coming away bloody.

Cerne's eyes flared, green burning to gold. "I would like a word with you privately."

"Why don't I walk you back to your rooms?" Tayen muttered, taking Brenna's elbow.

She yanked free. "That was barbaric. You said this was a safe place and no monsters lived here."

"Go to your rooms, Brenna. I need to speak with your sister." Cerne's voice was that of a fae lord, regal and measured, but Meara heard the rage rooted beneath and she was eager for it to bloom. She wanted to see him just as disheveled as she felt.

"Go, I'll be there shortly," she murmured. With a scoff, Brenna whirled and marched away. Tayen jogged after her, his words getting lost in the wind.

Wrapping her arms around her middle, Meara faced Cerne.

His jaw ticked. "You seemed so cautious. I never thought you'd wander off and get caught by the one person at that dinner who might harm you."

Meara scowled when she saw the dearg due had vanished during their conversation. Cerne tracked her gaze and exhaled harshly.

"So you will do what, make her pay a fee? That's hardly a fitting punishment when she defied the Lord of Autumn." Her tone grew acerbic.

"You have no idea what I will do." Cerne said, his words clipped. Meara took a step back, and Cerne advanced until her knees hit the bench and she sank onto the cushion.

His voice dropped, a lethal lullaby that sent her heart racing. "What I would do. I could rip her apart with my bare hands," he said, gripping the back of her seat as he loomed over her. She inhaled sharply, unable to let the breath go until he finished speaking. "For daring to touch someone under my protection."

Her heart thrashed like a caged raven. Some dark part of her liked the idea of him taking revenge for her. As much as she feared the feral anger in his mossy eyes, that passion unfurled heat in her stomach.

"You are the Autumn Lord. Can you not do as you please?" she dared to whisper.

He raked his hand through the hair at the base of his antlers. With a dark chuckle, he straightened. "It would not fit the crime, unfortunately, and I am not a lord who breaks our laws for my own gain, no matter how strong my desires."

Meara stood, finding herself nearer to him than she expected. His pupils dilated before he looked away. "She will have to give up something of value, not money. Perhaps her time in servitude, or heirlooms that can bring power to the less fortunate." Cerne trailed off, and Meara found she didn't truly care about the punishment.

"This wouldn't have happened if I could defend myself here. Teach me to use my magic so I'm not helpless again."

"I will try," he murmured. Gingerly, he touched the tips of his fingers to her neck, circling the bite but never touching it. "We can start now, if you like."

"You have to get back to your guests and I am exhausted," she said, sucking in a shaky breath. The feel of his fingertips against her throat lingered. "My sister expects me."

"Of course," Cerne said. "I'll walk you back."

She wanted to tell him she didn't need his help, but after he rescued her, it felt foolhardy. When he offered his arm, she took it. The fabric was warm under her chilled fingers.

Her voice stayed silent as they walked the long hall. The remainder of the guests had disappeared, and they reached her room without seeing anyone. He nodded and turned away.

The moment the door opened, Brenna seized her hand and led her to their washroom. Meara stared at the dark stained glass windows as her sister wiped away the blood. "It looks good, not really bleeding anymore. They were small holes."

"Lucky, indeed," Meara muttered darkly.

Brenna tossed the cloth into the sink and propped her hands on her hips. "You said we don't know their customs or how to keep ourselves safe, and this proved it. So what do we do? We learn. Ask more questions. Figure out how to use our magic to keep us safe."

Her breath came out in a broken chuckle. "I suppose you are right. Now let's get out of these gowns. Mine will need laundering, I think."

Meara was tugging her chemise over her head when a knock sounded at their door. She straightened the garment and looked for some sort of covering. The door creaked open and Kirrily called out, "Lady Brenna, Lady Meara?"

"Yes," Brenna called, crossing the room to meet her.

"I heard you had some trouble. I thought some tea might help, and I wanted to see if you needed anything more."

"Maybe something stronger," Meara said, crossing her arms.

Kirrily smiled sweetly and pressed into the room, crossing the carpet and setting a tray on the small side table between the armchairs. She paused, looking Meara in the eyes. "Were you hurt?"

Her jaw clenched, a darkness in her veins when she thought of the evening's events. "I was cornered and bit by a faerie of the court, and then told it was all fine and good except that she didn't get Cerne's permission!"

The leaves in her hair rustled as she nodded. "I forget you were not raised fae, especially now that your true faces are revealed." She paused, eyes roving over Meara's features. "It is our way, and what keeps us strong. A dearg due can take the blood they want from anyone who cannot defend themselves. So we learn to fight or stay with those who can protect us."

"What about your weak or very young?" Brenna asked, her hands twisting together at her waist. "That seems wrong."

Kirrily shook her head. "There is honor. No one would take from a child in that way."

"What would you do if she came after you?" Meara asked bluntly.

While she poured the tea, Kirrily pressed her lips together. After she handed a cup to Meara, she shrugged. "I am not so easily bit." When Meara frowned, Kirrily ran a hand down her arm, and her skin shifted from its rough texture to something tougher, like actual tree bark.

"Isn't that something," Brenna said, huffing as she reached for a cup.

"I wouldn't have strayed if I was aware of the danger. What else do we need to know?" Meara asked.

Kirrily twisted a tendril of vine from her hair around her finger. "I don't know human culture. You should ask Tayen. He would know best."

"Thank you, Kirrily. Would you have some tea with us?" Brenna asked.

The dryad dipped her head respectfully. "I must get back. There are plenty of guests about still. But no one will bother you after Lady Brenna's display of power."

"Thank you," Brenna said, her eyes warm with affection.

Kirrily gave another shallow bow and slipped out of the room. Meara considered shoving some furniture in front of the door, but nothing was suitable, and she supposed Kirrily was right - Brenna had proven she could defend them. With a sigh, she sank into the second chair and cradled her forehead in her hands.

Her sister didn't speak, knowing Meara needed time to untangle her emotions. Brenna would be here when she was ready. Finally, Meara raised her head and stared into the dying flames. "I have to access whatever magic I have. How else can I keep us safe?"

CHAPTER SIXTEEN
Brenna

"Focus," Tayen coached, and Brenna's skin heated. She was never one to get angry, but frustration burned hot in her bones.

"I am focusing," she gritted out. The sparks in her hands solidified into a single flame once more, but she could not hold it for long, and it dissipated into smoke.

Growling, she stalked away and sat with her back against the wall. All of the furniture had been removed to avoid her accidentally lighting upholstery on fire.

Meara appeared in the doorway, worry written in every line of her face. "Are you well?"

Her hand swept out, gesturing at Tayen. "This faerie thinks I can sustain a flame in my hand as if I am a hearth."

Tayen laughed, flaming curls shaking with the movement. "I'm confident you can do this, but it will take time to build up stamina. Meara, would you like to stay for a while? I think she could use some encouragement and you should work on accessing your own craft, no?"

Groaning, Brenna pushed up to stand. Meara hovered in the corner, watching her as she arched her back and shook out her hands. Anything to clear the burn that felt like overused muscles.

"Instead of heat, let's focus on the light," Tayen said, pacing back and forth in front of her.

She flexed her fingers, calling forth the buzzing feeling from her blood. She focused on the bright feeling, shoving away the sensation of warmth. It fought her, the flames wanting to emerge. Her throat ached as she sucked down another lungful of air and waged the internal battle. Bit by bit, she drew out the light. Through her eyelids, she could see luminescence.

"Good. Don't contain it to your hands. Let it spread. There is no reason to make this task more difficult than necessary." Tayen's words relaxed a piece of her control, and Brenna felt the lightness flood her veins, up her arms, throughout her chest, up into her cheeks. "Excellent."

Her eyes fluttered open and the glow to her skin faded.

Tayen's feet halted and he grinned at her. "Did you feel the difference in containing it as opposed to letting it fill you up? There are times for both. But you are doing so well."

A flush painted her cheeks and she glanced at her sister. Meara's eyes were on her, but a frown marred her face. "How is it going?" Brenna crossed the space and reached out to touch her sister's shoulder.

"Poorly."

"Why?" Her voice pitched higher and Meara's lashes fluttered as she rolled her eyes and smiled.

"It's nothing. But no matter how I try, there seems to be nothing magical within me. I don't feel anything, so how can I use it?"

Brenna looked to Tayen, her eyes begging. "What else can she try?"

Shrugging, Tayen crossed his arms. "Perhaps emotion, or simply time."

"Emotion?" Brenna canted her head.

"Yes, like perhaps if she is upset, it will bring it forth. Or scared, or joyful. It can vary."

"I've been plenty angry and frightened since arriving," Meara said darkly.

"Then maybe you'll need to find some joy," Brenna said with a wink. She shimmied her shoulders and turned back to Tayen.

"Let's work on elevating a light. That's something I've always wished I could do," Tayen said.

She shook out her hands, exhaled slowly, and drew on that flickering flame under her skin. Sweat prickled over the back of her neck as she drew out the light, leaving the heat burning within her. Once she held it in her hand, she looked up.

"Try to raise it up a ways, and then higher if you can," Tayen urged. The light reflected in his marigold eyes.

Her jaw clenched as she focused, but the sound of voices pulled her attention away. The light dimmed, withering around the edges. Her efforts wavered, and she allowed it to fade. Scowling, Brenna turned to peer over her shoulder.

Tayen's sister, Ayala, leaned against the doorway, smirking as she spoke with Meara. From her stiff posture and the way her hands slid into her pockets, Brenna could tell her sister was angry. Brenna opened her mouth to call out, but Meara was brushing past Ayala and out the door.

The anger was back, embers sparking into a flame in an instant. Brenna stormed toward Ayala. "What did you say to her?"

The beautiful faerie shrugged. "I merely encouraged her to

unveil her magic."

"Bullshit," Brenna spat.

"You are dreadfully angry," Ayala observed. A single, thin eyebrow arched. "You may want to be cautious with anger and fire craft." With a flutter of flame colored hair, she slipped through the door.

"She is correct," Tayen said softly. Brenna whirled to scowl at him. "Your emotions influence your craft, but your craft also influences your emotions. You are quite literally heated right now."

The anger spiraling inside of her dropped off with the realization. Pressing her palm to her chest, she swallowed. "I've never been someone who got angry like this." She blinked, brows furrowing as she sought his gaze. "How do I keep this from happening?"

Tayen's smile was understanding and gentle. "Practice."

"Splendid."

CHAPTER SEVENTEEN

Meara

Hot, angry tears welled in Meara's eyes. It was easy to be furious with the viciously beautiful Ayala, but her words were true. Her body and mind felt heavy, sluggish, and full of dark emotions that threatened to burst out of her.

Meara's boots stomped across pine needles as she exited the manor house and flung herself into the trees. For a short while, she could pretend she wasn't a faerie, none of this had happened, and she was simply enjoying the forest as she had done for all of her life.

After spending the morning trying to summon some sort of magic from within herself, it hurt to see Brenna wield it so freely.

The scent of pine and rotting leaves soaked into her lungs. Things would be better with more time, rest, and effort. Her stride slowed, and her chin tipped up as she regarded the treetops. Hedge sparrows of umber and ash flitted through them, singing and calling to each other.

This was what she needed. Her exhale was smoother. Every step calmed her anxieties and unwound the knots in her stomach.

She stepped forward again and her body halted so suddenly she fell, her body folding over as her feet remained stuck in the dirt. Righting herself, Meara attempted to move forward, but could not. She stepped backward, but found the same unseen barrier behind her if she went another step. All around her stood an invisible wall, leaving her trapped in the center. She bent down, brushing away leaf litter to reveal a perfect circle of mushrooms.

A faerie circle.

After pounding against the magic until her palms ached, Meara sank to the ground and sat cross legged. She was not far from the manor house, but her pride kept her from screaming for help. Not after last night and the way Cerne had jumped over the railing and scaled the hillside to reach her. Eventually, someone would find her, preferably Tayen, or even Xurey or Seda, and undo the magic that held her. As long as it wasn't Cerne.

Nothing to do but wait. Her eyes drifted closed as she turned her concentration inward. She reached for some fire or energy within, attempting to pull out her magic. But there was nothing but shadows within her. Her lips curled, frustration pummeling her.

"Lady Meara, are you meditating?"

Her hair fanned out as she twisted, her disappointment clear across her face as she regarded Lord Cerne. Breath hissed between her teeth and blood pulsed in her skin, tinting her cheeks sweet briar.

"My lord," she began, forcing herself to continue. It would be even worse to hide her situation from him and be found out. "I'm afraid I stumbled into a faerie circle. I can't go anywhere at the moment." Each word felt bitter, but they were true.

"Oh, I thought I found the last of those pesky things." Cerne drew closer, his billowing shirt gaping open to reveal an expanse of chest. Why bother with a shirt when it hardly covers one's chest?

Crouching so they were level, he smirked. His hand hovered over the edge of the mushroom circle, and with a sweep, it was broken, stirring up the musty scent of fungus and decay. The pressure fell away, and Meara scrambled up and stepped out of the magical prison.

"Why do you even have faerie circles in your land? To trap trespassers?" she grumbled, hugging her arms across her stomach.

Cerne shook his head. "It is not something I created, nor any ruler before me. I'm not sure why they form. Xurey once told me it was a surplus of the magic we feed into our land coming back out like a blemish."

She nodded, beginning to walk. Cerne joined her, matching his gait to hers. A twig snapped under his soft boots.

"You spoke of your relationship with your land before," Meara mentioned, searching for any information that would teach her about these people they were supposed to belong to.

"Yes, we care for the land and it cares for us. Is that so different from the human kingdoms?"

"We don't think of it like that. And there is less magic involved, obviously." She tugged on her bottom lip with her teeth for a moment, sorting through her thoughts. "I was wondering, does it snow here? I mean, do you experience the change of seasons? Because it's currently autumn for everyone."

For the second time, she heard Cerne's true, deep laugh. It rumbled out of his chest, filling the space. He sounded like a crackling, cozy fire and warm spiced cider. She couldn't help but smile. "Yes, we have the change of the seasons, but it's still a bit like autumn all year. Such as spring flowers blooming under leaves of orange and gold, as they are now."

"Truly?" she murmured, eyes flitting up to the branches above their heads.

Cerne caught her off guard by stepping closer and raising his hand. His knuckles skimmed her exposed upper arm. The impulse to pull away warred with the desire to move closer to him, and she settled on shifting her weight awkwardly, keeping her feet planted.

"You seem upset."

"Yes, it's been a difficult few days, as you're aware," she replied. Speaking her mind to this powerful faerie seemed to override her good sense. Words tumbled out of her. "As you know, we were chased by an angry mob, relocated from a human queendom to a faerie court, and then I was assaulted by a dearg due just last night. And all the while, I'm trying to find whatever magic is inside of me and *nothing is coming out.*" The last four words were sharp and slow.

Blinking, she raised her hand to her mouth. That was more words than she had ever spoken together to *anyone* - aside from her sister or mother. She scowled at his pleased smile. Those moss-studded umber irises seized her soul as his lips curved handsomely.

"I have been abundantly impressed by your fortitude while facing all of those challenges." He studied her, weighing his words before continuing. "To be clear, Meara, even if your magic never surfaces, or perhaps it does and it's something unremarkable, it will not matter. You are worthy of admiration as you are."

His smirk widened into a true smile. "And even without magic, I know you could gut me." His hand dropped from her elbow to her waist, coming to rest atop the blade sheathed high on her thigh. Meara's gaze followed his hand as it lingered on her hip before falling away.

"Thank you," she murmured, dropping her eyes to the ground. The moment felt too intimate. "I'm afraid your praise is wasted. All I've done is fight to survive, like anyone would."

"But you've done it so beautifully." His bold stare banished her doubts. He was flirting. The realization mired her thoughts, slowing them like thick honey.

It meant nothing. He flirted with many ladies in his court, she was sure. However, she had never been spoken to in this way and her heart pounded. Before her flaming cheeks could betray her, she cleared her throat and spoke. "I doubt Ayala would appreciate you saying that to me."

"Why?" he asked, enjoying watching her squirm as she opened her mouth and closed it again like a fish.

Meara folded her arms and set her weight onto her back foot. "Considering how she all but sits in your lap at gatherings, it is reasonable to assume she is your lover." Her pulse thrummed in her throat.

"She is not. Not anymore."

"I'm sure she mourns that fact."

Cerne laughed again, the warm rumble soaking into her blood and relaxing her muscles. His voice was a low purr. "So insightful for someone new to my court."

What did he want - for her to throw herself at him and beg the handsome Autumn Lord to bed her? She'd rather strangle him for the smug look on his face.

"I am sure you have plenty of women in your court who are interested in filling that role." She pressed a hand to her chest. "Not me, of course. But I saw more than a few beautiful, young women watching you as we walked through the shops."

His eyes widened and lips parted the slightest amount. It was the barest hint of surprise, but she felt victorious. She forced her smile to stay small, instead of grinning like a dolt, and focused instead on walking away as gracefully as she could manage.

"Glad to know you were watching that closely," he murmured, falling into step beside her. He offered his arm, and she begrudgingly took it. This time, the pose felt comfortable. The thin linen of his loose shirt was feather-soft under her fingertips.

"You have such a high opinion of yourself."

"It's warranted, don't you think?" His rumbling laugh sounded again, now familiar, and she found she liked arguing with him. The challenge in his eyes was playful, drawing her from her darker emotions. Perhaps he wasn't so terrible after all.

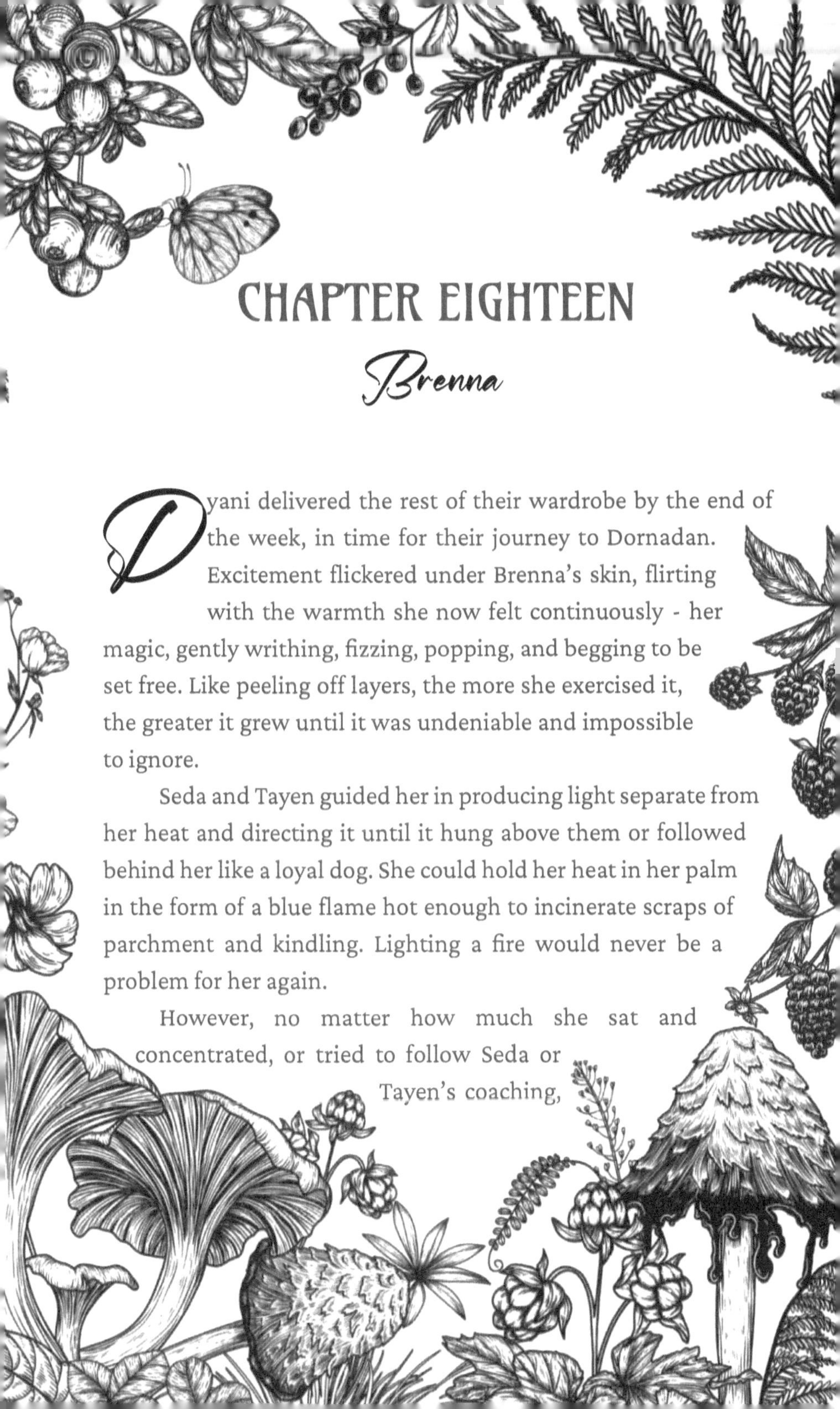

CHAPTER EIGHTEEN

Brenna

Dyani delivered the rest of their wardrobe by the end of the week, in time for their journey to Dornadan. Excitement flickered under Brenna's skin, flirting with the warmth she now felt continuously - her magic, gently writhing, fizzing, popping, and begging to be set free. Like peeling off layers, the more she exercised it, the greater it grew until it was undeniable and impossible to ignore.

Seda and Tayen guided her in producing light separate from her heat and directing it until it hung above them or followed behind her like a loyal dog. She could hold her heat in her palm in the form of a blue flame hot enough to incinerate scraps of parchment and kindling. Lighting a fire would never be a problem for her again.

However, no matter how much she sat and concentrated, or tried to follow Seda or Tayen's coaching,

Meara had yet to produce any sort of magic. Brenna's heart ached for her, and she fiercely hoped that visiting their mother would help.

Kirrily tucked a second dress into her pack as Brenna selected the leggings and tunic for the traveling day. She stowed them among silks in shades of bronze and champagne. They would only spend the evening in Dornadan, followed by time to visit their mother in the morning before returning home. It would be a long day traveling, but unweighted by the gifts given, the return trip would be quicker.

"How are you feeling?" she asked Meara as her sister passed her with garments in hand. Water droplets plinked against the window, and Brenna found her gaze straying to the darker treetops as rain stained the scenery darker.

"Excited to see our new home." The corner of Meara's mouth quirked up. Brenna reluctantly agreed. She picked at the braided crown around her head. Meara's matching style looked like an obsidian circlet.

Packed and ready, the sisters strode through the long hallway and out into the courtyard. The rain had dissipated, leaving damp soil and the scent of petrichor.

A groomsman laid blankets across the horses and settled packs across their haunches. Tayen stood beside Eirlys. He looked up as they approached and smiled, "Good morning!"

Brenna ran her hand down the mare's snowy neck, and Eirlys turned and nuzzled her shoulder. "Good morning. Who is coming with us?" She surveyed the clearing.

Eirlys closed her lips over Brenna's shoulders, and she shrugged away before the mare could bite her.

Tayen exhaled in a hint of a laugh. "The six of us."

"No attendants?" Her voice rose in pitch. The idea of a noble traveling without servants was unfathomable, and while she didn't consider herself of a high station, she expected the Autumn Lord and his retinue to behave like nobles.

Tayen grinned. "Brenna, I believe you've grown accustomed to a pampered lifestyle." She scowled at him, and he snickered. "We'll do fine on our own. We are made from the wilds."

Brenna turned the words over in her head. He was right. She was no longer human, and her old expectations did not apply anymore. It was freeing.

Meara was given a slender black gelding named Bran who tossed his head, making her sister glance anxiously at the groomsmen. Cerne assured her that he would ride beside her and keep Bran from mischief. Brenna enjoyed watching her sister's internal battle shine through her expressive lilac eyes until she gave in.

The sturdy buckskin mare selected for Brenna greeted her by pushing her velvet nose into Brenna's open palm. Her name was Clover, and she instantly adored her. Soft blankets were provided for padding for the longer journey.

Cerne opted to ride a gleaming bay stallion instead of traveling in his stag form. Brenna suspected this had to do with Meara. The dignified equine stomped his feet when Cerne ran his hand along his shoulder and then leapt astride.

With a click of his tongue, Cerne led their party down the path and southward. Roven fell away quickly, and soon they were surrounded by only trees.

The forest was warmer than Brenna expected. The breeze was cool but not chilling. It felt welcoming, like it wanted to play with her flame.

They walked in pairs, Tayen and Ayala leading the way, followed by Cerne and Meara. Xurey plodded along beside Brenna and Clover in her horse form, a silent companion. From the way her ears swiveled, Brenna was sure that Xurey was attentive to her, but she did not feel like having a one-sided conversation.

The towering trees gave way to newer growth and the forest brightened and thinned. The heavy sensation she had grown accustomed to faded, and her magic felt a bit itchy, like it couldn't get enough air to burn as brightly as it would like.

Cerne and Tayen laughed and traded comments between them while Ayala glanced back haughtily from her perch atop Airgid. Brenna listened to their voices on the wind and watched the landscape change. The forest chattered around them, joining in on their conversation.

As the hours melted away, she settled into the sway of Clover's gait and let her mind wander. It was strange to be returning to the human lands. A royal function was far from the rural life she knew, but she suspected it wouldn't impress after the grandeur of the Autumn Court. She was still looking forward to it, and seeing their mother would be worth the trip regardless.

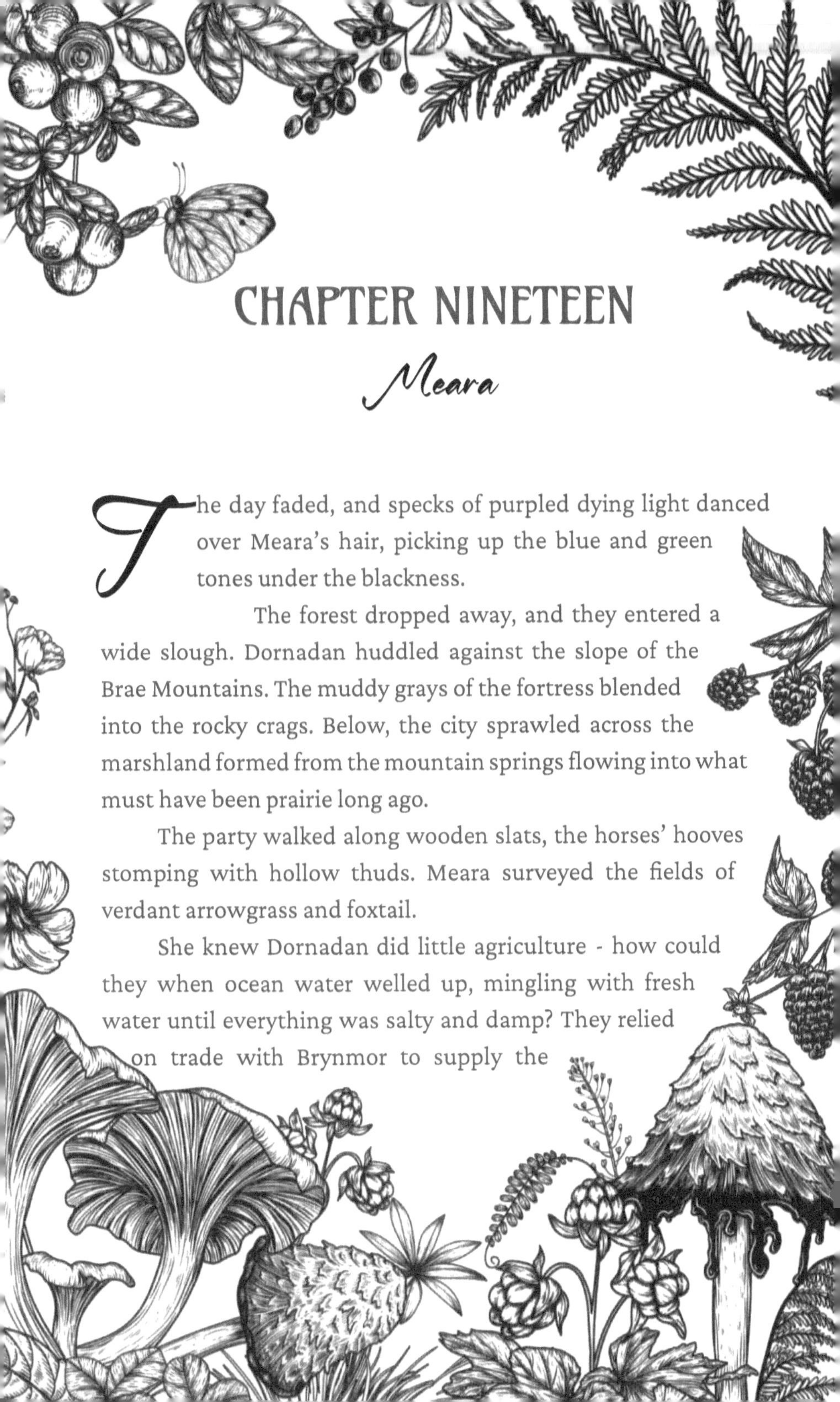

CHAPTER NINETEEN
Meara

The day faded, and specks of purpled dying light danced over Meara's hair, picking up the blue and green tones under the blackness.

The forest dropped away, and they entered a wide slough. Dornadan huddled against the slope of the Brae Mountains. The muddy grays of the fortress blended into the rocky crags. Below, the city sprawled across the marshland formed from the mountain springs flowing into what must have been prairie long ago.

The party walked along wooden slats, the horses' hooves stomping with hollow thuds. Meara surveyed the fields of verdant arrowgrass and foxtail.

She knew Dornadan did little agriculture - how could they when ocean water welled up, mingling with fresh water until everything was salty and damp? They relied on trade with Brynmor to supply the grain and produce they required.

The outermost row of buildings stood evenly spaced with wide troughs between them. They were canals, drawing water out of the city and draining it into the fields. The structures were raised on embankments, and as they reached them, the path turned from slats to dirt.

The residents looked up as they passed, but quickly returned to their business. Women pinned freshly laundered clothing to lines tied between the timber trusses supporting peat roofs. Wood-clad walls held shuttered windows above the dark stone that made up the lower half of the homes.

The path wove through winding streets at a steep incline, and Meara leaned forward in her seat as Bran climbed toward the watchtowers seemingly built into the mountain itself. As they grew closer, dwellings gave way to shops and businesses. One of these might be her mother's new apothecary. Meara couldn't help but check the signs nailed above the doors painted in shades of charcoal and ash.

More faces turned their way as they ascended. The men wore their hair in braids down the center of their skulls with the sides shorn off. Silver and black beads decorated beards and braids. The style revealed more than a few humans with a slight point to their ears, and she wondered how many half-fae had taken refuge in Dornadan. Or conversely, how many faeries visited this city and found the comfort of a human lover, resulting in hybrid children?

The ground evened out as they broke from the twisting labyrinth of shops and stepped into the stronghold's courtyard. Guards in black uniforms edged in silver fastenings strode between doorways, long swords hanging at their thighs.

Sleek horses of every color followed their masters, for Dorandan was known for their equine husbandry. Her lips parted as she watched the beautiful creatures. Surely, the Autumn Court's horses came from this stock.

Cerne dismounted and offered to help Meara down, but her pride wouldn't allow her to accept. She slid down Bran's side and landed in the gravel softly.

"My lord," a brusk man exclaimed, bowing to their group. He lacked a sword and had the look of steward with the softness of his middle. "We are blessed by your presence. Let my groomsmen take your horses and I will show you to your rooms so you can refresh yourselves before the feast tonight."

Tayen ducked his head, leaning close. "Where have you placed the party from Liosliath? We would like to avoid any unnecessary conflict."

"Of course, Lord Tayen. They are in rooms along the south side, and I have prepared suites closer to Sablewood as I know you prefer."

"Good man." Tayen patted him on the back, an easy smile on his face. Perhaps Tayen was this friendly with everyone, but Meara sensed a familiarity befitting an ambassador who made regular visits.

They trailed behind the steward as he led them to the left. Colorless stone rose up in sheer walls. The man pushed open a nondescript door and bowed his head as Cerne strode inside. A dark, cold sitting room opened to three small bedrooms. At least the sleeping spaces had windows cut into the stone high on the walls, sending down shafts of gray light that clashed with the pools of warmth from the flickering oil lamps.

Xurey stuck close behind her, and Meara turned, dropping her voice. "What do you expect for sleeping arrangements?"

"You and Brenna will share a room. That is your preference, correct?"

"Does that mean you have to share with Ayala?" Meara pressed her teeth into her bottom lip.

Xurey shook her head, a light laugh punctuating her words. "Oh, I don't expect Ayala will spend the night here. Nor Tayen."

Meara frowned, but Xurey was already moving away, claiming the smallest bedroom for herself. Figuring Cerne would take the grandest room with the canopy draped over the bed, Meara decided on the middle room for herself and Brenna.

Their bags were delivered moments later, and she stood by, holding items when requested as her sister aired out their dresses.

"I wonder if Mum knows that we are here," Meara mused.

Brenna nodded, laying out the linen pouch that held their borrowed accessories. "When do you think we can see her?"

"Now?"

"I'm not sure there is time before the party. The day is growing late already. But tomorrow we have time set aside."

Delicate fingers untied the laces and folded back fabric to reveal a collection of jewelry. Brenna murmured, "I cannot believe we are attending a king's betrothal party."

Meara turned over the hair pins in her hands. The darkened gold would disappear amongst Brenna's curls, but they were still beautiful. The tourmaline gemstones would add sparkle, and that befitted her sister's cheery nature perfectly.

"Stop glowering at the jewels and come wash up," Brenna said.

"I wasn't." Meara pressed her lips into a line. With a sigh, she followed her sister to the washroom. They scrubbed their faces and arms and then set about preparing for the feast.

Much to Meara's distaste, Ayala set out her gown in Cerne's room and promptly sat at his dressing table brushing out her long hair. Her auburn waves flowed over her shoulders and down her back like a length of fine silk.

Ignoring the fae female, the sisters retreated to their room and took turns styling each other's hair. Brenna braided the front pieces of Meara's hair and tucked them back, leaving the rest smooth. Once they traded places, Meara tucked the gemstone pins into Brenna's curls, holding the front pieces back leaving the rest loose.

Xurey appeared in the doorway with a subdued smile and an ebony dress hugging her statuesque frame. Sheer fabric flowed over her shoulders.

"You look gorgeous," Brenna said, beaming at her friend.

"Thanks. I was wondering if you needed any help." Xurey perched on their bed, her hands folded loosely.

"Thank you. Is there any advice you have for us as far as fitting in with the nobility here?" Meara said, an anxious edge to her words as Brenna untangled her darkly iridescent hair.

"They're used to us. Do not feel as if you need to conform to human styles," Xurey said quietly.

Ten minutes later, the girls tied the laces on their dresses and stepped into the shared sitting room. Ayala sat on the settee with her legs crossed and her foot twitching impatiently. Her body dripped with liquid bronze, the fabric conforming to her body. Metallic beads flashed in spiderweb braids adorning her long, lush hair. Painted lips thinned as she regarded the sisters.

Meara tugged her dress. It was the most conservative style Dyani had created for her. Silk the color of wet soil rose to her collar, scooping lower in the back. Her hands rose to cover her exposed upper arms.

Brenna's dress rustled as she moved. Skirts the same shade as dogwood blossoms layered over a bodice of gilded ocher that clasped at the nape of her neck. Metallic stitches formed vines that feathered out over her waist and hips.

"You look lovely," Cerne said, his voice brushing across Meara's skin as he appeared in the door. Meara was surprised to find Cerne's eyes sweeping down her body and up to focus on her face. She looked away, swallowing.

"Thank you," Ayala said, a small smirk brightening her face.

Cerne rolled his eyes as he crossed the room and sank into an armchair. "Are we ready to go?"

Tayen glanced toward the door. "We have some time yet."

Xurey perched beside Ayala, nibbling at her lip. "I apologize, but I am offput by this betrothal. I mean, he is four times her age." Her naturally quiet voice rose with indignation. She must have been stewing about this for some time.

"That is common among the upper class in the Queendom," Brenna said apologetically, her brows drawing together as she regarded her friend.

Ayala shrugged, unbothered. "It makes her a queen."

Xurey scowled. "She is the sole child of a king. Wouldn't she have become queen some day anyway?"

Shaking his head, Tayen explained. "Malacia did not make Elysia her heir when she and Barrach wed. But this marriage will bring peace between two rivals. Eldric and Elysia both know this. I imagine that is enough motivation."

Sitting back, Xurey crossed her arms. The crease between her brows deepened. "She could have married one of his sons."

"Emeric is single." Ayala said, her eyes sliding to her brother. "Though I'm not sure if he has similar preferences as Eladin or not."

"Prince Eladin does not care for...?" Brenna said, cutting herself off and raising a hand to her mouth as her cheeks tinged pink.

"It's not that Eladin dislikes humans, it's that he prefers a *particular* faerie," Cerne said, winking at his friend.

Tayen ignored them, though a blush crept up his neck. "Get all this talk out of your system now. It's about time to leave, and I'd like to at least appear composed."

"I'm ready," Ayala said, rising and brushing off her metallic dress.

As they walked toward the door, Cerne paused, turning to face the sisters. "It would be best if you did not discuss your prior lives. It would be unwise to risk the guards of Liosliath catching wind of your history."

"So no discussing our old home," Brenna muttered. "What about our mother?"

"Maybe keep your mouth closed," Ayala hissed with her fist propped on her hip. "We will be unacceptably late if we stay here prattling on."

Cerne inhaled, his eyes narrowing, and began walking, forcing Ayala to double step to return to his side and take his arm. "Ayala," he rumbled, so quietly Meara almost missed it. The reprimand brought a small, justified smile to her face.

The air had chilled, and dust plumed from the many humans in the courtyard. Sweat and the scent of burnt charcoal assaulted Meara's nose.

Guards swarmed among Dornadan citizens looking for a chance to glimpse the royal visitors from Liosliath. The crowd parted and Cerne led the way to the formal entrance of the keep. Once ushered inside, they paused at the massive blackened iron plated doors leading to the great hall.

Stewards bowed and heaved the doors open to reveal a tapestry of rich brocade and jewels lit by hot firelight as the scent of smoke, sweat, and musty furs enveloped them. Crimson spilled over the shoulders of Liosliath nobles intermixing with the blacks and mixed metals of Dornadan courtiers.

Heads turned as the steward called out, "Lord Cerne, ruler of the faerie Court of Autumn Harvest, and his guests, Lord Ambassador Tayen, his sister Lady Ayala, Lady Xurey, Lady Brenna, and Lady Meara."

Meara stiffened at hearing her name announced like she was worth everyone taking note. From the gemstones glinting at the throats of every person in the expansive space, she knew she did not belong here. She would have turned away, but she walked with her fingers resting in Tayen's grasp, and his hold on her tightened as if he sensed her hesitation.

Meara's stomach twisted, watching Ayala's haughty sneer. She stayed on Cerne's arm as he spoke with a few human men wearing expensive mink coats, one with massive sapphires for buttons. Another's hands glittered with white stones as he shook Cerne's hand with a smile that made her skin itch.

Anxiety took hold and Meara crowded closer to Tayen and her sister. Tayen expertly threaded through the throng, towing them along.

As they neared the center of the gathering, Tayen smiled at her over his shoulder encouragingly. Despite the knots in her stomach, Meara raised her chin. She was a faerie among these human nobles. She would not cower before them.

CHAPTER TWENTY

Brenna

Four tables spanned the length of the room, with the middle left open for revelry. They were made of massive logs, hewn down and joined together with deep grooves between them. The make was rough compared to the fine furniture she had grown accustomed to in the fae court.

Nestled between her sister and Tayen, Brenna felt safe enough to study the humans around them. It was easy to spot the visitors from Liosliath from the native nobles of Dornadan. They wore reds and browns to honor their queen and sat mostly on the far side, closer to her side of the dais.

King Eldric looked over the seated crowd, a proud gleam in his dark eyes. The high table stretched the width of the platform, drawing every guest's attention to the ruling families. King Eldric sat in the center.

Deep grooves marked his tan face, his eyes shaded by thick black brows threaded with the same silver that streaked his braids and long beard.

Beside him, Princess Elysia looked frail with pale skin and auburn hair coiffed into a loose chignon that left curls tumbling down her back. Her petal pink lips pursed as she gave the king a demure smile.

Brenna couldn't help her gaze straying to the royals of Liosliath. She had never seen them in the flesh and the portraits hung throughout the queendom bore little resemblance to the figures before them.

Barrach, Queen Malacia's newest king consort and king in his own right, wore his long, black hair tied back, revealing weathered olive skin over high cheekbones. Beside him, Malacia sat primly with a wicked twist to her smile. Her chocolate hair was styled into an elaborate updo with her diamond crown glittering from within. Her signature blood red lips sent a shiver through Brenna. This woman wouldn't hesitate to order her death if she was aware of their story.

King Eldric pushed his chair back with a scraping sound. He raised a hand, and a seething silence settled over the room. His crackling voice boomed over the crowd. "My people, thank you for joining us for this monumental occasion. Isn't my bride beautiful?" Princess Elysia raised a gloved hand to cover her mouth, hiding her expression. "Together, we will turn rivals into allies and open up a new era of trade and collaboration."

The crowd's whispers built until murmurs of cheers trickled across the room. Eldric smiled with a regal sweep of his hand. "So enjoy my wine and feast. This is the beginning, and we shall come together again on Yuletide to seal this union. Huzzah!"

The room surged, hundreds of voices echoing his exclamation. Brenna's lips traced the word, her voice silent.

Eldric's three sons raised their glasses and drank to their father's betrothed, their faces pleasantly bland. Brenna wondered how they really felt about Elysia's age and citizenship.

The crown prince, Emeric, sat stoically. He was a broad man with rune tattoos running up his neck to skim his square jaw. She would have thought him devastatingly handsome if it was not for her time among the faeries.

The younger prince, Eladin, had finer features and a mirthful glitter to his dark eyes. His skin appeared bare until he turned to face his adopted brother, and Brenna spied runes along the sides of his scalp. Beside him, Rydan replied to whatever Eladin said with a frown. His skin was darker, as was his hair, styled into locs, and his tattoos ran down his inner arms and across his hands. A bronze circlet sat atop his head, simple compared to the bejeweled crowns on Emeric and Eladin's heads.

Dozens of servants in matching gray tunics placed a myriad of platters and serving bowls in the center of the table. Glistening ham, rack of lamb in a well of mint jam, steamed mussels and clams on a bed of cabbage leaves, and pale, round loaves of bread.

A few weeks ago, she would have drooled while loading up her plate and then ate until her stomach hurt, but after living in the faerie court, Brenna found the food unappealing. She struggled to fill her plate. Meara's plate was similarly sparse, her face tense and her eyes on the line of Liosliath guards along the far wall.

"Relax. We are guests," Brenna murmured, gratified when Meara's shoulders loosened.

Yet again, Brenna was grateful to Tayen as he led the conversation with the humans around them. She tried to smile and nod along, answering the questions and comments directed at her. Eventually, the humans around them stopped trying to address Brenna and spoke with Tayen only. She listened with her best approximation of a courtly smile plastered across her face.

It was a relief when the plates were cleared away and small dishes of custard tartlet were placed before them as a final course. She would give anything to be back at Roven, enjoying a meal with the Autumn Court. Sucking in her cheeks, she scooped a bite of the dessert and tasted it. Despite her improved faerie senses, it tasted dull.

The tables went silent a second time, and Brenna cringed, her eyes slowly roaming the length of the room to the dais. Queen Malacia stood alongside her consort. Barrach held her hand up and kissed it, watching his wife with obvious adoration as she addressed the crowd.

"What a lovely occasion. We thank you for hosting us and celebrating this marriage, and we look forward to many years together, knitted into a single family caring for our people with generosity and wisdom. Now, let us enjoy dancing."

No sooner had Queen Malacia spoken, the crowd rose. Attendees shuffled aside, gathering in small groups to talk. Brenna clung to Meara as they followed the Autumn faeries to the side of the room.

Servants efficiently moved the tables aside and arranged the chairs for those wanting to rest. Once the center of the room was cleared, the first notes of instruments echoed through the room.

The royal families watched from their seats on the dais, mildly interested as the room was transformed for dancing. Finally, King Eldric rose and offered his weathered hand to the princess. Elysia descended the steps gracefully. Once at the center, she allowed Eldric to turn her and take her other hand in a dancer's stance. The music began playing in earnest, and the guests watched the couple move through the steps.

Brenna's stomach soured as she watched Elysia turn her face away from her betrothed. How sad it must be to be a royal marrying for an alliance to someone so ill suited.

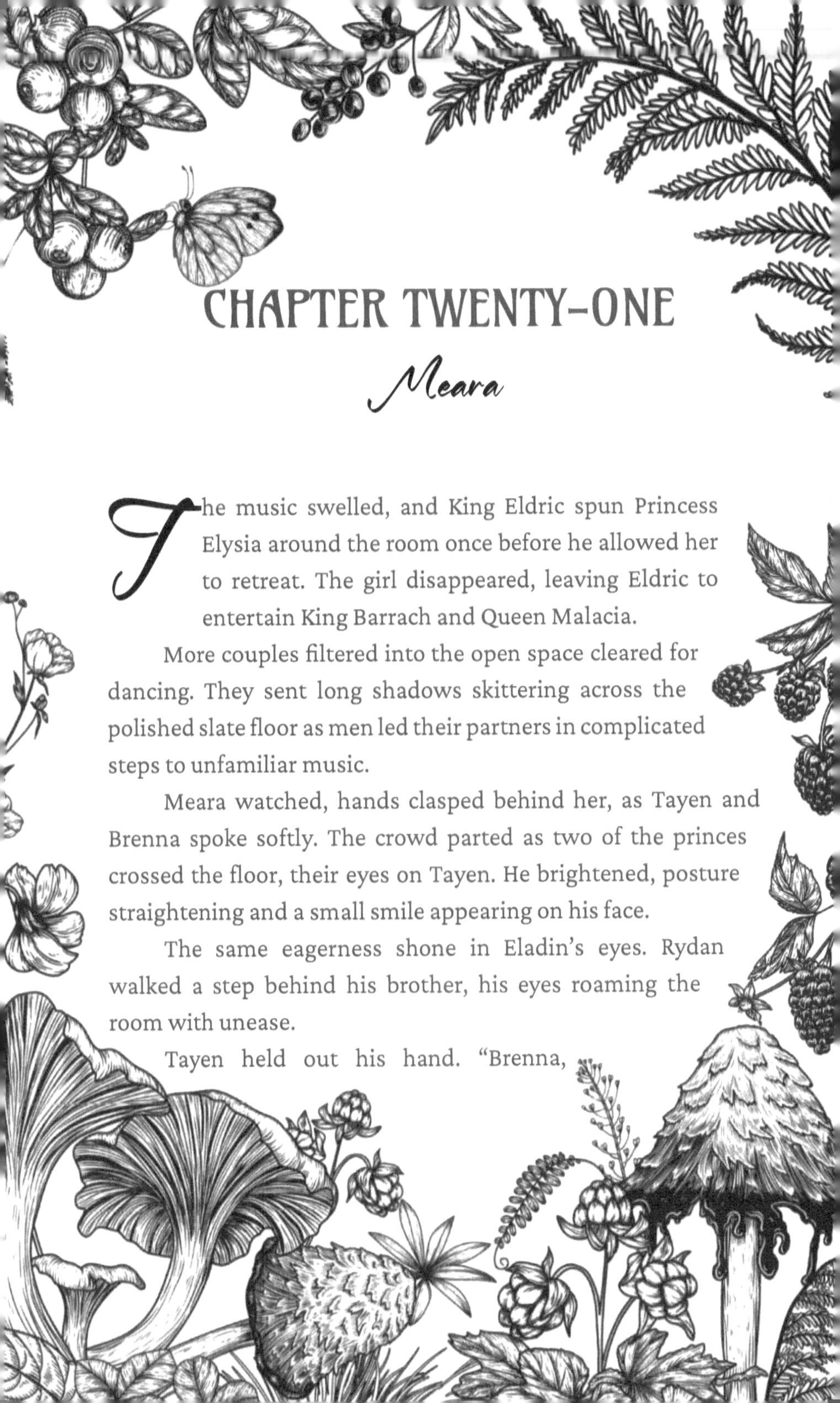

CHAPTER TWENTY-ONE
Meara

The music swelled, and King Eldric spun Princess Elysia around the room once before he allowed her to retreat. The girl disappeared, leaving Eldric to entertain King Barrach and Queen Malacia.

More couples filtered into the open space cleared for dancing. They sent long shadows skittering across the polished slate floor as men led their partners in complicated steps to unfamiliar music.

Meara watched, hands clasped behind her, as Tayen and Brenna spoke softly. The crowd parted as two of the princes crossed the floor, their eyes on Tayen. He brightened, posture straightening and a small smile appearing on his face.

The same eagerness shone in Eladin's eyes. Rydan walked a step behind his brother, his eyes roaming the room with unease.

Tayen held out his hand. "Brenna,

Meara, this is Prince Eladin and Prince Rydan."

"Pleasure," Eladin purred. "Welcome to our home."

"It's lovely," Brenna said, folding her hands against her stomach. "Thank you for hosting us." The prince's smile widened.

"We should dance," Tayen said, taking Brenna's hand.

Meara took a cautionary step back, but Eladin smirked and swiped her hand from its place resting against her hip. "Surely we shouldn't leave Tayen and your lovely sister on their own," he said. She scowled but had no argument to voice as the prince dragged her into the spiraling crowd.

She knew none of the steps, but Eladin was an excellent dancer. He led with gentle pressure, even spinning her when the dance called for it. Tayen and Brenna moved past them, and in the distraction, she missed a cue and stepped on Eladin's boot. Cringing, she opened her mouth to apologize, but he cut her off with a laugh. "The song will be over soon, no need to maim me."

"I apologize," she spluttered, the tension in her frame leading her to miss another step. Eladin kept clear and used a firmer hand to lead her through the rest of the dance.

It was unbearably stuffy as the fires roared and dancers sweated. Meara finally escaped the dance floor and turned, looking for her sister and finding only Tayen.

"Meara," he said, his smile distracted as his eyes tracked Eladin's lazy progress winding after Meara. "Brenna went with Xurey to refresh herself. May I leave you with Cerne and Ayala? I have others needing my attention."

His eyebrows rose as he awaited her permission. Her anxiety about being in this room lessened as she met his kind eyes. "Of course. Go enjoy yourself." His smile bloomed at her answer. "So, where is Cerne?"

"He is speaking with Emeric, I believe," Tayen answered as he led her toward the front of the long room.

Cerne lounged against the steps of the dais, holding a goblet loosely in hands decorated with thin rings that caught the light as he moved. The dark green doublet he wore hugged his broad shoulders and stretched across his chest as he leaned back.

"Meara, this is Prince Emeric," Tayen said.

The eldest prince stood and took her hand, feathering a kiss over her knuckles. "Why have you not come to visit us before? This wretch is here drinking my wine every chance he gets. The least he could do is bring along better company." His smile was charming but nonthreatening, and Meara felt herself relax.

"We joined the Autumn Court only recently," she said, sinking down beside Cerne.

"Where did you come from?" Emeric asked as he settled back onto the steps on the Autumn Lord's other side.

"Well, that's none of your business," Cerne snapped, almost snarling.

The prince held his hands up to pacify him. "I apologize, I was merely trying to make conversation." Meara watched the two males, sensing the dominance rolling off of Cerne, like heat or perhaps magic brushing against her soul. She folded her hands neatly, her fingers squeezing together until the tips turned white.

"Are you going to take your lady to dance, then?" Emeric said, a challenge in his voice.

"I don't think I will." Cerne said, taking a long drink from his cup. "And don't even consider it." Emeric snapped his mouth shut.

Irritated, she reached out, pinching Cerne's shoulder. He turned so quickly, wine sloshed over his wrist as his free hand shot out and caught her arm. Those glassy eyes sharpened and his lip curled to show sharp canine teeth. A growl rumbled from his chest, and she wasn't sure if it was from the wasted wine or the brazen pinch. She bared her teeth in response, trying to pull her hand free. "Just because I am staying with you, it does not make me your property."

"You are of my court," he said, the words slow and lazy. "I am your lord."

"And what a fine lord you are," she said, rolling her eyes.

"Right you are," he said, tipping his head back as he laughed. His hold on her wrist loosened and she yanked it back.

Her eyes traced the line of his lips as they parted. Even sloppy drunk, he was magnetic. She thought the draw to him would fade, but it was stronger than ever. Standing, she smoothed her skirt and pressed her lips into a line.

"I'm going to return to our rooms. I've had enough of this," she said, waiting for Cerne to protest or insist on walking her back. He did neither. Disappointed, she swallowed and nodded. "Good evening. It was nice to meet you, Prince Emeric."

"Good evening, my lady," the prince answered with a warm smile.

She wound through the crowd, her face burning. Stewards bowed deeply before opening the door for her. As she stepped into the night air, she finally took an uninhibited breath.

Stars littered the black sky. Guards lined the wall and the townsfolk had gone home, leaving the courtyard quiet. She crossed the barren space, retracing her steps and grateful she took careful note of the route.

She eased the door open slowly, worried perhaps she had the wrong rooms. It was the same dark hall. She stepped in, her feet halting as she looked up. Two figures leaned against the wall at the end of the shadowy room.

Tayen's disheveled hair fell over his cheek as he closed his mouth over the prince's neck. Eladin arched his body, eyes squeezed shut and head pressing back into the wall as his hands ran over Tayen's shoulders, shrugging his doublet off.

So this is what he meant by others needing his attention.

Eyes wide, she fumbled with the door behind her, trying to escape unnoticed. Tayen's head shot up, the gold of his irises a thin ring around his blown pupils. His grin was devious without a hint of shame being caught with the prince.

Eladin lowered his chin, following his lover's gaze. "Hello, my lady."

"Sorry!" she squeaked, finally catching the knob in her palm. Before she could flee, Tayen winked and returned to his task, his hands pulling at Eladin's shirt. She stepped back into the cold with Eladin's throaty laughter following her. With her heartbeat pounding in her throat, she clicked the door shut and leaned her back against the wood.

The times she had witnessed young lovers in their village, it was nothing like that. She was used to seeing light kisses, hands cradling faces, clumsy embraces. Nothing like the way Tayen's hips pressed into Eladin and caged him against the wall. The way his teeth flashed as he devoured his skin. Her face warmed and she tipped her head back, letting the chilled breeze cool her.

She wouldn't bother them again, but she didn't want to go back to the great hall full of wealthy strangers and a particular drunk faerie. But perhaps Brenna and Xurey had returned or she could discover where they were. She nibbled the edge of her lip as she thought. Even the promise of seeing her sister wasn't enough to drive her back into that crowd.

Meara turned, looking for any answer to present itself. The soft nickers of horses drifted through the air. She followed the sound, hoping a quiet hour or so admiring horses in the stable would fill the rest of her evening nicely. The solitude would give her time to think. She passed the castle's main entrance, the ground sloping downward slightly.

Before she could find the stables, gruff male voices echoed off to the stone wall to her left. Their accents were familiar. Liosliath guards. She turned, frantic to hide herself, but short of sprinting, there was nothing for her to do. They ambled into view, their sharp gazes focusing on her with intent that seized her muscles.

"A faerie!" one called, throwing his arm over his friend's shoulders.

The friend sneered. "I've never actually seen one before. She's odd looking."

She ignored them, changing direction to stride toward the great hall. The men were faster, surrounding her in seconds. Her instincts urged her to run, but they were tall and lean and she doubted she could outpace them. Attempting escape would be unwise. It would excite them. So she turned and raised her chin defiantly. "I am a guest of the King, so please excuse me and go about your business." She was proud of how steady her voice was, hiding the fear. Even if she had a weapon, it wouldn't make a difference. These were trained soldiers and at least five of them circled her like a wolf pack closing in.

"Good evening, Lady Meara." Prince Rydan strode into the group, his face calm despite the tension bristling in his muscled frame. He stood broader than any of the guards and just as tall. "Sirs, I suggest you return to your posts."

With mumbled apologies, the guards dispersed. Rydan watched them until they were out of view.

"Are you alright?" His soft question gentled her icy anger.

Her hands curled into fists against her hips, and she took a slow breath. "I didn't need you to do that."

"I thought faeries could not lie." Raising his eyebrows, Rydan assessed her. "Except that you believe it."

"I am sorry, Your Royal Highness." She kept the sarcastic edge from her words, but it had been a long day and her words were sharper than she intended. "Surely you can understand my frustration when I am harassed by guests of your kingdom and then forced to play damsel and rely on you to rescue me."

Cerne or Tayen would have argued or teased her, but Rydan merely nodded. "Why did you leave the feast?" he asked plainly, unbothered by her acidic tongue.

She sighed, biting the inside of her cheeks for a moment. "I find large groups difficult to tolerate. I was going back to our rooms and found them occupied. So now I'm wandering around like a fool." She paused, surprised by the way his mouth twisted into a wry smile, as if he knew exactly what she had stumbled upon. Clearing her throat, she continued, "I thought to see the stables and the horses you are so famous for."

"Allow me to escort you. It's the least I can do."

"I couldn't impose. If you would point me in the right direction," she protested, wrapping her arms around her waist defensively.

"The stables are my favorite place in the city, so humor me and allow me to join you. I would love the excuse to avoid the rest of the celebration."

Meara smiled, the prince's humility and calm demeanor putting her at ease. "Thank you," she muttered, falling into step beside him. He didn't hold out his arm, so she kept her hands clasped at her waist, twisting her fingers around each other anxiously. It wasn't far to the wide doors leading to the royal stables.

"There are other stables that our masters of husbandry manage, but these are my personal stock." He spread his arms, reaching for a horse that poked its head out from its stall. "Sorry I woke you," he murmured, stroking his tattooed knuckles over her soft nose. "This is Kemuri."

"She's beautiful," Meara said, softly touching the mare's smokey jaw.

"She is a blue roan," Rydan said, his eyes shining with pride as he scratched along her neck.

Wandering down the row, she couldn't suppress her smile as she peeked over doors and observed the beautiful creatures sleeping. Some lay in the hay, others slept where they stood. Their glossy coats ranged from silvery white to darkest ebony.

"They do not have horses like these in Liosliath," she muttered.

Rydan frowned. "How do you know that?"

Turning, Meara clenched her jaw, trying to think of an explanation. "My mother lived there for a time," she said vaguely. His dark eyes moved to her ears, perhaps questioning if she was half-fae, though he kept silent. "It is not a place I intend to visit again."

Rydan turned back to Kemuri, chuckling as she bumped his shoulder with her nose. "Perhaps with this alliance, Liosliath will learn to not fear the fae and it will be a place you are welcome."

"I doubt that." Meara frowned. "Do you sincerely think the queen doesn't know what the fae are truly like? Fearing them keeps her people in line and reliant on her for protection."

His brow furrowed as he glanced back at her. She stepped closer, feeling bolder. "How do you feel about this betrothal?" At the slight widening of his eyes, she retreated. "I apologize, that was inappropriate."

"No, I understand your reason for concern." Rydan brushed his locs over his shoulder. "My father is benevolent and just. The princess will not want for anything." He paused, looking back at Kemuri. "I suspect she will be safer here than in Liosliath."

She chose her words carefully. "I heard guests asking why she did not marry the crown prince instead."

Rydan's shoulders rose and fell with his exhale. "Liosliath was rather uncompromising, and the queen would not accept Emeric." His expression turned wry. "He was not disappointed."

Silence stretched between them, but she felt his unsaid words building. Finally, he continued, "It is important this treaty does not fall through. The terms tied up both trade, military, and land. It will bring lasting peace, but there is no margin for failure."

"Then I hope it succeeds," she said, trying to soothe the worry lines in his forehead.

He bobbed his head and reached for the nearest rope, recoiling it and straightening the tack hung upon the wall. Meara twisted her fingers together, unsure of what to say. She opted to change the topic of conversation. "Do you ride often?"

"As often as I can," he said, brightening. "You should come back soon and we can go riding together. Perhaps when Tayen cannot stay away from Eladin and comes for another visit." He huffed a laugh.

"Perhaps," she echoed, smiling back at him. It was a lovely suggestion.

The sounds of revelers leaving the great hall broke their comfortable silence.

"It sounds like the celebration is ending. I should go back. My sister is likely worried." She swayed, eyeing the exit.

"I'd rather not have Cerne unhappy with me for keeping you," he muttered, jerking his head in a request for her to follow.

Scoffing, she fell into step beside him. He made no effort to hold a frivolous conversation and Meara felt as if she walked with a friend.

Nobles drifted across the gravel, dissipating from the great hall. Rydan led them diagonally, steadily northward to where her fae friends would likely be.

"There you are!" Brenna broke from the crowd streaming from the hall and wrapped her arms around Meara. "Prince Rydan," she greeted with a graceful curtsy.

"Good evening," he responded, dipping his head before

walking away.

Cerne draped his arm over Meara's shoulders and she tensed. "I see you got acquainted with Rydan." His voice was husky in her ear. Brenna strode ahead with Xurey, leaving Meara to shrug Cerne's arm away. He stayed close like an annoying insect.

"He was kind enough to assist me when Liosliath soldiers bothered me." She watched his teasing amusement drain away, leaving a smoldering anger. "Don't worry, I'm fine. I can handle a few guards."

"You should have stayed with me."

"You were occupied. Besides, I couldn't possibly take Ayala's place at your side. How else would she wheedle her way into your bed again?" She regretted the bitter words as they left her mouth, but she was tired and had drank enough to shorten her reservations.

Cerne's eyes narrowed dangerously as his lips curved into a smile. "You seem awfully concerned about my bed."

She sucked in a breath to protest, but his index finger touched her lips, halting her words. "Don't worry yourself. Ayala will have found a bed more to her liking by now. She has many friends among the human kingdoms and faerie courts alike. She wouldn't waste an evening with me, no matter how *skilled* I am."

Meara's nose scrunched as she sneered at him. "You think highly of yourself."

"You are welcome to discover the truth of it for yourself."

She gaped at him and his lewd invitation. With a wink, he strode past her. Meara shut her mouth with a snap of teeth and stormed forward.

They turned the corner to reach their rooms. Xurey stopped at the door, and Meara yelped, "Wait!"

"What?" Xurey frowned.

"I think..." She halted, embarrassed to say what she

interrupted. "I saw Tayen." Blood rushed to her cheeks, heating her skin.

Cerne barked out a laugh behind them. "I guess they couldn't make it back to the prince's quarters." Behind him, Brenna frowned, bemused.

Xurey rolled her eyes and huffed before opening the door. Meara clutched a hand to her chest, waiting to hear evidence of Tayen's rendezvous. The rooms were silent and empty.

"I guess they moved on," Cerne said, grinning at her. "Too bad. We could have doubled up our rooms. I would make room for you."

"I'd rather sleep on the floor," she hissed, ignoring his chuckle. Tayen had the right idea. The prince's rooms must be opulent and blissfully free of annoying Autumn Lords.

Brushing past Cerne, she steered toward her room. With a great, heaving sigh, she flopped onto the bed and squeezed her eyes shut.

"Wasn't that lovely?" Brenna asked as she trailed into their chosen room. Meara sat up, raising an eyebrow. "Is it terrible that I hated the food? We are spoiled."

"We should learn to cook the way the fae do before we leave," Meara suggested as she unlaced Brenna's dress. Her sister didn't answer, but there was a sad turn to her mouth as she stepped out of the dress.

"I noticed you disappeared. Where did you go?" Brenna asked as she turned to undo Meara's dress.

"Nowhere," she muttered, "I just made a fool of myself."

"What do you mean?" Brenna pried, following her as Meara hung her dress over the chair and threw herself back onto the bed.

"Truly?" Meara said, dropping her voice and drawing closer to her sister. "I came back here and walked in on Tayen and Eladin. *Together.*" Brenna's eyes widened. "I stood there like an idiot, apologized, and ran away."

Brenna exploded in giggles. "Is that what Cerne meant with his comments? That sounds wildly exciting."

"It was awkward. He winked at me."

"Tayen or the prince?"

"Tayen. The prince laughed."

"What did you see?" Brenna asked, rolling over and propping her chin on her folded arms.

Meara shook her head, reticent to go over the memory again when she had barely gotten it out of her head. "He had him pinned up against the wall. Tayen pinned the prince, I mean. He was kissing his neck." Her cheeks burned as she buried her face in her hands.

Hopefully, by the time he returned, Tayen will have forgotten her accidental voyeurism.

Brenna sighed. "It sounds very romantic."

"Romantic?" Meara rolled onto one elbow.

"Well, not courting romantic, but like a romance novel romantic."

Laughing, Meara stood to pull on a shift. "Perhaps those books are a poor choice to fill your thoughts."

"They are the best choice," Brenna sniped, grinning to soften her words. "I could sleep for a week. It feels like it's morning and we've been dancing through the night."

Humming her agreement, Meara unfolded the blanket and laid it across them. Brenna snuggled down and fell into sleep instantly. Meara listened to her steady breathing and replayed the evening in her head, suddenly grateful they didn't go straight to Dornadan with Brenna's untrained magic sparking out of control. Her fingers traced the tapered tip of her ear. It was hard to imagine their life in Dornadan in the future. It didn't feel like home, but she was afraid nowhere would again.

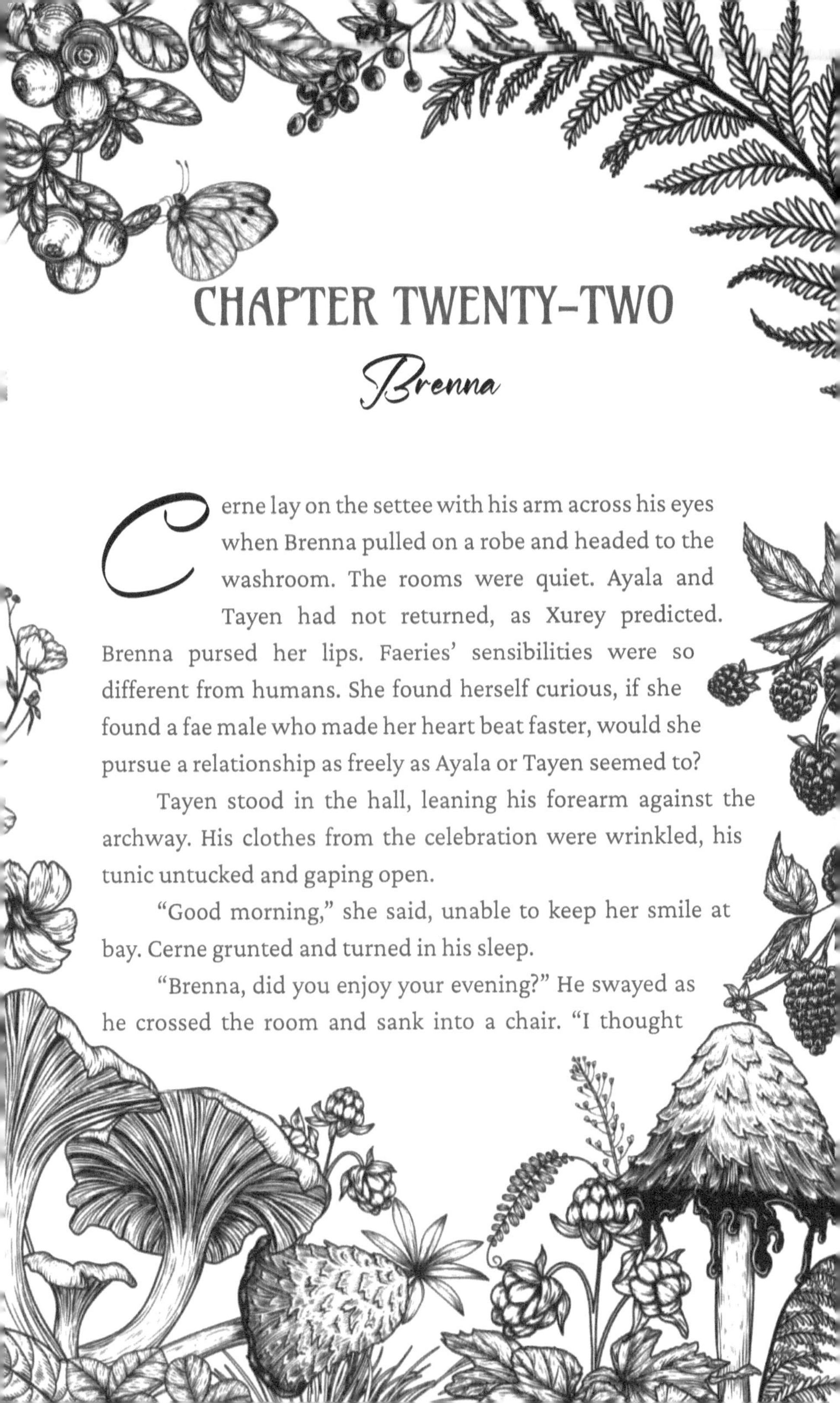

CHAPTER TWENTY-TWO
Brenna

Cerne lay on the settee with his arm across his eyes when Brenna pulled on a robe and headed to the washroom. The rooms were quiet. Ayala and Tayen had not returned, as Xurey predicted. Brenna pursed her lips. Faeries' sensibilities were so different from humans. She found herself curious, if she found a fae male who made her heart beat faster, would she pursue a relationship as freely as Ayala or Tayen seemed to?

Tayen stood in the hall, leaning his forearm against the archway. His clothes from the celebration were wrinkled, his tunic untucked and gaping open.

"Good morning," she said, unable to keep her smile at bay. Cerne grunted and turned in his sleep.

"Brenna, did you enjoy your evening?" He swayed as he crossed the room and sank into a chair. "I thought you'd like to see your mother before we set off today."

"Yes, please." Brenna clapped her hands together. "Let me wake Meara up." Tayen nodded, leaning his head back and closing his eyes.

When Brenna emerged with a bleary-eyed Meara in tow, Cerne was sitting up talking with Tayen in low tones. He paused as he glanced up at them. Meara blushed furiously and strode past him toward the door. Chuckling, Tayen rose, straightened his clothes, and followed.

Gray morning light coated the fortress, turning the brown crushed rock beneath their feet sepia. A small selection of guards stood by the grand entry, but they turned the other way and headed into the surrounding market.

Their mother's shop stood in the row of buildings nearest to the gate. It seemed to nestle into the inner wall, with a small courtyard tucked beside it, giving it space from the closest neighbor. A freshly painted sign hung above the door: an alder tree cradled in a bowl. A pestle poked out from the side of the bowl, denoting the shop as an apothecary.

The door was closed and locked. Tayen stood back and allowed Meara to knock a familiar pattern. Their mother threw the door open and stared at them, her eyes filling with tears. "My beautiful girls," she crooned, wrapping her arms around both of them and dragging them inside.

"Good morning, Miss Aldridge," Tayen said with a tip of his chin.

"Hello, my lord. Do you want to join us?" Their mother asked over her shoulder.

Tayen shook his head. "I'll be back later this morning to retrieve them. Have a nice visit."

Brenna waved, overflowing with gratitude for her friend's support. Seeing her mother brought back so many emotions in a rush, she had to wipe at her eyes. Their mother pulled them through the shop and into her personal rooms. They sat around a wobbly second-hand table while she added additional slices of sausage to the heavy iron frying pan over her wood-burning stove in the corner.

A stable door led to the garden beyond, the top half swung open while the bottom stayed closed. Around it, herbs hung drying for both cooking and the shop's salves and tonics. Jars lined the tall shelves, and the edge of the long, stone counters. It was similar to the old shop, except the structure was primarily stone instead of wood. The thick walls held in the heat of the hearth, and the entire space felt cozy. The scent of herbs filled the air, but had yet to soak into the walls and floor.

Their mother beamed at them as she served her daughters eggs with runny yolks over shredded potato pancakes she explained were popular in Dornadan. The spices in the sausage were unfamiliar, but the meal warmed Brenna through.

"Everyone has been friendly," their mother said, sipping the bergamot and black tea blend she had prepared for them to share. "Despite the harsher landscape, this land is kinder."

"And the people will accept us when we return to you," Meara said.

"Oh yes, the fae are welcome here. Many of my neighbors have faerie heritage. It's been fascinating. But I am curious about your experience the last few weeks."

Brenna described the Autumn Court and all of the wonderful shops, including Dyani's dressmaking studio. "And Lord Cerne's house is the largest structure I've ever seen. Not as large as the king's fortress here, but that's not really one building, is it? This is one giant house and it covers the side of the hill. You can look out the back windows and it drops off into a valley with a lake. It's beautiful."

"Would you like to come see it?" her sister asked quietly.

Their mother stroked her hand. "I don't think so. I am happy here and the new business is quite busy. I'll have to hire an assistant soon."

Meara's brows furrowed. "Can't you wait until we join you?"

"No dear, I will not tie you to the shop in that way. You are under no obligation to join me in the business, and I know you do not love treating patients." Her forehead creased as she raised her eyebrows and gave Meara a meaningful look. "Besides, it seems to me that you are not done with your time in the Autumn Court."

"Brenna has gained great control over her magic."

"Yes, but you have not. And there is no rush. You are growing into your true selves and I am so proud of you. You may even stay among the fae if you wish to. You are faeries after all. And you're only a day's ride away." Her knowing smile made Brenna chew her lip. Their mother was right. Brenna loved the Autumn Court and had no desire to return to a human life.

Meara shook her head stubbornly. "Of course we are coming home to you."

"My daughter, many children grow up and move away. And I am doing fine without you. You gave me a great blessing by moving me here. It is a wonderful opportunity. Now seize your own opportunity and live among the faeries if you wish to."

"Thank you, Mum." Brenna leaned forward and kissed her mother's cheek. "We will see what happens. But I do like it there."

"Now I'd love to see what you can do with your magic."

She led them into the small garden, and Brenna stood in the stone pathway between rows of new seedlings. "So far I can do light and heat, together or separately," she explained. She took a moment to center herself, drawing on that buzzing power that felt stilted this far from the fae court. But it came willingly, and soon she held a small flame in her palm.

"Remarkable," her mother murmured, drawing closer and reaching out as if she would touch her wrist, but halting a handbreadth away. Brenna grinned and recalled her flame, drawing forward a light that floated higher for a moment before it flickered and faded. Exhaling, she focused on sustaining her light.

As she let it go, Brenna shook out her hands and grinned. Her mother clapped, lavishing her with praises.

They returned to the shop, and Meara questioned their mother about the new shop. They worked side by side, processing raw ingredients into salves and tonics.

Brenna sat on the stool beside them, telling their mother more about the Autumn Court. She described the friends they had made, her time training with Tayen, and all the delicious food they had shared.

Their mother seemed particularly interested in the sweet honey cakes. "We will bring you some when we return," Meara promised.

Tayen knocked on the open door. "Lovely ladies, I'm afraid it's time to depart. The Autumn Court calls."

Their mother hugged Tayen and then held each of her daughters for a moment until she released them. She spoke softly into Meara's ear for a moment, giving the encouragement her somber daughter needed.

Brenna sighed, her shoulders hunching and falling as they left the shop and crossed the yard to their waiting party.

The trip back was smooth and quick, unburdened by the gifts Cerne and Tayen had presented King Eldric and Princess Elysia. Their steps were lighter and each measure of the journey felt like coming home.

They returned late in the evening and went straight to bed. Brenna slept hard, her muscles sore from riding and dancing.

In the morning, Kirrily brought pastries filled with egg and cheese, and the sisters ate by the window, watching the morning sun climb higher as the colors reflected across the lake turned from pink to gray.

"I think we should focus on your magic," Brenna suggested. "I know you have been, but I'd like to help." Perhaps if Meara unlocked her own abilities, she'd be keener on staying.

"If you'd like," Meara said. She drained the last of her bright green tea and set the cup down. "I suppose it couldn't hurt."

They found the veranda empty and sat upon the rug in the middle. Meara closed her eyes and Brenna watched her brow furrow.

"Focus," Brenna coached.

Meara scowled. "I am!"

Smiling, Brenna held her hands out and called forth a soft glow. "Can you feel the hum of magic in you? I can feel mine under my skin."

Her sister opened her lilac eyes and pursed her lips. "No, I can't. There's nothing there. Just blood and bone."

"Tayen can sense your magic, it has to be there."

As if summoned, the flame haired faerie appeared in the doorway. He watched the sisters with raised eyebrows.

"I can feel *your* magic," Meara growled.

"You can?"

"Yes, it's buzzing like bees."

Brenna frowned, turning her hands over and watching the glow under her skin. "So you can sense mine, but not your own. Is it possible it's still locked down somehow? Tayen, are you sure the suppression enchantment over Meara was fully broken and lifted?"

"I would say so. I was thorough," he said, drawing closer. "Let me see."

His hands settled over Meara's shoulders, and she exhaled slowly as his magic brushed over her.

"I can feel that too. It's different, more like a breeze."

"Interesting," Tayen said. "There's nothing residual on you. I see no reason why you'd be having such difficulty. Have you explored the emotional connection we discussed?"

"Of course," Meara said, crossing her arms.

"Including joy? You haven't been particularly cheerful," Brenna teased.

"Forgive me if I can't manufacture emotions."

Tayen cleared his throat, straightening. "Look, I was coming to see if you'd like to join us for training."

"That's what we are doing," Brenna said, smiling sweetly.

"No, I mean physical defense training." Tayen cocked his head. "We try to train with Seda when we can, and she has new recruits coming in a few days, so it's our last chance for a while."

"I'm not sure," Meara said. "We aren't familiar with your methods. Maybe we can observe?"

"We have to try." Brenna propped her hands on her hips. Meara reluctantly agreed.

They followed Tayen out of the manor house and to the northwest side of the structure. Brush and saplings were cleared away to create training circles, currently occupied by Seda, Xurey, and Ayala.

Seda looked up, her sharp gaze inspecting them. "Come to train?"

"Yes, thank you!" Brenna smiled, ignoring the flip in her stomach. She was not the athletic sister, and this was likely to be a disaster, but it would be good for Meara.

Seda led them through paces. Despite her strong fae body, Brenna's arms burned as she held poses mimicking weapon stances. The movements felt clumsy.

Xurey and Ayala stood before them, each moving through the exercises flawlessly. Tayen laughed as he fumbled a movement, and Brenna couldn't help but smile. As she peeked at her sister, she was grateful to see Meara smiling too.

Finally, Seda released them and they flopped onto the ground. Brenna wiped the sweat away from her neck.

"Well done," Seda said.

"Lovely, thank you for your patience with us," she said to the commander.

"Of course," Seda replied as she stretched her arms over her long legs. "How did you enjoy Dornadan?"

"It was good. We got to see our mother." Meara said, crossing her legs and resting her forearms on her knees as her dark hair fell around her like pooling ink. They began to chat about the half-fae living in Dornadan and how it was different from Liosliath, and Brenna lost interest. Her gaze trailed to Tayen who was watching the leaves sway about their heads.

"Now that we are past the betrothal celebration, do you think we could look into the question of our parentage?" Brenna asked Tayen, dropping her voice.

Tayen brushed hair away from his brow, looking perfectly put together. "Yes, I have been thinking on the subject. Cerne has begun to draft a list."

"Thank you."

Seda interrupted them. "Listen, I was preparing a challenge for the new recruits, and I was hoping my friends would help me test it."

Ayala sat up sharply. "What do you mean by a challenge?"

"A game of sorts," Seda said, smiling.

"That sounds fun. I would like to try," Brenna found herself saying. She liked the burn of her muscles as she trained and the way her fae body responded. Her balance and stamina were greatly improved and she wanted to test herself further.

"Alright, how about this evening before dinner?"

"Alright," Tayen said. "I will make sure Cerne comes as well." He pushed to stand. "I'm due in a meeting with him anyway."

"Perfect," Seda said, her smile a bit too wide.

Meara watched her warily, but Brenna trusted their friends. Seda was a protector. She would not put them in the path of harm. Shaking out her muscles, Brenna stood and offered a hand to her sister.

"Let's freshen up," she said. Meara nodded and followed.

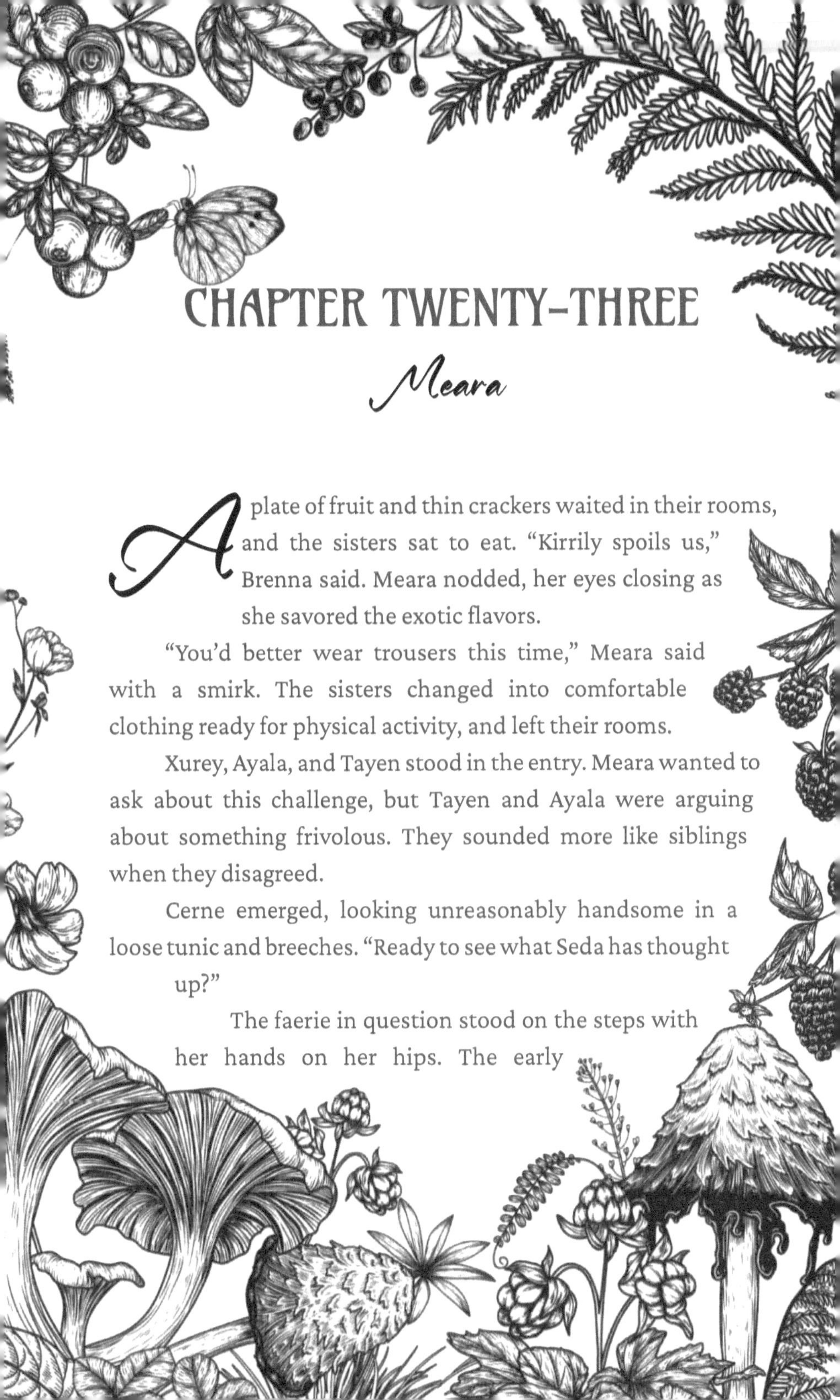

CHAPTER TWENTY-THREE
Meara

A plate of fruit and thin crackers waited in their rooms, and the sisters sat to eat. "Kirrily spoils us," Brenna said. Meara nodded, her eyes closing as she savored the exotic flavors.

"You'd better wear trousers this time," Meara said with a smirk. The sisters changed into comfortable clothing ready for physical activity, and left their rooms.

Xurey, Ayala, and Tayen stood in the entry. Meara wanted to ask about this challenge, but Tayen and Ayala were arguing about something frivolous. They sounded more like siblings when they disagreed.

Cerne emerged, looking unreasonably handsome in a loose tunic and breeches. "Ready to see what Seda has thought up?"

The faerie in question stood on the steps with her hands on her hips. The early afternoon sun illuminated her dark skin to a warm mahogany. "I will be testing potential new recruits for the Autumn Guard this week. While you were gone, I set up an obstacle course. I would like to see it completed before turning the youngsters loose on it."

Tayen cocked his head. "Why do I get the feeling you're simply looking for entertainment?"

Seda's full lips tugged into a sly smile. "Perhaps, but it will be good for all of you to challenge yourselves physically. When was the last time you trained with the guard?"

"When was the last time you broke my toe?" Tayen muttered.

Ignoring him, Seda clapped her hands together. "Is everyone agreeable?"

"Very well," Tayen grumbled. Cerne laughed, and gave his own agreement.

Brenna wrung her hands nervously, but Meara tugged them apart and threaded their fingers together to calm her.

"So what do we do?" Ayala drawled, picking at her nails.

"You will form teams. The challenge starts with tracking. Once you locate the course, you must reach the token and bring it to me before the other team." Seda shrugged like it was the easiest task possible.

Meara shifted her weight, glancing at the others' faces to gauge their reactions. Was this a typical occurrence in the Autumn Court? Tayen's eyes gleamed with eagerness and even Xurey smiled. She exhaled slowly, trying to relax.

"Do the winners get a prize?" Ayala asked, drawing out her vowels like she was bored, but Meara didn't miss the competitive edge to her tone.

Cerne's eyes narrowed and his chin lifted, "Bragging rights." Smirking, he stretched his shoulders, pulling open his half buttoned shirt with the motion and revealing a swath of golden skin.

"Sounds good to me," Meara said, keeping her gaze away from both Cerne's distracting body and Ayala's sneer.

"I have chosen teams and I am accepting no complaints." Seda surveyed them, looking like the leader she was. "First team is Tayen, Meara, and Xurey. Second team is Brenna, Ayala, and Cerne."

Tayen turned to Meara, grinning, and motioned her and Xurey closer. She glanced at Brenna, concerned, but her sister had a determined set to her jaw and was eyeing her two teammates. She would be fine. Ayala was not antagonistic to Brenna the way she was with Meara, and Cerne was there too.

"I suggest you begin!" Seda laughed and folded her arms.

Brenna jumped as Ayala grabbed her wrist and dragged her into the trees. Cerne broke into a jog, leading the way.

"Meara!" Tayen called. She blinked, realizing she was being left behind. She fell into a jog beside Xurey.

Huffing, she spoke between breaths. "So how are we supposed to track down an obstacle course? Do you know what it will look like?" They slowed and stopped, and Meara frowned. "Well, do we have a strategy?"

"Patience," Tayen hummed. He nodded to Xurey. The faerie's curtain of dark hair swayed as she approached the nearest tree. Her mouth pinched and she let out a low whistle. In a flash of auburn, a robin flitted to a lower branch and warbled to her.

"What is she doing?" Meara whispered.

"Asking the animals." Chuckling at her shocked expression, he explained, "Seda gave us Xurey because her magic is not too different from Cerne's. Both are useful for this type of thing."

Xurey spun, her face bright. "It's this way!"

Meara's calves warmed as they jogged. After a while, Xurey paused to ask a squirrel which direction to go. It was surreal watching her stare into the creature's adorable face and knowing she was communicating with it. A pang of jealousy streaked through her. It would be incredible to have magic like that.

Her face was flushed by the time they reached their destination: a great brute of a tree with ropes extending from its high branches to another tree until leaves concealed the course.

"We are climbing that?" she gasped, bending at the waist to rest her palms on her knees.

Tayen snagged a bow and quiver of two arrows from the base of the tree. "What are those for?" Xurey asked. They stepped back and peered upward.

"We could simply climb it. The bow and arrow could be unrelated," Tayen mused.

"Or a distraction." Meara squinted up at the lowest tree limbs, far above their heads. A flutter of crimson drew her attention. Walking sideways around the tree, she tried to see a clearer view without any success. "I can't tell, but I think there is a target painted up there."

Glancing behind them, Xurey said, "We should hurry. The second team will be here soon."

"Meara, can you shoot?" Tayen stepped closer to her and craned his neck back while she pointed at what might be a target.

"Not well, sorry."

"Don't worry. Xurey, can you shoot? I'm going to attempt to guide the arrow." With a sharp nod, Xurey gripped the bow and notched one of the two arrows. She followed Meara's directions and carefully aimed at the shock of red.

Tayen stood behind her, arms raised on either side of her. His eyes narrowed and his jaw ticked as Xurey loosed the arrow. It soared straight and the greenery in its path swayed out of the way as the arrow flew past. The sharp head embedded into the target and with a resounding snap, a rope unraveled and tumbled down to rest at face level.

"Excellent!" Tayen's hands fell, his shoulders slumping.

Cerne dashed into the gathering, Ayala and Brenna on his heels. Xurey surged forward and grasped the rope, keeping it from Ayala's hands. Without hesitating, Xurey reached higher on the rope and set her feet onto the trunk. As she climbed, Meara rushed to scale the rope behind her.

Ayala snarled at them and paced away. She snatched up the bow and looked around for a target. A moment later, a second rope unfurled, and Ayala began climbing. Meara pulled herself upwards, wincing at the burn in her palms as the rough fibers dug in.

"Climb!" Tayen urged, his voice breaking into laughter as he blocked Cerne with his body. In response, Cerne grabbed his shoulders and shoved him to the ground. The males grappled, both grinning madly.

Xurey reached the tree limb and released the rope, turning to heave Meara up beside her. They grabbed the branches above their head and stepped onto the next limb until they reached the ropes stretched between the towering trunks.

Behind them, Ayala and then Brenna scrambled onto the first bough. Brenna's eyes were wide, but she grit her teeth and crept after Ayala. Meara felt the twigs under her hands snap as her grip tightened. She didn't like to see her sister in any danger, even if it was a game.

"So onward to the next tree?" Xurey asked, her voice wavering. Meara nodded. Two ropes, one above the other, stretched between trees. Xurey gripped the top rope and cautiously stepped onto the bottom one. It wobbled but held her. She took a deep breath to steady herself and then shimmied out into mid air.

Ayala reached the branch, and Meara knew she would muscle past her given the opportunity, so she flung herself out onto the ropes behind her friend. Xurey tensed but continued working her way across the rope. Hand over hand, feet skating forward, Meara edged further. Her balance tipped too far forward, and she had to yank herself up with the upper rope.

"This is ridiculous. I'm a puca, not a wind sprite," Xurey muttered as she leapt onto the wide bough of the next tree.

The rope swayed in her hand as Ayala stepped across. Her movement was graceful and confident, and Meara's throat constricted. Brenna watched with wide eyes as she clutched the trunk behind her.

"You're almost there!" Xurey chanted, gripping a branch with one hand as she strained to reach Meara with the other.

The rope wobbled, and Meara paused, clinging to the rope as it shook. Her hair whipped against her neck in a sudden breeze. She glanced wildly at Ayala, but she stood upright with one hand stretched toward them with her palm facing out.

"You've got to be kidding me," Xurey hissed. "Meara, you need to move!" Wind slammed into her, shoving her feet off the rope below her. She swung from her hands, feet scrambling to find the rope as her hair whipped over her eyes. Her hands screamed with the pressure of holding her full weight dangling from the rough rope. Xurey's voice sounded distant. "Ayala, stop!"

The air battered her, prying her fingers from the swinging rope. Blood rushed in her ears, competing with the whooshing air. She was going to fall. Each breath felt like drawing needles into her lungs.

"Don't touch my sister!" Brenna screamed.

For a moment, her hair slipped back and Meara caught sight of her sister. Brenna's eyes blazed gold and her gleaming curls tumbled from their braid. Light poured from her hands like magma flowing outward. Ayala threw her hand up to cover her eyes. The wind died away instantly.

Meara pedaled her feet, searching for the bottom rope. They made contact and she pulled herself to stand. She looked to Xurey and edged forward. Brenna let out a startled shriek and the rope fell out from under her feet.

Shoulders screaming, Meara caught herself with one hand. She used her momentum to swing forward and catch the lower branch that Xurey stood upon. Her palms split under the rough bark. She hauled herself up with the last of her adrenaline, and threw her arms around the trunk, panting.

The remains of the bottom rope smoldered, uselessly dangling from her perch. Ayala floated down, her descent slowed by her own magic and her brother's. Tayen held his hands up, his face tense with concentration.

Meara's heart leapt into her throat and her breath caught as she scanned the forest floor for her sister. Brenna huddled against the trunk, her eyes squeezed shut, unharmed.

"That bitch burned my tunic!" Ayala howled from below.

A hysterical laugh burst from Meara, the relief euphoric. Ayala raised her palms, her teeth flashing as she snarled, but Cerne grabbed her wrist and tugged her back.

"Enough," he growled.

Looking up at Xurey, Meara blurted, "I think we are sure to win now." Her heart pounded in her ribcage like a sparrow fighting to escape its cage.

"Then let's finish this task so we can get out of these trees." Xurey edged around the trunk and began to climb.

Meara reached for a higher branch and heaved herself upward, grasping the vertical rope that Xurey scurried up. With a resigned exhale, Meara followed her.

Sticky blood congealed on her palms. The pain felt further away as a vicious sense of triumph grew in her chest. Her teeth clenched as she finally reached a platform of planking set across several boughs.

Gold streaked the sun drenched leaves across the highest layer of the canopy. Clouds meandered overhead, softening the effect. Meara's heart soared at the scene.

"Are you injured?" Xurey asked, her voice soft in this quiet haven. Scratches marred her arms, but her concern was for Meara.

"I can handle it." Her smirk was fringed in pain. "It'll be worth it to beat Ayala."

Xurey chuckled and they turned, searching for the next task. "There!" She pointed at a square of red fabric tied to a branch.

Squinting, Meara wrinkled her nose. "How are we supposed to retrieve that?"

"I hate to say this, but Ayala could easily reclaim it. Maybe Tayen could have, though I am grateful he is on the ground in case one of us falls."

"Can you ask a bird to get it?"

Xurey sighed, chewing her lip. "If we ask nicely, they may help. But creatures only do what they want to."

"Better to ask than attempt to reach it ourselves," Meara muttered. The spindly branches above them swayed in the gentle breeze. She flinched, the memory of Ayala's magic nearly blowing her off the rope too fresh.

She watched Xurey close her eyes, working her magic craft. Moments passed, and Meara feared that Ayala would attempt the climb again and steal this victory from them. Finally, a speckled starling settled on a branch beside Xurey. A moment later, it flitted away. They watched as it wove between branches and paused near the fabric token. And then it darted away. Xurey cursed under her breath.

"We can try another bird," Meara suggested.

"Unless you have some fruit or nuts in your pockets, I'm afraid they have no motivation to help."

Exhaustion seared Meara's muscles. They came so far, only to have no way to retrieve the prize. She could not accept failure, not after shedding her blood on the rope and branches along the way. Gritting her teeth, she reached for a higher branch.

"What are you doing?" Xurey's voice pitched higher.

Without looking back, Meara pushed herself up and reached higher. The trunk split again and she was left clinging to a tediously thin bough. "Tayen will catch us if we fall, correct?"

"Yes, but I wouldn't stake my life on it."

Shrugging, Meara reached higher. "I spent my childhood climbing trees, and I've never quite given up the habit."

Xurey circled the tree in an attempt to counterbalance her. Meara resorted to tugging the highest branches to her, lower and lower until they bent. She had to use both hands, leaving her balanced precariously on a branch far too thin for her comfort. She was so close, she could not abandon the task.

As Meara leaned farther, her bloody fingers reached the red fabric and she seized it. Her shout of victory turned to a shriek as the bough she teetered on slipped from under her feet. Branches lashed her ribs and whipped her face. Reaching wildly for purchase, she managed to slow her descent before her hands lost their grip and she was free falling.

Something slammed into her, knocking the air from her lungs. Terror struck her, seizing her muscles and throwing her heart into a hammering rhythm. She gasped for air, and felt the ground meet her back and slowly press into her as she was placed upon it by an invisible force.

Brenna fell to her knees beside her. "What were you thinking? That was so foolish!"

Another painful breath, and Meara was able to answer, "We won." Brenna smacked her stomach. "Ouch! Please don't hit me, I'm in enough pain already."

A scrap of red fabric fluttered down, and Brenna snatched it from the air. Too weak to protest, Meara raised a hand, reaching for it. Shaking her head and tutting, Brenna passed it to Tayen, who presented it to Seda.

Ayala stood beside Cerne, her tunic singed and torn away at the waist. Her cold gaze promised murder. Despite her discomfort, Meara's lips curved into a smile.

"I'm so sorry about the fire. I didn't mean to," Brenna began.

Meara raised a hand. "You were brilliant. It looked intense. Have you produced that light before?" Brenna shook her head. "You should try again during training." Her distraction worked and Brenna relaxed.

"Well done," Seda said. "That was quite the showing. Are you sure you don't want to join the guard?"

"Absolutely not, I could never," Brenna said, her voice rising in pitch.

Meara frowned. Cerne watched her as Ayala whispered into his ear. When he ignored the beautiful faerie, Ayala growled and stalked away, wind whipping her hair into a frenzy.

Turning to Tayen, Meara said, "Thank you for catching me."

"Ayala tried to make her fall," Brenna sputtered, her face flushed and eyes burning. "She could have died."

Cerne shrugged. "Tayen would have caught you. Or maybe you would have broken something and we'd visit a healer."

"She doesn't have a way to defend herself," Brenna argued.

"I wasn't in any true danger," Meara argued, hoping it was true. She trusted Tayen, even if his sister was a monster.

"Then I suggest she find her craft," Cerne said. Brenna glared at him, but Meara had to agree.

"I'm ready for a luncheon," Xurey declared. She leapt from the lowest branch and crossed to stand beside them. "Next time try to refrain from falling." With a smile, she offered her hand, grasping

Meara's wrist to avoid her injuries. Meara rose to her feet and brushed herself off. New bruises ached along her spine, her hip, and her stomach, but she was victorious and that pride drowned out the pain. She limped as they made their way through the woods and back to the manor house, her mind going over the herbs she could use to create a salve for her hands.

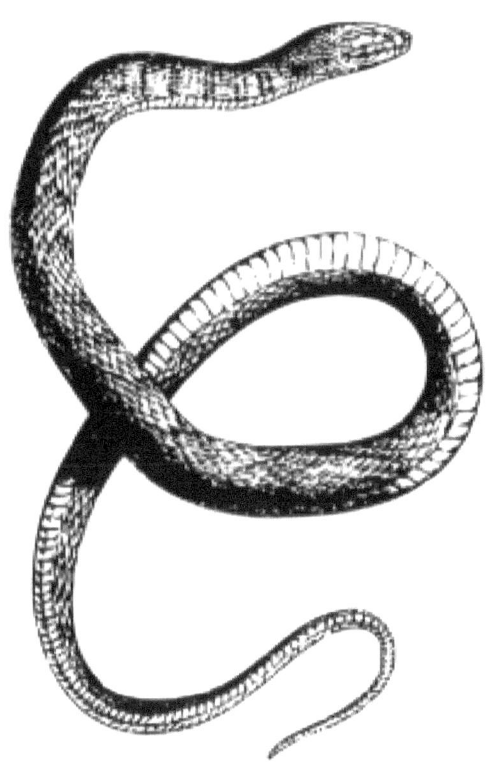

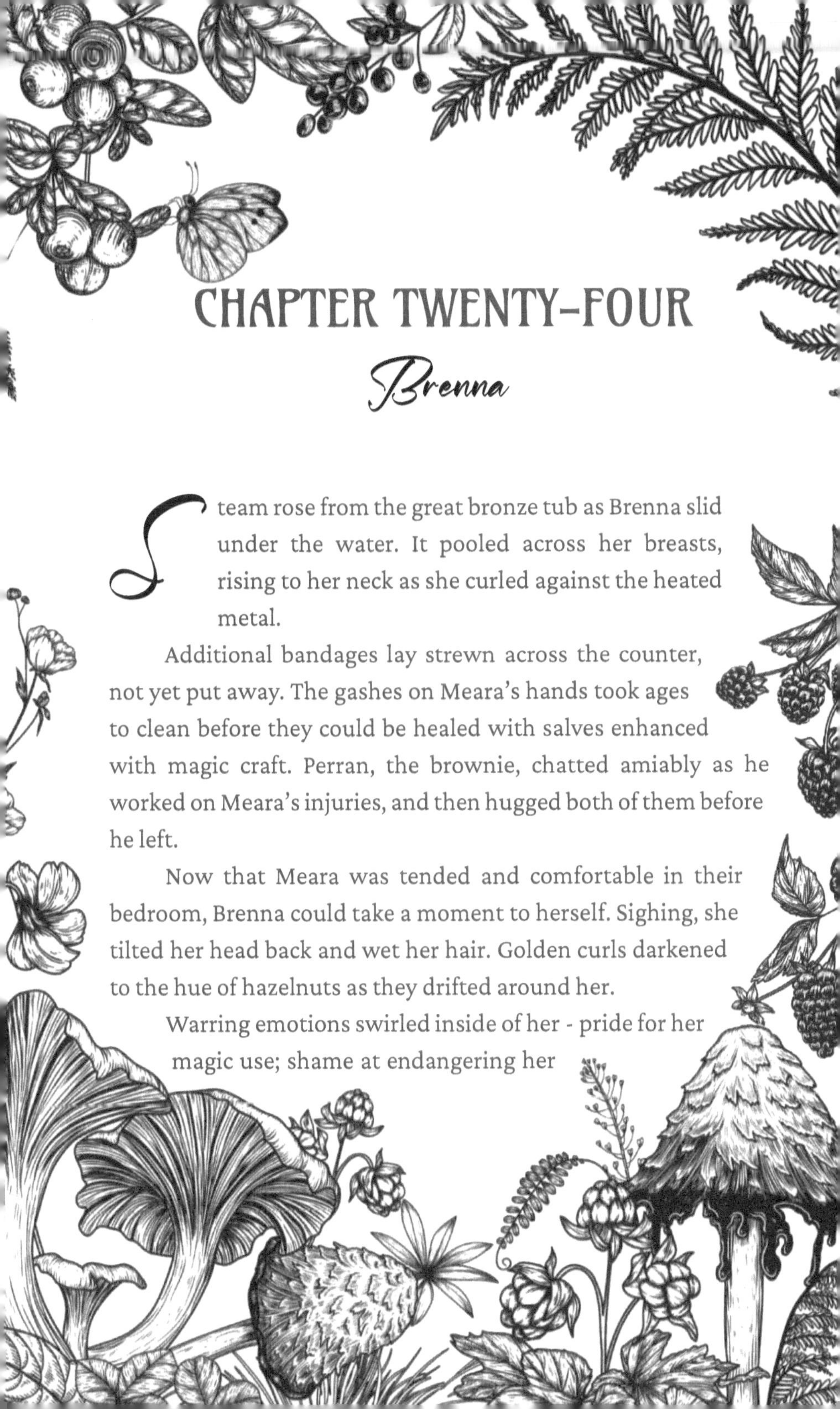

CHAPTER TWENTY-FOUR

Brenna

Steam rose from the great bronze tub as Brenna slid under the water. It pooled across her breasts, rising to her neck as she curled against the heated metal.

Additional bandages lay strewn across the counter, not yet put away. The gashes on Meara's hands took ages to clean before they could be healed with salves enhanced with magic craft. Perran, the brownie, chatted amiably as he worked on Meara's injuries, and then hugged both of them before he left.

Now that Meara was tended and comfortable in their bedroom, Brenna could take a moment to herself. Sighing, she tilted her head back and wet her hair. Golden curls darkened to the hue of hazelnuts as they drifted around her.

Warring emotions swirled inside of her - pride for her magic use; shame at endangering her sister; ebbing shock at the entire event; anger with Ayala for her actions. Face flushing, she slipped under the water. She let the heat burn away the worst of her turmoil until her lungs ached. Slowly, bubbles slipped from her mouth. When she could no longer hold back the need to breathe, her back slid up the tub and she sucked in a lungful of fragrant air.

She would give herself ten minutes to sulk, and then she would focus on the positive and rejoin her sister with a smile. Reaching for the soap, she scrubbed the dirt clinging to her nails. She worked until her skin was bright red and raw and she felt in control once more.

Her worries faded away as she toweled off and she wrapped herself in a silk robe. The fabric whispered against her skin, soothing her. How could she go back to living among humans after experiencing fae luxury?

Straightening her shoulders, Brenna left the washroom. Meara huddled on the window seat, her long, pale legs stretched out. She smiled when Brenna entered.

"Are you hungry? I'm starving."

Meara nodded. "Kirrily was fetching us something light. Cerne wanted to take everyone to the tavern tonight."

"That sounds enjoyable." Mood brightening, Brenna pulled open the wardrobe and brushed her fingers down her small collection of dresses. She imagined having a full wardrobe like a noblewoman, including riding clothes, night dresses, and fine undergarments. Her hand stopped on a simple yet elegant flaxen dress that allowed her hair to shine. Laying it out, she perched on the edge of the bed and dragged a comb through her hair.

A gentle knock sounded. "Good afternoon." Kirrily peered through the doorway, smiling sweetly, a tray balanced on her hip. "I hope you like soup. If you need anything, let me know. And don't wait too long to eat, it's best warm." She lowered the tray onto the side table.

"Thank you, Kirrily. I don't know what we would do without you," Brenna confessed.

"It's my honor." The dryad dipped into a graceful curtsy and slipped away.

Meara was happy to help Brenna lace up the back of her dress but refused to change out of the soft pants and loose tunic she had donned.

"You look like a man," Brenna grumbled.

"It's practical, and I am not here to attract a husband," Meara stated patiently. "Besides, Xurey and Seda are typically in trousers." Brenna supposed that was true. Some things about fae culture were odd to her.

They settled at their small table and removed the cloches. Bowls of bright orange soup swirled with cream sat beside thick slices of sourdough, studded with pumpkin seeds. Brenna picked one off and popped it into her mouth.

Meara dunked the bread in the soup, scooping up some of the cream. She chewed thoughtfully. "So you seem to have better control over your magic. Should we discuss returning home? I do not think I will manifest any magic."

Frowning, Brenna picked up her spoon. "Of course you will. And we aren't nearly ready." Pausing, she looked up. "And I'm not sure I want to. Besides, don't you want to learn about our parentage?"

Meara's shoulders tensed defensively. After a moment of brittle silence, she met Brenna's gaze. "You know that I don't."

Her next breath was harsh with frustration as Brenna stirred her soup. She had no interest in repeating the same argument.

Tayen fetched them with a rhythmic knock on their door. "Ready to celebrate?"

"We'll see," Meara said, wrinkling her nose.

Undeterred, Tayen chuckled and offered his arms. With one sister on each side, he led them to the entry where Cerne and Seda spoke quietly with their heads leaned together.

Ayala stood with a hand on her hip. She reached up and dragged her fingers through her vibrant hair and shook her head, the glossy strands flashing in the warm evening light. Brenna glared at the faerie, mentally replaying how she attempted to knock her sister out of a tree.

"Let's go," Tayen said brightly as Xurey emerged from another hall. "Brenna?"

She attempted to smooth her features and smile, but her anger sparked back to life at Ayala's smug expression.

"Love, you are glowing," Tayen said. "What is it?"

Her hands rubbed over her arms, trying to dispel the light. "I apologize, I guess I am still upset about the," she paused, "incident."

Tayen sighed, looking between Brenna and Ayala. "Then I suggest you talk to her."

"What?" Brenna's eyes widened as she pulled away from Tayen.

"There's no reason to stew over it. Confront her and let's be done with it. Then we can enjoy our evening."

Ayala huffed. "I don't know what she has to complain about. I'm the one who was burned and tossed out of the tree."

"You tried to do that to my sister!"

Meara raised her hands, but her mouth opened and closed silently, clearly unsure of how to help. It wasn't in Brenna's nature to confront, but she found herself eager for the conflict.

"Alright, I will apologize to her, and you may apologize to me," Ayala said, raising an eyebrow. "Meara, I am sorry I tried to use my craft to remove you from the challenge."

Meara raised her chin defiantly. "I promise to pay you back in kind the next time we are in a similar situation."

Ayala's lips curved into a smile. "I supposed that is fair." Turning to Brenna, she crossed her arms expectantly and waited.

Swallowing bitterly, Brenna worked her jaw and pulled together an apology. "I am sorry I burned you. It was not my intention."

"Fine."

"Wonderful. Now that we are all on good terms, can we go?" Tayen said, humor in his voice. Rolling her eyes, Brenna nodded, her anger finally diffusing.

The group strolled down the steps toward the village. The residents of the Autumn Court often waved or nodded in greeting as they wandered down the cobblestone street. The day's work was done and now the residents mingled as they made their way home.

A faerie with scales over his head and cheeks turned, waving to a dryad with golden vines throughout his beard. Down the road, a family of huldra walked hand in hand away from the shops, likely heading home. It was a beautiful tapestry of fur, claws, and fanged smiles.

The buildings were lit up with cozy lamplight, casting a comforting glow to light their way. As they passed the empty forge, now a dark cavern, Brenna reached up to brush Cerne's shoulder. He turned, eyebrows rising.

"Who was the friend you built the forge for?" She wasn't sure where the curiosity came from, but something about the cold building bothered her.

Cerne rubbed his jaw. "It's not a very happy story, or a very interesting one." Meara's head turned, her interest peaked as well, though she stayed a step behind them.

"I'd like to hear it, if you don't mind." Brenna pressed her lips into a thin line, hoping she hadn't asked too much.

"Alright." He sighed. "His name was Daryan. He was a mentor

to me when I became the Lord of Autumn. He ruled the Spring Court then."

"No longer?"

Cerne's dark curls swayed as he shook his head. "It is led by his son now." He stared blankly ahead for a moment and Brenna was careful to not disturb him. He would continue when he was ready. "He isn't dead. He was banished by King Argyro."

"Oh."

"It was a pity." His voice dropped. "Daryan's family was attacked by the Lord of Summer, and in retribution, he killed him."

Brenna's eyes widened and her hand went to her mouth. "What did the Summer Lord do exactly?"

"Killed his two younger children."

"That's terrible." Brenna's hand slipped down to press to her chest, empathy for Cerne and this faerie she did not know a dull, aching twinge behind her breastbone. "I can understand your distaste for the Summer Court."

"Yes, working with them is difficult. The Summer Lady, Aletris, has always been unpleasant, but any friendship I had with her son was ruined when he held me responsible for his father's death, for my support of Daryan."

"I'm sorry, Cerne."

"We are here to enjoy ourselves, so no more discussion of tragedies." His charming smile was back, and Brenna nodded along.

The tavern loomed ahead. Tayen held the door and waved them inside.

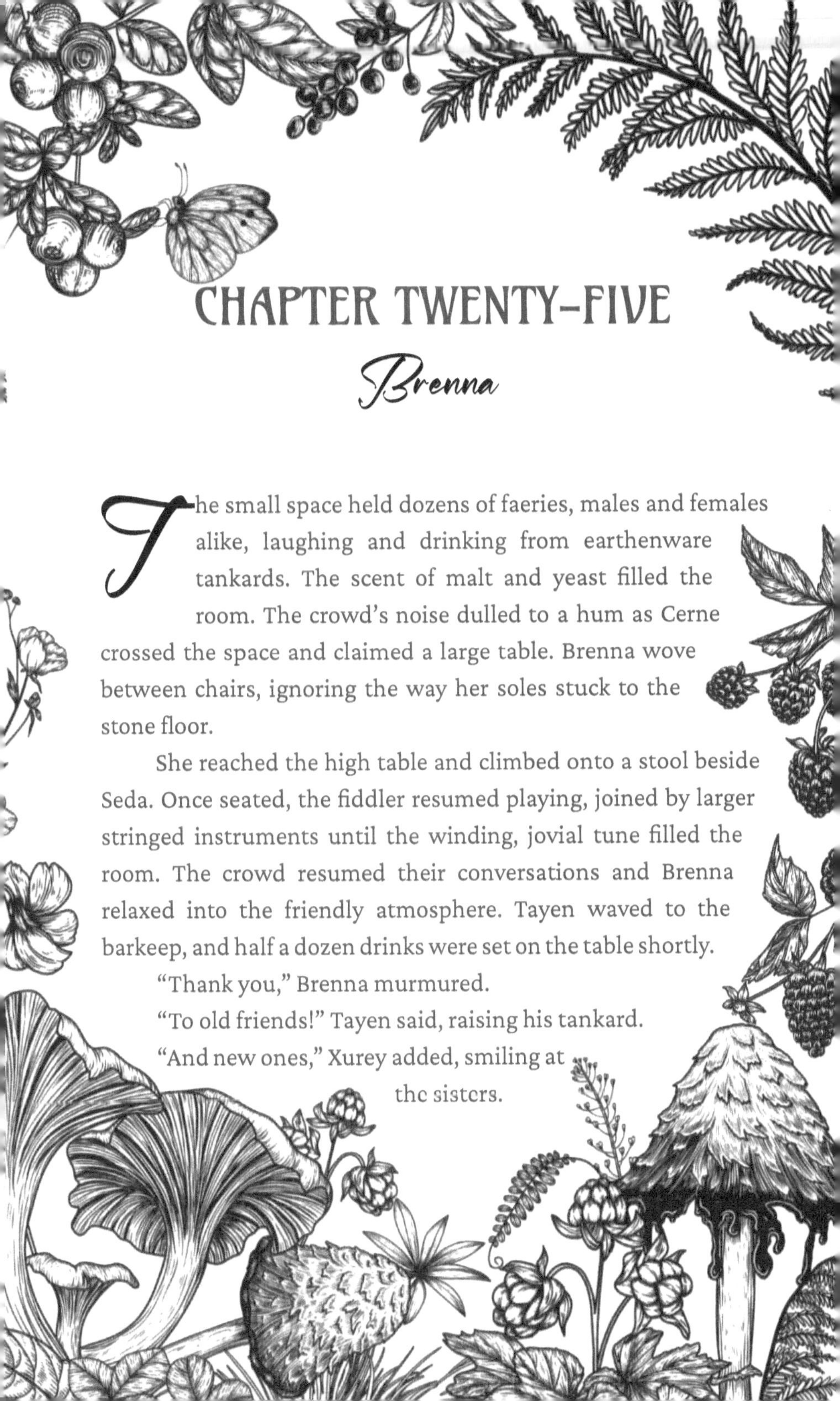

CHAPTER TWENTY-FIVE

Brenna

The small space held dozens of faeries, males and females alike, laughing and drinking from earthenware tankards. The scent of malt and yeast filled the room. The crowd's noise dulled to a hum as Cerne crossed the space and claimed a large table. Brenna wove between chairs, ignoring the way her soles stuck to the stone floor.

She reached the high table and climbed onto a stool beside Seda. Once seated, the fiddler resumed playing, joined by larger stringed instruments until the winding, jovial tune filled the room. The crowd resumed their conversations and Brenna relaxed into the friendly atmosphere. Tayen waved to the barkeep, and half a dozen drinks were set on the table shortly.

"Thank you," Brenna murmured.

"To old friends!" Tayen said, raising his tankard.

"And new ones," Xurey added, smiling at the sisters.

"And handsome human princes," Brenna teased Tayen. Cerne threw his head back and laughed. Brenna joined him until she had to wipe tears of mirth from her eyes and her ribcage ached.

Their laughter fell away to the warm glow of contented smiles. She sipped her ale, letting the sour taste override the myriad of scents in the tavern.

Meara had a pink tinge to her cheeks and a hand rubbing at the collar of her tunic. Cerne tilted his head, watching her. "Tayen, I'm afraid you may have scandalized Meara."

Xurey stifled a laugh, and Meara's brows jumped up before they lowered into a scowl. "Nothing of the sort," she stated, folding her arms across her chest.

Tayen leaned his chin into his hand. "Sorry about that. But don't fret, Eladin likes the attention."

Her mouth opened and closed.

"You aren't really a part of the group until you've caught Tayen in a compromising situation," Cerne joked.

Tayen huffed, his mock outrage softened by the laughter in his eyes. "Or Cerne. The fact you haven't stumbled across him and some court lady is a miracle."

The redness in Meara's cheeks darkened, the blood glowing under her pale skin. Her gaze lingered on Cerne. "I don't," she started, but the sentence never came together.

"The fae differ from humans in this way," Tayen said, rescuing her sister from her mortification. "Anyone without a partner can be with whoever, and it is not looked down upon."

"Even partners don't keep things as private as humans might expect," Seda said with a pointed look at Tayen. He shrugged and shifted in his seat, his grin widening.

Brenna chewed on the inside of her cheek, considering Tayen's words. "Are those expectations the same for females and males?"

"Of course," Cerne said, frowning as if her question was confusing.

Leaning forward, Meara's mouth curved downward. "You are aware expectations among humans are largely inequitable between men and women."

The males' smiles fell away. "I would never allow that sort of culture in my court," Cerne growled.

"I'm sorry, but things are not entirely equal here either," Ayala interjected.

"How so?" Cerne said, his voice rising with argument.

Ayala, Xurey, and Seda sighed collectively, and Brenna couldn't help her small smile at the sense of feminine solidarity. It was Seda who addressed the Autumn Lord. "Cerne, we may be better, but that doesn't stop male faerie from pushing into the role of protector. It makes it harder for women to claim positions of power."

Nodding, Ayala set her folded hands on the table primly. "It might seem equal, but the moment a female falls pregnant, you feral beasts become quite oppressive. And it's difficult to claim any sort of power without opportunity." Their words turned over in Brenna's mind as she worked to reconcile this perspective.

Cerne drummed his fingers. "I'm going to take that into consideration."

"I'm happy to bring this up at a later date," Seda said, her smile wolfish. Brenna had a feeling this fae female never lost an opportunity to train anyone within the Autumn Court, including Lord Cerne.

"Do the fae marry? I haven't heard anyone mention being wedded," Brenna asked, the thought striking her.

"Occasionally," Xurey answered.

Ayala pursed her lips, annoyance flashing across her face. "It's hard to make that commitment when it's for such a long time."

"Marriages tend to be political," Tayen said. "Most faeries simply have partners, but in bonded partnerships, they can share magic. That is the sign of commitment most faeries desire. It can't be falsified, and your connection must remain strong. No one can deny your relationship when you use each other's magic craft."

Brenna's mouth formed an "O." Tayen laughed, though it felt like laughing *with* her and not at her expense.

"Do they know nothing about us in Liosliath?" Seda asked.

Brenna shook her head.

"Well do you have any other silly questions we can settle before you embarrass yourself at the next formal event?" Ayala asked. Despite her irritated tone, it was the closest the faerie had come to being kind to them.

Meara's crossed arms leaned on the table as she said, "Actually, I have a question. I apologize if this is rude, but I've been wondering how old everyone is."

Ayala's eyes narrowed. "How old are you?"

"Twenty-six."

"It's not rude," Tayen said. "Not among friends. I am fifty-two and Ayala is forty-nine." He ignored the daggers Ayala stared into the side of his head.

"Thirty," Xurey said, shrugging.

"Oh, really?" Brenna said brightly, happy to find someone closer to her age.

Seda sighed, folding her arms across her knee. "I am eighty-seven and this male is eighty-four."

Cerne dragged his fingers through his hair, looking sheepish. The dynamic between Seda and Cerne made sense when she realized Seda treated him like a younger brother.

"That's quite an age gap," Meara muttered, and Brenna laughed, fiddling with the sleeve of her dress.

"Anything else or can we get to drinking?" Ayala drawled.

"Not that I can think of," Meara said, a sarcastic bite to her voice. She was becoming bolder, and from the curious way Cerne watched her, she wasn't the only one noticing.

"I propose a game!" Tayen said, raising his tankard. "Truth or tale, two stories, one true and one not. Those that guess wrong will drink, and the teller drinks if they fail to fool us."

"I'm going to need more ale for that," Seda muttered.

"I can go first, I am prepared," Ayala said, waving her hand to gather their attention with a flourish. "First of all, when my magic craft manifested as a child, I leapt from our family's cottage roof, convinced I could fly." Brenna drew in a sharp breath, and Tayen gave her a knowing smile. "Secondly, over the years, I have stolen silver cutlery from every single court. Now which do you think is my truth?"

Brenna's eyes went to Tayen, trying to gauge his thoughts as her sibling. He leaned back, crossing his arms. "Don't look at me. I happen to know the answer, so I am recused."

"Was it jumping off the roof?" Brenna guessed.

"I think it's the silverware," Meara said. Ayala raised a single eyebrow.

"I'm trying to remember," Cerne said, rubbing his jaw. "I recall something about your family and the roof, so I believe that is the truth."

Ayala's feline smile widened. Seda's eyes narrowed as she watched her. "I've seen your cutlery collection in your rooms, so I have to say that is the truth."

"Yes, that sounds true," Xurey said.

"Truth," Ayala said, nodding. "It was not *I* who fell from the roof." Tayen huffed.

"You?" Brenna asked.

"I'm afraid so. I had merely moved a few objects at that point and I had no understanding of my true craft." Tayen's freckled skin brightened with pink. "I broke my ankle. It is not even my turn. Cerne, would you please?"

The Autumn Lord chuckled at his friend's chagrin. "Fine. Let's see. When I was twelve or so and my antlers first grew in, I got my head stuck in a stair railing when visiting the high court." Xurey let out a giggle, and Cerne's serious demeanor cracked. His words held a smile. "And when I was younger, I had a problem with squirrels following me around for weeks."

Everyone looked to Seda. "I never joined him in Court Tara. My duties have always been here. I cannot help."

"Damn. Alright, I have to guess the incident in Court Tara is your truth," Tayen said.

Canting her head thoughtfully, Meara said, "I think it's the squirrels. That is quite an embarrassing incident that I cannot believe you would have imagined for yourself."

"I hate to agree, but I've seen animals following you," Ayala said. It was a simple statement, but it eased something inside of Brenna to hear the fae female agree with her sister. It was a sign they were moving forward.

"Brenna?" Cerne asked.

"Oh, squirrels, for sure," she said with a grin.

"You do have a rather large head, so getting it stuck is my guess," Seda said, crossing her arms and giving Cerne an inscrutable look.

"I have fooled three of you! Drink, my friends. It was a family of mice that trailed me for weeks. Though I also had an otter admirer who snuck into my quarters once and more than a few foxes that followed me whenever I went into the woods." Laughter echoed around the table.

"To Lord Cerne's *animal* magnetism," Tayen said, raising his cup and taking a long drink despite the fact he guessed correctly. Brenna swallowed more of the ale. The warmth spreading through her may have been the alcohol, or it may have been her magic loosened by her drink, but she was too relaxed to care.

"I supposed it's my turn." Tayen straightened and cleared his throat. "Let's see, I unintentionally dated Kyrell, heir of the Court of Darkness," he added when Brenna frowned, "for a few months the first time I visited. I thought he was merely an attentive host." He shrugged. "Secondly, the first time I was going to be kissed, I got so excited that my magic reacted and he hit his nose on my shield and refused to try again."

"Is that why Kyrell wrote to our court so often all those years ago?" Cerne asked with an eyebrow raised.

"You are ruining the game," Tayen snapped. Cerne's laughter filled the room.

"So no bungled first kiss?" Seda asked.

"Oh that was true, but he was willing to try again," Tayen said with a wink. "I think we all must drink this round."

Brenna took a long draught of her ale and set it on the table with a thunk. Beside her, Meara wiped her mouth with the back of her hand, her mannerisms relaxed. Brenna loved seeing her sister at ease and enjoying herself in this new group of friends.

"Alright, my turn," Seda said. "When I completed my trial to join the guard, I sliced my foot open but kept it secret from my mother. I stitched it myself."

Brenna recoiled, flexing her foot within her boot.

"Secondly, at one point I didn't want to take up my mother's post, and instead planned to become a fletcher and craft the finest arrows."

"Oh really," Cerne said, one eyebrow rising. Brenna frowned, trying to interpret his meaning.

"I believe it is the foot injury," Ayala said.

Meara nodded, "Agreed."

"I can't picture you as a craftsman, so that is my vote," Tayen said.

Xurey frowned, looking between them. "I think it must be the injury as well."

Seda's smile was smug as she raised her hand to show a thin scar across her palm, hidden near a crease. "It was my hand, and Cerne did the stitching."

Brenna gasped, looking at Cerne. "You sewed up a wound?" He shrugged, leaning back in his seat with a smug smile.

"Drink," Cerne said. "And I think it is Xurey's turn."

Sighing, Xurey leaned her arms on the table, her teeth dragging over her full bottom lip as she contemplated her answers. "The first time I shifted, I couldn't figure out how to shift back and I spent three days wandering the Observatory as a horse. Secondly, the Autumn Court is my favorite court."

"Well that is obvious," Cerne said. "We all know we are your favorite. You should drink twice for that."

"Sorry," Xurey said, raising her hand to cover her mouth. "I was only stuck for a few hours, but I couldn't think of anything else." Tayen reached forward and nudged the bottom of the tankard clutched in her hand. Rolling her eyes, Xurey lifted it and took a long drink.

"Brenna? Would you like to go next? Give us a proper challenge?" Cerne said with a grin.

"Alright, let me see." She giggled, raising her fingers to her lips. The ale saturated her, leaving her feeling light and giddy. "When we were kids, a boy was teasing Meara so I pushed him into the stream."

Giggles and guffaws circled the table, emboldening her. "And then my first kiss was a boy in the village, the butcher's son, and he was awful. He licked at my teeth and then told me thank you and that he wanted to see someone else." Surprised that the words escaped her, Brenna covered her flushing face with her hands.

Tayen laughed so hard he wheezed. "Surely they are both true." Brenna shook her head. "Alright, I think it's the first kiss."

"Pushing the boy into the stream. You are too kind hearted for that," Cerne said.

Brenna braved a glance to her sister. Meara scowled. "Kipp, really?" A flush darkened Brenna's cheek.

"Well?" Ayala asked, sounding irritated she had to wait to find out the truth.

"It was Meara who shoved a boy into the creek, and it was Kipp because he made me cry after that kiss."

"I wish you had told me why. I would have found a deeper river to throw him in," her sister grumbled.

Xurey wiped a tear from her eyes, her giggles dying away. "I would have helped. That sounds like a terrible first kiss."

"It was." Brenna took a long drink of her ale. Her friends' teasing and laughter comforted her. This must be what it felt like to belong to a circle of friends. A third round of ales was called for, and she lost herself in laughter as Xurey told them about the time she was lost and ended up wandering with a herd of wild horses.

Meara gripped her hand, squeezing her fingers, and Brenna leaned her head against her sister's shoulder.

As the evening continued, the stories and ale flowed freely. A sense of closeness wrapped around Brenna, like a cozy blanket. She would give anything for this to be her usual end of week gathering of friends. For a time, she imagined this was one of many evenings laughing and playing with her friends. Nothing could convince her to give up her life as a faerie and return to the human lands. Meara would have to understand.

CHAPTER TWENTY-SIX

Meara

Meara didn't remember the walk back. Fae ale ran through her blood, relaxing her and filling her with a fizzing energy. Not unlike the faerie wine, but this was comforting, grounding. She liked it a lot. All her worries fell away.

She found herself lingering in the hall, unwilling to go back to her rooms. Brenna disappeared, unable to keep her eyes open. Meara wandered until her feet led to the veranda, the same one she lost her humanity in. She felt further removed from that life than ever before, especially with a contended warmth buzzing within her.

She settled against a pile of pillows and gazed over the lake where a million stars reflected, glittering and winking as the water moved. Absently, her finger traced up her ear, trying to remember what it felt like rounded. She was forgetting what being human felt like.

"May I ask what that keen mind is contemplating?" Cerne asked, standing in the archway.

"No, you may not," Meara responded, her difficult attitude overriding her manners. Something about this male shattered her sensibilities. His casual confidence irritated her. She had never felt that self possessed in her entire life, and he wore it like a second skin.

He ignored her prickly demeanor and sat beside her. "Regardless, you owe me a truth or tale," he said, one side of his mouth quirking in a lopsided smile.

"I couldn't think of anything," she protested.

He shifted in his seat to face her. "No adventurous stories or humorous anecdotes from your life before you met me? Thank fate we found you and rescued you from a life of boredom."

She scoffed. "That reminds me. Here is my truth or tale: I once met a handsome rake in the woods who dragged me away to his home and incessantly bothered me, wanting to be entertained."

Cerne's laugh rolled over her, wearing away at her defenses until a smile bloomed on her face. He shoved his fingers through his hair and brushed it back. Her gaze lingered on his dark lashes and the cut of his cheekbone. Moonlight pooled on his features. From his demeanor to his beauty, everything about him spoke of magic. She could almost see it under his skin.

"What is bothering you?" Cerne said, his voice dropping. Her eyes tracked his movement as his hand rose and his thumb brushed over her furrowed brows. Instinctively, she relaxed her features. His hand skimmed her cheek as it dropped.

"Nothing."

"Do not tell me tales now. The game is over." His sincere plea pierced her, layering guilt over her feelings of inadequacy.

"You don't have to concern yourself with my problems."

"Don't I?"

She scowled, and the feeling of her brow wrinkling reminded her of his touch. She intentionally released the tension in her face.

"I meant my worries and emotions. I understand your jurisdiction over my possible magic."

He nodded, turning to look out over the moonlit treetops. She took the opportunity to study the line of his jaw under his close shorn beard, far too aware of each breath he took. It was the first time they were alone together since that day in the forest.

Silence stretched, and the urge to share more with him built until she spoke. "I wish I could figure out my magic. It's the unknown that bothers me." Cerne stilled. "But I'm afraid of what I'll find. I've always protected Brenna, and now she is the one protecting me. Nothing is as it should be."

"Ah." Cerne tipped his chin up. "There is more than one way to protect the ones we love. She might have the *firepower*," he said, smirking at his own wordplay, "but she still needs you."

She pressed her lips together, trying to hold back her final confession. "I feel powerless."

He turned, irises of umber and evergreen meeting hers. "No one could look at you and think you are powerless."

A laugh burst from her. "I don't think anyone else sees it that way."

"Then they aren't paying attention," he whispered.

She parted her lips to thank him, but his hand swept up and skimmed her cheek. It was the lightest touch, but it reverberated through her. They were a breath's width apart, and she didn't know if he had moved closer or if she had. Gravity had shifted and a heavy weight pulled her into him, and her muscles ached at the effort to keep herself from collapsing into his chest and burying her face in the crook of his neck. He would be so warm and comforting. His body heat teased the exposed skin of her arms.

His hand turned, brushing his knuckles over her jaw. No male touched a female this gently, stared into her eyes, leaned in this way without wanting more. And she found she wanted the same. Every cell of her body yearned, but she was frozen, afraid to move and break the spell.

Her tongue wet her lips, and his pupils flared. It sent a thrill through her, one she tried to ignore, but it was no use. "If you'd like to kiss me, I wouldn't push you away." The scratch to her voice betrayed her nonchalant words.

"Really?" His sensuous lips pulled into that smirk that made her want to smack him and yank him into her all at once. He delighted in the moment, his eyes sparkling as they roamed over her.

She should move away, cut her losses and save herself the embarrassment that was surely waiting for her when he laughed at her. Shame crept up her neck, heating her skin. Swallowing, she leaned back, her dark lashes flicking down.

Calloused fingers slid in her hair, pressing into the back of her neck and firmly guiding her forward. Her gaze shot up and she spied a tiny constellation of freckles above his brow before her eyes closed and his lips met hers.

She froze as he brushed his lips over hers, kissing her again before the first one ended, pressing harder until her mouth opened and she moved her lips against his, melting into him.

A cold fire ran through her veins, an icy sting. Her blood sang and her heart pounded. His hand trailed from her hair across her neck and over her collarbone. She was sure he was painting her with moonlight.

Her hand reached for his shirt, twisting the linen against her palm. His skin radiated heat that soaked into her as she drew closer. It was all the encouragement he needed. His hands closed over her waist, lifting her into his lap until she straddled him. Their breaths competed, chests rising and falling as they pressed together.

Her hand moved from his shoulder to grip the lowest spike of one antler. He let out a feral growl at the touch. She broke off their kiss with a gasp, her eyes wide as she leaned back to study his face as her hand slipped down to rest against her thigh. His lips curved into a satisfied smile. Around him, there was nothing but darkness.

Jolting, she twisted. Darkness blanketed the veranda, and as her lips parted in shock, the blackness swirled, lapping at her legs. "What?" she yelped. This wasn't the absence of light, like shadows, but something fluid that absorbed the flickering flames and sparkling starlight. It seemed if she touched it, it would have a velvety texture.

"Ah, it looks like you've discovered your craft," Cerne said, his lips brushing below her ear as he spoke. The words processed in her mind and she began breathing again.

"This is me?" she asked shakily.

"Relax and it'll fade," Cerne prompted. "Probably." He tucked her against his chest, smoothing his hand over her hair until her tension ebbed. As the charge in her veins lessened, replaced with a deep tiredness, the darkness lowered like a receding tide and faded until it was nothing.

"What if I can't get it back?" she asked, feeling ridiculous.

Cerne's chuckle vibrated through her. "Then I guess I'll have to kiss you again."

Meara pushed off him and turned to scowl. "Is that your answer to everything?"

"No," he said, winking at her. "Just anything concerning you."

Her breath hitched, all pithy words dropping out of her mind. He disarmed her. But considering the magic that filled the veranda, it was best she stopped. If things went further, she couldn't imagine what the darkness would do.

Exhaling, she straightened. "I am going to return to my rooms and see my sister. Thank you for your *assistance*. It was a lovely night."

Cerne chuckled at her formal response, and she felt her cheeks flame anew. "Goodnight, Meara," he said, folding his hands behind his head and leaning back.

She crossed the room, keeping her eyes on him. She tried to look calm, but her heart still pounded in her chest. She discovered her magic. And the Autumn Lord kissed her. She decided the magic was more notable, though the feel of his beard against her cheek and his fingers on her waist whispered in the back of her mind.

CHAPTER TWENTY-SEVEN

Brenna

renna smoothed her hand over her champagne silk skirts as she walked beside her sister. Meara glided along in a smokey slip of a dress that was not befitting a breakfast, but she didn't seem to care and Brenna was simply happy she was in a dress and not trousers.

Cerne sat in the antechamber, leaning forward with his forearms resting on his knees as he spoke with Tayen. The younger faerie held a letter in his hands. It flashed with gilding, and Brenna caught sight of the heavy, sharp script of a calligrapher.

As they entered, Cerne rose. "Morning, ladies."

"Good morning," Brenna said. Meara pressed her lips into a line, seemingly unsure of what to say. Brenna frowned at her. "Is something going on?"

"We are being summoned to the high king's court," Cerne said. Tayen rose and held up the paper. A crest inked across the top depicted a silver griffon. "Court Tara."

"Summoned?" Meara echoed, crossing her arms. Brenna reached out and brushed her upper arm. She pulled back imperceptibly. "Why? When?"

"High King Argyro is not patient," Cerne said with a shake of his head, his throat working. "We will have to go immediately."

"What is the reason?" Brenna asked.

"You are being asked to present yourself to his court."

"So it's fine. Right?"

"It's not typical," Cerne admitted.

"They simply want to meet you." Tayen said. "How about we eat and we can discuss it."

Ayala swept in, looking between them. She spotted the summons in Tayens hand and snatched it. "Argyro heard about them? How?"

"I was hoping you could tell me," Cerne said dryly. Ayala's eyes narrowed.

Brenna followed Tayen into the dining room, settling into the cushioned seats. A spread of cranberry scones, spiced eggs, salted pork and petite layered desserts covered the table.

Cerne sank into his seat and took a long drink of his cider. "It will be fine, but I prefer to avoid Court Tara."

"I'm sorry," Brenna said quietly.

His gaze landed on her. "You did nothing wrong. But I would like to know who is reporting back to the high king. I don't care for the idea of spies." Ayala huffed, clinking her goblet down. Cerne tipped his head toward her. "Except for you, of course."

Eyebrows shooting up, Brenna peeled her eyes off Ayala and focused on her plate. The fae female was a spy. Brenna wondered if she chose this path for herself, or if it was inherited like Seda and Cerne's positions.

Tayen set the layered dessert on her plate. "Try this, they don't have it in the human kingdoms."

"Thanks."

Everyone ate quietly, and Brenna used a small spoon to scoop a bit of the top layer. It was whipped cream flavored with something floral. She inspected layers of some sort of creamy soft cheese or yogurt, crushed nuts, oats crumble, fruit, and a dark syrup. It was delicious.

The fire crackled behind Cerne. He rested his head in his hand and watched the table. Not the table - specifically Meara. Brenna peered at her sister. She kept her gaze on her food and pushed it around her plate as if she was nervous. Suspicion crept in, making Brenna's observations sharper. A soft flush suffused Meara's cheeks and the tips of her tapered ears pink.

"So when do we leave?" Ayala asked, swinging the goblet in her hand and taking a sip of whatever bubbly liquid sloshed within it.

Cerne's attention snapped to her. "We should leave today so we can reach it tonight. Best not to keep the high king waiting. And hopefully, we can outpace the rainstorm that's been darkening our horizon."

"Good plan. It would be miserable to ride in the rain," Ayala said. The pinch to her mouth suggested there was more than the potential for rain bothering her.

"Who will be joining us?" Brenna asked.

Tayen eyed Cerne before answering, "Most likely the five of us in this room. Xurey left early this morning for her next journey, and Seda must stay." His eyes shot back to his lord, and Cerne gave a slight nod.

Ayala set her drink down and pushed back to stand. "As lovely as this breakfast is, I have a lot of preparations to make, especially if we have to prepare to bring these two to the high king's court."

Cerne nodded. "Would you please assist them?"

"As if I am a servant," Ayala quipped, sweeping out the door. She paused, looking over her shoulder. "Of course I will, do not get yourself in a bunch."

Brenna stared at the empty doorway once Ayala disappeared. She offered to help them.

"You've won her over," Tayen said, smiling at the sisters. "That's not easy to do."

Shrugging, Brenna dug back into her breakfast, making sure to eat plenty so she would have the energy she needed for a long day of travel. It was easier to focus on preparations than the swirling, anxious thoughts of being presented to the high king and queen of the faeries.

Back in their rooms, Kirrily was already at work, laying out dresses and travel clothes. The dryad's nimble fingers smoothed the fine fabrics.

"This one won't do," Ayala said, pointing to a cream dress Dyani had made for Brenna. "Too informal."

Kirrily replaced the dress with a more structured and fitted style without hesitating.

"I liked that one," Brenna said. "So how much do we need to bring? It's just one day."

Ayala's gaze was sharp. "You will be presented, and then there will be some sort of dinner or banquet at the minimum. Those are standard, but we do not know if the king and queen will want to see you again the next morning. While we'd like to avoid the attention, it is an honor. You must be prepared with garb appropriate for their presence."

"This still seems excessive," Meara muttered.

"Best to have a few days worth of court clothing and not need it, than to rewear a dress." Her fists rested on her hips, her mouth thin as she waited for Meara to challenge her.

"Whatever you say," Meara said, raising her hands in surrender.

"Brenna, please braid Meara's hair tight so it has some wave to it when we arrive." Hand fluttering in a dismissive wave, Ayala turned away from them and moved to inspect the jewelry Kirrily was placing into a linen travel pouch.

Meara plopped into the armchair and flipped her hair over the back. Brenna left Ayala to order Kirrily around and went to work weaving Meara's hair into a series of braids coming together at the back of her neck.

"That should do it. I will see you shortly," Ayala said, sweeping toward the door.

"What is Court Tara like? How will we know what to do?" Brenna asked, anxiety fighting to the forefront of her thoughts.

Ayala paused, looking her up and down. "Don't worry. Tayen will prepare you, I am sure. He's always taken good care of his pets."

The insult didn't have the same bite as before, so perhaps she was accustomed to Ayala's acerbic nature, or they really had forged a friendship with her. Flame colored hair blew behind her as the faerie disappeared into the hall.

"Is there anything else I can do for you?" Kirrily asked.

Brenna sighed. "Thank you, Kirrily. Again, we could not manage without you." With a nod, the dryad curtsied and left them.

The sisters changed into trousers and tunics, pulling cloaks over their shoulders. Despite her love of luxury dresses, Brenna found comfort in the familiar, similar fabric and practical cuts, even if she'd prefer that fabric was a work dress and not trousers. But fae females wore pants often, and she was trying to adjust.

A servant took their bags, and they trailed after, repeating the same process as their trip to Dornadan, but with a new destination in mind. Brenna's stomach churned.

Tayen mounted Eirlys, patting the mare's white coat. "Let's get moving!" Her snowy mane gleamed like platinum as she tossed her head.

Ayala nodded and swung up onto Airgid's back. The dappled stallion stood calmly, ignoring the hoof stamping coming from Eirlys.

A groomsman brought Clover to Brenna with a shallow bow. A thick pad sat atop the mare's back, and after her soreness from their last ride, Brenna was grateful for the padding.

She ran her hands over her golden coat and sooty snout. "Ready, my friend?" Snorting, she tossed her dark mane. Brenna allowed Ryles to boost her up, and she swung a leg over Clover's back and settled into place.

"Thank you," she said. Ryles nodded and moved to help settle packs on the horses' haunches.

Meara sat atop Bran's black back, her fingers tangled in his mane. Tayen pulled Eirlys around, and Ayala sat still atop Airgid. Only Cerne stood alone, his bay stallion nowhere to be seen. With a shimmer of russet magic, he shifted into his stag form.

"I guess he didn't want to talk," Brenna muttered to Clover, whose ears twitched. She scratched along the mare's neck affectionately.

The party set out, following Cerne's stag form as he led the way. Brenna watched the tawny tines of his antlers sway. The overcast day tinged the forest in celadon. The trees forced them into a single line, so there was little conversation, only the occasional snap of a twig under a hoof or the snort of a horse.

Brenna's heart rose to her throat as she thought about entering an unknown king's court. Hopefully soon they could speak with Tayen and learn what was expected.

They worked their way around the west side of the valley until they walked directly north. Hours slipped by, and Brenna found herself lost in thoughts of banquets and fae nobles. The terrain grew steeper downhill, and Brenna leaned back in her seat. Clover was steady and cautious, but she still sighed in relief when the ground leveled.

The sound of hooves broke through the forest sounds, and Ayala pulled Airgid around, looking for the source. Cerne moved to put himself between their party and the noise. They caught glimpses of riders in the distance, weaving through the trees at a much faster pace. Within minutes, they were pulling level.

The leader called, "Ho!" Three horses slowed to a walk and then stopped.

"Farran!" Cerne called, stepping forward in his faerie form.

"Who are they?" Meara asked, sidling Bran closer to Tayen and Eirlys.

Tayen eyed the riders. "Rangers. They are half-fae nomads who go between the faerie and human lands."

Their leader swung down from his golden stallion and approached. He walked with the grace of a faerie, but he was heavily muscled and a close cropped beard shaded his jaw. Sleek, black hair swept into a tie at the back of his head. Keen eyes studied their group, landing on her momentarily before moving on.

Cerne met the man and they clasped arms, smiling. "Farran, it's good to see you. Where is your bride?"

Frowning, the man spoke with the accent of Brynmor or another southern kingdom. "I left Melisande home. We are headed to Court Tara but I am afraid it is not with good tidings."

"What is wrong?" Cerne asked. Tayen dropped from Eirlys' back and joined them. Tension tightened his shoulders, defining the muscles through his tunic.

Farran ran a hand through his hair. "Dornadan and Liosliath are bringing demands to King Argyro. Princess Elysia was abducted."

"What?" yelped Brenna. Clover stepped sideways nervously. She stroked her neck. "Sorry, baby."

"That is surprising and unfortunate. Do you know any details?" Tayen asked.

"She was taken by shadows."

Silence fell at his words. Dark resignation shone on every face. She chewed her lip, waiting for someone to explain.

Tayen stepped back, reaching for Eirlys. "We shall see you at Court Tara. We were summoned to present our new friends. This is Meara and Brenna."

Farran smiled widely, his lined face warm and friendly despite the obvious tension in his followers. "Well met, my ladies. I am Farran, leader of the Rangers. This is my second, Lorand." He motioned to the man on a black mare. Slightly tapered ears poked through glossy, black hair. "And Cahira." The muscled woman rode a gelding painted with splotches of reddish brown across its white coat. Her own burgundy hair shone against her olive skin. She nodded in greeting but made to move to dismount.

"I'm afraid we must also be on our way. We should report to Argyro as soon as possible." Farran was already striding to his stomping mount. He swung onto the stallion's back in one smooth movement, and they were off. Clover nickered as the Rangers rode out of view.

"That will not make our visit better," Cerne grumbled before shifting into his stag.

Brenna chewed her bottom lip as they rode, unsettled by the news of the princess. If she was taken by shadows, it must be a faerie. But why? She couldn't imagine what someone would want with the delicate human princess.

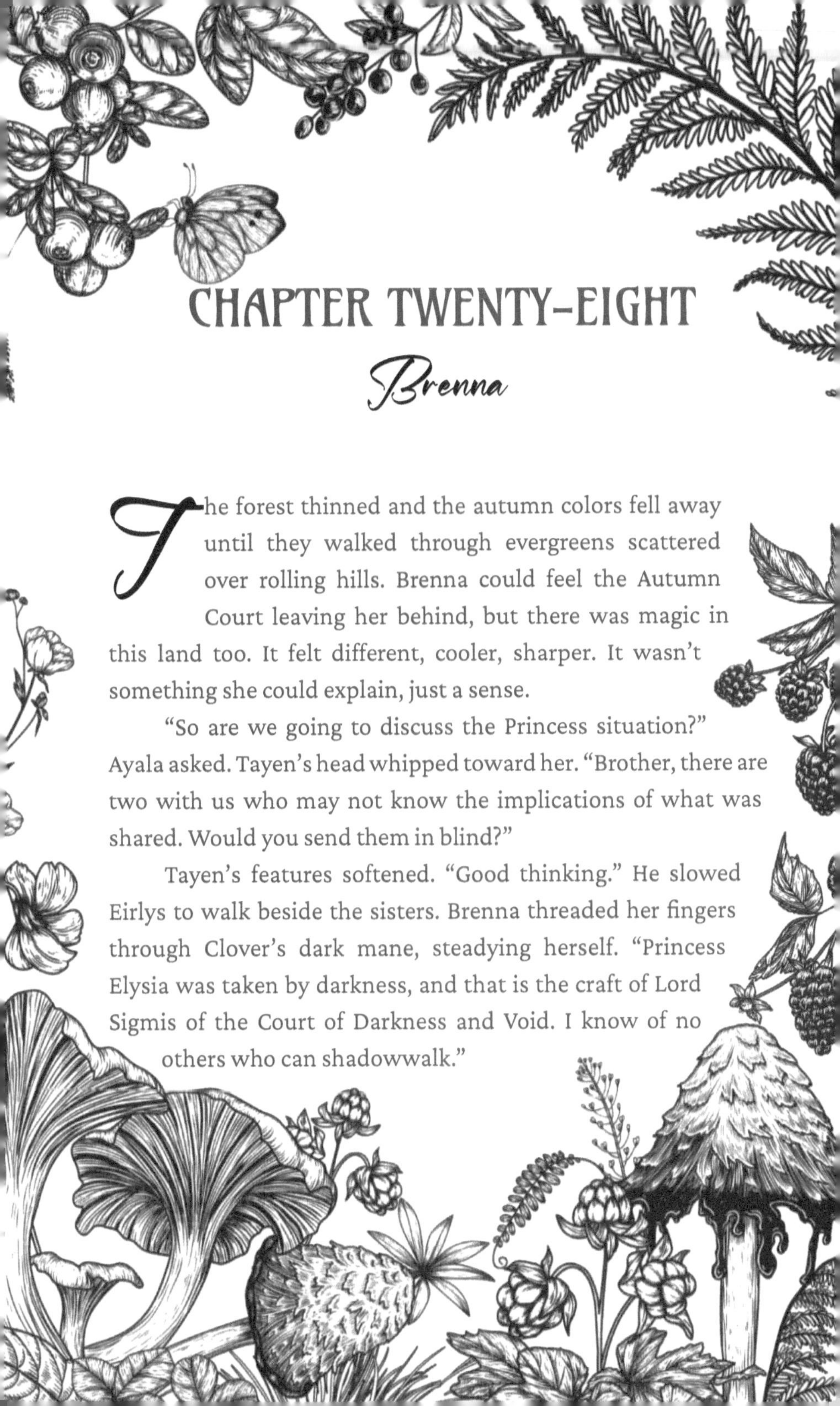

CHAPTER TWENTY-EIGHT

Brenna

The forest thinned and the autumn colors fell away until they walked through evergreens scattered over rolling hills. Brenna could feel the Autumn Court leaving her behind, but there was magic in this land too. It felt different, cooler, sharper. It wasn't something she could explain, just a sense.

"So are we going to discuss the Princess situation?" Ayala asked. Tayen's head whipped toward her. "Brother, there are two with us who may not know the implications of what was shared. Would you send them in blind?"

Tayen's features softened. "Good thinking." He slowed Eirlys to walk beside the sisters. Brenna threaded her fingers through Clover's dark mane, steadying herself. "Princess Elysia was taken by darkness, and that is the craft of Lord Sigmis of the Court of Darkness and Void. I know of no others who can shadowwalk."

"Why would he take a human princess?" Meara asked.

"I don't know." Tayen sighed, looking out over the hills.

Ayala turned back in her seat. "His younger brother, Kyrell, likes pretty things."

"That's one way to put it," Tayen said, scrubbing his hand over his face. "But I don't know how he would have known of Elysia."

"She's part faerie," Brenna added. "I think her mother was half."

His hand dropped. "You didn't think to share that sooner?" She shrugged and he raised his voice. "Cerne, did you hear that?" The stag tossed his head in response.

"Sigmis is unpredictable," Tayen said darkly. "We will see what happens."

As they crested the hill, a confluence of rivers spanned the valley before them. Sparkling water stretched wide, separating and rejoining around an island that rose up like a crystal jutting from the earth. The sparkling, white stone was carved, and as Brenna studied it, she saw a network of buildings, stairs, and terraces making up what must be Court Tara.

"Welcome to Court Tara," Ayala said, a hint of sardonic humor in her cool voice.

The river ran deep until it crested a ford. The water streamed over the wide platform, bubbling and frothing as it tumbled over the far side. This was where they crossed, their horses' hooves sending up a spray of glittering river water. Brenna dropped her hand and felt the water sprinkle across her fingers.

On the far side, they passed through a wide, ornate archway of stone. Silver veins ran through the white stone, and Brenna realized that was the source of the reflective quality she admired. Even the ground under their feet was the same stone, carved away to leave a rough texture, making it easy to scale the hill.

Balconies and windows covered every wall, and most were draped with greenery, filling the air with the verdant scent of leaves and flowers. Between the windows, ornate columns and corbels decorated every solid surface. It was the most decadent architecture Brenna had ever seen. Her lips parted in awe as she took it in, letting Clover guide her.

Faeries of every variety surrounded them. They formed a living, breathing rainbow of colors, sizes, and shapes. She spotted fox ears, rounded horns, whiplike tails, claws, whiskers, bright red eyes, scaled skin, and every shade of skin and hair, many of which were not possible with humans. The bustle was quiet compared to the peasants in Dornadan. Every faerie moved gracefully, going about their business and stopping to speak quietly with their friends or neighbors. She smiled, loving the way the mass moved as if it was choreographed. A dance in a city center.

Part of the way up the winding path, Cerne stopped. With a shake of his head, he shifted back and reached for a door. The white stone was carved with falling leaves. An array of antlers branched out from the top of the door frame, marking it for the Autumn Court. A pair of grooms, short, stout faerie with goat's legs, appeared, offering to take the horses. Brenna slipped off Clover and patted her hindquarters as she was led away.

Cerne stood in the doorway, scowling at the other side of the road. It was an identical door, this one carved with waving wheat and a rising sun. Light shone from within the windows, diffused by sheer ivory curtains. His lip curled. "Good to know Luce is here."

"Luce?" Brenna asked.

"The heir of the Summer Court," Tayen answered, coming up behind her. Cerne's exhale was derisive, and with one last glare, he pushed the door open and walked inside. Brenna raised an eyebrow, and Tayen leaned in. "Cerne's least favorite person."

Brenna followed him into the Autumn Court's quarters. While their rooms in Roven were luxurious, nothing prepared her for the decadence of Court Tara. White wood and silver trappings made up all of the furniture, with ivory linens draping upholstery. Massive pillows welcomed her toward the settee.

Light poured in from floor to ceiling windows along the wall, broken up by glass doors opening onto a balcony. Brenna was frightened she would mar the beautiful decor with her touch. Doors stood open along the side wall, revealing spacious bedrooms beyond. Cerne moved within one of them, and Tayen claimed another.

Meara stood in the center doorway, beckoning Brenna into the room they would share. Clasping her hands together, Brenna crossed the room to join her sister.

A four poster bed draped in sheer, white organza stood in the middle of the room. The headboard was a complex carving of silver, depicting leaping deer, dashing foxes, great trees, and hundreds of tiny mushrooms. She ran her fingers over the polished design, marveling at its intricacies. It shone under the bright afternoon sun pouring in the open door.

"We have our own bathing room," Meara said, and Brenna followed her voice into the second room. A porcelain tub stood in the center of the space with a silver faucet arching over it. A huge mirror covered the wall above dual washbasins, and Brenna blinked at the crystal clear reflection of herself. Her fingers went to the pink of her cheeks and lips, the glow of her skin. It complimented the warmth of her hair. The top layer had lightened with all of the time she'd spent in the sun since they left Liosliath.

"Yes, you are lovely," Meara teased. "Tayen said we should dress for court. Nicest dress, apparently. He said that twice, so I think he's concerned I'm going to stay dressed as I am." She chuckled, and Brenna smiled, grateful for her efforts to cheer her.

Meara hated when Brenna was the morose one, and she would do whatever it took to bring back Brenna's good spirits, so Meara could be the grumpy pessimist once more.

"Sounds good. Which dress do you think?"

Drifting back into the bedroom, she scanned the dresses Meara had laid out. Something urged her toward the dress the color of burnt caramel, like the darkest shade of her hair. Iridescent webbing embroidered with pale yellow vines threaded along the top layer, stitched with dozens of flowers rising up the corset and trailing down the hips: blush roses, burgundy ranunculus, and ivory peonies. Hundreds of miniscule chips of tourmaline gemstone sparkled at the sweetheart neckline, forming a field of wildflowers across her bust. Once on, the sheer sleeves swayed around her wrists, more gems twinkling as she moved.

"You look incredible," Meara said quietly as she tied the last lace in the back.

Brenna pressed a hand to her corseted waist. "I'm glad, it's a bit tighter than what I've grown accustomed to. Who knew I'd grow to prefer the flowy faerie dresses?"

"Formal court wear tends to be more structured. That's why I picked that." Ayala stood in the doorway. Her gaze flicked down Brenna's figure. "Meara, get dressed," she snapped, closing the door sharply.

Sighing, Brenna helped ease Meara's dress over her head. It was yards of black fabric, dark enough she could barely see the shadowy lace embellishing the bust. The silk skirts draped over her hips in a cascade of gleaming obsidian fabric, fading into the deepest shade of blackberry around her feet. Meara eased the coordinating capelet over her shoulders. It was simple, save for the raven feathers sewn along the top. They framed her shoulders and softened her features.

"This is all so sudden, I feel as if I will stumble over my own feet and then say something crude, and get us imprisoned," Meara muttered.

Brenna let out a bark of a laugh. "That is quite the imaginative disaster. Relax. You almost never fall over your feet. Just hang onto Cerne's arm. I know you want to," she teased, fluttering her lashes. She was gratified when Meara's face flushed.

"I don't, absolutely not," she protested, a blush spreading to the tips of her tapered ears, reflecting pink in the silver ear cuffs. She scowled, giving her head a little shake. "Come, let's go."

Meara pushed the door open and they faced the sitting room. Cerne turned, dressed in the darkest emerald from his doublet to his fitted pants. The bright light in the room reflected off a copper crown on his brow. It was shaped like a laurel wreath with realistic leaves encircling his head. Metallic threads draped between the tines of his antlers, tiny chips of garnet and topaz catching the light in a sparkling spiderweb. As he turned his head, Brenna spied a chain across the back allowing the crown to fit around the base of his antlers. It must have been made specially for him. The effect was stunning, she had to admit, with his long, dark lashes framing those mossy eyes lined with kohl.

Ayala stood against the frame of the front door, tapping her long nails against her arm impatiently. The warm chocolate silk of her dress set her hair aflame, reflecting off gold flakes across her high cheekbones. The burgundy shade of her lips enhanced the effect.

"You look beautiful," Brenna told her, happy to stay on good terms with the female.

"Of course I do," she said airily. "Now come sit, I'm afraid the high court requires a bit more gilding." With sweeping movements, she urged the sisters to sit and produced a small, threaded jar and brush. Brenna lifted her chin and allowed Ayala to swipe cosmetics over her cheeks and around her eyes.

She pressed her lips together to hide her smile as Ayala did the same treatment to Meara, who squirmed in her seat. "It looks lovely," Brenna reassured her. Meara's nose scrunched, but she stilled.

Ayala snapped the lid back and set the tools aside, her eyes flicking between them as she surveyed her work. "That will do."

Tayen exited his bedroom, his jacket a deep wine, like the richest of autumn leaves. The bright stitching along his lapel depicted antlers, making it clear who he was loyal to. Gold already dusted the top of his eyelids, while the bottom was lined with kohl. "Ready to face the court?" He offered his arm to the sisters.

Cerne stepped closer, holding out his hand. "I believe Meara wanted me to escort her."

Meara's eyes flashed as she glanced at Brenna for a second before facing the handsome antlered faerie. She took his arm with a reluctant smile. Brenna hid her grin, looking at the floor as she took Tayen's arm. Ayala took his other side, seemingly unbothered by Meara taking the place beside Cerne.

The light was fading, and warm sunset tones reflected off the stone of the citadel, bouncing back and forth in a riot of peach and cerise tones on every glittering facet.

Brenna allowed herself to look around greedily, trusting Tayen to lead her. Many of the faeries inhabiting the city were absent at these higher levels as they climbed toward the palace at the peak.

As they reached the second gate, her mouth fell open. Two massive griffins stood just inside the courtyard. Sharp black beaks gleamed below pairs of intelligent, ammolite eyes. Tawny feathers melted into fur and a lashing lion's tail. Their wings lay against their backs, but Brenna was sure they would stretch at least five or six meters across, maybe more.

Tayen smiled knowingly. "Magnificent, aren't they?" It was the only word that fit them. She nodded mutely and allowed Tayen to lead her forward.

The entrance to the high king's fortress gaped like an ivory maw. Guards in silver lined the entrance, tipping their heads in respect as Cerne approached and paused. Nobles walked around them, wearing a rainbow of shades and styles from each of their courts. Cerne allowed them to pass, turning and facing Meara and Brenna.

"We will visit the throne room, and they will introduce us. The king and queen will want to look you over and they might ask you to show your magic craft. Brenna, you should show them a small flame. Meara, you should decline."

"I don't have much choice," Meara muttered.

"Anything else?" Brenna asked, her heart rising to her throat.

"Address them as my queen and my king, and don't be rude," Ayala said dryly.

"Relax," Cerne muttered to Meara, rubbing his hand over her forearm. Meara bristled but her chest rose and fell in deliberate calming breaths. Brenna smiled as they climbed the steps to the king's palace.

Two servants opened the door and allowed them entrance. Brenna inhaled in a silent gasp at the throne room before them. Faeries filled the open space, leaving a center aisle open. In the center, two massive thrones sat atop a raised platform. Arched windows rose behind the thrones, allowing the setting sun to stream in. The golden glare obscured Brenna's vision until they drew nearer.

She gripped Tayen's arm until her fingers locked up, but he kept them moving forward. The faeries in this space spoke quietly, the hum surrounding them as they walked the aisle.

Harsh voices emanated from the thrones, and Brenna glanced up, seeing the outlines of a tall, bulky fae male on one throne and the familiar shape of Farran beside him, speaking with his hands waving animatedly. The other throne was occupied by a female with long, straight hair over her shoulders. Her silver dress reflected light, highlighting her curvy figure.

"Presenting Lord Cerne of the Court of Autumn Harvest, and his guests, Lady Meara, and Lady Brenna, along with Lord Tayen and Lady Ayala," a steward called.

They drew close enough for the thrones to cast shadows across their faces and allow her to see the high king and queen clearly. The king's silver beard was long but tidy, his hair much shorter, and his face lined. Beside him, the leader of the Rangers stood stiffly. King Argyro turned from Farran and glanced over them, his lip curling. "We do not have time for this. Let them come tomorrow."

Brenna stiffened, and Tayen broke his stride. This was one outcome she had not prepared for. She looked to Cerne, brow pinching.

Queen Araluen sat forward. Her chestnut hair was streaked with silver, but her face looked young. Deep sapphire eyes studied them. "Argyro, they came here on our summons. I would like to see them."

The king scoffed, but leaned back on his throne. "If you insist, my love."

The queen stood, stepping off the dais to approach them. The crowd quieted. "Hello, Cerne," she said softly, offering her hand to the Autumn Lord who kissed her knuckles. "Good to see you again."

"My queen," he said, bowing his head.

"Who have you brought to me?" She looked over Meara. Brenna cringed as her sister attempted to curtsy and looked as if she was ducking to avoid a low-flying bird. A demure smile formed on the sovereign's features.

"This is Meara," Cerne said.

"What is your craft, Meara?"

Meara's lips pressed together as she picked her words. "Shadows, my queen, but I am still working on summoning them in bright places such as this. I'm afraid I have no display of magic for you."

"Very well. And your sister?" Queen Araluen looked at Brenna. As their eyes met, Brenna felt herself relax. "Your magic feels familiar. What is your craft?"

"Light and flame, my queen," Brenna answered.

"Show me."

Brenna released Tayen and cupped her hands, calling forth a tiny ball of flame. She glanced up, looking for the queen's reaction. Instead, her gaze caught on a male.

He leaned one arm against the throne, clearly comfortable beside the king. Reddish-brown eyes pierced through her from a pale face. He had sharp features, high cheekbones, and dark hair slicked back. He stared at her, something knowing in his eyes. Her breath caught and her flame flared. She refocused on her hands, pulling the flame back into her skin.

"Interesting." The queen clasped her hands at her waist and stepped back. "I am Queen Araluen, and I welcome you to my court. You will join us for a banquet tonight. But first, we have urgent matters to address, so please join our court." She smiled, and it felt forced, like political politeness. Tayen bowed and Cerne dipped his head, and their group moved into the crowd.

"Now that's over," grumbled King Argyro, "someone needs to call Sigmis. I want him here *now*."

Brenna resisted the urge to tuck herself into Tayen's side. No one was looking at them any longer. No one except the male who was now watching her with a smirk, his arms crossed and back leaning against the silver throne. She met his eyes and his tongue darted out to wet his lips. She nearly choked on her own spit, her hands gripping Tayen's arm firm enough to wrinkle the fabric. She looked back at the king and swallowed, trying to ignore the feel of the male's eyes on her.

"You have five minutes to get Sigmis here," bellowed Argyro. Beside her, Tayen tensed. She gentled her hold on his jacket. He tipped his head and murmured, "Don't worry. You did great."

She didn't trust her voice to thank him, so she nodded and took a slow breath.

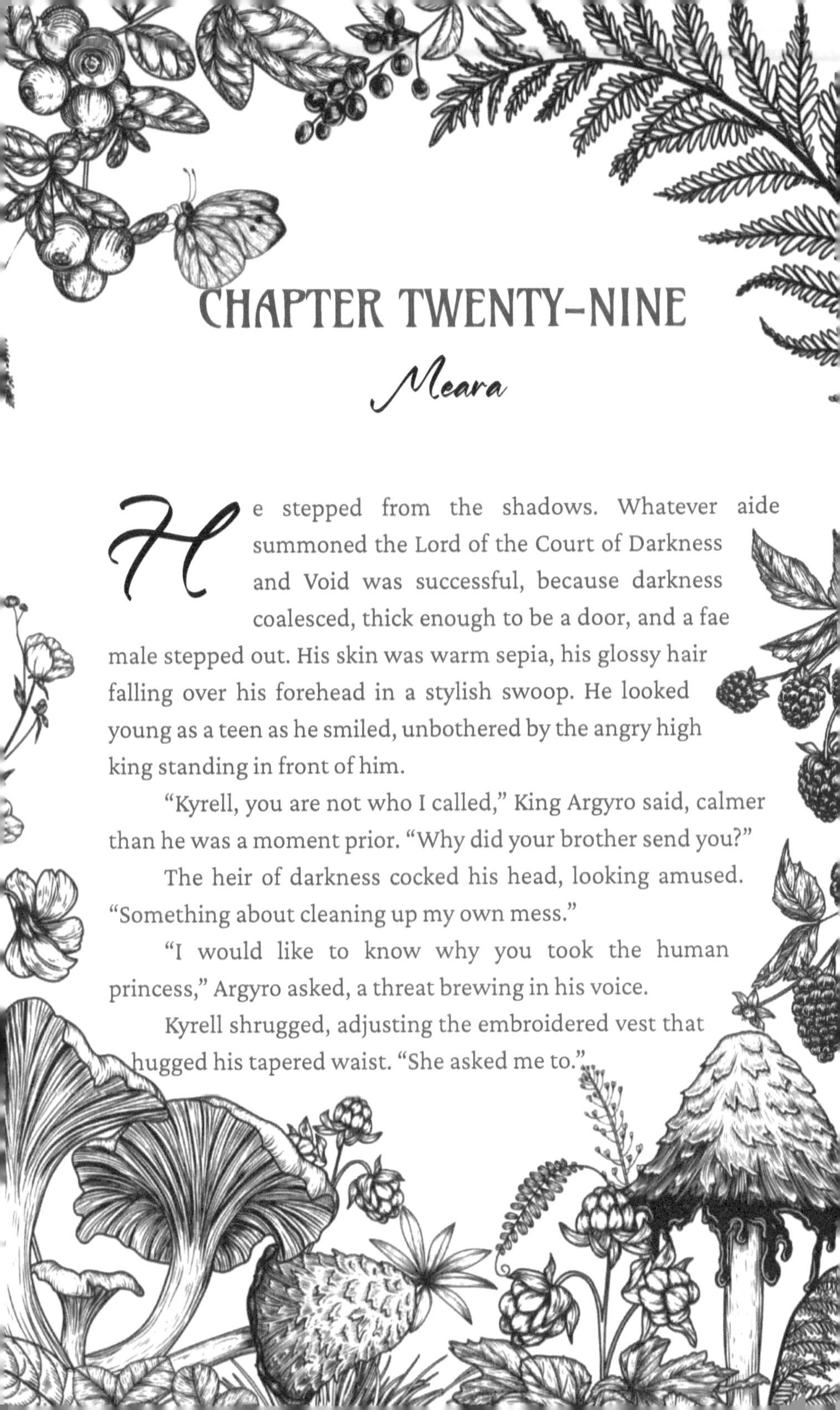

CHAPTER TWENTY-NINE

Meara

He stepped from the shadows. Whatever aide summoned the Lord of the Court of Darkness and Void was successful, because darkness coalesced, thick enough to be a door, and a fae male stepped out. His skin was warm sepia, his glossy hair falling over his forehead in a stylish swoop. He looked young as a teen as he smiled, unbothered by the angry high king standing in front of him.

"Kyrell, you are not who I called," King Argyro said, calmer than he was a moment prior. "Why did your brother send you?"

The heir of darkness cocked his head, looking amused. "Something about cleaning up my own mess."

"I would like to know why you took the human princess," Argyro asked, a threat brewing in his voice.

Kyrell shrugged, adjusting the embroidered vest that hugged his tapered waist. "She asked me to."

"Her parents and her betrothed are demanding her return," Farran interjected, his hand resting on the dagger in his belt. Meara's pulse pounded in her throat. Surely violence would not break out in the high king's throne room. She wished for her hunting dagger, stashed in her bag in the Autumn Court rooms.

"Don't fret. I'll send her back if she asks me to," Kyrell stated.

"Child," the king said, "you will not defy me in this. You will return the girl who is not yours to have."

Kyrell straightened, his expression turning stony. In that instance he went from a careless youth to an ageless fae. His voice stayed cool, casual, but the gleam in his dark eyes promised violence. "She is mine, and there's nothing you can do to change that."

Argyro nodded to his attendants and two armed guards moved toward Kyrell. As one reached for him, shadows flashed and a hand grabbed the guard's forearm, forcing him back.

Another faerie stepped out of the darkness, this one an older version of Kyrell. Endlessly dark eyes glittered as he said, "If you lay your hand on my brother, I will remove it at the wrist."

"Sigmis," Argyro said. He wore his courtly smile, but his hands clenched into fists at his sides. "You realize the human kingdoms are threatening war if they do not get their princess back. She is in a marriage contract."

"I will not return my brother's plaything. I suggest the human kingdoms forge a new treaty, one that does not rest on bartering a girl." Without waiting for a response, Sigmis spun, his dark cloak whipping behind him and raising shadows that swallowed the two males, leaving an empty floor and shocked mutterings breaking out among the courtiers watching.

"Damn it!" Argyro said. "Everyone out! Go enjoy the banquet while I clean up this pile of griffin shit." He waved his hand dismissively.

The chatter of the crowd rose, debates breaking out all around them. Meara gripped Cerne's sleeve in an attempt to keep the chaos from overwhelming her sensitive fae hearing.

Queen Araluen rose and kissed her husband on the cheek before leaving the room. The crowd filtered out behind her and Cerne led them into the middle of it. No one bumped or pushed, but she stayed close to her escort.

Tayen had coached them on what to expect - delicate bites of food, faeries drifting between conversations as they strengthened their social alliances, and of course, dancing.

As they breached the doors, there was no formal announcement. The tightness constricting Meara's lungs loosened a fraction.

The court members lounged around in seats, leaning against the soaring pillars, laughing and drinking. Faerie wine covered the long table on one side of the room, beside the spread of food, and most guests held a flute in their hands already. The mood was lighter, jovial, compared with the tense atmosphere of the throne room below.

Sunset was dying, the series of arched doorways leading to balconies darkening as the light from hundreds of tiny crystals from chandeliers above their head shimmered over them.

At her side, Cerne looked over the gathering. The tilt of his chin was regal, and she drifted closer, brushing his side.

She was on his arm at a court function. They made it through being presented to the high king and queen and perhaps won the queen's approval. She had every reason to feel good, but it was the memory of his kiss that surfaced. She wanted to do it again.

Lilting music hummed in the background, similar to what they enjoyed in the pub but refined, lighter, brighter. Her hips swayed. Cerne smiled and leaned closer to speak to her. "Hungry?"

She nodded and he guided her to the table spread with food, Tayen and Brenna trailing behind them.

Meara took the plate that Cerne offered. Everything on the table was meant to be a single bite. Miniature tarts, stuffed dates, little pieces of meat skewered on stems. Cerne placed a bite of cheese on her plate that he thought she would like. She reached for a sliver of bread topped with a terrine that smelled of olives and wild boar, her mouth watering.

"Here, I know how you like these," she said, putting a tiny cake topped with pomegranate on his plate. It felt intimate. He leaned closer to speak in her ear when a flash of gold caught her eye. Cerne stiffened beside her.

Garbed in deep turquoise trimmed in gold, a tall, broad fae male strode through the crowd. The spear that peeked over his shoulder seemed to shimmer with magic. His hair was the same molten gold as Brenna's, and his skin a rich tan that seemed to glow. She squinted, trying to determine if it was magic or simply the slight glow of sunset on his skin.

"Who is that?" Meara muttered.

Cerne lowered his face toward her, and she shivered as his lips brushed the shell of her ear. "That is Luce, the heir of the summer court." He didn't have to say he disliked the male, it was apparent in his tone and curl of his lip as he straightened.

"Let's find a place to sit," Tayen suggested, his hand resting on Cerne's wrist where the faerie gripped his plate hard enough Meara was surprised it hadn't broken. Cerne blinked and then nodded, allowing Tayen to locate a group of seats at a small table along the edge of the room. Meara's eyes traced the columns upward where they arched into a vaulted ceiling. Shadows revealed intricate carvings of white marble.

"Can we get some of this at the Autumn Court?" Brenna said, covering her mouth with her hand as she chewed a bite. Her other hand held a round pastry topped with pale green icing.

Tayen chuckled. "That's a specialty of the spring court. Do you like it? Maybe I can arrange something."

Brenna's eyes crinkled as she grinned. "I was kidding. But yes, it's incredible." She took another bite. "Don't worry, I love our food at the Autumn Court too. I could never go back to eating human food again." Meara pressed her lips together and looked away.

Cerne's hand drifted to her thigh. His fingers skimmed the silk, settling above her knee. It was a casual gesture, but it felt like a public claiming and her heart rate accelerated.

Without looking at her, he leaned closer. "I apologize, but I must go speak with the Rangers again. Farran looks... unsettled." He glanced at Tayen. "I'll bring news." His hand released her reluctantly, fingers tracing over her knee as he stood. She watched his antlers gleam ivory in the crystalline light as he walked away.

Brenna giggled at something Tayen said and Meara turned. "You guys should dance," she said, catching her sister staring at the couples whirling across the marble floor to the string instruments' tune.

"We couldn't leave you," Brenna protested.

Meara took a bite of creamy cheese and swallowed before answering, "I will be absolutely fine." Her gaze met Tayen's and she raised her eyebrows.

Understanding her silent command, Tayen stood, offering Brenna his open palm. "We are still in the same room, and no one here would harm her while she is under Cerne's protection and in the high king's court. Not so publicly, anyhow."

Brenna's brows furrowed, but she tucked her hand into the crook of his arm and walked onto the dance floor. Meara watched them fall into the steps of the dance and twirl away as she ate her last bite of food. Frowning, she noted her empty plate. Time for a refill.

As she moved back toward the banquet spread, she heard the distinct sound of whispers and smothered giggles. It had been weeks since the last time she received such treatment among humans, and she had grown accustomed to moving through public spaces without gossip or mockery following her. Her shoulders tensed, refusing to turn and look for the petty gossip mongers.

Despite her lack of acknowledgement, her skin heated with a clammy sort of anger. Perhaps it wasn't directed at her, but somehow she knew it was. She set her plate on the tray of a passing server and turned back. The room was too warm, stifling, and she could not fill her lungs without feeling like she was choking. This shouldn't affect her like this, but after the last few tumultuous days, she felt raw. Vulnerable. She scanned for reprieve and her eyes fell on the closest balcony, the door open a sliver. She fled.

Sliding into the night air, her heart slowed and her panic faded to a bearable hum in her mind. The quiet rush of the rivers below and the zing of nighttime insects soothed her and the tension wound taut in her chest slowly unraveled. Exhaling slowly, she drifted toward the railing and peered over the dark water.

Moonlight coated the treetops and sloped grassy hills. Rivers wove like ribbons through the landscape until they disappeared into blackness. She knew the sea was somewhere in the distance. Leaning her forearms on the railing, she studied the shining line of water and let the chilled breeze cool her flesh.

"Find something interesting out there?" A low voice asked. She spun, a hand to her mouth as the summer heir materialized. He must have followed her out or emerged from the far side of the wide balcony, but she had not heard him. He ignored her surprise and looked over the railing. "Those hills are the edge of the summer court, just as the autumn court ends in the trees there. If you could see west, you would see our shared agriculture."

Blinking, she stared at the golden faerie. He was Cerne's rival. And he was standing beside her explaining the geography around them. Wavy hair the color of dried wheat fell over his brow. Everything about him was broad, from his defined jaw to his shoulders. He looked like he personally did most of the threshing of their courts' shared harvest.

She waited for some sort of introduction, some shred of decorum, but he simply leaned onto the railing and stared over the landscape beside her.

If he had no manners, she would have to take the lead. It was a way to place formality between them. "Apologies," she said, her voice rough. She cleared it. "We have not been introduced."

"I am Luce, from the Summer Court, and you are Lady Meara." He stated it so plainly. Then, with a note of curiosity, he asked, "Did you enjoy meeting Queen Araluen?"

The question caught her off guard. He didn't sound like someone making idle conversation, nor did he carry the hostility she expected from Cerne's near-enemy. When she hesitated, he turned to look at her. Thick lashes framed eyes of two different colors, one the deep blue of a summer sky, and the other a complex honey brown. Her breath caught as she was caught in their depths.

"No, it was fine," she stammered. "I didn't know what to expect, but she was kind."

He stared at her for a moment and then nodded. "She is."

Meara dragged her bottom lip through her teeth, unsure of what to say. Those bicolored irises unsettled her.

"I would have remembered you if we had met before," he continued. "Where did you live before you joined the Autumn Court?"

Her inhale was measured as she gathered her thoughts. He was not a safe person to confide in, in fact, she was sure he was one of the people Cerne seemed to worry about.

"If you will not speak to me, I can accept that," he said quietly, taking her silence for rejection. "But do not fault me for attempting it again when we meet at Samhain." A hint of a smile warmed his rugged features.

The door swooshed open and the shards of light scattered across the stone floor, shifting over her feet as the glass moved. Familiar antlers stood out, marking the silhouette as Cerne's.

"Luce, what are you doing?" His voice had a friendly air, but Meara sensed the threat under his words. Cerne was skilled at those courtly games, sounding friendly while promising retribution. She turned, her hands gripping the railing as she pressed the small of her back against it.

Luce glanced back, looking unconcerned. "You could have introduced me. It would have saved your lady from some distress."

Meara scowled. "I am not in distress. But being approached by a stranger with a spear strapped to his back is not a common experience for me."

Cerne stepped closer, offering her a hand. She placed her fingers in his warm palm, feeling the draw to him as his fingers closed over hers. Luce sighed behind her, and she glanced over her shoulder in time to see the light catch the golden stubble on his jaw as he turned back to the view.

"Good evening," she said, trying to assuage the discomfort of the situation. Cerne's lips thinned into a hard line as he pulled her away. "Is there anywhere else we could go? It was a bit warm in there." She searched his face, her heart jumping at his soft expression.

Luce straightened and strode past them. "I could never leave a lady in discomfort. I will leave this space to you. Good evening, Meara."

"You have my thanks, Luce," Cerne said. The sharp tone felt like a defense she was tucked behind. His arm looped around her, emphasizing the feeling. The familiarity was a balm, and she melted into him, letting him warm the icy parts of her. He spoke into her hair. "I'm going to have to have a word with Tayen about leaving you."

"Unsupervised?" she added. "I do not need a bodyguard nor a chaperone. No one else here has one."

His finger tipped her chin up until their eyes met. "No one else is brand new to the court with magic craft that has barely been discovered. Craft you cannot wield. Yet. And trouble seems to find you, though I cannot blame it. You are beautiful."

She wanted to argue, or at least glare at him, but his hold on her waist tightened and his mouth lowered to hers. She tipped her chin up, feeling his lips brush over hers. He paused, giving her a chance to pull away. She prayed the shadows provided privacy and the entire ballroom wasn't watching as she met his kiss hungrily, pressing into him. His fingers dug into her skin, the pinch of pain adding to the delicious strokes of his tongue against hers.

"Dance with me?" he murmured, leaning back to look into her eyes. The softness of his forest eyes comforted her after the shock of Luce's intense gaze.

"I'm afraid my dancing has not improved." He chuckled at her confession. "But wait," she said, raising an eyebrow, "you were too drunk to dance with me at our last banquet. So perhaps I am a wonderful dancer and you are a terrible one."

"Only one way to know," he said, his hand sliding down her arm to grip her wrist and tug her into a twirl. She turned under his arm and then fell back into his chest. His mahogany curls fell over his cheeks as he dipped his head to capture her mouth again. She kissed him slowly, savoring the slide of their lips together.

When she released him to take a shuddering breath, he smirked. "I thought we were going to dance. It is the more socially acceptable option of the things you make me think of doing."

Meara shivered, wanting to press nearer to him, closer until she crawled into his ribcage and lived in his confidence and warmth. His voice was rough and low. "It's up to you, my lady. To the dance floor, or shall we find a more private alcove?"

She ran her teeth over her lip again, trying to sort out her racing mind. Every rational thought swirled into a mess as his mouth trailed over her jaw and he pressed a kiss to her earlobe. Her hand went to his hair, pulling him away. "You cannot expect me to make a wise decision when you kiss me like that."

"Sorry." His grin said otherwise. In fact, he looked wildly pleased with himself. He ran a hand down the inside of her raised arm, tracing her ribs and dipping to the small of her back.

Scoffing, she rolled her eyes. "You haven't been sorry a day in your life."

His rakish smile widened. Her stomach flipped, and she tipped her head back, offering her mouth. Her eyes fluttered shut, anticipation coiling within her, when raindrops splashed onto her cheeks.

The clouds rumbled, and rain began to pour in earnest. Throwing his arm around her, Cerne rushed them back under the edge of the roof. His arms enveloped her, shielding her from the chill and mist of the rain drenching the ground a mere footfall from where they huddled.

She stared into the landscape as rain obscured the darkened rolling hills. His breath was hot on her neck. "Should we go back to our rooms?"

Her hands wrinkled the fabric of his shirt. "As appealing as that idea is," she murmured, her words slow and halting, "I think we should rejoin our friends."

His chuckle was dark, but his hold on her loosened, giving her space to breathe. "If you desire a dance, I promise to not complain about any stomped-on feet."

"I don't-" she protested.

"Of course - I promise to not step on your feet. Better?" She nodded. Slowly, he peeled away until a hand width separated them.

Leaving one hand on the small of her back, he guided them into the ballroom where they joined Tayen and Brenna in a dance. The steps were slower, thankfully, and she allowed Cerne to guide her. Only once did she step on his foot, and he gave her no reaction. In his arms, the overwhelming crowd of the room didn't bother her. Everything fell away until there was only his arms twirling her and her sister's smiling face as they passed each other on the ballroom floor.

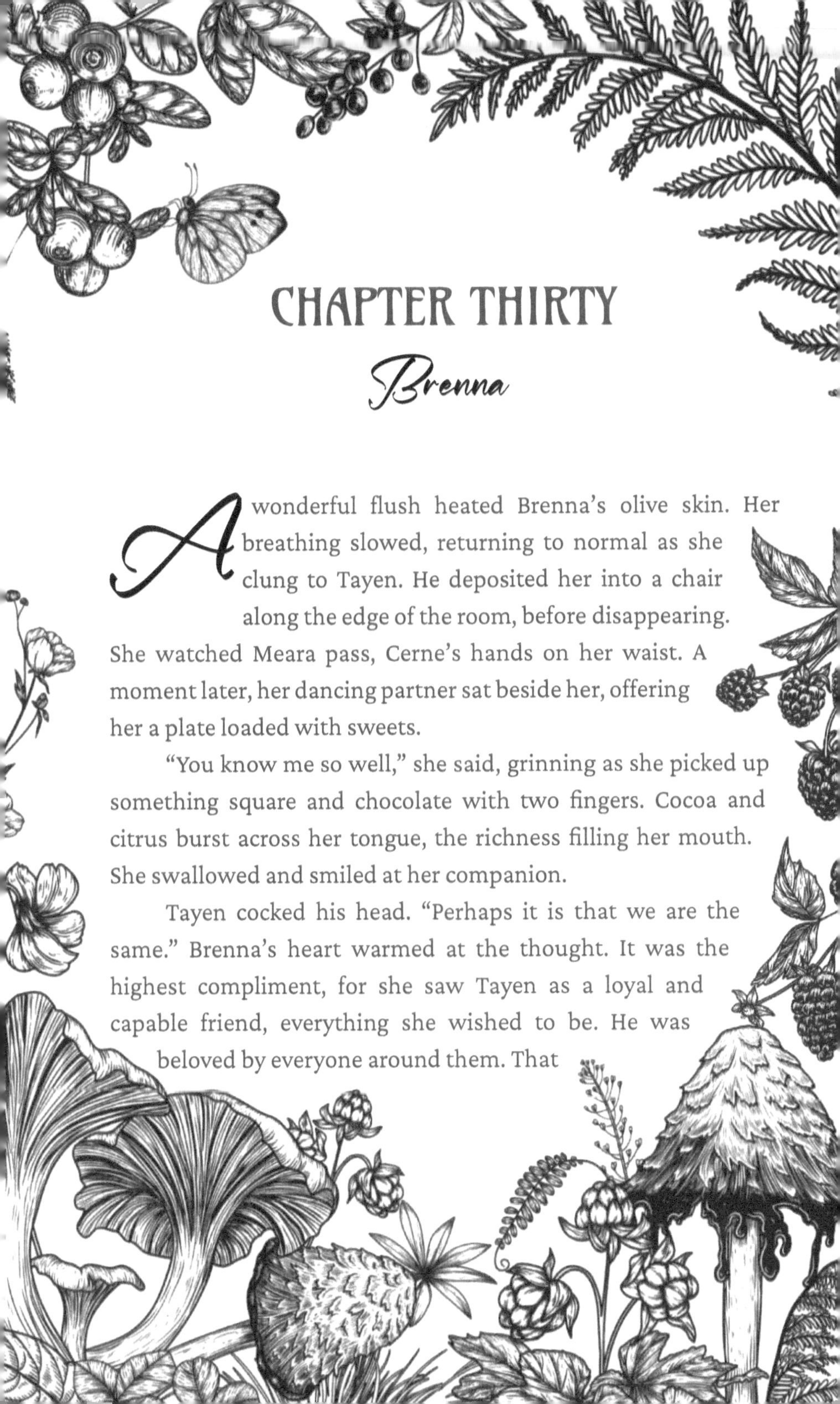

CHAPTER THIRTY

Brenna

A wonderful flush heated Brenna's olive skin. Her breathing slowed, returning to normal as she clung to Tayen. He deposited her into a chair along the edge of the room, before disappearing. She watched Meara pass, Cerne's hands on her waist. A moment later, her dancing partner sat beside her, offering her a plate loaded with sweets.

"You know me so well," she said, grinning as she picked up something square and chocolate with two fingers. Cocoa and citrus burst across her tongue, the richness filling her mouth. She swallowed and smiled at her companion.

Tayen cocked his head. "Perhaps it is that we are the same." Brenna's heart warmed at the thought. It was the highest compliment, for she saw Tayen as a loyal and capable friend, everything she wished to be. He was beloved by everyone around them. That sense of belonging was her deepest craving.

They cleared the plate and she leaned back in her seat, hands folded over her soft stomach. She was grateful for the gentle corset built into the dress for it allowed her to breathe while highlighting her curvy figure. The boning was stitched with viridian up the sides and under her breasts, like vines coming out of the spray of ranunculus and peony. For the hundredth time, she mentally praised Dyani for such a beautiful garment. It gave her the confidence to raise her chin as she looked out over the crowd.

Her gaze snagged on intense russet eyes and glossy black hair. Cheekbones so sharp, he could never pass as human. Even with dancers crossing their sightline and intermittently blocking his stare, she felt as if he was stripping her soul bare. Her hand went to Tayen's arm. "Who is that?"

Tayen's sunburst hair whipped against his cheeks with how fast he turned to follow her gaze. His muscles tensed under her hand.

"Well?"

"It's the king's advisor, Emrys."

Her brows furrowed and she tore her eyes off Emrys so she could gauge Tayen's emotions.

He leaned closer and dropped his voice. "He is a prince in his own right, and serves Argyro using his blood magic. He is one of the most powerful faeries here, but he is not safe."

The male stalked through the crowd toward them.

"What do we do?" she asked.

Tayen stood, drawing her up with him. "I will speak." He didn't have to say the rest - *you keep quiet*. She bit into her cheeks, her fingers digging into the fabric of his jacket's arm. "Don't worry," he murmured, keeping his eyes on the approaching fae male.

Emrys slowed, his posture falling into a casual stance that did nothing to hide the predatory grace with which he moved. "Tayen," he said, nodding in greeting, "and Lady Brenna. So glad you could join us at court."

"Good evening, Lord Emrys." Tayen's voice was formal.

"How is the Autumn Court?"

Brenna felt brittle, listening to the males exchange pleasantries like the courtiers they were. Only her fear of sounding foolish held her tongue. Tayen placed his hand at the small of her back, rubbing small circles that reassured her.

"Quiet. We are preparing for Samhain with the summer court."

"Perhaps I will attend this year," Emrys said. "Lady Brenna, I noticed that you are an elegant dancer. Could I tempt you into another?"

She should decline. Tayen would sweep her away, keep her protected from anyone who was less than kind and trustworthy. But something about Emrys kindled a burning curiosity. In that moment, she desperately wanted to take a closer look at this beautiful, dangerous faerie.

"That would be lovely." Tayen's eyes darkened in warning. She patted his arm. "I will be back in a few minutes."

"I'll be right here waiting," Tayen said, the wariness in his voice reminding her of Meara.

"Excellent." Emrys' smile was feline and painfully handsome. Emrys held out an arm clothed in fine black fabric tailored to show the line of his sculpted figure. She hesitated, her hand hovering before she placed it over his forearm. Muscles rippled under her fingers, and a thrill coiled in her core as her awareness narrowed to that small point of contact.

The overhead light cast shadows in the hollows of his cheeks. He was made of sharp angles, the high contrast of midnight hair and pale skin, and stretches of lean muscle and sinew making her heart pound.

As they drew close to the line of dancers, he turned to face her, one hand going to her waist and the other taking her fingers in his. "Ready?"

"Yes." She drew in a lungful of air and let it go in a rush before he guided her into the flow of dancers, and they began to move with the lilting music.

As if influenced by his presence, the music slowed, becoming haunting. He adjusted their speed, pulling her closer, moving one hand to her waist while the other gripped her hand securely. While Tayen's touch had felt warm and comforting, Emrys' burned like ice. She suppressed the urge to shiver.

"I must say, I was fascinated by your flame. Does fire craft run in your family?" he asked, dipping his head closer. A rogue strand of hair fell over his temple, marring his perfection in a way that drew her in.

Blinking, she opened her mouth and closed it, unsure of how to answer. There seemed no harm in a small measure of honesty. "I am not sure. I was adopted," she admitted.

"Really." One eyebrow rose, and with it, her heart rate.

Swallowing, she reprimanded herself for falling for a pretty face. She shouldn't even be dancing with him, yet she couldn't bring herself to regret it.

"You do not know your family of birth?" he asked lightly. She shook her head, her brows pinching. "I apologize, that was rude," he said, his voice velvet. "I simply desire to get to know you."

His merlot irises held hers, full of knowing intention. For a moment, her assumptions wavered. Her fingers tightened in his grip, and a warm smile spread over his face.

Sighing, she returned it with a tentative smile of her own. "It's true. Though I had a wonderful mother who raised me. But I never imagined I'd be in the high court."

Emrys listened with such attentiveness, she felt her boundaries fraying. Subtle reactions flashed over his face, too fleeting to interpret. "We are lucky then, for your presence brightens this court. It would be a cold night if you had not come."

"Thank you," she said, her cheeks tinging pink as her gaze wandered downward, to his trim waist and then over shined shoes crossing a glittering stone floor striped with the shadows of dancing beings. "What about you? Have you been in Court Tara for long?"

Emrys hummed, a dimple pressing into his cheek as his expression turned thoughtful. "I was sent here as a youth. My uncle was Lord of Summer, and he insisted I spend time among civilized folk. I was to learn leadership from the high king, and I never left. I've served him most of my life."

Brenna tilted her head, trying to guess at his age, but she didn't have the courage to ask. Not without some alcohol easing her reservations.

His dimple reappeared and she focused on it as he spoke. "It's my home now. I haven't seen my father in a decade or two."

"Do you wish to?" she asked gently.

His smooth expression never faltered. "No."

The music shifted again, the tempo accelerating. Emrys' feet never stumbled, and his gentle hold guided her into the quicker steps.

"So you've seen my magic," she said, her confidence rising with the swell of the music. "Tell me about yours."

He twirled her and brought her back flush against his chest. They slowed, swaying in the center of the open floor. Other couples swept around, but her world shrank to just him.

Emrys brushed a chaste kiss over her knuckles. A gallant gesture, until he turned her hand and his lips closed over her fingertips in a languid kiss. Heat prickled up her arm.

With a smirk, he closed his teeth over the pads of her fingers with enough pressure to prick the skin. His irises dilated at the soft gasp that escaped her.

As he lowered her hand, the barest smear of blood painted his bottom lip. Brenna froze, unable to look away as his tongue darted out to capture it.

"Blood magic," she whispered, fascination warring with her fear. Everything felt strained within her, waiting to see what he could do with a taste of her blood.

His brows pinched for a split second, confusion flickering across his face. It softened the sharpness of his features, making him more beautiful. His tongue dragged over his lip a second time and her own lips parted.

"I could make you feel things," he purred. "Like happiness, or comfort."

He pulled her into the steps of the dance once more, and as her feet followed his, a foreign warmth welled in her chest. She stumbled and he steadied her as she pressed a hand to her chest.

"Are you influencing my emotions?" she asked, trying to separate the alien feeling from her internal fire.

His chin dipped, his eyes dropping to her hand.

The music swelled into a final crescendo. The feeling intensified in a smokey, hazy heat. "That is incredible, but I'd prefer it if you didn't," she managed to say.

The sensation vanished. His smile was unrepentant. "Of course."

"Thank you." She cleared her throat. "What else can you do?"

"I can tell if you are being deceptive." He twirled her, pulling her close once more. "But not much else unless you'd like to give me your blood often and build up a connection."

The suggestion shouldn't sound appealing, but from his lips, it was pure temptation. She shrugged, feigning indifference as their feet slowed and the song ended.

The crowd thinned and their world of rustling skirts and enchanting music faded away. Emrys held her at a polite distance before he released her entirely.

"Thank you," she murmured.

He raised his chin, that delicious smirk returning. "Until next time."

Brenna twisted, orienting herself to the room while searching for her friends. Tayen stood with his arms crossed, an inscrutable expression hardening his handsome features.

Beside him, Cerne stood with Meara tucked against him. Brenna's heart stuttered as her attention caught on the nearness between them, and the way Meara leaned into him.

"Brenna," Meara said, her voice carrying. She snapped from her trance and jerked into motion, closing the distance with a giddy smile on her face.

"Enjoy your dance?" Cerne asked. She nodded.

Tayen said nothing. Brenna's exuberance ebbed, guilt overtaking it. She would make it up to him somehow.

"Well, let's retire and get some rest. We can ride home in the morning."

"That soon?" she asked, frowning.

Antlers flashing in the candlelight, Cerne turned. "Considering the current political tension, yes, we should go home sooner rather than later." Meara peered past him, her mouth a tight line.

Nodding, Brenna followed him out, hardly feeling the chill of the night as they descended stairs and strode down the stone road to the quarters designated for the Autumn Court.

Stars glittered overhead like shards of glass. Echoes of a sleeping city surrounded them, footfalls of other guests returning to their rooms, the guards on patrol.

Cerne pushed the door carved with leaves open with a heavy sigh. They filed into the opulent space, and Brenna felt her tension ebb.

"You certainly stayed later than I expected," Ayala quipped from her position lounging across the ivory sofa. Her decadent gown was replaced with a slinky black slip. "Was there adequate debauchery for a court celebration?"

Cerne plopped into a plush armchair. "Almost none. The queen's gathering was practically wholesome. You would have been thoroughly disappointed."

"Glad I pursued entertainment elsewhere."

Tayen tapped his sister's foot until she bent her knees and made room for him on the sofa. "And was this entertainment fruitful?"

Brenna chewed on her lip, settling into a seat opposite Cerne. Meara perched on the arm of the chair.

"Not particularly," Ayala grumbled. "What did you learn at the banquet?"

Tayen rubbed at his forehead, his eyes squeezed shut. "Everyone was concerned about the way Sigmis disrespected Argyro. It cannot be allowed to stand. But the king has few options when the Court of Darkness is so distant."

"And independent," Ayala added.

"Sigmis has always been an arrogant bastard," Cerne said, tipping his head to rest on the back of the chair.

"Yet this was the first major problem he has caused for all courts," Tayen mused.

"What about the humans?" Brenna asked. Meara nodded, her hands clasped against her thigh.

"I expect Argyro will send an assassin," Ayala stated and four sets of eyes snapped to her. She shrugged. "It's what I would do. It would punish Sigmis and end the human's motivation for bringing violence. The treaty between the two kingdoms will dissolve, and Court Tara can bully them into peaceful compliance."

Meara scoffed. "You sound like a sadistic dictator."

"Thank you," Ayala said with a smirk.

"I'm not sure those are the terms of their treaty," Tayen added. "It could still lead to war, or more likely, the two human kingdoms go to war with each other."

"Neither of those outcomes are acceptable," Meara snapped.

Ayala tilted her head back, highlighting her sharp jaw. "What would you prefer they do?"

"I'm wondering why he took her to begin with," Brenna muttered. She clasped her hands together, rubbing the pad of her thumb over the tips of her fingers bitten by Emrys. There was no mark, but they tingled.

Tayen's voice was tired. "It could be as simple as wanting to possess something beautiful that belongs to others."

"Have we considered that Kyrell was honest and Elysia wanted to be taken?" Meara asked. Her silken hair darkened the shadows on her face as she leaned forward, chin resting on the heel of her hand.

"This is futile." Ayala rose, stretching her arms above her head and causing the hem of her shift to rise up her thighs. "We should all sleep if we are going to leave before noon tomorrow."

Brenna raised a hand to cover her mouth, her nose scrunching as a yawn forced her mouth open. "I'm tired too," she said.

With a tilt of his head, Tayen caught her attention. "Would you stay and speak with me for a moment?"

Dread curled in her gut. He had never addressed her in such a serious manner. "Of course."

Pausing, Meara looked between them, reluctant to leave her. Brenna waved her away, and she pressed her lips into a thin line before leaving Brenna alone with Tayen.

The lines in his face aged him. He rubbed at his jaw, his eyes pleading with her. "You danced with Emrys."

Warmth fizzed through her veins. She swallowed. "Yes, it was just a dance."

"Drawing his attention is unwise. Hopefully he will forget you," Tayen said, causing Brenna to clench her jaw. "If he had gotten you alone and tasted your blood..." He trailed off.

She should tell him what happened, but she couldn't. He would think the worst, and she was quickly deciding that Emrys was not a danger to her.

"He was a gentleman and I felt safe in the ballroom with you and Cerne nearby," she protested weakly, her voice more apologetic than argumentative.

Tayen sighed. "You are too sweet and trusting, my dear. Let's hope he doesn't decide to attend Samhain."

"Hopefully," she echoed, lacking any conviction. Tayen seemed too tired to notice. He stood, straightening his clothing. Brenna nodded, pushing off the chair to stand. When he took the door to the left to his room, she turned right and slipped into the bedroom she shared with Meara.

Her sister stood by the dressing table with a hairbrush in hand. "What was that?"

"He was concerned about that faerie I danced with. I guess he is powerful and somewhat unsavory."

Meara clicked her tongue. "Alright, no more dancing with villains. Next time I will have to approve all of your dance partners, and none of them will be good enough." Brenna's heart lightened with her teasing. She hummed in pleasure as her sister undid her braids and brushed out her curls before twisting them into a loose bun for sleeping.

"Thank you," Brenna murmured. Her movements grew clumsy as sleep threatened to overtake her. They helped each other with their dresses and then curled up under the covers together. She hardly remembered her head touching the pillow before she was lost to a heavy sleep.

CHAPTER THIRTY-ONE
Meara

Meara awoke to find the Rangers in their rooms. Clutching her robe firmly, she scowled at Farran as he lounged across the settee. Ayala stood in her doorway with a similar expression.

Cahira sat quietly while Lorand stood with his back against the wall and observed the room. Tayen reentered the room and handed a cup of tea to Farran.

"Good morning, lovely Meara," the half-fae leader of the Rangers called out. "Come join us for breakfast."

"Give me a moment, please," she replied, shutting the door of her room. Brenna sat up in bed, bleary eyed. "The Rangers are here."

Brenna scrambled from bed and began dressing. The sisters fell into their familiar routine of tightening dress laces and brushing out each other's hair. Meara found comfort in the gestures, especially when everything else in their lives had changed.

When Meara returned to the sitting room in her loose travel tunic and trousers, Cerne was closing the front door behind his back.

"Any word?" Tayen asked.

Cerne sighed heavily. "We have leave, but Argyro is still in a foul mood. I do not think he found any solutions. It's in the hands of King Eldric and Queen Malacia now."

"We will travel back and see what we can negotiate," Farran declared, slurping his tea. Lorand accepted a cup as well, though he was better mannered.

Meara perched on a plush bench and accepted a cup of tea and a sweet pastry shaped like a flower. Beside her, Brenna nibbled at the treat happily. Cerne occupied the armchair beside her, and his arm reached out, hand settling on her thigh. There was no hiding the contact in such a small circle, and her heart leapt into her throat. Brenna's mouth tugged into a smile, but no one else reacted.

"I wish you safe travels," Cerne said.

"Thank you. I'm sure we will see you soon. I suspect there will be a lot of back and forth required to sort out this mess." Farran stood and brushed crumbs from his leather vest. "Shall we?"

Lorand pushed off from the wall, and Cahira rose, both following her leader. With a tip of their heads, the Rangers exited.

The moment Brenna closed the door to their bedroom, she spun to face Meara. "What was that?"

"What?" Meara felt a blush creeping up her neck.

"Cerne's hand." She stepped closer, eyes sparkling. "On your leg."

Meara bit her lip. She didn't want to lie to her sister, but sharing what happened felt strange, as if it would make it real. Fingers twisting together, she confessed, "Cerne kissed me."

Brenna seized her shoulders. "You're jesting."

A smile fought it's way over her face. "He kissed me after the tavern, but I thought it was a drunken mistake. But then he did it again last night on the balcony."

Spinning, Brenna clenched her hands into fists and threw her hands out in victory. "I knew it!" She turned back. "This is wonderful. It will secure our place in the Autumn Court."

Meara's heart stuttered. She was fond of Cerne and enjoyed kissing him, but it did not negate her desire to return to their mother. As Brenna twirled and chattered about the future while packing their belongings, Meara gripped her elbows across her body and sagged onto the end of the bed, feeling utterly torn in two.

The forest embraced them, the shadows of old growth bathing her in their shadows. Meara felt the dregs of magic that stirred in her bones when she kissed Cerne and again in Luce's presence. It teased her, small glimpses of something she should be able to summon whenever she liked. Yet it stayed elusive. She sat atop Bran, swaying to his gentle gait, and searched for the piece of her that drew upon shadows. Frustration built, until her face turned tart and Tayen frowned when he looked her way.

She wanted to grind her teeth together and growl her frustration until it built in a shrieking scream. Instead, she pressed it down. Like all the times before, she buried the thoughts and tamped down the rage she felt until it fit within her ribcage, a cold sharp bundle.

One, two, three. She counted her slow breaths, emptying her mind of the chaos.

The horses shifted positions and Tayen guided Eirlys to walk beside her. "What are you stewing over?"

Scowling, she let her exhale hiss through her teeth. "I am frustrated about my magic."

"Have you summoned shadows again?"

"They made an appearance on the balcony at the banquet." She turned the events over in her mind. "It was dark and I think that made it easier. But what's the use if I can only work shadows in the night?"

He nodded thoughtfully, staring ahead at Cerne's swaying antlers. "It's nothing to worry about if it takes you a while to learn to wield your craft."

Meara's eyes narrowed. Brenna rode ahead, so she lowered her voice to keep her words between the two of them. "My sister summoned flame and light within a day of unlocking her magic. Magic so strong it shattered the enchantment placed over us. Clearly, I do not have the strength she does."

Tayen's lips pursed. "I am not sure that is true. But if you stop training and working on your craft, it will become true. You will impose limits upon yourself that were never meant to be."

"You are doing nothing for my frustration," she deadpanned.

His exhale turned to a laugh. "I am afraid I have no words of wisdom that won't aggravate you today. You are short tempered when you don't get enough sleep."

There was no use in arguing. She wrinkled her nose and turned forward, denying him her attention. He must have felt the matter was settled, because he nodded to her and urged his mount forward until he rode beside Brenna.

As the trees thickened and forced them into single file, Meara's mood stayed sullen. Brenna sensed that she needed time, and gave her space to brood. She was grateful to reach the Autumn Court and retire to quiet solitude.

A week passed quietly. Meara spent her days focusing on her magic, and yet she couldn't conjure so much as a wisp of darkness. After long, frustrating days, she took her dinner in her rooms and avoided Cerne. Thoughts of her eventual return to Dornadan soured the blossoming relationship between them.

Brenna sat with her, sharing encouraging words, though it only made Meara feel worse when Brenna flicked droplets of light between her fingertips when she grew bored.

Tayen was busy with politics, Ayala disappeared entirely, and Xurey did not return. Even Seda was busy training her new recruits, and Meara knew her sister was lonely. She sat with Kirrily and sipped tea as Meara stared out the window and agonized.

Finally, she reached her breaking point. With a frustrated growl, she threw herself onto their bed. Brenna moved to sit beside her, stroking her hair. "Meara, you need to stop. You're driving yourself mad. You've barely eaten, you haven't seen Cerne in days, no wonder you cannot access your magic."

Meara rolled over and narrowed her eyes. "And I am supposed to rely on that male to manifest my magic?" The fact she had only brought forth shadows when assisted weighed heavily on her, and she was feeling sensitive.

"No, but you deserve to be happy. And you aren't going to figure out your magic by punishing yourself," Brenna said, firmer. "Tomorrow, we will take a walk in the woods and relax. Perhaps that will help you."

Exhaling harshly, Meara buried her face in the covers. Brenna's nails pressed into her shoulder blades. "Fine," she mumbled. Happy, Brenna patted her back and rose.

The next morning, the Autumn Guard assembled. Seda held meetings of her lieutenants, and as Brenna and Meara walked the halls of the manor house, they passed an open door revealing the circle of faeries. Dull green tunics wrinkled under pieces of cinched leather armor. They were dressed for training, lacking the sleek armor of battle, and they looked tired.

Seda's dark eyes rose to meet theirs, and a nod passed between them. Meara could read the stress in her eyes, the chafing responsibility to prepare her guard when a conflict was looming.

A nervous energy filled the manor, and Meara was relieved to step outside. Brenna tucked her hand into the crook of Meara's arm, their shoulders bumping together as they walked.

Meara's boots crunched the ever present autumn leaves. Brenna's feet were quieter in soft leather slippers, hidden under her simple linen dress. The caramel color of the garment was a shade lighter than her warm skin, causing it to look like it was glowing against her neckline.

Brenna slowed, and Meara turned to face her. "How about here?"

She looked around. The trees were spaced further giving them ample space to work. "Show me what you've got." Meara smiled, loving the way her sister's face lit up.

Brenna shook out her shoulders and then her hands, her lashes fluttering against her cheeks as she focused inward. Brightness started at her palms, coalescing until it took shape. Meara squinted, unable to look directly at the ball of light. It flickered like flames, but she felt no heat from it.

With a look of strained concentration, Brenna drew the light up into a column. It blazed, turning Brenna white and splashing the same blinding light across the tree branches nearest to them.

Meara threw an arm up to cover her eyes. "That is incredible," she murmured.

Brenna's smile widened. Her nose wrinkled as she clenched her hands into fists and extinguished the light. "And now heat." Her exhale slowed, no visible sign of magic appearing, but then

Meara felt warmth emanating off of her skin. It was like standing beside a burning hearth.

"Is that uncomfortable?" she asked. Brenna shook her head. "Does it feel hot to you? I would be sweating."

A giggle escaped her sister. "No, it's like being wrapped in a blanket."

"You'll never be cold again," Meara mused.

"That's enough of that," Brenna said, relaxing her stance as the heat faded. "I can hold it longer, but it's exhausting. Besides, this was a motivational display. I really want to see what you can do."

Meara pursed her lips. "I haven't been successful as of yet."

"Do we need the Autumn Lord's assistance?" Brenna teased. "I'm sure he would be thrilled to help."

Meara's gaze could have sliced stone. She exhaled and stretched out her hands before clenching them. Unsure of what to do, she stretched her neck, tipping her head from one side to another, trying to relax herself. Mentally drawing into herself, she looked for that feeling, the icy sense that felt more like an absence than magic within her. Her chin dipped down, her chest rising and falling slowly. After a moment, she looked up.

Brenna shrugged, her cheeks rising in an apologetic half-smile. "Nothing, sorry. Or nothing that I could see. That doesn't mean you weren't working magic."

Her hands rose and flopped back to her sides, palms hitting her brown trousers as she let out a growl of frustration.

"Try to relax," Brenna said, crossing her arms and hugging herself.

"Honestly, this might be worse," Meara said, twisting where she stood. "Before, I didn't know what could happen, now I know I have a bit of magic but it's unreliable and inaccessible."

Brenna grabbed her arms. "You just need time."

"Like you did?" Meara snapped. Her sister's face slackened, brows pinching together as her beautiful amber eyes turned glassy. "I'm sorry. I didn't mean that. It's only that it seemed to come so easily to you."

"I've worked really hard, actually." Brenna's lips pressed together, her tone brittle.

"You're right. You've been diligent, and it shows," Meara said softly.

"I have, but you've been wrapped up in your own worries. You're missing all the wonderful things around you," Brenna chided. Frowning, Meara bit her lip. "You have Cerne's attention, he obviously adores you." Meara opened her mouth to argue, but Brenna held up a finger to stop her. "And we have friends here, nice rooms to stay in, every need met. You have no reason to be unhappy."

Meara's shoulders slumped. "I'm sorry. I do appreciate all those things. But it feels temporary."

"Maybe," Brenna said, "but that's true of everything in life." She rested her head on her shoulder, and slowly Meara relaxed against her. "Come on, try again. Maybe let's go to a shady place and your shadows will feel more at home."

Meara laughed, the tension draining from her. Even if things fell apart, she had her sister. Her sister who now had powerful magic. She allowed Brenna to tug her away from their small clearing and into the smattered shade of swaying treetops.

She sighed, settling her feet into the soil and counting out her breaths. Brenna's words repeated in her mind, a mantra of positivity, and if she believed hard enough, maybe it would unlock the magic she knew was within her.

The stomping of horse hooves drifted through the trees, and Meara's eyes snapped open. Within minutes, a group of horses drew near. She didn't recognize them, and from the white and gray of their clothes, she did not think they belonged to the Autumn Court. She gripped Brenna's arm, ready to pull her sister to safety.

Brenna tugged herself free. "I can handle myself," she muttered. The riders noted them, and the leader peeled off, shouting orders for the rest to continue. His midnight black stallion trotted forward, and the faerie swung from his back with the grace that comes from power and a lifetime of experience.

"Lady Brenna," he exclaimed.

Meara narrowed her eyes, studying his features. He was familiar, but it wasn't until Brenna stepped forward with a bright smile and said, "Emrys!" did she place his face - the king's advisor Brenna had danced with.

His dark hair fell around his face, disheveled from riding hard. He raked his fingers through it, smoothing it back. Everything about him was cold, from his blue-black hair to his marble complexion, but most startling, his eyes shone a reddish brown. His smile revealed canines a bit longer and sharper than the faeries she had grown accustomed to.

"Why are you here?" Brenna asked, drawing near to him. He took her hand and kissed the back, holding it between them longer than necessary. Meara bit the inside of her cheek, resisting the urge to interfere.

Emrys dipped his head, worry darkening his eyes. "Unfortunately, I bring concerning news."

"What?"

"It's best discussed with Lord Cerne. May I escort you back to the lord's manor?" His gentle way of speaking and soft smile felt calculated, like every motion was practiced. Meara bristled.

"Yes, I would love that." Brenna turned, a rosy tinge to her cheeks. "Meara, are you ready to go back, or do you want to stay longer?"

"It's fine," Meara said. Even if she wished to stay longer, she wouldn't leave Brenna alone with this fae male if she could help it.

"Excellent." He looked up, the dappled light painting his pale skin ivory. She had to admit he was handsome, and from the way her sister looked at him, she found him exceedingly appealing. Brenna tucked into his side, wrapping her hands around his arm. He leaned down to speak to her as they walked. The black stallion fell into step alongside them.

Emrys' companions waited at the manor house. He whistled and his horse trotted over to stand with the others milling about, nosing at shrubs and clumps of grass to eat. Five tall fae warriors stood in a line. Seda spoke with the nearest, her hands propped on her hips. Her jaw ticked and every muscle in her arms and back tensed.

"Captain." Emrys greeted Seda. "Is Cerne here? We should speak."

"Yes. We should." She regarded him with a hint of disdain that made Meara want to smile. "Come inside." Begrudgingly, she led the way into the manor house.

CHAPTER THIRTY-TWO

Brenna

renna and Meara followed Emrys and Seda into the manor house and to the meeting room they passed earlier in the morning. Cerne looked up, his eyes flashing. "Emrys," he said, his voice carefully neutral.

Seda stepped to the side, tucking her arms behind her. Her jaw tensed and her words were sharp. "What has happened?"

"The human kingdoms have officially declared war. Liosliath troops have moved into Dornadan, preparing to move on our lands."

"Shit," Cerne said. He turned away from them, his back flexing as he clenched his hands into fists. "What is Argyro doing about it?"

"We are mobilizing the high guard and sending summons to each court to provide forces." Emrys stood against the wall, shoving his hands into the pockets of his jacket.

Cerne looked to Seda and she cleared her throat. "They are ready, all but the newest recruits we discussed. What do you want us to do?"

"Set patrols in place, but have them spend as much time with their families as they can. We will be ready when Court Tara moves."

Emrys withdrew a letter from his jacket and set it on the table. "Here is Argyro's direct orders. Let me know your questions."

"Give me some time," Cerne said, motioning to Seda. She sat at the table and Cerne pulled out a chair and sank into it, his shoulders tense.

"I have to depart before sunset, my guards will stay." Emrys straightened, rolling his shoulders.

Without looking up, Cerne replied, "I will update you before you go."

"Certainly." Emrys strode from the room.

"Are we?" Brenna asked Meara quietly, jerking her head to the door.

She shook her head. "In a moment. I'd like to see what the details are," she muttered. "I'm going to stay a bit."

Nodding, Brenna slipped from the room. She spun in the hall, looking for Emrys' retreating back, but he wasn't walking away. He leaned his shoulder against the wood paneling, his eyes on her. The dimpled smirk on his face told her that he had been waiting for her to follow. Her heart leapt into her throat and she felt the familiar buzz of her magic rising as her emotions intensified.

He pushed off the wall and stalked closer. As Emrys leaned into her space, the warm scent of copper and salt washed over her. She wanted to take it into her lungs until it became a part of her. His voice was smooth. "I'd like to take you for a walk."

"Yes." She fought to keep her eyes open, overwhelmed by his close presence. She leaned toward him as he pulled away, leaving her swaying in the space between them. "Lord Emrys, are you influencing my emotions?"

"No, would you like me to?" His hand brushed down her upper arm, leaving sparks in its wake.

"No, thank you. I merely wondered if my emotions were true." She wrapped her hands around his arm and let him lead the way through the manor house and out the ornate doors. The warmer midday air greeted them, rich with the scent of sharp pine sap and musty, decomposing leaf litter.

"What were you feeling?" Emrys murmured, leading her down the path until the river branched off.

"Unexpected ones," Brenna said, her cheeks flushing. "I didn't know if I would see you again, and it was a glad surprise."

"How could I stay away?" he said softly, causing her stomach to flip. "You look lovely."

"Thank you," she said, looking up at him. They wandered along the edge of the hill, the rushing water to their left until it curved further east and the ground leveled out.

He halted, reaching up to brush a curl off her cheek. "Brenna, I am concerned about this conflict. I would like to take you back to Court Tara and away from here."

"Why? I'm safe here."

"The Autumn Court borders the human kingdoms, and this is most likely where any battles will take place. If nothing else, the humans will be testing our resolve in these woods. You would be safer at the high king's palace."

"With you?" she asked, her face heating further when she realized how blatant her words had been.

He smiled, and her heart leapt at the sight. "Some of the time. But I am focused on ending this war before it begins, though I am not sure it's possible at this point." His expression faded into a frown, and it was her turn to run a hand up his arm comfortingly.

"I am confident you'll find a peaceful solution."

"I hope so." He caught her wrist, turning it over to kiss the inside of her palm. He cradled her hand, holding it against his lips for a moment. Disappointment prickled her as he lowered her hand, though he kept ahold of it, twining their fingers together.

She resisted the urge to glance at the place their hands joined. She had met a powerful faerie, second to the high king, and he was interested in her. Her pulse fluttered, speeding as his dimple reappeared. He cocked his head, studying her. "So will you come back with me?"

Her teeth scraped her bottom lip as her eyes flickered from his mouth to his eyes. "I'd have to talk with my sister."

"Of course," he said, looking away from her and breaking the intense connection. "I can stay here for a time, but I must travel north soon."

"To where?"

"I have been tasked with collecting someone from exile to help with the potential fighting."

"Someone from exile?" she echoed, her voice pitching higher.

Emrys chuckled, rubbing his thumb over the back of her hand. "Don't worry. He isn't dangerous to me. Honestly, I don't agree with the decision to exile him." He paused, shrugging. "I understand his reasons for what he did and they aren't likely to repeat."

"Really? What did he do?" She couldn't help her curiosity.

"He killed another faerie who had killed his children."

"Is it Cerne's mentor?" she asked, remembering the story. Every time she thought of the empty forge, she felt a surge of pity for the stranger.

"Daryan?" he asked, raising his eyebrows. "I am surprised he would tell you that story about his friend."

"You think he was justified?" she asked.

Emrys nodded slowly. "Wouldn't you kill someone who had killed someone you loved?"

"I don't know," she admitted. "I can't imagine killing anyone."

"You are exquisite," he murmured, brushing her hair over her shoulder, then skimming his knuckles down the side of her neck and over the skin he had uncovered.

Her breath faltered, and she fought to keep her voice even. "What I don't understand is why another lord would kill his children. That seems tragic."

Emrys' dimple indented as he pursed his lips thoughtfully. "There was a prophecy. The seers of the Winter Court often provide prophecies whenever an heir of a court is born, but this one was tricky."

"What did it say?" she said, her brows furrowing.

"That one of the babies would lead armies of darkness. Or something like that. I don't remember the details. You'd have to ask the Winter Court."

"Oh," she breathed. "So the Summer Lord wanted to eliminate the threat before anything bad could happen. That's still terrible of him."

"Yes, and he paid with his life."

"The whole story is so sad," she said, comforted when he looped an arm over her shoulders and pulled her into his chest.

"It is, and it was a terrible decision Elio made, but I understand it. Just as I understand Daryan's revenge against him."

Brenna wanted to ask him if he found it abhorrent or if he justified the sacrifice, but she was too afraid of his answer to voice the question. Leaders had to make horrifying decisions.

"Enough talk of tragedies. I would love to see your magic again," he murmured, his breath on her hair. "If you would be so generous."

She was reluctant to move away from his warm embrace, but she also wanted to please him. Straightening, she held up a hand and called forth a small flame. "I can do more than this," she said, augmenting the flame until it was blue at the base and much hotter.

"Impressive," he said. "Many faeries with fire craft can simply light a candle or kindling."

Her earlier sadness burned away and she grinned. Biting her lip, she pulled back the heat and increased the luminescence until she held a ball of light so bright it hurt to look at.

"Incredible," he said, reaching out to touch. His hand glowed red as the light shone through his skin, illuminating blood and bone. She let it extinguish, her chest rising and falling faster.

"Can you tell me more about your magic? You said you could do more with those you have a connection with?"

"Are you asking for a demonstration?" he asked slyly.

Her heart rate sped, nerves gripping her. "Maybe. Is there any risk to me?"

His expression was wholly sincere as he said slowly, "I would never hurt you." He raised her hand to his lips, placing a kiss on her wrist. She tensed, waiting for the pierce of teeth, but he drew her closer and pressed his lips to the inside of her forearm. She gasped as he trailed kisses to the crook of her elbow.

She leaned back as he pulled the inside of her arm to his mouth. His dimple appeared as he smirked, his mouth still against her skin. She felt as if her knees would have given out if it wasn't for his grip on her arm.

The moment heated, her stomach clenching and pulse pounding in her ears, before he closed his lips over the tender skin in the crook of her elbow and bit.

Instinct spurred her to pull away, but his grip on her arm was steel. He removed one hand and wrapped it around her waist, supporting her as she sagged against him. The pinching pain of his bite faded, leaving the strange pull of him drinking her blood. His adam's apple bobbed and she watched in fascination as he swallowed.

His hold on her arm released suddenly and he pressed his hand into her back, easing her back onto her feet. "I'm sorry," she muttered, a flush rising up her neck. "That was unexpected."

"Did you feel pain?" he asked softly. Brenna shook her head. "Ready to see what else I can do?" He raised one eyebrow, inviting her curiosity. Gingerly, he turned her arm to show blood running from the punctures. She swayed on her feet, feeling faint, and his hold on her tightened. "Stay with me. I can make it better. Watch."

He wiped his thumb over the marks, cleaning the blood away. The tiny holes were gone, the skin unmarked.

She took a breath and rubbed at the spot. "You can heal."

Emrys nodded. He sucked the blood off his thumb, grinning at her while he did it. Her lips parted as she watched his movement. She wanted that touch on her mouth.

He had drunk her blood twice, kissed her skin, but had yet to kiss her mouth. She ached for it. The need consumed her until she could hardly think straight. Her breathing grew shallow, caught in his snare. His palm skimmed her upper arm, joining the other at her waist.

"Brenna!" Meara called.

She leapt back from Emrys, her blush deepening as he let out a low chuckle. Ignoring him, she waved at her sister, who strode toward them. Her hair streamed out behind her like a raven cape.

Behind her, Cerne transitioned from stag to male in a shimmer of magic.

"What's wrong?" Brenna asked, taking a step toward her sister.

"There was a raiding party of humans on the south side of Roven," Cerne said, his words clipped. "It's not the time to be wandering in the woods."

With those words, her blood went from hot to chilled. If Cerne was worried, it must be serious. Emrys moved to her side, his hand settling on the small of her back. Protective. Her attention wavered between Meara's worried expression and Emrys' serious frown.

"We need to go," Meara snapped, reaching for Brenna's hand. Giving in to her sister's demands, Brenna allowed herself to be tugged forward. Cerne led the way and Emrys fell into step behind them. Brenna felt his eyes on her back like a phantom touch.

They rose up the hill, only going a short way before Cerne halted. Brenna bumped into Meara's back, the hold on her hand squeezing painfully. He looked back, his intense focus settling on Emrys for a split second. Silent communication flashed between them.

"What is happening?" Meara hissed.

"There is someone nearby. It sounds like several people, and they are moving too loudly to be faeries."

Meara pulled a familiar blade from her pocket. Brenna felt powerless, but she knew that wasn't the case. She rolled a small flame between her fingers, reminding herself of all she could do. She could burn the skin off an attacker if they got close enough.

"There," Emrys said, his voice low and dangerous. Meara tensed beside her, and Brenna took a deep breath, readying herself for whatever came next.

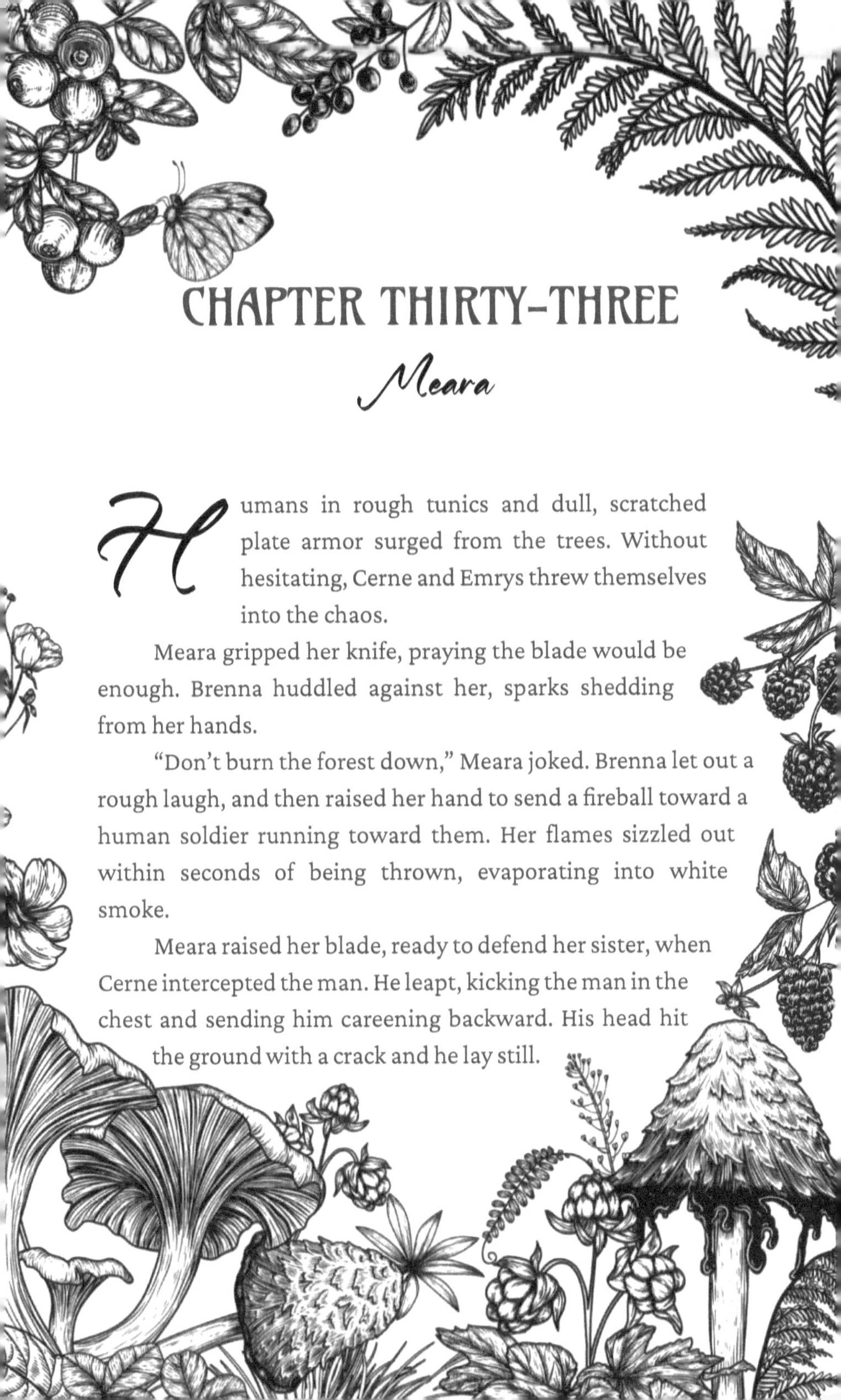

CHAPTER THIRTY-THREE
Meara

Humans in rough tunics and dull, scratched plate armor surged from the trees. Without hesitating, Cerne and Emrys threw themselves into the chaos.

Meara gripped her knife, praying the blade would be enough. Brenna huddled against her, sparks shedding from her hands.

"Don't burn the forest down," Meara joked. Brenna let out a rough laugh, and then raised her hand to send a fireball toward a human soldier running toward them. Her flames sizzled out within seconds of being thrown, evaporating into white smoke.

Meara raised her blade, ready to defend her sister, when Cerne intercepted the man. He leapt, kicking the man in the chest and sending him careening backward. His head hit the ground with a crack and he lay still.

Cerne spun, moving on to the next opponent with the fluid grace of a predator.

Fear seized Meara's muscles, causing her hand to shake. She squeezed the handle of her blade tighter and focused on breathing and staying vigilant. Emrys moved through the men, slashing and stabbing with the dagger from his belt. Cerne had been unarmed, but now he wielded a short sword he took from one of the attackers.

A tall warrior swung his sword at Cerne who leapt back to avoid being sliced open. With his free hand, he knocked the man's arm aside and dove in, striking him with the butt of his weapon. He collapsed and Cerne was already dancing away to face the next enemy.

Several of the men turned and ran and the fae males did nothing to stop them. A few humans lay on the ground unconscious or moaning in pain, blood dripping from broken noses. Cerne turned, looking Meara up and down.

A zing pierced the air, followed by a sickening sound of flesh being pierced, and Brenna shrieked. She fell to her knees, grasping at her stomach.

Meara screamed, staring at the man sitting up, his hand still raised from throwing a dagger. Emrys let out a snarl and swung his blade, slicing the man across his throat in one vicious movement.

Brenna whimpered. The short knife stuck from her ribs, blood welling around it. Meara grabbed her sister under the arms and eased her back into her lap. Emrys hit the ground on his knees, pressing his hands around the wound. Brenna blinked at him, shock and pain seizing her features.

"Can you heal her?" Cerne asked, still scanning the area for more attackers.

Emrys bowed his head and placed his hands on Brenna's ribs. His magic was a dark haze in Meara's senses. Nothing happened.

"Not without more of her blood," he answered, his voice ragged.

"Don't take her blood," Meara snapped without thought.

"It's the only way I can heal her," Emrys replied, meeting her anger with a flare of his own.

"It's okay," Brenna said through the pain pinching all of her features. "Please."

"I've got you," Emrys said, using his dagger to cut the fabric away from her torso. "Hold her still," he instructed before grabbing the blade's handle and yanking it from her body. Blood gushed from the hole. Meara let out a strangled cry at the sight. Brenna stiffened, her breathing shortening into quick gasps.

Emrys lowered his face to her stomach and closed his mouth over the wound, drinking directly from the injury. Meara's stomach churned and she had to look away. Brenna's eyes remained squeezed shut.

With a growl, Emrys pulled back, blood on his lips. He covered the wound with his hands and closed his eyes. A moment later, Brenna relaxed and her breathing slowed and deepened. Emrys wiped away the remaining blood, revealing smooth skin with a faint white scar where the blade cut.

"Thank you," Meara choked out. "Did she pass out?"

"Sleeping," he said. "It will help her heal." Sighing, he sat back on his heels, wiping the back of his hand over his mouth.

"We need to get back now," Cerne said. "I can send guards to round up these fools and deposit them on the border. I'd rather not be here when they wake."

Emrys nodded curtly and slid his arms under Brenna's back and knees, lifting her in a bridal hold. Her head tucked against his chest. Meara bit her lip, wanting to shield her from him, but he was already off, walking toward the manor house.

Cerne stalked behind her with his stolen blade in hand,

continually looking for any new threat. He didn't relax until they reached his estate. Once indoors, he threw the sword on the ground, where it clanged against the hard floor.

Meara led Emrys to their rooms. Kirrily rushed in, fussing over Brenna and placing a pillow under her head as Emrys laid her across the bed.

He stood against the wall and watched Brenna as she slept. Meara tried to ignore him, but having a strange male in their room set her on edge. She kept her eyes on Brenna and ignored him.

Brenna's chest raised and lowered with a slow rhythm. Color tinged her cheeks, and Meara took that as a good sign.

"She will be fine," Emrys murmured.

Her lip curled. "Are you a dearg due?"

Emrys regarded her cooly, wiping away a smear of blood on his chin. "My mother was. I do not require blood to survive, so no, I am not."

"But you drink it," she stated.

"It's my magic craft and how I healed your sister." He met her suspicion with calm confidence.

She snapped her mouth closed and perched on the bed beside Brenna, brushing tendrils of damp hair from her cheeks.

"How is she?" Cerne said, filling the doorway. His hand buttoned up a clean shirt as he assessed the room.

"She seems well," Meara said. Brenna groaned and turned on her side, bringing her hand up to cover her face. Meara brushed her palm down her sister's limp arm. "How do you feel?"

"Like I got walloped by a tree," Brenna whined. Scrubbing her face, she eased up to sit. Her hand went to her exposed stomach, and her cheeks flushed as she remembered. Her fingers traced over the healed skin as she looked up at Emrys. "Thank you."

He crossed the room and crouched beside her. "Happy to do it, but please do not get injured like that again. It was distressing," he said with a smirk.

She scrunched her nose as she smiled back.

Emrys continued, "This is why I wanted you to come back to Court Tara. The Autumn Court will not be a safe place until this conflict is handled."

"What about all the other families and children?" Brenna asked, her brow furrowing.

Cerne folded his arms. "Those with children or unable to defend themselves are evacuating as we speak."

"I don't want to run," Brenna said, "but if it's helpful to have us leave, of course." Her sincere gaze moved to Cerne.

Raising a hand, Cerne interjected, "Another option would be leaving for the Samhain celebration a few days early."

"The Summer Court," Emrys muttered, frowning.

The lines forming around Cerne's mouth were the only indication of his irritation. "It's further than Court Tara and less likely to become a target if the humans were to march through my land."

"We will go to Samhain early," Meara said, laying her hand across Brenna's knee. "But if you don't mind, Brenna needs to rest and change into clothing that is not ripped apart."

Emrys exhaled, a sharp, rough sound. Face tipped up, he reached out. Brenna took his offered hand, and he kissed her fingertips. "I will come to Samhain, but first I have my tasks to accomplish. Will you be okay?" She nodded, her eyes turning glassy as a smile bloomed across her face.

"I will see you in the Summer Court, then." He nodded, releasing her hand reluctantly before he turned and exited.

Cerne scowled at his retreating back, and it made Meara want to kiss him. It felt good to have someone agree with her for once.

"Ayala will join you for Samhain, she returned this morning, but I am afraid I can't spare Tayen." He tilted his head, mossy eyes flickering between the sisters.

"That's fine. Now go," Meara said, a smile threatening to break through her serious expression.

With one last lingering glance, Cerne left, leaving Meara to prepare for their unexpected travel.

The forest faded into rolling fields of green grass, saturated gold in the afternoon light. Small copses of scrub trees scattered the landscape, huddling in the niches between hills.

The air warmed and Meara felt as if they had slipped back a season into the heart of summer. A sheen of sweat slicked her skin, cooling her. Bran tossed his dark mane, as if he was happy to visit somewhere other than the white stone fortress of Court Tara.

Small cottages of sun washed stone dotted the expanse. The faeries of the Summer Court were as diverse as those she had gotten to know at Roven, but their skin leaned darker, and she admired the multitude of freckles coating the skin of many fae they passed.

Their horses slowed as they climbed a hill ringed in low bushy trees in shades of muted chartreuse. As they cleared the brush, Meara drew in a breath.

The Summer Lady's estate rose up like a castle of pale yellow stones. Sunset turned the sides blazing white and the shadows a deeper honey, while the red clay roof tiles flamed. While the autumn manor house nestled into the bosom of the forest, the summer palace crowned the land proudly. From the higher vantage point, Meara could see fields of grain swaying in the light breeze to the southwest and rows of bushes and vines studded with vegetables further north.

"Welcome to the Summer Court," a slender faerie announced. Her skin glowed with a verdant luster, her hair a warm silver that looked almost transparent. It flowed around her as she moved, brushing over her loose linen tunic.

Ayala swung from her mount and addressed the sylph. Within moments, their bags were collected, their horses handed off to a groomsman, and they were striding through the summer manor.

The passageway was open on one side to the fields, with wide arches supporting the glass roof and defining the walkway from the outdoors.

The escort halted, and they followed his example, as a resplendent fae female approached with an entourage in her wake. Meara would have been able to pick her out of a crowd as Luce's mother. Her skin glowed bronze, only a few shades lighter than Brenna's.

The Summer Lady's hair fell around her waist in luscious waves, deep honey streaked through with platinum, like rays of sun. Delicate flaxen vines wound through her hair, curling at the ends. Even her dress was gilded with metallic beading across the bodice over ivory skirts that flowed down her waiflike figure.

Her thin lips curved downward at the sight of her visitors, and her fingers came up to brush her hair back. Rings glittered across her hands and up her tapered ears.

Ayala and Brenna curtsied, and Meara copied the best she could. She felt Aletris' eyes on her, and the disdain was like a dampness creeping over her body.

"So lovely to receive the Autumn Court," she said. As she moved, the golden diadem woven into her hair glittered with sheer jewels cut like leaves.

Ayala smiled, putting on graces she reserved for those she wished to impress. "Lady Aletris, thank you for receiving us. This is Lady Brenna and Lady Meara. They were presented at Court Tara recently."

"Welcome to Elhora. What brings you earlier than expected?"

"How could we resist the allure of your court?" Her delicate brows arched.

Meara let out a smothered laugh. After the stress of the day, her tolerance for staying silent was waning. Aletris looked up sharply, and Meara lowered her face, praying the Summer Lady would think the noise had been a cough.

"It is always so lovely here," Ayala rushed to say, "and we appreciate your hospitality."

"Of course," Lady Aletris said, her frown deepening. "Though I am not sure your entire party feels that way. Please, return to the Autumn Court or whatever hole you came from if you do not wish to be here."

Brenna tensed as Ayala worked to soothe the ruler. "My lady, we truly are blessed to be in your lands, but it has been a long and difficult day."

Aletris studied them, the silence stifling. "There will be no formal meals or events until Samhain, so you'll have to entertain yourselves." She waved her hand in a courtly dismissal. "Until then."

"Thank you," Brenna said.

"Ladies, if you would please follow me," the ethereal steward said, gliding down an interior hallway.

Meara seethed, ashamed of her blunder and furious at the haughty Summer Lady. Ayala drew closer as they walked through the passageway. "Relax. She would have found some fault in you regardless." With a flick of her hair, Ayala sauntered ahead. Meara blinked, her lips parting in surprise. That was remarkably kind coming from Ayala.

Brenna slowed, looking over her shoulder at her sister. "Come on, let's go." Meara hated the sympathy in her gaze. Swallowing her remaining irritation, she surged forward to loop her arm through Brenna's.

Ayala swept into the guest apartments ahead of them, surveying them with a curl of her lip. "You might as well take the biggest room. I doubt Cerne will stay the night. Tayen might, if he can come."

"Will you be staying in the rooms?" Meara asked, raising one eyebrow.

"Not if I can help it." Ayala sighed, as if the entire situation was terribly tiring to her. "We are invited to a gathering tonight. Cerne never likes to go, but I find Luce's friends entertaining." She tugged the curtain open to let purple light pour into the space, illuminating a bouquet of campion flowers set on a low table surrounded by comfortable seating.

"Friends?" Brenna asked absently as she trailed her finger across the book spines stacked on a pale wood bookcase with a curved top.

"Yes, of course. I have friends everywhere. Those loyal to Luce are generally trustworthy, so they rarely give me any information intentionally, but you can learn a lot when you watch closely."

Meara smiled, shaking her head as she walked into the room Ayala suggested they take. A massive four poster bed covered one wall, and a door led to a private bathing chamber. Everything was shades of wheat and grass with glimmers of gold. The oak furniture gleamed, freshly polished. Despite the fact they arrived earlier than expected, their rooms were immaculate.

Servants entered and placed their bags upon the bench at the foot of their bed, and Meara joined her sister in hanging their dresses to air out.

Task complete, Meara wandered back into the sitting room. Linen seating circled around a central table, but all the places were empty. Ayala had disappeared already. Rolling her eyes, Meara returned to their bedroom and sat by while Brenna brushed out her hair.

"So what do you think of the Summer Court?" she asked.

Brenna shifted where she sat, and her voice sounded as if she was grinning. "I think Samhain is going to be wonderful. But I'm not sure what we will do until then. Perhaps they have a library."

"What do the fae do for Samhain?"

"Well," Brenna said, chewing on her lip. "It's to celebrate the end of the harvest season, and the Summer Court and Autumn Court both celebrate that. So we will see."

Sighing, Meara relaxed into her seat as Brenna recalled everything she knew about the Summer Court and fae traditions around Samhain. She had been listening and learning, while Meara was stewing over her blocked magic. Thank goodness one of them was having success in these fae lands.

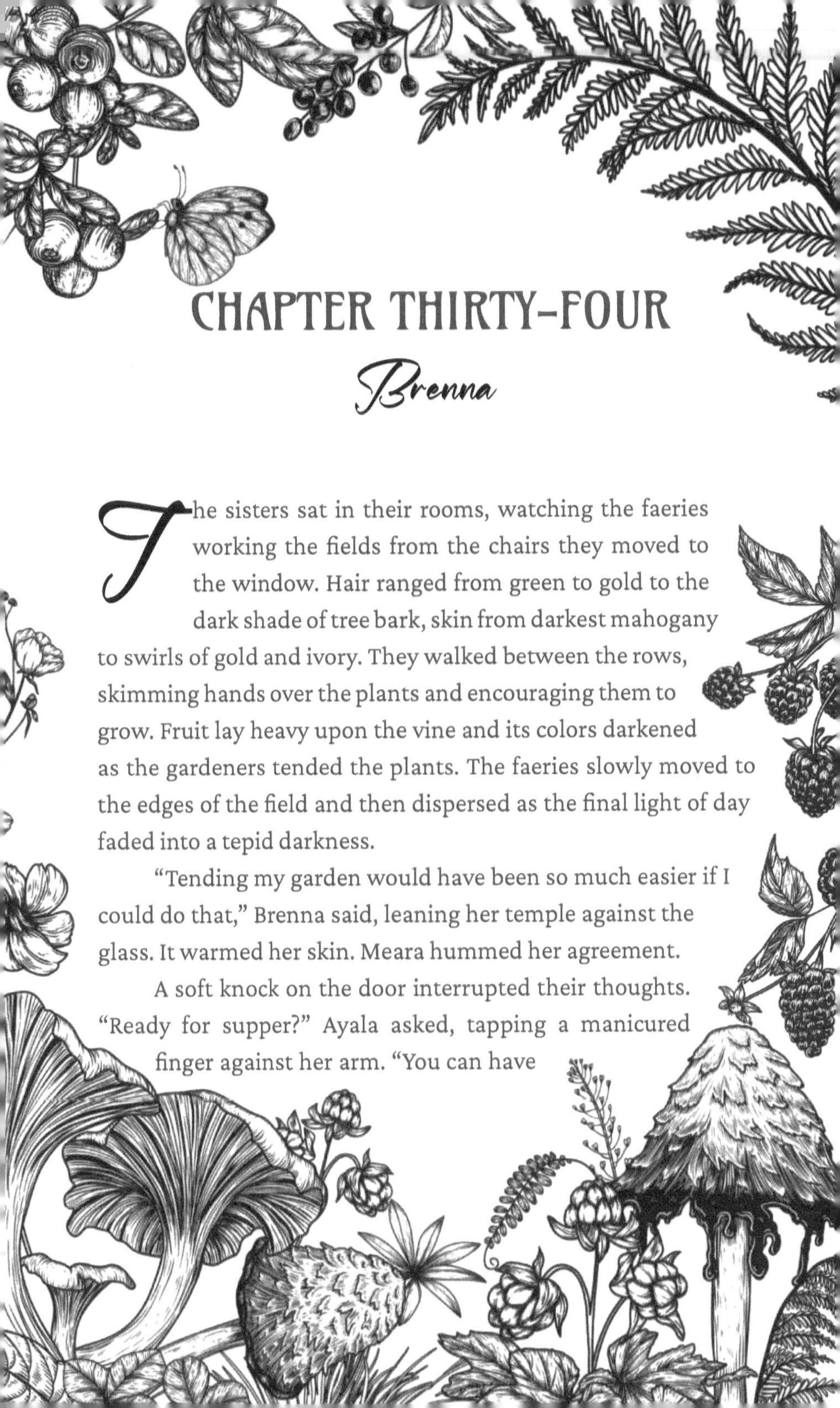

CHAPTER THIRTY-FOUR
Brenna

The sisters sat in their rooms, watching the faeries working the fields from the chairs they moved to the window. Hair ranged from green to gold to the dark shade of tree bark, skin from darkest mahogany to swirls of gold and ivory. They walked between the rows, skimming hands over the plants and encouraging them to grow. Fruit lay heavy upon the vine and its colors darkened as the gardeners tended the plants. The faeries slowly moved to the edges of the field and then dispersed as the final light of day faded into a tepid darkness.

"Tending my garden would have been so much easier if I could do that," Brenna said, leaning her temple against the glass. It warmed her skin. Meara hummed her agreement.

A soft knock on the door interrupted their thoughts. "Ready for supper?" Ayala asked, tapping a manicured finger against her arm. "You can have food brought to our rooms if you don't feel like socializing."

"We are coming," Brenna said, smiling. She tugged on Meara's sleeve, and her sister rose with a huff. Most likely, she would rather eat in their rooms alone, but Brenna needed some cheering and making new friends would do the trick.

Ayala sashayed down the hall as if she owned the summer palace. While it would have bothered Brenna in the past, now it provided comforting familiarity. Even Meara's steps lightened as they passed beautiful tapestries of sun bursts falling over sunflowers and grains.

Their hall opened into a wide terrace. Ornately carved marble columns the color of wheat rose up with sheer curtains draping between them. Two faeries lounged across sofas, and they straightened when Ayala greeted them.

"I hope you haven't missed me too terribly." She flashed a brilliant smile and sank onto a cushion.

The female laughed. "I hear what you aren't saying, Ayala. You'd prefer to stay in the Summer Court with us. You do not have to hide it." Her slender frame relaxed back into the cushions, a riot of white gold curls fanning around her head.

"I know that's *your* dream," Ayala quipped, waving the sisters forward. "Brenna, Meara, this is Vasara," she motioned to the female beside her, "and Harin." The male could have been her sibling, with the same tan skin and pale gold hair. A tidy beard shadowed his jaw.

"It's nice to meet you," he said, leaning forward to take Brenna's hand. She tensed, not wanting another male to kiss her hand after Emrys touched her so tenderly, but he merely raised it in the air in a short greeting and released her. Leaning back, Harin rested his hands behind his head. "So what is the news from the Autumn Court?"

Ayala scoffed. "Are you mining me for information?"

"Maybe," he said, a devious smile widening his full mouth. Not a hint of guilt. From the way Ayala watched him, Brenna wondered if they were close. Perhaps Harin collected information the way Ayala did.

"You'll have to work harder than that to get anything out of her," Vasara said lightly as she reached for a small plate. Brenna studied the spread. Small flatbreads lay stacked in a round dish, while bowls surrounded them with various toppings. Vasara scooped a smooth beige dip onto her flatbread, followed by a spoonful of diced tomatoes and something green. Brenna breathed in the scents and tried to pick through all the new smells. Was that cucumber?

"Have some. It's not going to poison you," Vasara said, her soft smile turned on her. Brenna nodded, taking a plate and copying her choices. Her first bite of flatbread was floury and dense, layered with the rich, salty dip and bright, acidic tomatoes.

Vasara motioned to a bowl of pomegranate pearls. "Try those too. They're delicious."

"Vasara, stop flirting. She is smitten with a high court faerie," Ayala said, rolling her eyes.

Cheeks flushing, Brenna opened her mouth to protest, but Vasara interrupted. "Just for that, I won't be chilling your drink for you," she said, scrunching her nose.

Both women laughed, but when Ayala raised a goblet of sparkling drink, Vasara held her palm up in refusal. "Oh, you are the worst." Ayala pouted, sipping her drink.

Meara and Brenna accepted their own goblets, and Brenna took an experimental sip. It was lighter than wine and it fizzed across her tongue. The tang of alcohol was softened by a sweetness that reminded her of peaches.

A flash of burnished brass caught her eye.

Luce, heir of the Summer Court, stepped in the room and

halted, his brow furrowing as he took in their guests.

Brenna's flush of embarrassment shifted to one of indignation. From the curve of his lips, Luce clearly did not want them here.

"Sit down, Luce, and be friendly. Cerne isn't here," Vasara said.

Exhaling, the golden prince settled into a chair as far from them as possible. Brenna pressed her lips together, trying to not be offended, but his rejection stung. It shouldn't. He was rivals with Cerne, and not someone she wanted to associate with. From Ayala's easy smile, she was unbothered. Beside her, Meara was so tense, Brenna worried she would break. Her food sat untouched.

"Eat," Ayala said softly, eyeing Meara. Brenna felt a surge of gratefulness for the prickly fae female.

Luce sighed audibly, and Brenna focused on her plate. It was Vasara who broke the awkward silence. "So there was word that the humans are moving against us?"

"Yes," Luce said, rubbing his forehead. "We've already received a request to mobilize whatever forces we can offer."

"Us too," Ayala added. "We had to deal with a few humans testing our borders already."

Brenna rubbed at her ribs, phantom pain twinging in her gut. "That's why we came early. To stay out of their way."

"Wise," Harin said, nodding knowingly.

Luce laughed bitterly. "I don't know what they expect from us. Our guard is well trained, but it is small. We are a land of farmers, as you are craftsmen." He swept a hand toward Ayala and the sisters.

"I hope they can negotiate a peaceful solution," Brenna said.

"Unfortunately, I believe we are past that."

Meara's grip on her skirts tightened, wrinkling the fabric. "So will the fae march on the humans?"

"Absolutely not. We will only respond if they move against us," Ayala said, her confidence unwavering.

"Perhaps they won't," Meara said, though it sounded hollow.

"Enough of this saddening news," Vasara said. "We are here to have fun." She raised her goblet and took a long drink. "Let me tell you about my day."

Stories bled into each other, and Brenna drank and laughed. Even Meara relaxed and smiled. The moon was high by the time they trudged back to their rooms.

Birdsong awoke them. The summer finches and jays were louder than the soft whistles and chatters of the forest birds in the Autumn Court. She turned, smiling at her bleary-eyed sister. Meara grunted, dragging herself out of bed and to the washroom.

Brenna followed, washing her face in the ivory basin and gazing out of the arched windows painted the saturated yellow of marigolds. The fields glistened and glittered with dew before the heat of the day burned it away. Fresh flowers covered the table beside the white porcelain soaking tub pushed up against the windows. She wasn't sure she could bathe in that tub when the windows were clear glass. The entire court would see her. That was a problem for later.

"Ayala is gone," Meara said, her voice gravelly. "I thought she was here last night."

"She's a spy, so the sneaking around shouldn't surprise us," Brenna said with a dry laugh. "Let's go look for food. I'm starving. We didn't eat nearly enough last night."

Meara nodded and dressed in her typical trousers and loose tunic, while Brenna selected a dress that would work for an active day. She might as well be comfortable if there was no formal gathering today. They had the entire day free, and tomorrow the rest of the guests would arrive and the celebration would commence.

"Where do we go?" Meara asked, easing the door to their rooms open.

Brenna shrugged. "I suppose we should find someone to ask." They took a few tentative steps into the hall, and when no one appeared, they started walking. Brenna tried to remember the way to the terrace from last night, knowing that path would not lead them to any private bedchambers or office that could get them in trouble.

"Ayala!" Meara yelped.

The female closed a door behind her quietly, her orange hair falling around her in voluminous waves, as if it had been mussed recently.

"Shush," Ayala said, darting toward them and crossing her arms across her chest. "What are you two doing?"

"What are you doing?" Brenna asked, raising an eyebrow.

"Going back to freshen up," she snapped.

"Whose room is that?"

Ayala wrinkled her nose. "None of your business."

"Was Harin working harder to get information from you?"

"Shut up!" Ayala crossed her arms and started to walk away, pausing to look over her shoulder. "Keep going straight and you'll find the kitchens."

"Thank you!" Brenna chimed. Ayala raised her middle finger over her shoulder as she walked away.

Meara pressed her hand to her mouth. "Sounds like she had a nice evening." Brenna grinned at her.

The kitchens were at the end of the hall, and a trio of brownies prepared breakfast for the estate. Egg quiches cooled on the stove, melon was being sliced, and glaze glistened on hand pies. The chefs loaded up two dishes with sticky sweet bread and slices of a vermillion melon with a green rind.

It was early enough that most of the court still slept, so the sisters crossed the hall and stepped onto the grassy hills surrounding the Summer manor.

Strolling along, Brenna admired the rainbow of flowers growing along the edge of the estate. Were they intentionally cultivated, or was the land responding to the magic within the walls?

Meara's steps faltered, and Brenna turned. "What?"

"Luce is there." Meara tipped her chin, directing Brenna to the edge of the field a short ways down the hill.

The heir of the Court of Summer Harvest stood looking out over the ocean of stems. The stalks before him rippled, something moving through the field toward him. Brenna gasped as a huge hound burst from the tall grass. Its tongue lolled from its mouth and its tail wagged. Its head snapped to her, and the creature was bounding up the hill before she could turn to run.

Luce threw his hands up to cup his mouth and called, "He is friendly. Don't be afraid."

The creature barreled into Brenna, and only Meara's hold on her arm kept her upright. She steadied herself and lowered her hands to scratch at the beast's neck. He sat, his long, thin tail sweeping the ground and scattering wisps of dried twigs and leaves.

"Aren't you the sweetest boy?" Brenna crooned, letting the dog lick her hand with so much enthusiasm, his butt lifted from the ground as he scooted closer to her skirts.

"Sorin, down," Luce commanded, and the dog settled. His deep brown eyes begged for more attention, and Brenna couldn't help but scratch below his ear. His tongue fell from his mouth. "I apologize. He is spoiled."

Brenna shook her head. "Don't worry about it."

Meara watched Luce warily, so Brenna straightened and put

on her sweetest smile. "We understand there are no organized events today. We can stay in our rooms, but what else might we occupy our time with?" The dog nudged her hand with his wet nose, and she ran her fingers over his head.

"You are welcome to explore. Although I understand you are still training in your magic. Would you like to join us this morning?"

"Join for training?" Meara clarified.

Luce nodded. "I train with Vasara and Harin. It's good to learn from others."

The sisters exchanged glances. Brenna was intrigued, while Meara hesitated. "Yes," Brenna agreed. "We would appreciate that."

CHAPTER THIRTY-FIVE

Meara

Meara was grateful that Brenna braided her hair into a long rope down her back, because she was already sweating. Wisps of hair clung to her neck and she adjusted the neckline of her tunic.

They followed the summer heir around the side of the estate and down the hillside. Luce's crew trained in a barren circle with the morning sun beating down.

Vasara waited for them and Luce greeted her warmly. She grinned, her dark skin gleaming a burnished bronze in the strong light. "I'm glad you came. I can't wait to see what you can do."

Brenna bit her lip, eyeing the fae female. "What is your magic?"

"Nothing you have to worry about," she said with a conspiratorial wink. "Luce told me you displayed fire craft at the high court?" Brenna nodded, and Vasara brought her hands up. Frost covered her fingers and she flicked water away as the heat melted it.

"You have ice magic," Meara said.

With a nod, Vasara explained, "Yes, one of my parents is a frost sprite from the Winter Court."

"Why do you live in the Summer Court? Is it not uncomfortable for you?"

"I can keep cool better than most, and my mother is from here. She's more fun to be around than that freezing bastard." Shrugging, Vasara waved her hand, sending a wave of coolness over the sisters.

"Oh, that feels lovely," Brenna said, tipping her chin up to cool her neck. "It really is quite warm here. I am concerned that I will require a bath today, but the washroom in our suite has windows near the tub."

Vasara laughed. "The windows are etched. They look clear from inside, but I promise they are obscured from outside."

"Truly?"

"Yes, I swear. Take a look." She pointed up the house, and Meara squinted, scanning the windows until she spotted a smaller one that could have been a bathroom. Indeed, it looked cloudy and she could not see in clearly. She located several windows like that. "Don't take my word for it. You can look closely at the glass when you return and you'll see the marks."

"Good to know," Meara muttered.

"Thank you, Vasara." Brenna said with an embarrassed giggle. "I think you've saved me from offending the entire court with my smell."

"Brenna!" Meara exclaimed, but her sister only laughed harder. Luce shook his head and turned away while Vasara threw her head back and joined in the laughter.

"We are here to train," Vasara said, wiping a tear from her eye with the back of her hand. "Fire faerie, you should go work with Luce. He has enough light craft he should be able to show you a few things. And Meara, you are with me."

Meara went still, watching as Vasara rolled her shoulders and jumped on the balls of her feet, her mass of snowy hair shimmering as she moved.

"I haven't been able to access my magic consistently," Meara warned.

Brenna brushed past her and murmured, "Give it another try. You'll figure it out."

"What can you do?" Vasara asked, beginning to pace before her.

Meara swallowed, wiping her sweaty palms along her trousers. "I've summoned shadows a few times, but not often. Or even on command, really."

"What about under pressure?" Vasara asked.

Shaking her head, Meara admitted, "We were attacked by human raiders and I could do nothing."

"Then let's spar. We can get your body moving, relax your mind, and see what happens." Vasara didn't wait for confirmation, but swept her foot out.

Startled, Meara leapt, landing hard on both feet. She overbalanced and raised her arms to catch her balance. The ice faerie moved in quick, swinging with her hand as if she held a blade. Meara blocked but was pushed back a step. Vasara slowed, allowing Meara to loosen and begin to meet her blows. Soon, she was swinging and kicking too, the physicality of it bringing a smile to her face.

Vasara turned, gaining some distance. She waved a hand and summoned a blade of ice. Water dripped from the tip, but it would pierce all the same. Meara sucked in a breath, refusing to let surprise paralyze her. Vasara swung for her, and as Meara pushed her back, Vasara said, "Call your shadows. Do it, now!"

Meara blinked, trying desperately to reach inside of herself and find something that had been absent every other time. Vasara moved faster, shoving her back. Meara threw up her arms to block, and Vasara pushed her down, holding the knife over her as water dripped onto her chest and down her neck.

"Nothing?" Vasara said, disappointment drawing out her word as she gracefully rose.

"No," Meara said, scrambling to her feet. She raised her fists, unsure if Vasara would come at her again. The blonde faerie turned away, chewing on a long nail while she thought.

Brenna held a ball of light and slowly the brightness widened until Meara could not look in her direction. She fisted her hands against her thighs, wanting to scream. Her sister would advance in her magic and gain more respect until she wouldn't even want Meara in the same room. She would be the magical dud, shunned and alone.

When the light faded, Meara looked up to see her sister frowning at her, pity in her eyes. Meara's anger doubled. Behind her, Luce watched with a detached curiosity, and beside him, Harin folded his arms. All three approached Meara, and she forced her hands to relax.

Luce spoke first, his low voice rough. "What were you feeling when you summoned shadows at the high court on the balcony?"

Brenna's head tilted, one eyebrow rising.

"Nothing," Meara said. "It was dark, and I was upset. But it wasn't intentional."

Luce frowned, turning to Harin. His friend nodded and said, "Meara, I think I can help. Our craft may work in similar ways. Are you willing to try?"

"I have been trying," Meara said, her shoulders taut. She

wanted to get out of here. The sun was too bright, making her eyes water, and everyone was surely judging her failure as they wielded their magic craft effortlessly.

Brenna squeezed her hand. "Give him a chance. You're about to have a breakthrough, I can feel it."

"Are you a seer now?" Meara snapped, instantly regretting the hurt in Brenna's eyes. Her sister smiled and took a quick breath. "I'm sorry, Brenna. I'll try."

Luce and Brenna retreated, leaving Harin facing her. He stood a head taller, and she scowled as he drew nearer, forcing her to look upward. His face was stoic but gentle. "Can you feel your magic within yourself?"

Meara's eyes narrowed. "Not really." She looked him up and down. "What are your abilities?"

"Illusion." His answer came without hesitation.

"Like what?" Meara tilted her head.

The corner of Harin's mouth pulled up into a smirk as he raised a hand. Meara jolted as the people around them disappeared and she stood alone in the sparring ring with Harin. Feeling panic rising, she took a shaky breath and confirmed, "This isn't real."

Harin's hand dropped and the illusion evaporated.

"Well that has to be useful in certain situations," Meara muttered. He chuckled. "So how can you help me when no one else could? Because I've been trying and trying and I'm starting to think it's hopeless."

"Stop," he said, his voice dropping. She looked up, her stomach churning at the understanding in his eyes. "For most faeries, their craft comes from within. Fire or ice in their blood, and it fights to come out. For me, there is nothing - until I use it. Only then can I feel the energy. So what do you feel when you summon shadows?"

She dragged her teeth over her bottom lip, trying to

remember. "It was cold. Well, not really. It felt uncomfortable in the same way being cold is uncomfortable. Hurt a little."

"That's your magic."

"So how can I summon it when I desire?"

He shrugged. "That depends on you, we are all different. But start by reaching outside of yourself."

She remembered how her shadows came at night when darkness surrounded her. If it didn't come from within her, maybe it was from beyond her body and mind. Eyes squeezing shut, Meara turned her inward focus out, searching for any buzz of magic around her. Her inhale sucked in through her teeth, the sensation of magic all around her roaring to life. She could feel Brenna's bright, burning magic, something cool and sleek within Vasara, and a steady healing light from Luce. Wisps of magic clung all around her, and when she reached for them, they came to her. Her eyes opened, and her mouth fell open as the whispers of shadows swirled around her palm.

"How about that?" Harin said, holding his arms and stepping back. Meara basked in his proud grin.

"Meara!" Brenna squealed, clapping her hands. "Look at that! You're incredible."

As her attention moved from the magic in her grasp to her sister's beaming smile, the shadows faded and fell away entirely. She frowned, but Brenna threw her arms around her. "That was amazing. You can do it again and again until it's easy."

"That sounds exhausting," Meara muttered. Already a heaviness hung over her limbs. "I need a nap now."

Luce stepped closer, his brow furrowed. "You summoned them, but will they be of any aid to you in a fight?" He withdrew a spear from his back, not the golden shining spear from the high court, but a simple wood and steel spear like any guard might hold. He tossed it to her, and held out his hand. Vasara tossed another to him.

Meara gripped the length of the spear, feeling the worn wood under her fingers. Luce stalked sideways, and she had to turn to keep him from circling her.

"If you can't summon your craft when it counts, it is useless to you." He darted forward, bringing his weapon down. She blocked him, but the force shoved her back a pace, her heels digging into the dirt.

Luce spun, swinging sideways, and when she blocked the second powerful blow, it threw her off balance. She stepped back, but he pressed forward, and she could not regain her footing. Struggling to block and also catch herself, Meara tumbled to the ground. She attempted to scramble up, but a spear pressed into her chest, forcing her to lay back.

"What will you do now?" he said, each word a threat.

Meara braced herself and threw her consciousness outward, drawing up all the shreds of magic until darkness swirled around her. If she was lucky, she could blind him until she could get away. With all the conviction she had, she flung the shadows at him. Darkness rushed upward, and Luce stepped back. She wasted no time rolling away and leaping to her feet.

When the shadows dropped away, Luce sought her out and nodded his approval. "Well done. It is a start."

Vasara rubbed her hands over her arms. "That felt like a waking nightmare."

Brenna shivered, plastering an encouraging smile as she looped her arm with Meara's. "That was fantastic. I think you've earned a good meal. Is there food to be had?"

"Yes, I need a drink after that," Vasara huffed.

As they entered the manor house, Luce excused himself, leaving the four of them to lounge around the small dining room. Harin sent for food, and Ayala joined them as it was delivered.

Unease still churned in Meara's gut, but she had to admit she was slowly warming to Ayala's friends in the Summer Court.

They ate seasoned and steamed river fish over a bed of greens dressed with lemon and oil. The bitter, sour taste cut through the oily fish. Vasara produced a white tea that tasted like sunshine with a hint of blueberry and rosemary.

Harin shared about his recent visit to the Observatory and the art and music being produced. Brenna was fully relaxed and giggled in response to his storytelling. Meara wished she could trust their companions and enjoy herself the way Brenna did. Only when she glanced up and met her gaze did Brenna's brow pinch with concern.

Back in their room, Meara watched Brenna while she fussed over their dresses. She sighed, having had enough. "What is your concern?"

"Nothing," Brenna said, her answer too quick.

"Brenna." Meara crossed her arms.

Her sister huffed and perched on the end of the bed. Meara waited. Brenna pressed her lips into a line, fiddling with her fingers in her lap. Finally, she spoke. "I'm so happy you figured out how to access your magic, but it felt dark."

"It's shadows," Meara deadpanned.

"It felt scary. Terrifying actually."

Unsure of what to do with that information, Meara stood and turned in place, considering walking out of the door.

Brenna rose, moving behind her. "I'm not sure demonstrating that magic in front of a bunch of faeries we don't know is wise. Perhaps you should learn to separate the shadows from that awful feeling before you go showing them off."

Twisting to face her, Meara snapped, "I don't have any intention of showing off my magic. I'm not going to parade around with a fireball in hand every chance I get."

Brenna froze, hurt filling her eyes. "I understand." Her words were clipped, and she spun away, grabbing the hairbrush and plopping into the seat before the dressing table.

"I'm sorry," Meara said, crossing to her and crouching beside her chair. "I know you're watching out for me. I appreciate you being conscious of those things."

An angry tear tracked down her cheek as Brenna stubbornly ignored her and dragged a brush through her hair. Meara laid her arm across her sister's lap and rested her chin on it. After a few minutes, Brenna brushed her fingers over Meara's hair.

"I know it's been hard for you not having your magic while mine came so easily. I wish I could have done more to help."

"Nonsense, there is nothing you could have done, and you've been there with me the whole time," Meara said with a forced smile. "Let's take a walk in the fields before dinner. I want to see the preparations for tomorrow's celebration."

The girls wandered the estate, rested and ate, and when Brenna was distracted with a book, Meara snuck into the empty bedroom and summoned her shadows. Her heart raced as they gathered around her. It felt effortless, though she tired quickly. If this was how Brenna's flames felt, no wonder she was displaying them so readily. Exhaustion snuck up on her.

The second morning, Ayala joined them for breakfast and the girls enjoyed quiet companionship. The three of them waited, knowing that at some point, Cerne and hopefully Tayen would join them.

Meara locked herself in the spare bedroom and spun shadows around her fingers, let them swirl around her ankles and crawl up the feet of the bed frame she sat perched on. It felt freeing, though her anxiety rose when she thought about showing this magic to others. Not after even her sister recoiled from it.

When the daylight began to fade, Ayala proclaimed they

should get ready for Samhain, and the dumb boys would arrive whenever they managed to get their asses there.

Brenna begged Meara to let her style her hair, and Meara acquiesced. She spent the better part of an hour braiding her hair into a complex design that dripped down the back of her head over a layer that Brenna had left loose. Once she was done, they had little time left to change, and both girls struggled into their dresses and took turns doing up their laces.

"Lovely," Brenna murmured, running her hands down the bronze silk of her skirts. Lace ran from the waist up over her breasts, providing structure to the dress that was otherwise nothing more than layers of diaphanous silk flowing over her body. A slit ran up her thigh, but she seemed unbothered by it.

Meara glanced at herself in the mirror, wondering if Dyani had sensed something about her magic. Her dress was cut much the same, but thin vines snaked over her chest and shoulders, draping down her back and merging to hold the dress together. It was perfect for a harvest celebration, except for the fact everything was a dusky gray, so the vines looked like shadows crawling over her skin.

Brenna held out a piece of black molded fabric, and Meara frowned at it. "What is this?"

"It's your mask. Here." Brenna raised it to her eyes, and Meara pressed it in place while Brenna tied the ribbon into her hair. Turning, she took in the silk arching over the bridge of her nose, dipping around her eyes, and lifting up at the corners with a design that mimicked feathers.

"What am I?" She tilted her head.

"I don't know. A blackbird?"

"What are you?"

Brenna held up a gold mask that curled around her eyes and met with a sunburst tiara. She settled it into her hair and grinned.

"Do I look like a princess?"

"Always," Meara said, her mood lightening at her sister's joy.

"Are you two ever ready on time?" Ayala snapped. She wore a gold dress that Meara recognized as one of her favorites. It clung to her skin as if it was wet, showing every curve of her lean body.

Brenna rolled her eyes and smiled, striding after Ayala with a confidence that warmed Meara's heart. Hopefully this would be an enjoyable evening.

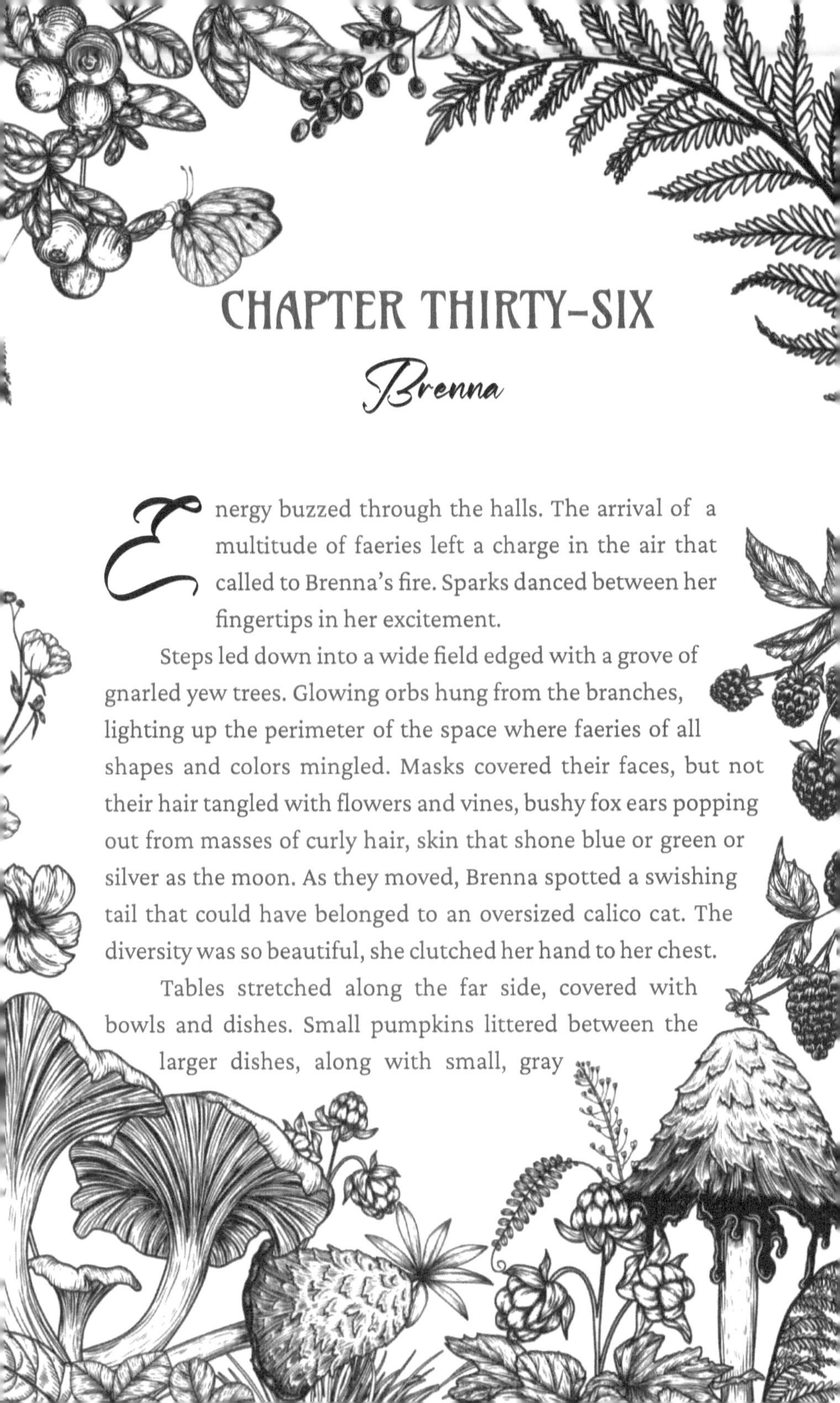

CHAPTER THIRTY-SIX

Brenna

Energy buzzed through the halls. The arrival of a multitude of faeries left a charge in the air that called to Brenna's fire. Sparks danced between her fingertips in her excitement.

Steps led down into a wide field edged with a grove of gnarled yew trees. Glowing orbs hung from the branches, lighting up the perimeter of the space where faeries of all shapes and colors mingled. Masks covered their faces, but not their hair tangled with flowers and vines, bushy fox ears popping out from masses of curly hair, skin that shone blue or green or silver as the moon. As they moved, Brenna spotted a swishing tail that could have belonged to an oversized calico cat. The diversity was so beautiful, she clutched her hand to her chest.

Tables stretched along the far side, covered with bowls and dishes. Small pumpkins littered between the larger dishes, along with small, gray items that looked suspiciously like animal skulls.

The crowd hushed as Aletris raised her hands. Gold lace curved over her cheekbones and along her brow.

"Welcome, kindred spirits. Tonight we stand between dusk and dawn as the year ends. Join me in revelry while we celebrate life and remember those that have passed on. They have joined with the land that provides this harvest.

"May your magic craft be strengthened with the ancient magic that flows through our blood and within our land. Do not forget your offerings, both of our harvest but also from your bodies. Raise your voices, give yourself over to the wildness that roots us to this land, and celebrate with your spirit!"

The Summer Lady raised a massive golden goblet and took a sip of a dark, thick liquid. Everyone stood still and silent as she passed it to her companion, who took a drink and passed it to the next faerie. It moved through the crowd, and Brenna's sense of apprehension and excitement grew until her magic was buzzing under her skin.

"My fire sprites and salamanders, please help us in lighting the bonfires," Aletris called.

Brenna felt the urge in her soul, and she stepped forward to join a small, curvy faerie with hair that faded from red at the roots to gold at the tips that skimmed her hips. Together, they lowered their hands to the small pyre closest to them. Firelight blazed around them as faeries lit the other bonfires. With a mere thought, heat flowed from her hand into the wood. The faerie beside her dripped flames from her fingertips, catching the bundled kindling. Their bonfire flickered to life.

Meara raised the cup, eyeing it suspiciously. Brenna nodded, urging her to drink as she returned to her side. Reluctantly, she did, and Brenna took it from her, taking a sip for herself. The liquid seared down her throat. It was heavily spiced and the cinnamon burned her nose.

She passed the cup to those beside her, and a cool hand brushed hers as they took it from her grasp. Bemused, she looked up into dark eyes that glowed red in the firelight.

"There you are," Emrys said softly, drawing closer to her, but not touching her again. She smiled, reaching out to brush the satin fabric of the darkest crimson vest gracing his frame. His black mask shielded his sharp cheekbones and shaded his long lashes. She wished to rip it from his face and see him properly.

Voices rose around them, a chant coming together and resonating through the trees. The entire gathering glowed with dozens of bonfires. The music swelled, a hundred voices blending into a type of magic that reverberated in her bones.

"There's Cerne. I'm going to go speak with him," Meara said, surging into the crowd. Brenna smiled, watching her sister threading between faeries toward the pair of antlers jutting above the crowd.

In the absence of her sister, Emrys drew closer, and she leaned into him, savoring his stable strength and the way he curled around her. "Do you want to dance or eat?" he asked, his low voice near her ear. A shiver skittered across her shoulders.

"What are the offerings she mentioned?"

He sighed, the movement brushing their bodies together. "We can bring food to the forest, or offer them pieces of ourselves."

"What does that mean? Blood?"

Emrys laughed, slow and dark. It brushed over her skin, lighting up every one of her nerves. "As appealing as that sounds, it's usually a display of passion. Many of our festivals include *certain activities* happening in the darkness."

Her stomach lurched. Mouth dry, she studied what she could see of his expression. Was he suggesting..?

"Let's get you fed and we can do an offering," he said, taking her hand. "A food offering," he said with a deadly smile. "Though I could be persuaded to make other kinds."

Fingers entwined, they wove through the crowd. As the faeries parted, they paused to watch Lady Aletris as she held the ceremonial goblet high in the air and slowly poured out the remaining liquid into the flames of the largest bonfire. It fizzed and popped, sending sparks into the purple sky.

Faeries moved around her, dancing in a circle around the fire. Perhaps dancing wasn't the correct term. They moved wildly, legs kicking and arms waving in graceful arcs. It was chaotic and entrancing.

Emrys' arm was firm around her, and she leaned into his warmth as they crossed the meadow to the banquet tables. All sorts of breads and vegetable dishes covered the tables, but she was drawn to the tiny pumpkins littering every available surface. Emrys lifted one and handed it to her. She tugged on the stem to reveal it had been hollowed out and filled with a creamy soup. Steam that smelled of allspice and nutmeg wafted from the thick liquid. Emrys took his own and lifted it to his lips, taking a long drink. She mirrored him, letting the sweet and hot liquid pour into her belly.

When she lowered the pumpkin, Emrys reached forward and wiped her lip with his thumb, popping it into his mouth with a wicked grin. She wanted to drag him into the darkness of the trees and discover the activities he had alluded to.

Together, they filled a small plate with pastries, dried fruit, and a cluster of cherry tomatoes. Emrys led her to the edge of the trees where guests placed food around oil portraits. She looked up at the faces of those who had passed on, finding the one before them eerily familiar. Brooding heavy brows with fierce golden eyes - it looked like Luce, but with darker hair and much paler skin. Emrys noted her pause and spoke into her ear, "Elio, my uncle, the Summer Lord, and Aletris' mate."

"Mate? Husband?" she asked, twisting to peer at him.

"I don't believe they ever wed. It's not a requirement unless you are the high king and queen," he explained with a shrug. "If you can magic share, that is what validates the relationship."

Nodding, Brenna sat the dish of food down below the portrait.

"Have you ever had a partner like that? One you could magic share with?" she asked, her stomach clenching as she waited for his answer.

"Why are you asking, my light?" Emrys ran his hand over her shoulder and up her throat until he tipped her chin back. "Jealous at the idea of me with another?"

She shivered again at his touch, but she prayed he mistook it for the chill in the air. The longer she spent in his presence, the greater the effect he had upon her. He consumed the very air around her.

"I'm not sure. Perhaps." Her reply earned her a dark laugh that felt like a caress. Taking a shaky breath, she peeled her attention off his full lips and the way he loomed over her.

Her gaze swept the crowd, but she did not see her sister, nor Cerne. Ayala's bright hair caught the light and Brenna tracked her to a group sitting around a small fire on the fringe of the celebration.

"Do you want to go sit with my friends?" Brenna asked.

Emrys smiled wryly. "I would love that, as long as you promise me I can have you to myself later."

She tensed her shoulders, refusing to shiver a third time. Emrys draped an arm over her shoulder, pulling her into his warmth. The casual possessiveness sent a thrill through her.

The small group reclined around the fire, laughing and passing a cup between them. Ayala leaned against Harin with his arm over her stomach, and when she saw them, she nodded in greeting.

Brenna sat, pulling Emrys beside her. He leaned back on his hand and she nestled into his side. Beside them, Vasara's eyebrows rose, but she said nothing as she passed the cup to Emrys. He took a long drink and then held it to Brenna's lips. She opened and allowed him to pour the spiced cider into her mouth. Some slipped from her lips and down her chin.

Emrys passed the goblet to Harin, and then turned Brenna's face with his hand, kissing the corner of her mouth and then running his tongue over the trail of drink. Brenna felt as if she would burst into flames. She gasped, trying to regain any sense of time and space.

His mouth had been on her hand, the crook of her elbow, and even her stomach, but so near to her mouth - her heart stuttered, molten heat roaring through her. The drink blurred her thoughts further until she was delirious.

Glassy eyed, Ayala laughed into the cup before she drank, and Harin tightened his hold on her middle, his fingers pressing into her soft skin. Brenna watched these faeries she called her friends as she leaned into Emrys and enjoyed his hands running over her arm and settling on her hip. His lips brushed her ear as he murmured, "I can't think of a better way to spend Samhain than with you in my arms."

CHAPTER THIRTY-SEVEN

Meara

Meara watched Cerne speak with Aletris, the Autumn Lord and the Summer Lady. They were amicable but clearly there was no true affection between them. Cerne turned his charming smile on her, and Meara tensed. When was that smile genuine and when was it for show?

He picked up a cup and drank deep, draining it and reaching for a second. Faeries crowded around the leaders, and her shoulders slumped. He would be drunk soon at the rate he was going, and she had no interest in him in that state.

Exhaling through her teeth, she scanned the crowd, spotting golden curls and a sunburst hairpiece. Her sister was with Emrys, and her mood soured further. Brenna would be furious if she tried to intervene.

She reached for a drink of her own and took a swig of the spicy cider. Faeries moved around her, jostling her, some heading for the food while others moved between bonfires to join the wild dance.

Moving on instinct, she wandered further from the crowd. The trees whispered to her, shadows calling her into their comforting embrace. She sipped her drink and gave in to the impulse to lose herself in the darkness. As she stepped into the tree line, she felt magic coiling around her. Smiling, she pinched a thread of shadow between her fingers and drew it up, loving the way it floated like smoke.

A figure moved between trees in the distance. She watched, waiting to see if the faerie drew closer or kept their distance. A familiar set of broad shoulders and waving golden hair emerged from the dense gloom.

Clothed in ochre linen, darker than his usual ivory, the summer heir had a gilded mask over his cheeks and brow that was surprisingly plain.

"Lord Luce, are you hiding from your court's Samhain celebration?" she teased, letting the cider's effect relax her pose and loosen her tongue.

"It is not mine," he grumbled, crossing his arms as he watched her unravel shadows and draw them through the air.

"You are the heir of the Summer Court, which happens to be the court that is currently hosting Samhain. Therefore, I fail to see how this is not *your* celebration."

He chuckled at her sassy response and the warmth of it tingled on her skin. "I do not think I agree with your conclusion, but please continue."

"You should be enjoying the party," she said, scowling at him. "It's not the same without you."

"Why?" Bicolored eyes bore into hers, thickening the air around them.

She broke the contact and looked away while sipping her

drink. "You are summer embodied." She waved her hand at him, and how even in the dim, he seemed to glow. "Therefore, the Summer Court requires your presence."

"Summer embodied," he echoed, smirking. "What does that make you?"

Caught off guard, Meara canted her head, lines forming around her eyes. What was she?

"Nothing. Darkness. The absence of light," she muttered, looking down. Shadows seethed at her feet like a stream flowing over rocks.

Luce was in front of her, looking down intently. "You are not nothing." He did not touch her, but he held her attention so firmly in his grasp, she felt as if she could not pull away even if she wished to.

"Night is powerful because it devours the day. Everything ends in darkness. It's inevitable." Shadows licked up his legs, teasing the loose fabric of his trousers. Luce's eyes dropped. "Are you threatening me?"

"No," she said, fluttering fingers at her shadows as they crawled up his legs, sending them dancing in swirls around their knees. Not a threat, simply asserting her dominance. The thought made her smile.

Luce laughed again, and this one was warmer, like he found actual humor in the situation. He opened his hand and called upon his magic, shining light down to chase away the shadows. They scattered and faded.

"Call them back, I want to see if you can withstand my light," he commanded.

Meara's heart leapt, her excitement rising at the challenge. "I wouldn't want to smother your light," she said with a sly smile.

"You can't. I can take whatever shadows you summon. You won't hurt me, little moth," he said, stepping closer into her personal space.

She backed up, her back bumping against a tree. "Are you sure you want to discover if that is true?" Looking up at him, she couldn't help her devious grin. She felt powerful, going up against this prince of summer. Even now, her shadows twisted, coming closer to his luminous hands. "I would hate to make you a liar."

"Now, that does sound like a threat." He chuckled, his skin beginning to glow in earnest.

"I think threatening you may be my new favorite hobby," she murmured, her focus pouring into the magic in the air around them. It gathered, taking form for her, wrapping around Luce.

He looked down at his body coated in darkness and grinned. For a moment, his smile darkened, and a trickster shone through. That was all the warning she received before his radiance intensified. He blazed like a fire, breaking apart her shadows. She threw her arm up over her eyes as he burned before her.

"What the hell is happening here," Cerne growled, stalking toward them. Meara could make out the outline of his antlers and little else in the shining light. Luce faded, and lights wove across her vision as she took in the Autumn Lord, every line of his face tense with anger. He grabbed Luce's shirt and yanked him back.

"What are you doing? Stop!" Meara yelped, pushing off from the tree she had been leaning against and reaching for Cerne. His other hand shot out and grabbed her wrist to stop her.

The heir of summer glared at Cerne. "Is this how you treat your lady?"

"I don't let the heirs of murderers pin her to a tree and ravage her," Cerne snarled.

Luce's bicolored eyes flared. "Let her go."

Meara yanked her arm to free herself from Cerne's grasp. His hand tightened instinctively, and he pulled her back, further from Luce.

Meara cried her outrage, no true words forming, but before she could move, Luce twisted and swung his fist, landing a blow on Cerne's jaw.

The Autumn Lord released his hold on Meara and staggered back, landing in the brush. Meara dropped to her knees beside him, her hands going to his head and shoulders to keep him from injuring himself further.

Luce shook out his hand and growled, "Meara, if you want me to take you away from him, you only have to ask."

"What is wrong with you?" she muttered, brushing her fingertips over the bruise blooming on Cerne's face.

He clumsily rose, snaking an arm around her waist to pull her against him. His fae canines glinted as he bared them at Luce. "You will pay for that if you ever come near her again."

Meara pushed away from him, her anger gathering shadows around her so she was wading through black fog. "You are both brutes. I think you deserve each other." Hair whipping behind her, she strode away from both males and toward the light of the celebration.

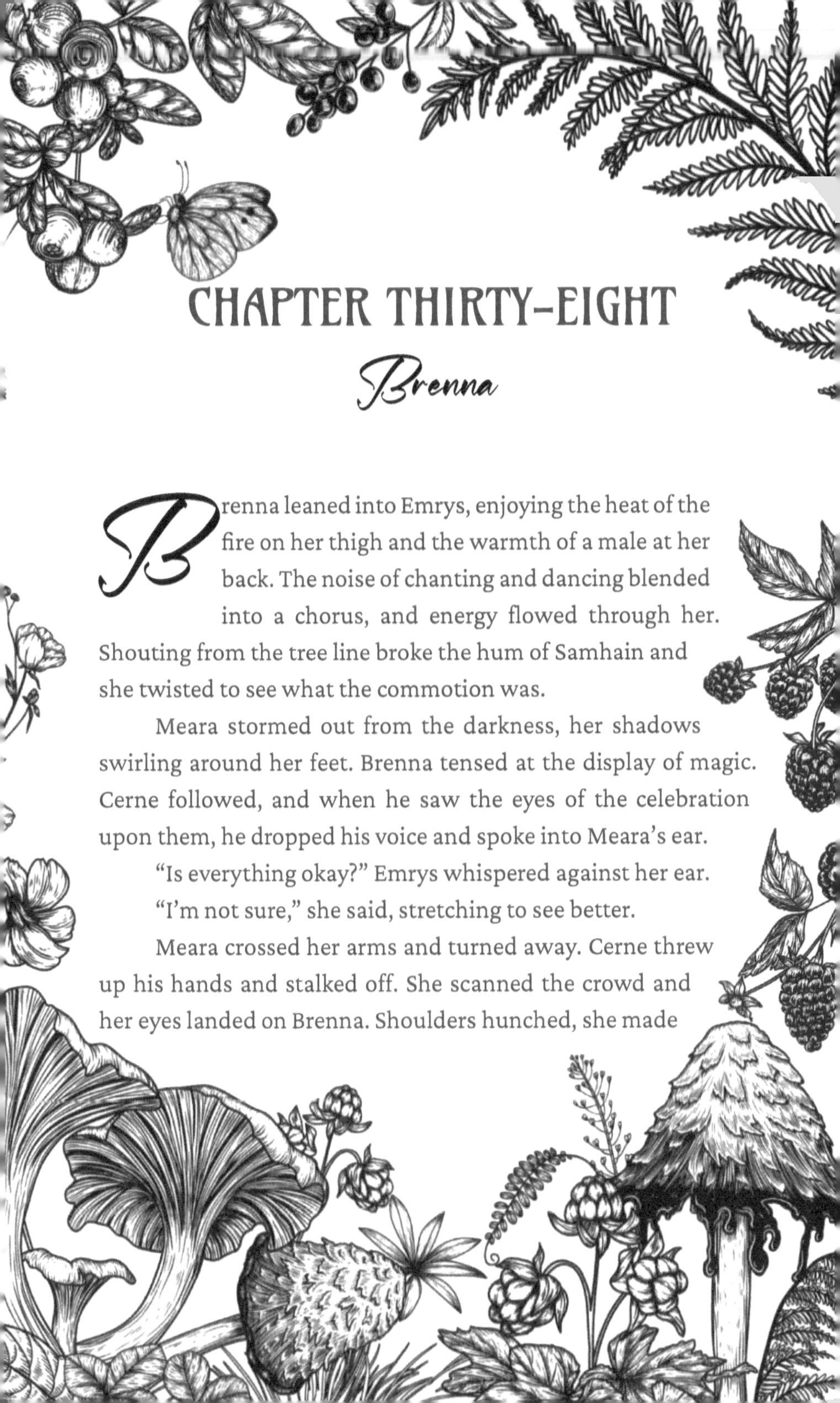

CHAPTER THIRTY-EIGHT

Brenna

Brenna leaned into Emrys, enjoying the heat of the fire on her thigh and the warmth of a male at her back. The noise of chanting and dancing blended into a chorus, and energy flowed through her. Shouting from the tree line broke the hum of Samhain and she twisted to see what the commotion was.

Meara stormed out from the darkness, her shadows swirling around her feet. Brenna tensed at the display of magic. Cerne followed, and when he saw the eyes of the celebration upon them, he dropped his voice and spoke into Meara's ear.

"Is everything okay?" Emrys whispered against her ear.

"I'm not sure," she said, stretching to see better.

Meara crossed her arms and turned away. Cerne threw up his hands and stalked off. She scanned the crowd and her eyes landed on Brenna. Shoulders hunched, she made her way through the clearing to reach their gathering. Around them, voices rose once more and the disruption was forgotten. As Meara reached them, Brenna spied the golden head of Luce ducking out from the trees and disappearing into the crowd.

"What was that?" Ayala asked.

Meara ground her teeth together, sinking down to sit beside Brenna, and finally said, "I was speaking with Luce and Cerne made some assumptions. Of course neither one would listen to me."

Brenna reached out and squeezed her hand. "That's frustrating."

"He can be such a fool," Meara said, looking over her shoulder at Cerne's antlers bobbing above the crowd. They dipped back as he drained another cup.

"Don't I know it," Ayala said with a giggle, taking another draught of her cider.

Meara rested her forehead on her arm for a moment. "Look, I have a headache. I think I'd rather go to bed."

"Did you get anything to eat?" Brenna asked, her voice rising.

Shrugging, Meara stood. "I'm not hungry. I'll be in our rooms. Don't stay too late."

"Do you want me to go with you?" Brenna asked, beginning to rise.

"No, stay here and enjoy yourself. At least one of us should have a good time." Meara sighed, disappointment pulling her mouth into a frown. "I'll see you later."

Once she was gone, Brenna leaned her head against Emrys' shoulder. "Why do they insist on maintaining this hatred?" she asked. "Surely, Cerne cannot hold Luce responsible for his father's actions, and Luce cannot hold Cerne responsible for being loyal to a friend."

"But they can and they will," Vasara said, taking a long drink.

"Why can't they let it go and get along?" Brenna continued.

Ayala scoffed. "I don't think you're going to find a way to end a feud that has been festering for a quarter century."

Frustrated, Brenna exhaled and turned, huddling closer to Emrys and resting her temple against his chest. His palm moved up her back, tangling into her hair.

Vasara and Ayala went to dance, and Harin rose to watch, leaving Brenna and Emrys watching the flames.

"Do you want to take a walk with me?" he asked, his low voice suggestive.

A thrill of anticipation raced through her veins. Nodding, she allowed him to pull her to her feet. With a hand on his forearm, she followed his lead as he strolled around the perimeter of the celebration. They ducked into the tree line, and she averted her gaze from a couple embracing nearby. He led her deeper, and she clung to him.

"What do you think will happen with the human war?" she dared to ask, her worries pressing in now that they were away from the light and life of the celebration.

Emrys shrugged. "They may march on us, and we will send them home soundly beaten. That will be the end of it."

"Will the fae attack the human cities?" Brenna asked tentatively.

"Why? We have no reason to," Emrys said. His matter-of-fact reaction comforted her. She slipped her hand down his arm and twined their fingers together. Emrys turned their joined hands, looking down at the fine veins under her golden skin. Her heart sped up as she imagined what he might do.

"Your sister seems to have learned to wield her magic craft," he said.

Brenna nodded. "Yes, finally. I'm really proud of her."

"She can summon shadows?"

"It seems so." Brenna's pulse thudded in the quiet. They had strayed far from the gathering. "Perhaps there is more to her magic, but we will have to wait and see."

"How has her disposition been toward you?" He glanced up at her, those russet eyes questioning.

"She's relieved, I think, to have overcome the challenge."

"Has she been cheerful?"

Brenna laughed. "Meara is never cheerful. Even as a child, she was cautious and serious."

Gathering her to him, her back pressed to his front, Emrys brushed a hand over her shoulder, pushing her golden curls over her shoulder to reveal bare skin. "You are quite different."

Pulling her lip through her teeth, she nodded. "Yes, but she is my other half."

"The dark to your light," he murmured.

Brenna frowned, not liking the comparison. Meara may wield shadows and look at things with a critical view, but she was also loyal, protective, and incredibly smart. Unsure of how to communicate this, she changed the topic. "Do you like living in the high court?"

"Yes. Argyro is fair and he loves his people. He can be harsh, but not without reason. He is more of a father to me than my own." His fingers lingered on her bare shoulder, trailing across her collarbone. "What about you?"

"What about me?" she asked, playing coy as a way to avoid questions she knew she was not supposed to answer.

His arms came around her waist and pressed flat into her stomach, his breath on her neck. "Where is your family from?"

All thoughts of secrets drained from her head as he brushed his lips over her neck. "Um, we were raised by a human mother, and we've only been away from her a few weeks. Meara wants to go back soon, but I'm not sure."

"And your fae family?" he asked.

She shuddered. "No idea."

"Interesting," he purred, finally giving her what she wanted as he dragged his sharp teeth over her skin. She arched, offering easy access as an embarrassing moan escaped her throat. "You want me to bite you, don't you?"

No words formed, all she could manage was a strangled hum. She waited for the pain of his bite, but instead he spoke against her skin. "Come to Court Tara with me."

"Why?" she said sluggishly.

"I want you safe."

"I am safe here. And I have my magic to defend myself," she protested weakly.

His hand trailed up her ribs, along the side of her breasts, and up to her throat. "Don't stay with Aletris. She is callous and cold. I want you with me in the high court. I want to know you better."

Brenna's breath came out in short huffs, her entire body shaking with overwhelm. "I'll think about it."

"Good," he said, turning her in his arms. For a moment, he cradled her jaw and their gazes connected, before his fingers pried her mask from her face. She reached for his, tugging the black silk off as he lowered his head.

His lips met hers. Every reservation melted away, and she gripped his shoulders to steady herself. His free hand tangled in her hair, sending fireworks radiating through her body. Every nerve sung, lit up like the blazing bonfires behind them. She moaned as he tipped her chin back and nipped at the delicate skin below her jaw. Slowly, his tongue ran across the crook of her neck.

The moment he sank his teeth into her skin, her groan turned to a guttural growl. The pain and pleasure blurred her vision until she saw nothing but the glow coming from her own skin and felt only the pull of his mouth on her neck.

CHAPTER THIRTY-NINE

Meara

Head throbbing, Meara rolled over and pulled her pillow over her head. Morning had come far too soon. Despite her better judgment, she dragged herself from groggy sleep and tuned into her senses. Brenna warmed the bed beside her. She stirred, flipping over from her back to her belly. The motion was as familiar as her own breathing.

Braving the light, Meara shoved the pillow off and turned over. Brenna's arm stretched above her head, bent at the elbow so her hand lay across her tangle of blonde curls. Her braids from the night before were half unraveled.

Memories of the fae cider and wine came back to her slowly. She shouldn't have grabbed a bottle on her way out of the celebration. Poor choice. She was as bad as Cerne. Their fight came back to her in a rush and she squeezed her eyes shut. Why must he be so wonderful in one moment, and so frustrating in the next?

Exhaling slowly, she sat up and crawled from the bed. Brenna let out a whimper as she rolled again. A purplish bruise marked her neck and Meara tensed. She stared at the mark, clenching her jaw and considering, but that was a confrontation for another time.

Regret weighed her down as she pulled a robe over her shift and stepped into the sitting room. Morning sun drenched every surface, reflecting in a riot of sunfire and saffron. Cerne lay across the settee, his antlers sticking off the end as his head rested on the arm cushion. He turned and blinked at her, his brows furrowing as his gaze focused on her. Pressing her hand to her forehead, Meara walked to him and sank into the nearest chair.

"I'm sorry," he said, his voice hoarse. Swallowing thickly, Meara nodded. She wanted to forget the reasons she had been distancing herself from him. Despite his flaws, she missed being close to him.

"Cerne," she began, "nothing was going on with Luce."

"I know," he said, looking up at the ceiling and the mural of clouds and white birds painted there.

"He was helping me figure out my magic. And it really helped."

Frowning, Cerne pushed to sit up. "How so?"

In answer, Meara called forth a wisp of shadow and twined it around her fingers. It was as easy as a thought, extending her awareness to the magic all around her. She felt Cerne's magic; it felt like fresh leaves budding on a tree, but she could not touch it. Plucking magic from the air around her, she gathered up shadows until a thick ribbon of darkness draped over her hand.

Cerne's eyebrows were in danger of disappearing into his hair. "So it really is darkness and not simply misused light magic."

She cocked her head, waiting for him to explain. He exhaled roughly and ran a hand through his hair, scratching at the base of his antlers. "I have to take troops back with me. We leave this morning. The Autumn Court is not a safe place for you until this is dealt with. I asked Aletris to allow you and Brenna to stay as long as needed, though if you don't want to, I can contact Amadi from the Spring Court or perhaps Xurey could take you to the Observatory."

"What if we want to come back to the Autumn Court and take that risk?" she asked, trying to bite back her irritation.

Cerne stood, his resigned gaze raking over her. "I won't allow that." Her teeth clenched as he strode out. Standing, she dug her nails into her robe, wrinkling the fabric as she stalked back into her bedroom.

Brenna sat up in bed, a goofy smile on her beautiful face. "Good morning, Meara. How did you enjoy your evening? Sleep well?"

Frowning, Meara perched on the edge of the bed. "Not particularly. How late did you stay out?"

"Not too late. I was told the dancing would extend until dawn, but I'm afraid I didn't last that long." She ran her fingers through her hair, her hand snagging on a knot. Meara sighed and scooted closer so she could undo her hairstyle and untangle the mess of her hair.

"Did you spend the whole evening with Emrys?" she asked.

Brenna's smile widened. "Yes. We talked and danced and it was lovely."

"Did he kiss you?" she asked quietly.

Brenna looked over her shoulder. When she saw Meara's frown, disappointment flashed in her amber eyes. "What if he did?"

Pausing, Meara weighed her words, knowing this would only bring more conflict but unable to help herself. "You hardly know him. One dance at a banquet and a single conversation in the woods does not make a deep or lasting relationship.”

“He saved me. He heals with his blood magic. He didn’t have to do that,” Brenna said, crossing her arms.

“You don’t owe him anything.”

“I know!” Brenna closed her eyes for a moment, exhaling slowly before she argued. “We’ve spoken about many meaningful things. He has opened up and shared his heart. I know him better than anyone else in the faerie lands, save for you.”

“Better than Tayen?” Meara asked, trying to reach her.

“Maybe,” Brenna said, her posture stiff.

“I don’t see why you are getting attached to him. This is temporary. We have a home back with our mother,” Meara said, pushing the issue. Brenna was pulling away, and it made her feel reckless.

“Mother told us to consider staying, and I think she is right. We have a wonderful life here.”

“We have no place here, no role to play where we are useful and earning our way. We are guests, and when the novelty of us wears off, we will have nothing but expired goodwill.”

“There’s more to life than working to prove yourself constantly,” Brenna spat.

Meara flinched. Pressing her fingers to her eyelids, Brenna reigned in her emotions. “Besides, you have endeared yourself to Cerne, so surely he would extend his hospitality. We are a part of his court now.”

“That is not reliable. I will not depend on such a mercurial relationship.” The sisters stared at each other for a moment, finding themselves utterly at odds for the first time in their lives. The chasm between their desires had grown until it felt like they would split apart.

Brenna wet lips, glancing toward the door. “Look, let’s go eat some breakfast. We are both hungry and tired.”

"I'm fine," Meara said automatically.

"Clearly," Brenna said, raising one eyebrow and planting a hand on her hip. Cowed, Meara rose and began dressing for breakfast. This argument would have to be dealt with later.

The breakfast room glowed a pale gold, and at the head of the table, the Summer Lady sipped at a tea that looked like liquid light while she laughed at something her silver haired companion said. Ayala sat a few seats away from her, leaning close to Harin while they spoke quietly.

"Ah, Meara and Brenna, glad you could join us," Aletris said, her eyes piercing Meara. The massive glass doors stood open behind her chair, allowing bright morning light diffusing through sheer curtains to illuminate her outline. She set her goblet down with a clink, and Meara had to look away. "Cerne asked me to play host. He is leaving this morning, taking my guards along with my beloved son. So how much longer will we enjoy your company?"

Ayala leaned forward. "My lady, we are unsure of our exact day of departure, as I am sure Lord Cerne discussed with you. We wait for news as eagerly as you do."

"I cannot imagine that," she said dryly. "But yes, I will tolerate your presence a while longer." She sat back and listened to something her companion whispered in her ear.

The sisters took seats as far down the table as possible, keeping a distance between them and the Summer Lady. Meara ran her fingers over the intricate carvings in the pastel wood. The table was covered in sweet breakfast items - peach cake topped with chunks of honeycomb that dripped down the sides, bright tomatoes gathered at the edges of platters of fluffy breads, ribbons of zucchini cradling poached eggs drizzled with a bright orange sauce. Small bowls of salad were decorated with edible flowers.

Tiny pots of jam decorated the table, and Brenna took a slice of bread and slathered it with a golden jam that smelled of citrus.

Meara was tempted, but her stomach curdled at the conversations around her. Discussions of war. She leaned closer to her sister and quietly spoke. "I think we should get Mother away from Dornadan."

"Why?" Brenna frowned. "She is safe in the city. Whatever humans march on fae lands will be the ones to suffer the consequences."

"Those are our people too," she whispered.

"No they aren't. We are fae." Brenna crossed her arms.

Meara's eyes burned and her throat thickened. Her sister felt entirely out of reach. "We have a human mother and this feels like betraying her."

"Betraying who?" Aletris broke into their private conversation as she leaned forward in her seat. The sun reflected off the jewels woven into her hair, scattering fractured light across the table and over their plates.

"Excuse me, my lady," Brenna said, dipping her head. "We have friends in Dornadan. It is heartbreaking to be estranged from them. They are trapped in a war they did not want."

"I suggest you do not have relationships with humans or mixed breeds. You are young, but they are short lived and so weak," Aletris sniffed. "Hopefully Luce and his guard can slaughter the humans quickly and this entire embarrassing ordeal can be over with."

"How can you say that? There is still hope for a diplomatic solution, and even if it comes to battle, our goal should be minimizing the loss of life." Meara clenched her fists in her lap, feeling her emotions slip out of her control.

"Do you really think the humans will agree to a diplomatic solution?" Her second laugh was crueler and colder. "We should wipe them all out and be done with it. Then we can seize their land

and resources and not have to bother with tedious trade."

"That is terrible!" Meara said, her voice rising. Brenna brushed down her arm, a silent request for Meara to calm down. She yanked her hand away. "No! I will not stay quiet and entertain the idea of slaughtering an entire group of people for the simple reason they wanted their kidnapped princess returned."

The Summer Lady stood and the vines along the colonnade writhed and reached for them through the open glass doors. Her tone dropped. "I suggest you learn to hold your tongue if your opinions are so treasonous."

Meara's face flushed, fear blossoming under the deep pool of anger in her gut. Brenna spluttered an apology, but Meara stood, shoving her chair back. She had to get out of here.

Brenna snagged her wrist, tugging her back, whispering a demand for an apology. The room closed in, the color fading, and Meara was quite sure she was about to faint.

Brenna's voice broke through, but the words were jumbled. Meara sucked in a breath, but nothing helped. Shadows rose up, out of her control, and swallowed her up. Everything blurred.

One moment she was drowning in the darkness, then next, she rose above it. Dark feathers covered her body, and she was different. Lighter, smaller. She moved on instinct, black wings beating as she rose above the table and shot out of the open doors. The screams of the faeries no longer mattered as she climbed higher on a draft of warm air coming off the stone of the castle.

Her thoughts were simplistic. She needed to protect their mother and the other humans who were about to march to their deaths. She had to end this conflict or at least try. With a beat of her wings, she turned south, her sharp vision following the line of the river that led to Court Tara and then further to the Autumn Court and finally Dornadan. With hardly a thought, she angled her body and air rushed around her. She was off.

CHAPTER FORTY
Brenna

Brenna flung her chair back and leapt to her feet as her sister transformed in a flurry of shining, black feathers and a wickedly sharp beak. The huge raven burst into flight, careening from the room and out of sight. She ran to the balcony and watched the dark avian circle the field and turn southward.

Ayala joined her, gripping the railing as she leaned forward to catch a glimpse of the raven. "What the fuck was that?" she asked.

"I have no idea," Brenna said. "I'm not sure she knew she could do that."

"And she just up and flew away," Ayala said, throwing her hand out in a sweeping gesture. "How am I going to explain this to Cerne? His precious pet is quite literally a bird now. As if we needed another emotional shifter in the court."

Brenna gasped in a deep breath, her

mind stuttering as she fought to reconcile Meara's transformation. "What do we do?"

"What can we do?" Ayala said, storming back into the dining hall and taking her seat again. Brenna blinked after her. Her thoughts clumped together like mud as she looked over the fields and across the clouds. Birds of ivory and brown flitted to and fro, but she could no longer see the gleaming black bird that was her sister.

Pressing her palm to her forehead, she tried to sort out a plan - anything she could do that would help the situation. She needed help. Her feet stumbled into motion, and she crossed the dining room, muttering apologies.

She jogged down the corridor and out the front doors of the estate, darting towards the guard assembled down the path. Cerne's antlers caught the light, a head's height above the soldiers. She ran for him, but arms closed around her middle, snagging her, and she fell against a strong frame.

"Brenna," Emrys breathed, "what is wrong?"

Peace crashed over her, almost sickening in its relief after her panic. "Meara is gone!"

"Gone?" Emrys repeated, gathering her up in his arms. She leaned against his chest and tried to match her frantic breathing to the slow and steady rise of his chest. "Tell me what happened."

Wiping at her eyes, Brenna tried to order her words. "We were at breakfast with the Summer Lady, and she was being quite terrible, and Meara got upset, and she turned into a raven and flew out the door."

"What's happened?" Cerne asked, jogging toward them. Brenna filled her lungs with Emrys' scent, trying to find the strength to tell Cerne what Meara did.

Emrys saved her from having to repeat the words. "Meara shifted into a bird and flew away."

"A bird?" Cerne repeated dumbly.

"A raven," Brenna said, nodding.

Cerne crossed his arms, his forearms flexing as tension coiled in his muscles. "Well, that is unexpected."

"Is there a problem? It's time to move out." Luce strode toward them.

Cerne faced Luce, his lip curling. "Meara's magic, that *you* helped her access, overwhelmed her and she shifted into a raven and flew away to goodness knows where."

Luce paled and his jaw clenched. Brenna looked between the three dominant males. The tension between them stifled her.

"You can decide where to place blame later. Right now, Brenna is distressed at her sister's disappearance," Emrys growled. He lifted Brenna, one arm under her knees and the other against her shoulders, and cradled her against his chest as he stalked away from the bickering faerie leaders. She closed her eyes, allowing him to protect her. Without releasing her, he swung up onto his horse and settled her against him.

"What are you doing?" she asked, twisting to meet his warm eyes.

Emrys exhaled and leaned forward, directing his horse to walk forward. "I'm taking you with me to Court Tara. It's possible Meara will go there. It's not far."

"What if she goes to the Autumn Court?"

"I will send guards to look for her and bring her to safety."

Brenna fell silent, her thoughts consumed with worry over her sister and where she would go. Was Meara even in control?

Emrys bent to kiss her hair. "I won't tell you to stop worrying, because I know this was upsetting for you. But I'm going to take care of it."

Sniffling, she arched in her seat and tipped her face up until she could kiss him. Their lips met, her tears wetting their kiss.

Tenderly, he kissed her lips, her cheek, and her forehead. It centered her and her heart rate finally slowed. "Thank you, Emrys. I don't know what I would do without you."

"Anything for you," he murmured. He tucked her against his chest and waved his other arm to signal his guard. They moved out, heading back toward Court Tara and whatever conflict awaited them.

The ride went quickly, as Brenna's anxious thoughts built up again, spiraling out of control. After a ways, Emrys leaned down to kiss the crook of her shoulder. "I can hear your worries, they are so loud."

"I'm sorry," she said automatically.

"Don't apologize," he said, and she could hear the frown in his voice. "I am concerned *for* you. You have done nothing wrong. You've had to face so much in the last few days."

She let out a weak laugh. "Not enough so that I turned into a bird. I am still shocked she did that. It was the last thing I expected." Frowning, she wound the horse's mane through her fingers. "Is it possible I can do that too?"

"Faeries who shift into animals are not common, but I suppose it's always possible if your sister can. But you would not be a raven."

"Oh, really? What would I be?" He brought a smile to her face and she leaned against him gratefully, feeling her strain ease.

"Perhaps a phoenix," he said.

"A firebird? How would that be possible?"

He laughed. "You already produce flames. Is that so far a stretch?"

"True," she said. Sighing, she placed her hand over his. He turned it, threading their fingers together and squeezing. It felt as if he was squeezing her heart.

He kissed the top of her head. "You would be a magnificent

firebird."

His horse climbed the next hill and they were rewarded with a view of Court Tara. Emrys tightened his hold on her while he signaled to his team. "What are you-?" Brenna began to ask when he leaned forward in the seat, pressing into her, and the horse broke into a canter.

Brenna squealed, grabbing for the horse's mane, and not finding purchase, so she reached back and grabbed at Emrys' sleeve. He chuckled and adjusted his hold on her. "Relax, my light."

With another shift of his weight, the horse increased his speed into a full gallop. Brenna sucked in a breath, opening her mouth to scream, but it fell away as they broke from the trees and rode through a meadow full of golden wildflowers that rose up to brush her toes. They whipped past in a haze. Their motion tore petals from their stalks, sending them fluttering through the air, trailing behind them.

She felt free and light, as if her worries were behind them in the dirt stirred up by the horse's hooves. She grinned as her hair whipped against Emrys' chest. She was safe in his arms for this wild ride. The horse leapt over a fallen tree and her heart jumped into her throat.

Her heart was racing again by the time they neared the river and the horse slowed to a trot. They crossed the river in the shallows and rode into the white city, circling upwards to the king's palace. The faces of the resident fae were pinched and drawn, and Brenna could feel the stress of the current conflict weighing upon them. Her fears crawled back in - war and ravens.

At the entrance to the palace, Emrys slid from his horse and reached up, gripping her hips and lifting her off. Her thighs ached as she straightened her skirts. He took her hand and began shouting orders for the stables to prepare for the incoming troops. Messengers were sent off to the barracks. She admired his confident stance and broad chest as he instructed those around him. Satisfied, he led her into the glittering white stone palace.

"Is Meara here?" she asked, glancing around as if her sister would leap out from beyond the soaring arches.

Emrys slowed. "I will find out. Are you tired?"

"A bit hungry. I didn't eat much breakfast before Meara's outburst."

"Of course."

She followed him to an alcove where ivory sofas formed a circle. A bay of tall windows framed the seating area, filled with intricate stained glass showing the river in shades of blue and ivory.

Emrys urged her to sit. "Give me a few minutes to make arrangements." Her eyes tracked his retreat, until she was left alone. The quiet settled over her.

Emrys returned with a steward in tow. The huldra bowed, her furry ears flattening with the movement. "My lady, we have rooms prepared for you and a meal will be delivered."

"Thank you," Brenna said, her hands gripping her skirts anxiously. "I appreciate that, but I don't want to be any trouble."

Emrys kissed her hair. "I have work to attend to. I will come to you later. If you need anything, just ask. I've instructed the staff to attend to whatever you desire."

"Really, I don't need much," she protested, but Emrys was already striding away.

The huldra bowed again before leading her down a hall. They walked past the public rooms she remembered from their visit and into areas that were quiet and private. Her skin prickled with the feeling she should not be here.

"My lady," the steward said, holding a door open for her. She noted the flowers carved into its pale wood, hoping she would recognize it again. The last thing she wanted was to get lost in the private wing of the palace.

Brenna sucked in a startled breath as she stepped into the room and the door clicked shut behind her. Plush carpets in shades of peach and gold covered the stone floor. The bed rested against the wall with sheer curtains surrounding it, fluttering in a salty breeze from the open balcony door. Beyond, the river sparkled as it fed into the sea.

Chairs and a sofa surrounded an ivory hearth already crackling with a young fire. A tray of refreshments awaited her on the table. Fresh flowers overflowed from vases on every open surface.

"This is too much," she breathed. She had become accustomed to luxury in the Autumn Court, but this chamber should belong to a queen. Gold gilded the trim on the furniture, surprising her when the rest of the castle was done in silver and sparkling white.

Stomach grumbling, she settled into a plush armchair and tucked into the meal. Little tarts she recognized from the autumn court were made with a different, milder cheese. She finished the serving and began eating the fruit when a knock startled her. A servant held bags of her belongings. Her brows shot up. Emrys had sent so many of her things, he must have sent someone to pack up the belongings she had left in the Summer Court. The attendant placed them on the bench along the wall and bowed before disappearing.

She moved to the washroom. Mirrors covered the walls so she could see herself from every angle as she turned. Dirt smudged her plump cheeks. The massive marble tub took up an entire wall, big enough she could have swam in it. She might just do that later. For now, she washed her hands and face in the sink that was a piece of art with detailed carvings. Flowers climbed up the pedestal and vines wrapped around where the gold faucet extended. The towels were incredibly soft as she dried her hands and returned to her room.

While she waited for news, she unpacked her dresses then resorted to pacing the room. She would need books if she was to wait in Court Tara for any length of time, or some other distraction from her worries. Otherwise, she would wear a path into the floor or chew her nails bloody.

The afternoon light began to darken when Emrys returned. He had changed into a silken shirt the color of charcoal which made his pale skin luminant. His smile was lopsided, a piece of his hair falling over his brow. This relaxed version of Emrys felt familiar and warmer than the polished facade he normally wore.

"Any news?" she blurted, going to him.

He swept her up, folding his hands at the small of her back as she gazed up at him. "No, Meara is not here, nor has she arrived in the Autumn Court yet, but I expect we will locate her soon."

"Where could she have gone?" she murmured.

"Brenna." Her name was a prayer. "Let me take you for some dinner and distract you from your worries."

Her eyes glistened as she looked up at him. "I feel terrible enjoying such luxury while my sister is a raven flying around the wilds, perhaps lost, and our people are preparing for war."

"Those were not your choices. You bear no responsibility for them."

Sniffling, she nodded. Emrys brushed a curl behind her ear. Smirking, he made a show of looking around the room. "Besides, this seems an appropriate amount of luxury for you."

"Emrys, this room is fit for a queen."

"Yes." His russet eyes glowed as he stared into her soul.

She shifted uncomfortably, opting to change the subject instead of facing the intensity of his stare. "Still, I don't want to sit around being pampered when I could be helpful."

"You are helping," he said, lowering his mouth to kiss her temple. She tipped her face back to give him access, and he kissed her brow and then her cheek. "I have a lot of responsibility to handle, and having you here gives me peace of mind. You are supporting my work and enabling me to manage our forces."

Her cheeks flushed. She had never heard such a confession from anyone and she did not know what to say. Instead, she cupped his jaw and kissed him on the mouth.

His kiss was familiar now, and her lips parted eagerly. The slide of his tongue against hers sent jolts of pleasure through her limbs. His grip on her waist hardened, keeping her pressed against his muscular frame. She sucked on his bottom lip and released him.

"Is there anything else I can do? I have my magic."

Emrys ran his tongue over his bottom lip slowly, his eyes darkened with want. "If you are truly set on doing more, we can see if your magic lends itself to healing. Many faeries with light craft can heal."

"I would like that," she said, smiling at the thought. If she could heal, she could help with the war.

"Good. We can see about that for tomorrow. Tonight, you need to be fed, and I need more time with you." Reluctantly, he released her so she could take his arm and join him in walking to dinner.

CHAPTER FORTY-ONE

Meara

Her muscles moved on instinct, leaning and diving and rising up swells of air currents. Flying should have been terrifying, but Meara felt nothing but detached relief. Her conscious mind moved slowly, turning over her next steps in pursuit of her goals. There was no room for regret or worry about what-ifs.

She soared above a forest of orange and red, moving south until the trees fell away and dull marshland stretched below. In the distance, a gray fortress rose up at the base of a mountain. Somehow, she knew that was where she needed to go. Powering her wings, she accelerated and closed the distance.

She passed the walls, no longer bothered by the humans' boundaries. Wheeling in a circle, her sharp eyes scanned the streets until she located a familiar walled courtyard lined with teeming garden beds. She tucked her wings in and dove, leveling out and fluttering to land between rows of herbs.

A woman appeared in the doorway, her brown hair loose around her shoulders. Meara ruffled her feathers, puffing herself up, until smokey magic washed over her and she returned to her two-legged self. For a suspended moment, she stared at her human mother, clutching at her chest, before Meara collapsed to her knees. Dark hair spilling over her face, she gasped, digging her hand into the dirt below her, trying to come back to herself as her emotions came rushing back.

Her mother fell to the ground beside her, hauling her up and pulling her into a desperate hug. She murmured Meara's name over and over while stroking her hair. When her limbs stopped shaking, Meara rose and hobbled into the kitchen. The pungent scent of herbs and medicinal compounds overwhelmed her senses, but it felt like home.

"Dearest, I'm so happy to see you, but it is not a safe time for faeries in Dornadan. Many of my half-fae neighbors have left for the countryside until this conflict resolves." She clutched Meara's hand across the table.

Resting her forehead in her hand, Meara took a deep breath. "That's why I am here. I'm so scared about what will happen, and I couldn't leave you defenseless."

"I wasn't about to march in the front lines," her mother said, a smile breaking through her concern.

Meara looked up, her violet-gray eyes serious. "They are terrifying in battle. I watched two fae males dispatch a dozen human raiders. It was effortless. They were unarmed, and it didn't matter, they took the swords from their hands and slaughtered them."

Her mother rubbed her chin, staring past Meara as she

thought the situation through. "That's concerning."

"What were they thinking declaring war?"

"I don't know."

Frowning, Meara leaned forward and caught her mother's gaze. "Some of the fae want to march on Dornadan and take it for themselves. I can't let that happen."

Worry lines creasing her face, her mother nodded. "I will have to tell King Eldric. Maybe knowing can help."

"I'll tell him," Meara said.

"No!" She stiffened, eyes widening. "You are the enemy now."

Shaking her head, Meara argued, "I'll make him understand I am on your side. I know Rydan. He will vouch for me."

Her mother pressed her lips together in a line. "Where is your sister?"

Meara closed her eyes for a moment, regret threatening to overtake her. "She's at the Summer Court. She does not feel the way I do. I don't think she will return."

Her mother ran her thumb over Meara's wrist. "Perhaps that is best."

With a hood pulled up over her head to hide her inhuman traits, Meara moved through the crowd toward the king's keep. Her hair hung down her back in a braid, keeping the iridescent black strands from drawing attention. She moved past the entrance and headed east. In the light of day, she could see stables everywhere, but she kept going until she found the royal stables that Rydan favored.

Groomsmen rushed around, but she raised her chin as if she belonged and strode forward with a confidence she did not feel. Her audacity paid off when she spied dark locs in a stall with a stunning roan horse. Leaning against the gate, she chewed the inside of her cheek and waited. Rydan ran his hand down the creature's neck and murmured softly to it.

Finally, he turned, his brow furrowing when he saw her. "Lady Meara?"

She waved her hand to quiet him. "Please, I need to speak with you! And I would prefer if I didn't get discovered and arrested before I can explain."

Rydan nodded thoughtfully. "Alright, my lady. So what is the explanation of being in your enemy's kingdom, in the king's stable?"

Scowling, she opened her mouth and paused. She had not thought much further than reaching Rydan and getting his attention. "I want to help. I'm scared of how strong the fae are, and I don't want to see your people die. I want to protect my mother."

"Your mother," he repeated. "And you aren't a spy sent to sabotage us?"

"A spy? Are you serious?" Meara exclaimed.

"Prove it."

"How am I supposed to do that? How can someone prove what they are not?" Her voice rose in pitch until she looked back at his face and realized he was teasing her. "You know, this seems like a serious matter."

Rydan shook his head, flipping his hair over his shoulder. "Your mother is here, and you were only with the fae for a few weeks. I'm surprised you didn't come sooner."

"Why?"

"It's what I would have done."

She studied him for a moment, seeing genuine honesty in his warm brown eyes. "I want to help. What can I do?"

"Come speak with the king and my brothers. We could use whatever information you can share. None of our allies have come through for us in recent weeks."

"Will the king treat me as an enemy?" she asked.

"Most likely, so we will have to convince him," Rydan reassured her. "Once we explain, he will understand."

Meara hesitated, gathering her courage. "Let's go."

Rydan led her across the courtyard and into a door to the side of the formal entrance. They climbed stairs and hurried through dreary gray passages until he paused before wide double doors of the deepest oak.

"Stay calm. If he reacts badly, I will deal with it. But if you start wielding magic or pull out a weapon or something else equally as foolish, then he may never calm down and listen."

"Understood." She kept her hand from straying to her pocket and the small borrowed blade hidden there.

He nodded and took a deep breath before tugging the door open and leading her inside. King Eldric reclined in a chair at the end of a long table. Maps and scraps of paper scattered the surface in front of him. Emeric perched on a chair beside him, while Eladin sat nearer to them with his feet up on the polished table and a book in his lap.

"My king," Rydan said, bowing. Meara mimicked his movement, her fingers clutching the edge of her hood to keep it in place.

"Son?" Eldric dropped the papers in his hand onto the map in front of him and looked up at them. "Who are you bringing into our private meeting room?"

Rydan folded his hands behind his back and paced the length of the table. Meara scurried after him. Eladin's eyes widened in shock when he recognized her, but he said nothing.

Eldric frowned at Rydan, who cleared his throat and explained, "Father, do you remember how the apothecary had two daughters who were staying in the Autumn Court temporarily?"

"That sounds familiar," Eldric said, scratching at his beard. "They were fae?"

"Yes, though they did not know it. They grew up human. They are still loyal to humans and Meara returned to Dornadan to be with her mother."

"A faerie came here?" Eldric asked, his voice booming as he looked her over. No guards were in the room, but Meara was sure some would arrive quickly. She tensed and held her ground. She had to trust Rydan.

"She is loyal to Dornadan and she wants to help us," he said.

"That seems unlikely," Eldric said, his mouth twisting into a severe frown.

"Sire," Meara said, hoping her interruption wasn't too great an offense. "My goal is to protect my mother and prevent the unnecessary loss of life that I fear is coming. I've seen the fae fight and it is…" She paused, carefully selecting her words. "Terrifying. I cannot stand by while your citizens are massacred. Let me help."

"You think I do not know of how the fae fight?" Eldric growled, slamming his fist down. His chest heaved as he calmed himself. "Sit and answer my questions so we may judge your sincerity and usefulness."

"Of course." Meara lowered herself into a nearby chair and held onto the arms, her knuckles locking up.

He crossed his arms, his bulging muscles shaded with dark hair. "So you are a traitor to your people?"

She bit the inside of her cheek, forcing the calm she did not feel. "As far as I am concerned, I have only been a faerie for less than a season, and it was something forced upon me. My entire life up to this point was as a human. Besides, even if that was not the case, is it so hard to believe that I would have compassion? My mother lives here. I am worried the fae will decimate your army and then take your kingdom simply because they can and you've angered them."

Emeric's frown deepened. "You think so lowly of us?"

"How have your raids gone? What do your warriors report back?" She didn't mean to be cruel, but there was no room for egos when people were set to be slaughtered.

"You have knowledge of the fae's plans to take our lands and conquer our people?" Eldric asked.

"It is not what the high king has stated, but I have heard some lords and ladies advocate for it. I do not know the fae well. I have had only small glimpses into their politics. Certainly not enough to make an accurate prediction. But would you take that risk?"

The anger on Eldric's face drained away, leaving him looking haggard and tired. He sank into the seat and rested his chin on his fist. "Angering Argyro was not something I wanted to do."

"Then why declare war?"

Clenching his fists, Emeric explained, "It was not our choice. We are locked into a treaty with Liosliath. Without Elysia, we have few options. If she had simply rejected the betrothal and gone back to Liosliath, we would be free of these constraints. But Liosliath will seize our kingdom if we do not join them in marching upon the fae lands."

"They would have our army anyway and the war would continue," Eldric said dryly.

"What if something were to happen to Queen Malacia? Could the treaty be broken then?" Meara asked quietly.

"It would have to be at the hands of the fae forces."

"So there is no way out. We have to face them in battle," Emeric said darkly. "Malacia made sure of it. She's got us by the balls."

"I want to help," Meara said.

"What can you even do?" Eldric's tone was dismissive. It was obvious he saw no value in her presence.

She would not accept the lie that she was useless. Even without her magic, she had power, but now that she had access to shadow craft, she was formidable. With a slow exhale, she gathered up the threads of darkness in the room and spun them around the table.

Eladin jolted at the sight, cringing at the feeling of fear that came along with Meara's ability. Eldric turned at her, brows furrowed. "What is this?" he demanded.

"My magic."

"And you would use it against the fae?" Eladin asked, speaking up for the first time.

Meara fixed him with a stare. "To protect people from dying needlessly? Absolutely."

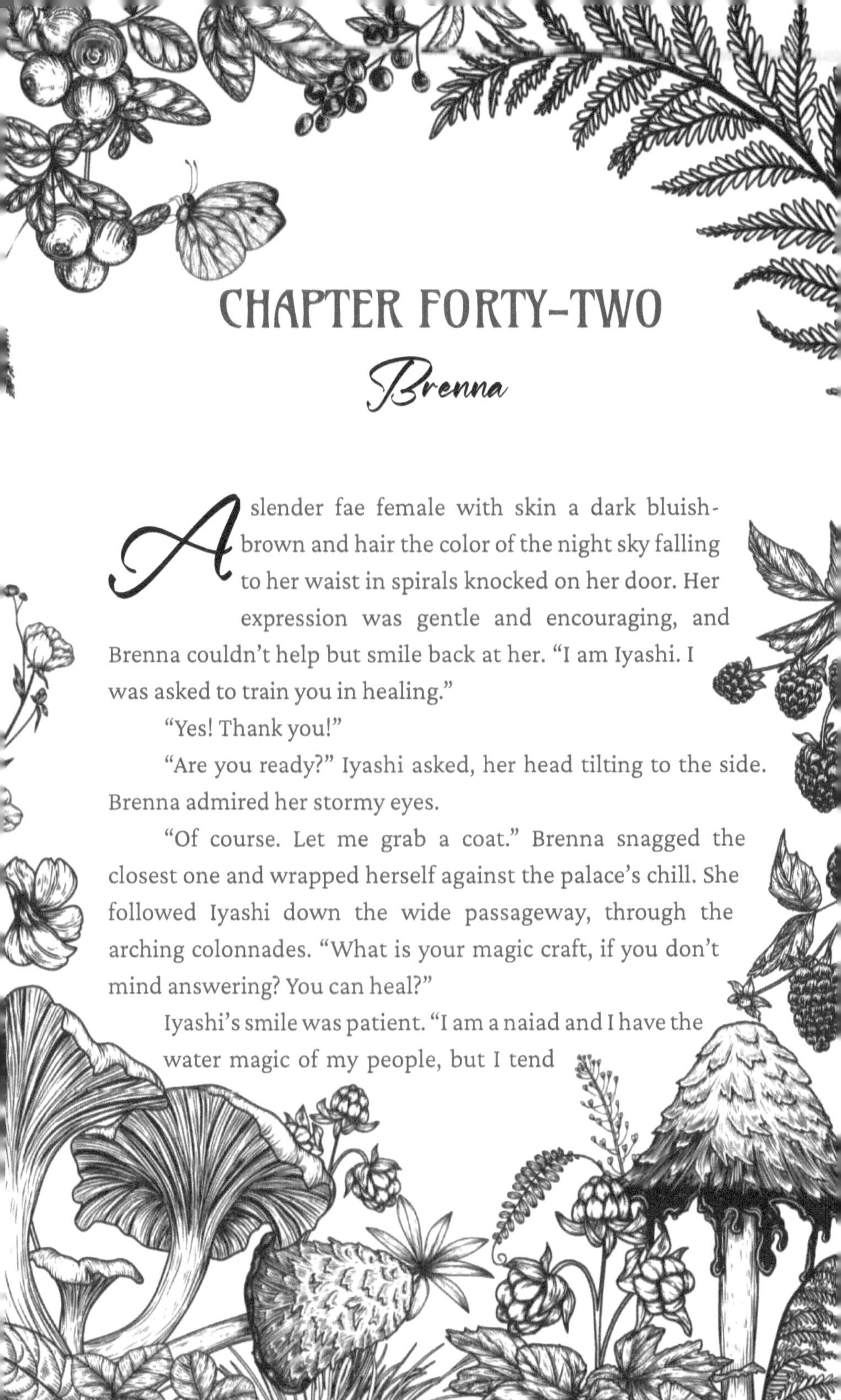

CHAPTER FORTY-TWO
Brenna

A slender fae female with skin a dark bluish-brown and hair the color of the night sky falling to her waist in spirals knocked on her door. Her expression was gentle and encouraging, and Brenna couldn't help but smile back at her. "I am Iyashi. I was asked to train you in healing."

"Yes! Thank you!"

"Are you ready?" Iyashi asked, her head tilting to the side. Brenna admired her stormy eyes.

"Of course. Let me grab a coat." Brenna snagged the closest one and wrapped herself against the palace's chill. She followed Iyashi down the wide passageway, through the arching colonnades. "What is your magic craft, if you don't mind answering? You can heal?"

Iyashi's smile was patient. "I am a naiad and I have the water magic of my people, but I tend towards healing. The body is made of water. And energy," she mused. "I am not the strongest healer, but my power is elemental like yours, so I hope I can show you how to use your craft to heal."

"I would appreciate that. It would be good to help people," Brenna said, clasping her hands together against her skirts.

The healer's ward sat low in the king's palace of Court Tara. Large windows let in the breeze, and Brenna could taste a hint of salt from the ocean in the distance.

Columns and arches defined stations, and some rooms had faeries stretched out. She spied a nasty cut on a young soldier, and a male with silver hair and curling rams horns leaned over it, muttering. He wiped a cloth along the injury, revealing angry red skin where a gaping wound should be. The soldier's face relaxed.

Iyashi paused outside of his alcove, waiting until he stood up and turned to them. Stubble, a darker color than the silver of his hair, dusted his cheeks, and Brenna realized he was young. Bright blue-green eyes creased as he smiled at her.

Iyashi bent in a shallow bow. "This is Master Sage Galen. Master, this is Brenna."

Galen wiped his hands on his apron. "Excellent. Lord Emrys said you showed potential as a healer. You possess light craft?" he confirmed.

"And fire," Brenna clarified.

"Ah, you must be powerful. We will see what you can do. Adept Iyashi, please take her onto the terrace and work through a meditation. Prepare her to access energies."

Nodding, Iyashi led her to the end of the hall where doors opened up to an expansive open space. Vines grew up the railing and across the overhead beams, giving them broken shade. They settled onto cushions, and Iyashi sat cross legged with her hands on her knees.

Brenna wished she had worn trousers for once, because

Iyashi seemed far more comfortable in her billowing pants and the top that wrapped over her chest, all made of the same pale purple fabric that Galen also wore.

After a quiet moment, she asked, "Can you sense the magic energies of those around you?"

"Um, I don't think so. I can feel my own magic," Brenna admitted.

"Good, that is a start. I want you to access that magic, and then look for the same in me."

Brenna closed her eyes and focused, feeling the sparking magic within her chest. She knew its vibration well. With effort, she pushed out further, looking for the same outside of herself. When she reached for Iyashi, it felt different. It was faint, gentle, like a trickle of water. "I think I feel it!"

"Good. Now under that, can you feel my life force? You shouldn't be able to touch it, if you know what I mean. But you need to find it, and then feed some of your magic into it. We don't want you to feed into my own magic, but directly into my life force. Then we will focus on concentrating it to a certain injury. It takes a lot of magic to heal, so you don't want to pour it into someone's entire body."

Iyashi was a patient coach. Brenna tried again and again, accidentally feeding a bit of her light magic into the naiad's power and causing her to jump. By the time she successfully connected with the gentle life energy of the faerie, Brenna was sweating and exhausted.

"It's time for a break. You need food." Iyashi helped her stand and steadied her as they walked back inside. "Then we will focus on turning that energy into healing. It's a bit trickier, but you seem to be a natural at this."

A simple meal was laid out on a low table where they joined the other healers. Galen sat at the head, while a pair of young women took their places nearby. When they looked up and smiled, Brenna was taken aback—their eyes were solid black, devoid of whites. Their tunics were cut away to accommodate the soft brown wings draping down their backs, and delicate feathered antennae rose from their mousy brown hair.

"How was it?" Galen asked, taking a bite of an apple.

Iyashi reached for a slice of bread. "Good. She has the disposition for it. We could test her with an injury soon." She sliced a peach and laid it across the bread.

"Healing an actual injury?" Brenna asked, nervously picking at the berries she had spooned onto her plate.

"Yes, generally that is what healing is for," Galen said with a flash of white teeth.

Brenna blinked, startled at his response, but when she saw the humor creasing around his eyes and mouth, she relaxed and returned the smile. "Of course."

Iyashi launched into a story of yesterday's visit to the training yards. The new recruits were struggling to fight in tandem with their teammates. She had a plethora of minor injuries to patch up, such as bloody noses, cuts, and bruises. There was no time to waste on healing naturally when they would march any day.

The warmth of the midday sun filtered through the open windows, casting a golden glow over the simple meal of bread, fruit, and meats. Brenna relaxed as she listened to the healers' quiet conversation and the soothing rustle of feathers as the winged healers shifted beside her.

Once the food was cleared away, Iyashi and Galen sat beside her. "Are you ready to try injuries?" Galen asked.

"I'm apprehensive," she said with a nervous laugh, "but I have to try or I'll never learn."

"Very well," Galen said. He produced a short knife from his pocket and rolled up his sleeve, nicking his forearm. Blood welled in the shallow cut. "Try to heal this."

Biting her lip, Brenna reached an open hand toward the injury and focused her eyes, sorting through the sensations around her to find Galen's life energy. She was not attuned to it the way she was to Iyashi's. It danced around her, ungraspable.

"I can't," she said, glancing down at the trail of blood down his arm. "I'm sorry!"

Galen's ocean eyes locked with hers. He gripped her hand and placed it on his forearm, over the injury. "Try again."

She scrunched her nose, concentrating. Warmth bloomed in her chest, and she was afraid she would burn him instead of healing. Then a soft magic whispered to her. Something gentle curled around her senses, guiding her until she could latch on to Galen's energy and direct her magic into it.

Her eyes popped open. Galen smiled, wiping away the blood to reveal whole unmarred skin. "I did that?" she asked, tilting her head.

"It was a team effort," he said, taking a rag and wiping his blood from her palm.

"I think it's best if you practice on yourself until you master directing your healing. That is what most people start with, because pushing it outward is draining and harder to guide."

"Yes, I felt that," she said. "So, myself first."

"And then we can combine skills until you can easily heal those around you," Galen added.

"Can you cut yourself?" Iyashi asked. She nodded.

Galen handed over the blade, and Brenna held it over her palm. She could prick a finger, but that made her think of Emrys. It was a distraction she didn't need. Clenching her teeth, she drew the blade across the meat of her palm. The sensation of metal through flesh turned her stomach. Hissing from pain, she dropped the blade onto the table beside them. It bled more than she expected.

"Direct your magic here," Galen coached. He cradled her hand with his own. As she closed her eyes to focus, she could feel his energy playing at the fringes of her awareness. It felt as if he was eager to heal her palm for her, but was restraining himself.

"Concentrate," he reminded her. His soothing voice guided her, and she honed in on the sting of her cut. "No, you're using your light craft. We want raw energy. Try again." His warm hand took her other hand and laid it over the cut. Blood wet between her fingers.

On the third try, Brenna managed to partially close the wound. Iyashi clapped, and Galen beamed at her. "Well done."

She was on the right course, she knew it. Gritting her teeth, she drew a line down the base of her forearm, close to the crook of her elbow.

"What are you doing?" Emrys said, his voice deadly cold. Brenna startled, nearly dropping the knife mid-slice. "Why are you cutting yourself?" He stood in the entrance to the ward, his eyes blazing.

"I'm learning to heal," Brenna said, her smile wavering. "I've already done it once."

"You thought it was best she injure herself to learn to heal?" he said, stalking further into the space.

Galen stood to face him, his hands folded loosely at his waist. "Yes, it is the typical process of teaching a new apprentice." His tone was calm, devoid of the anger she expected.

"She isn't typical," Emrys said. Brenna flinched.

"It's fine! They can heal anything I couldn't. I'm perfectly safe." She rose, stepping between Emrys and the healers. His lip curled, revealing fangs in a silent threat. She had never seen him like this. He wasn't the charming nobleman she had fallen for. This was a ruthless warrior sizing up an opponent.

He grabbed her wrist, twisting it to get a clear look at the cut. Cursing under his breath, he closed his palm over it, and she felt his magic knit the skin back together. Now that she knew what the feeling of magic mingling felt like, it was unmistakable. His craft felt like thick velvet brushing against her, luxurious and tempting.

"I think that's enough for today," he said, wrapping his arm around her shoulders. "We will have words before these lessons resume."

Others would have wilted under his intensity, but after a look at Brenna's hand, Galen simply nodded and returned to his work. Relieved, Brenna shot Iyashi an apologetic smile before Emrys ushered her out.

Emrys strode down the hallway and Brenna had to rush to keep up with him so he wasn't dragging her along. As they turned the corner, she spun, locking her legs and halting. Emrys' eyes narrowed dangerously as he faced her.

"I was uncomfortable with that," she said, waving her hand back toward the healing ward.

Emrys stared at her silently for a moment. "What exactly upset you?" he asked, slow, measured.

"I feel like we were disrespectful of the healers who were teaching me," she said, softening her words. Her desire to please him warred with her anger over the interaction.

He breathed out audibly, those crimson irises narrowing as his black pupils expanded. With the grace of a predator, he stepped forward, crowding her until her back pressed into the white stone wall. Keeping her gaze, he said roughly, "I apologize for upsetting you, but not for being angry when they instructed you to hurt yourself. I cannot help but protect you."

She opened her mouth to argue, but he placed a hand over her mouth, silencing her. "I know it seems like too much, but how can I stand by when everything in me demands that I defend you?" His lips brushed the shell of her ear as he spoke, low and silky.

Brenna melted under his intensity. Anger gone, she was nothing but desire. When he pulled back and removed his hand, she reached for him, dragging him against her until she was pressed between his hard body and the stone behind her. Her voice was husky. "You feel that strongly? I am not a mere diversion?"

He hauled her up against him, hands gripping her thighs through her skirts, and she was grateful for the thin layers of faerie fashions and her lack of a petticoat in this moment.

His voice was a growl. "I don't want anyone else touching you again. My very nature declares you are mine."

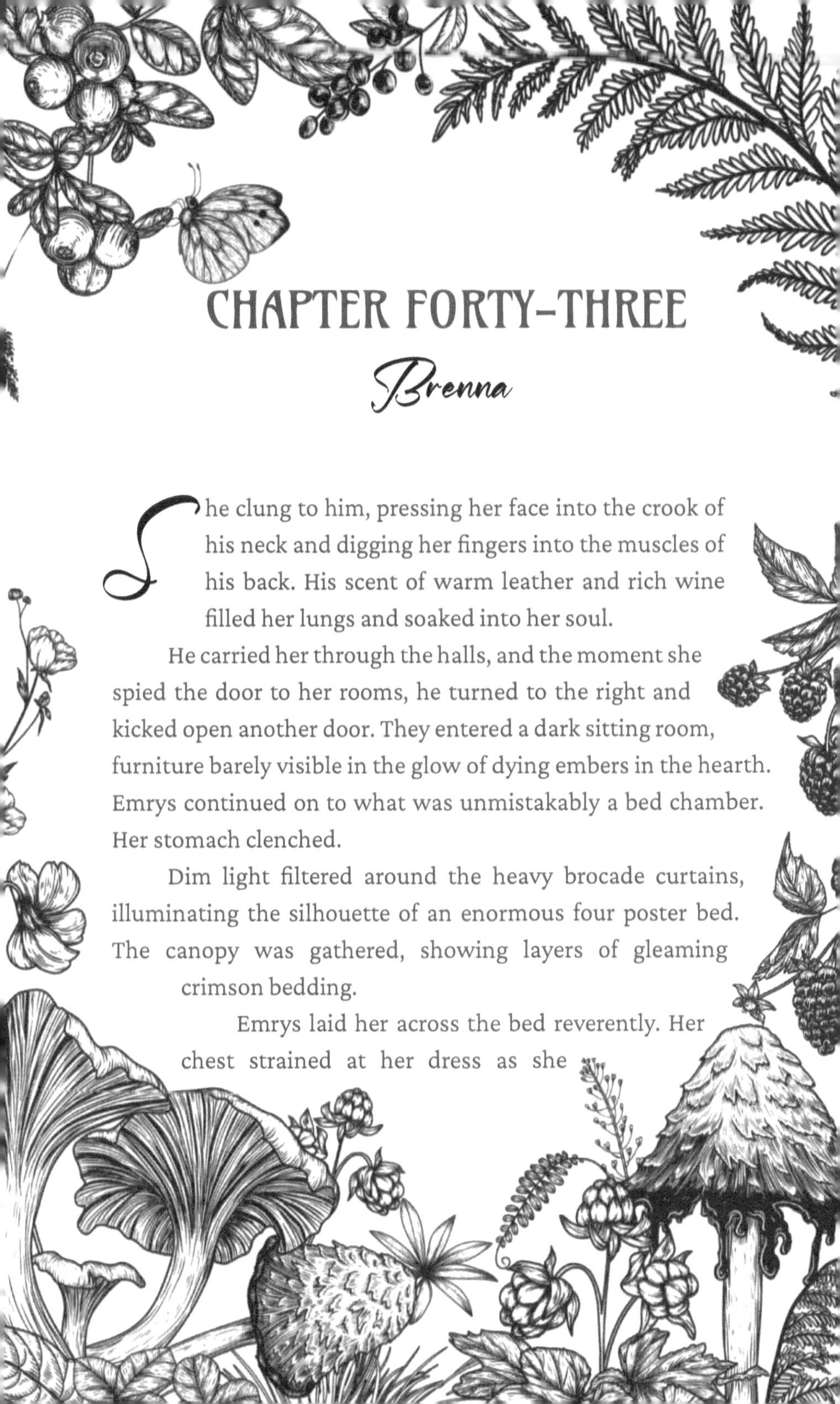

CHAPTER FORTY-THREE

Brenna

She clung to him, pressing her face into the crook of his neck and digging her fingers into the muscles of his back. His scent of warm leather and rich wine filled her lungs and soaked into her soul.

He carried her through the halls, and the moment she spied the door to her rooms, he turned to the right and kicked open another door. They entered a dark sitting room, furniture barely visible in the glow of dying embers in the hearth. Emrys continued on to what was unmistakably a bed chamber. Her stomach clenched.

Dim light filtered around the heavy brocade curtains, illuminating the silhouette of an enormous four poster bed. The canopy was gathered, showing layers of gleaming crimson bedding.

Emrys laid her across the bed reverently. Her chest strained at her dress as she struggled to gather enough air, her breaths turned to desperate, shallow pants.

As he pulled away, his fingers traced a slow path down her body, and for a moment, her thoughts melted into nothing. His intense russet eyes held her captive. Every part of this male was a study in contrasts, from his soft, full lips to the fangs they hid. He smirked, his mouth tugging up to reveal a single elongated canine that sent her heart racing.

"My light," he murmured, his voice low and rough, leaning closer until his dark hair fell over his brow. "Forgive me for being a brute... but you have taken hold of me."

She shivered as his lips brushed the sensitive skin just above her dress's neckline, her breath hitching. "I've done nothing," she whispered, her hands finding the back of his neck as his mouth trailed upward, lingering at the hollow of her throat.

"Then why can I think of no one else but you?" His teeth grazed her skin, making her gasp. He smiled against her pulse point. "If you walked away, I would follow. There is no part of me that can stay away."

With a soft groan, she turned her head, letting him scatter kisses along her jaw on his way back to her mouth. "I am insignificant."

His eyes shone crimson as he pulled back, his lip curling in dismay. "Do not speak those words." He cupped her face gently. "From the moment I saw you before the throne, with that flame in your hand, I knew. I've never craved anything the way I crave you."

His hands tightened at her waist, his grip possessive yet restrained.

"I felt the same." She couldn't think clearly when he touched her, every one of her words coming out breathy and broken.

"Brenna," he said, "my light, I want to make you mine. I want to have you in every way."

Her body turned molten at the words, all caution melting away. Nothing else remained, only his touch and the weight of him over her. "I have no desire but you."

"Thank goodness I am not alone in my devotion."

He devoured her, his mouth demanding, his tongue sliding against hers in a slow, claiming stroke. Heat flared within her, her body faintly glowing in the darkened room.

Her hands grasped at the tie of his shirt, trying to tear it from his body. Grinning, he removed the offending garment.

Brenna admired his chest for a split second before he flipped her onto her stomach. She whimpered into the coverlet as his firm hands unlaced her dress and peeled the fabric away. Cool air brushed her back. She tried to roll over, but his hand pressed into the nape of her neck to keep her in place. Slowly, he trailed kisses across the newly revealed skin.

The weight of him eased off, and she turned and propped herself up to watch as he knelt with a wicked grin on his beautiful face. His eyes roamed down her body and the stretch of skin exposed by the dress barely clinging to her breasts and stomach.

Loving the hungry gleam in his eyes, she tugged the loose dress further down. "I could use some help here," she said. A devious smile bloomed across her face as her confidence grew.

His movement was too fast for her to follow as he tugged her forward and stripped the dress down her hips. It fluttered to the floor and his hands returned to her body, exploring the expanse of tan skin.

She cleared her throat. "That was very effective."

Emrys growled. "Effective is not a word I'd like you to use in my bed."

"What should I say instead?"

"Only my name," he said, dipping his head to kiss her shoulder. "Or perhaps 'more' or 'harder'."

Her eyes widened, a flush staining her cheeks and the tips of her tapered ears. "Oh, really?"

"Maybe 'yes'." He kissed the crook of her neck and she groaned as his fangs scraped her skin. "Or 'again'."

"What about 'please'?" she choked out, reaching to run her hands over his muscled arms and up to his back.

"If you wish," he murmured, leaning forward to capture her mouth. She lay bare beneath him, reveling in the press of his chest against her breasts. The sensation was exquisite—intoxicating— and she wanted to lose herself in it forever, even as she ached for more.

"Eager?" he teased as she mindlessly fumbled with the ties of his pants. One eyebrow arched, sharpening his features.

Wrinkling her nose, she gave a harder tug on the laces. "It is only fair. I am laid bare and you are still clothed."

"Yes, but this way, I can give you the attention you truly deserve." His hand cupped her heavy breast, his thumb running over the silky skin.

"As lovely as that sounds," she ground out, "I'd appreciate if you removed your pants."

"Yes, my light."

He dipped his head, replacing his fingers with his mouth. She might have protested the delay, but the only sound that escaped her parted lips was a soft, wistful sigh as he moved to the other breast. Only when her breathy whimpers turned into a desperate mewl did he finally strip away the last of his clothing.

She responded instantly, rolling her hips against him. With a low growl, he caught her wrists, gathering them in one hand and pinning them above her head. Her body arched, stretched out beneath him, offering herself without hesitation.

His voice was rough with restraint. "So impatient."

Digging her heels into the mattress, she writhed beneath

him, seeking more. "Yes, please, Emrys, please," she chanted, repeating the words he supplied. He chuckled, rewarding her with a searing kiss as he pushed into her.

Heat radiated from her skin, and she prayed it wasn't too much for him. Forcing her eyes open, she found his lips parted, his gaze dark with need.

She cupped his face and pulled him into a kiss. He deepened it instantly, his mouth greedy as his hips moved in a slow, aching rhythm. A whimper slipped from her lips, swallowed by his. It was too much—too intense. Every touch, every movement sent a fresh wave of sensation through her, leaving her trembling beneath him. As he pulled back and thrust into her harder, her breath caught, breaking into a strangled gasp.

Emrys stilled, his forehead pressing to hers. "Did I hurt you?" His voice was low, laced with concern.

She shook her head. "No—it's just... I've never done this before."

"Never," he echoed with a raised brow. She almost missed his hand reaching between them, gently touching where their bodies joined. Embarrassment stung her cheeks as he brought up two fingers tipped in crimson.

A lock of dark hair fell over his brow as Emrys looked up, his mouth tugging into a smirk. Her breath stuttered. Achingly slowly, he slipped his fingers into his mouth and sucked them clean. Brenna's eyes widened and heat flared low in her stomach.

"I-" she started to say.

"Do not apologize for this gift," he said, his voice dark.

Emrys lowered himself down her body, the muscles of his back and shoulders rippling as he settled between her thighs. His hands spread her legs further to give him full reign over her body.

She threw her head back, curls spilling over the pillow. His tongue dragged over her, igniting a cascade of sparks through every piece of her. A feral groan ripped from her throat as he licked her clean.

Emrys laughed against her. He lingered, adding the firm touch of his fingers alongside his heated licks and gentle kisses. He explored her until she was in blissful oblivion, nothing but pleasure and white hot stars, building into an explosion she could not stave off. Brenna had the distinct sensation of falling over a cliff, tension seizing her and uncoiling until her body was limp and tears wet her lashes.

When she came back to herself, he was over her once more. With a grin, he swiped his thumb across his bottom lip to clean off the last of her blood.

Her lips parted, but no words came out. All she could think was *more*, *please*, *again*. As if he could read her thoughts, he pressed into her. This time, the discomfort gave way to glowing pleasure.

Her fingers tangled into his dark hair, further mussing his sleek style. She loved him like this, eyes dark and expression unguarded.

Though his movements were gentle and languid, the growls and soft grunts he made as she lifted her hips to meet him was what had her unraveling beneath him. If she could, she would crawl into his very chest and nestle beside his heart.

He stayed steady, until she was begging for more. She dug her nails into his biceps as she tensed and broke a second time, while he murmured praise in her ear.

Once she regained a glimmer of her composure, she urged him on, squeezing her thighs around his hips as his rhythm sped and stuttered. With a hiss of breath through his teeth, Emrys came undone. Brenna watched, fascinated, as his mouth parted in a soft expression and his brows furrowed, before his forehead fell against the side of her neck. His movements slowed, leaving both of them drawing in deep breaths to steady themselves.

"Beautiful," he said, dragging his thumb over her lip and down her throat, where his hand stretched over her neck in a momentary claiming. Her eyes wandered over his chest and lower as he withdrew from her and climbed from the bed.

He returned with linens to clean her. She blushed at his attention. Satisfied, Emrys tugged the coverlet around them, allowing her to nestle against his chest. Brenna sighed, her body buzzing and yet fully unwound. She wanted to bask in this warmth forever.

His fingers traced over her skin, swirling over her shoulder blades and brushing her curls back to expose her neck.

A knock interrupted their drowsy contentedness. Brenna jerked in surprise, but Emrys squeezed her arm and placed a kiss on her temple before he rose. She drew the warm blanket over her shoulders in his absence.

Tugging on pants, Emrys went to the door. The bed was too far from the entry for her to see the intruder, and it was impossible to make out what was said in hushed, quick words.

He returned in a moment, running his fingers through his dark hair to sweep it back from his face. He looked beautifully undone, something she selfishly wanted to keep to herself. Everyone else could have the polished prince. She wanted the growling fae male, the searing kisses, the possessive bites.

Emrys crawled into bed beside her and pulled her against his chest. She curled against him, her fingers gripping the tense muscles in his arm. He sighed, squeezing her tighter for a moment before he relaxed.

"I have news to share. Spies have informed me that Meara is with your mother in Dornadan," he said. Brenna froze. "Please don't worry. The fight will not spread to the human kingdom. Once the battle is won, you can safely reunite with her."

"So she's safe?"

"Quite," he said, stroking her hair.

Her exhale was heavy. "Thank you. That is a relief."

Pulling her hand up to his mouth, Emrys affectionately kissed each fingertip and then bit down on the meat of her palm, not hard enough to break the skin but enough to make her twitch in his arms. "See? Everything is well, my light."

She managed a soft noise of agreement as his lips moved to her wrist. He paused, and she met his gaze and hummed encouragingly. Only then did he sink his fangs into her skin. Heat flared within her again, subsiding into a soothing glow as he drank.

Stress melted away, her anxiety quelled and warm contentment thrummed through every muscle. Her hands roamed, gliding down his chest and lower. It was easy to entice Emrys to pull her down the bed, positioning himself between her legs, and let passion consume them once more.

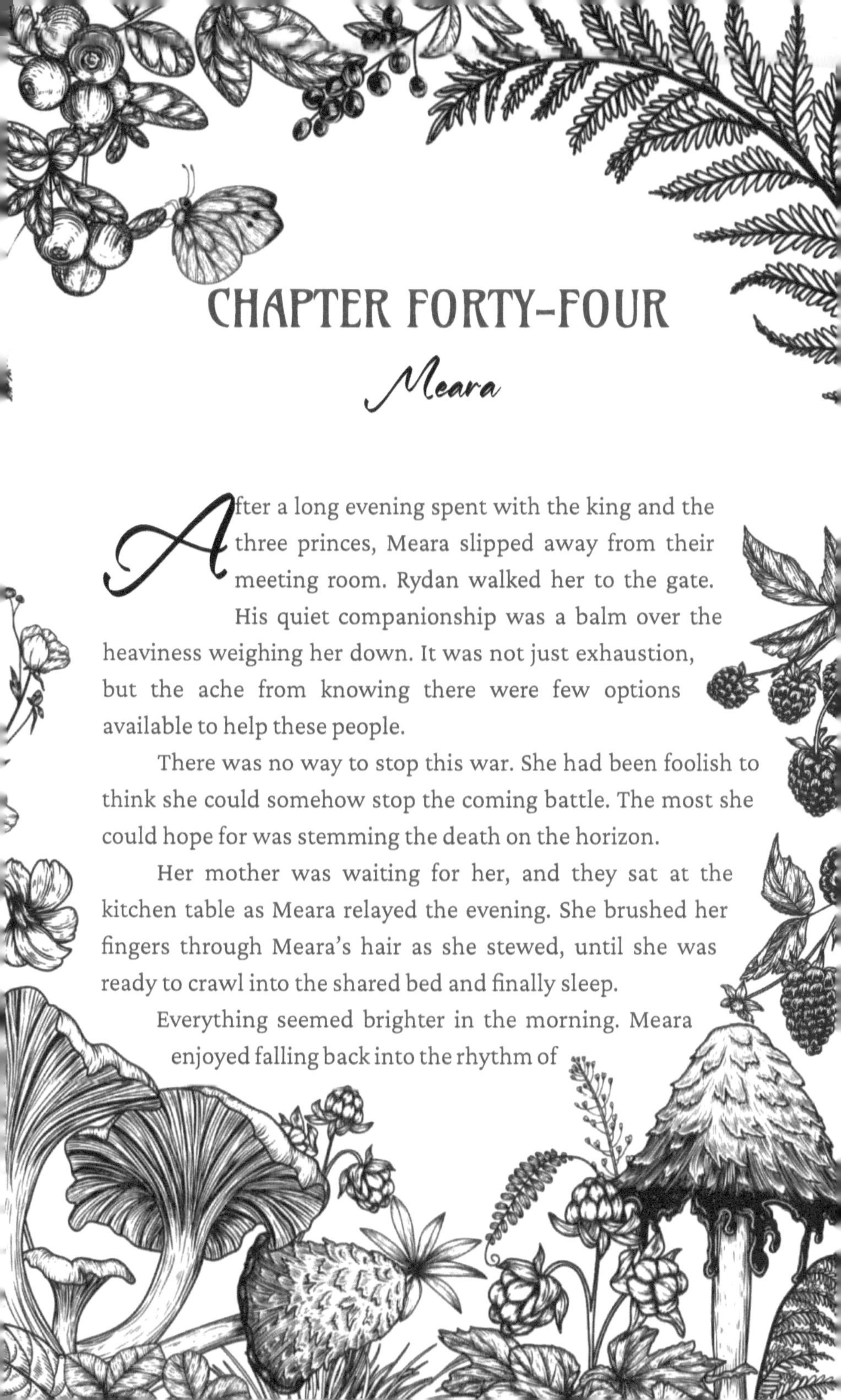

CHAPTER FORTY-FOUR
Meara

After a long evening spent with the king and the three princes, Meara slipped away from their meeting room. Rydan walked her to the gate.

His quiet companionship was a balm over the heaviness weighing her down. It was not just exhaustion, but the ache from knowing there were few options available to help these people.

There was no way to stop this war. She had been foolish to think she could somehow stop the coming battle. The most she could hope for was stemming the death on the horizon.

Her mother was waiting for her, and they sat at the kitchen table as Meara relayed the evening. She brushed her fingers through Meara's hair as she stewed, until she was ready to crawl into the shared bed and finally sleep.

Everything seemed brighter in the morning. Meara enjoyed falling back into the rhythm of preparing salves and prepping ingredients for teas and tonics. Her mother stayed busy with the front of the shop, but even with her dark hair over her pointed ears, Meara tried to not be seen. There was too much beauty in her features to pass as human if someone looked closely.

She waited to hear from Rydan or Emeric, but the day passed without any contact. Frustrated, she considered writing to Brenna, but she did not want to give away her location or put her sister under suspicion.

As night fell, she sat with her mother by candlelight and told her everything else she could remember of their time in Court Tara and the Summer Court. Eventually, they were too tired to continue, and she slept curled up beside her mother for a second night.

Rydan came for her the following morning.

"Lady Meara, are you ready to make yourself useful?" he said, his rugged face bright with a teasing smile.

Bristling, she pulled a spare cloak over the simple work dress she borrowed from her mother, pulled the hood over her hair, and stepped out the front door.

"Just Meara, please. I am not nobility."

To his credit, Rydan did not argue or attempt to mollify her. She was content with her status and had no desire to continue playing at nobility. She fell into step beside him, soaking in his confident and relaxed energy. "So what are we doing today? Training? Strategizing?"

"Later. This morning we are meeting a contact."

She frowned, turning to check his expression for sobriety. "A contact?"

Nodding, he continued, "Yes, a friend within the courts who has been aiding us. Perhaps the last friend that remains, it seems, aside from you." He paused and looked her over. "I believe you are trustworthy, but do you want to know who has been helping us? It is a risk to you both, but I feel you deserve to know you are not alone in this."

Meara swallowed and nodded. "I will join you."

"Good."

As they descended the mountainside toward the marshes, they were met by Eladin and Emeric on horseback, a smoke-coated Kemuri trailing behind them. Rydan swung up to sit atop his favorite mare. The princes looked between themselves, a silent discussion happening before her eyes.

"Lady Meara, you can join me in my saddle," Eladin said with a flirtatious grin. Memories of him in a dark hallway, Tayen kissing him, popped into her thoughts.

"No, thank you," she said, crossing her arms. "I can walk."

Rydan turned his horse back. "Here, sit behind me. It will be far more comfortable than the front of a saddle."

She muttered her gratitude and allowed him to pull her up to settle behind him. Her arms went around his middle and she leaned against his leather cuirass as the horses broke into a trot.

They crossed the marshland and into the trees, and her apprehension grew. Surely it was Tayen working to protect his lover. Or perhaps Cerne had a sense of loyalty after all. She chewed her lip, impatient to learn who they were meeting.

Once within the fringe of Sablewood, they slowed the horses and dismounted. Rydan tethered their horses, turning back to the trees with an expectant look.

Meara's heart raced, thudding against her breastbone hard enough she was worried it would burst. A flash of motion between the trees drew her attention.

"I wonder if he is late," Emeric grumbled.

She searched the landscape, and saw another movement. "Someone is out there."

All three princes turned, following her gaze. A figure covered in a dark cloak emerged. He was tall and broad, and Meara's heart sank when she realized it was not Tayen's slim frame.

The hood fell back, and angry mismatched eyes of gold and azure glared at her. "What is she doing here?"

"You?" she growled.

Luce stalked forward, jabbing an accusatory finger at her. "This female is loyal to Cerne, and her sister is in bed with the king's closest advisor."

He grabbed her forearm and she twisted, wrenching it free. "You are the heir to the Summer Court! Your mother speaks of slaughtering entire kingdoms of humans," she shot back.

The human princes looked between them, an infuriating expression of amusement forming.

"Why else do you think I want to help the humans my mother so callously dismisses?" Luce said, pressing forward into her space. "You are the one to not be trusted."

"My mother lives here!" Meara yelped, leaping back. "You are the one leading an army against us!"

"Stop yelling," he commanded. Light emanated from his skin in his anger, making him a beacon. He reached for her again, and she dodged, bringing her hands up and clenching them into fists.

When he came closer, she threw a punch, landing a blow to his cheek. He stepped back, surprise in his eyes as he lifted a hand to touch his face. Looking at his clean fingertips, his lips spread into a smile that chilled her. When his eyes rose, they promised violence.

She wanted to turn and run, but she grit her teeth and readied herself, calling shadows up around her. He moved far too quickly for such a large male. She twisted to escape, but he pulled her against himself, so her back pressed into his chest. His voice was against her hair. "This is not a safe place for you to work out whatever guilt you have."

"I can keep myself safe," she hissed.

She dragged her shadows around them, but the glow of his magic held them at bay. Snarling in frustration, she increased her effort. She would drown them in darkness if that was what it took, but his light would not fade no matter how hard she tried.

"What will you do now?" he asked, his anger turning to mockery. "Turn into a raven and fly away?"

She let out a frustrated scream, held back behind her teeth. "I don't think I can. It wasn't intentional."

"Like I said before, you need better control of your craft." He spoke against her ear, and the skin on her arms pebbled.

Eladin cleared his throat. "If you two are done with your rather sensual display, we have business matters to attend to."

Meara pushed away, expecting Luce to release her, but his hand closed around her wrist so she was able to unfurl from his hold only to be yanked back. Turning, she tugged her arm but he held fast.

His eyes darkened and he held up her hand. "What are these?"

She relaxed her fists and opened her fingers so the scars running down her hands were less noticeable. "Nothing. Old scratches from foraging."

"Foraging?" he repeated dumbly.

"Yes," she hissed, yanking her arm away. "I told you my mother was a human. She is an apothecary. I grew up hunting for medicinal plants in the forest."

He assessed her, eyes roaming over her face, ears, throat. "You grew up among humans."

"I thought I was one until a few weeks ago," she said, rubbing her wrist.

"I don't believe…" he started, and Meara threw her hands up.

"I don't give a flying fuck if you believe me, as long as you leave me alone." Spinning, she stalked into the trees and away from the summer heir that made her shadows seethe around her. She considered kicking a tree, but did not want to damage her mother's boots.

A second set of footsteps crunched in the leaves. As she turned, it was Rydan who followed her.

"I was ten when I was adopted by the king," he said. She was so taken aback by the change of topic, her mouth shut with a click of teeth. "My brothers had trained since birth, while I ran the streets as an orphan. They often reminded me of that fact as they beat me in our lessons. Over and over."

He ran a hand over his locs. "It took two years to be able to defeat Eladin. Another two before I could best Emeric. No one can keep you from working hard and becoming better."

"So I simply must work harder?" she asked quietly. "Excuse me, but I feel as if I have done everything I can. I don't think I can possibly do more."

He frowned, his warm brown eyes connecting with her violet ones. "Meara, I felt the nightmares in your shadows. You are anything but weak, especially if you use that terrifying talent. I cannot imagine what you could accomplish given enough time."

Rubbing her hands over her arms, she pursed her lips. "Time is something we lack."

"True, but you can use the time that remains. And learning to shift into your raven at will would be useful as well, though that may be well beyond the time we have."

Her hands curled into fists at her sides as her resolve hardened. "I suppose, I have my task."

Meara looked through the trees to where Luce stood with Emeric and Eladin. The summer heir's eyes rose to her, and her stomach flipped. Exhaling, she set her shoulders and strode back to the group.

Arms crossed, she listened as Luce detailed the size of the fae forces and the planned marching structure. Emeric took notes in a little book he kept in his vest. Rydan questioned Luce, and Luce answered most of them. Once their debrief was complete, Luce turned to leave.

"Wait!" she said. "How is my sister?"

Luce folded his arms. "Are you sure you want to know?"

Eyes narrowing, she mimicked his pose. "Of course I do!"

"She went to Court Tara and has been staying with Emrys."

"With Emrys?" she echoed.

His eyes fell to the ground, and reluctantly, he added, "In his bedchamber."

Meara's mouth fell open and she gaped at him. "Is she safe?"

"As safe as she can be with him. No one else will touch her, I can assure you of that. And I do not think he will let her near the battle to come, though she has been training as a healer."

"A healer," she echoed, running her fingers through her hair. "Thank you for telling me." Her thoughts rushed over each other, and she hardly saw Luce's retreating back.

Perched behind Rydan on Kemuri's haunches, Meara turned over the information in her mind. Her sister as a healer. She wasn't surprised at that decision, but she couldn't reconcile Brenna growing that close with the blood-drinking fae, Emrys. How could she be so reckless?

When they returned to the king's keep and dismounted, Eladin walked beside her. "How is Tayen?" he asked softly.

"I don't know," she answered honestly. "He did not attend Samhain with us, so I have not seen him in recent days. But I am sure he is concerned. He cares for you." It felt like too much to share, but if Eladin was going into battle soon, she would rather risk Tayen's anger than leave things unsaid and risk his regret.

Dark eyes stared into the distance, northward into Sablewood. "I miss him," he finally muttered before moving to the horses.

"Do you want to train with us?" Emeric called to her.

Meara sighed. "I need to work on my shadows. Unless you want me terrifying your forces, I should find a private place to work."

"I have a place for you," Rydan said, jerking his head to indicate the direction.

While the princes walked through their exercises, she sat in an empty yard and gathered as many shadows as she could, exercising her control and stamina until she was sweaty and shaking.

She found the princes finishing their own training. They led her to a small fire, and Emeric produced a cold supper to be shared. The flames crackled merrily, and Meara stretched her sore limbs out.

The chilled night air nipped at her skin as her sweat dried, and she bundled her cloak over her arms. She ate the dense bread and salted meat happily, listening to the princes share stories of their childhood together.

Eladin leaned against the bench with a smirk on his handsome face. He told about the time Emeric challenged a full grown guard to a duel and got his ribs broken for his trouble. Emeric replied with a story about Eladin being chased from a brothel as a skulking teenager.

Their camaraderie warmed her, but left her heart aching for her sister. Growing up, they had shared the same loyalty. Becoming fae changed everything. After this war ended, they would repair things and return to the same. She promised herself that.

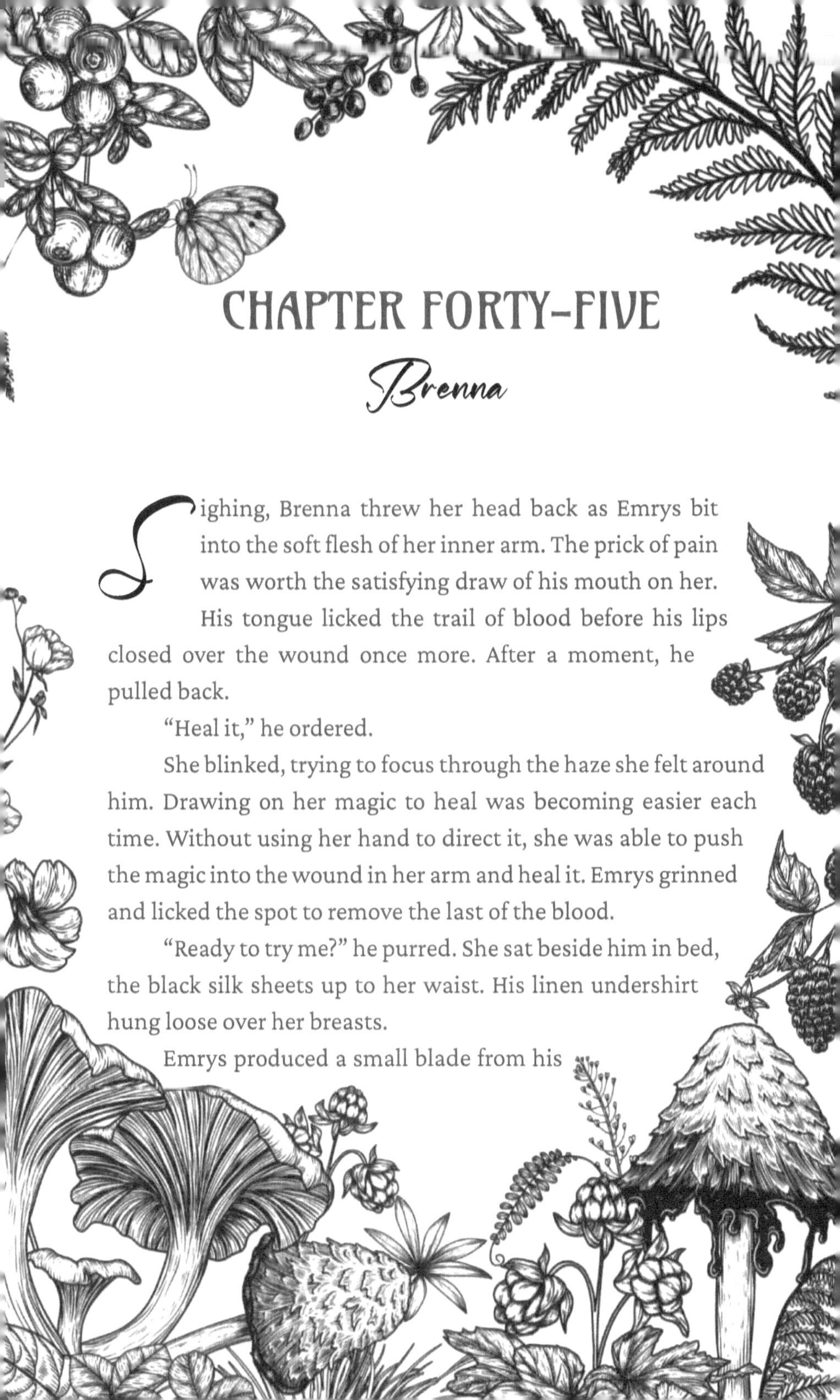

CHAPTER FORTY-FIVE

Brenna

Sighing, Brenna threw her head back as Emrys bit into the soft flesh of her inner arm. The prick of pain was worth the satisfying draw of his mouth on her.

His tongue licked the trail of blood before his lips closed over the wound once more. After a moment, he pulled back.

"Heal it," he ordered.

She blinked, trying to focus through the haze she felt around him. Drawing on her magic to heal was becoming easier each time. Without using her hand to direct it, she was able to push the magic into the wound in her arm and heal it. Emrys grinned and licked the spot to remove the last of the blood.

"Ready to try me?" he purred. She sat beside him in bed, the black silk sheets up to her waist. His linen undershirt hung loose over her breasts.

Emrys produced a small blade from his

bedside table and drew it across his bare chest. She rose up on her knees, pressing a hand to his chest. He leaned against the headboard, watching her while a smirk graced his handsome face. She tried to focus on his wound, but he was distracting.

"I cannot work when you look at me like that," she said.

His gaze darkened. "Taste it," he urged. "See if you can taste my magic."

The idea should revolt her, but she felt intrigued. Steadying herself, she dipped her face to his skin and tentatively dragged her tongue over his skin. Blood soaked her senses. It tasted like merlot, smooth and thick. His magic lay dormant in the crimson liquid she swallowed.

She closed her eyes and pressed her magic into the cut, closing it up after a moment of effort. Her lashes fluttered open and she inspected the perfect skin. Her hand trailed over the fine dusting of dark hair over his pale chest.

He sucked in a breath and she paused her exploration, looking up at him. "Don't stop on my account," he murmured. His smile revealed a pair of sharp canine teeth that stirred heat within her.

"I think," she said, pausing as she explored new sensations, "that I can sense your emotions." A flash of pride warmed her.

"Our bond is deepening. You have access to my magic," he said.

"Will I have to drink blood to use it?"

He cocked his head, keen eyes questioning. "Yes. Do you not wish to?"

With a giggle, she straightened. "Not particularly. I mean, *your* blood is one thing, but I can't imagine using it on anyone else." She frowned. "How often do you drink from others?"

Emrys brushed her hair over her shoulder and ran his fingers down her bare arm. "Not often. And rarely from biting them." His tongue darted over his bottom lip, fascinating her. "Argyro asks me to use my magic from time to time. The subject will be cut and their blood placed in a cup."

"Does that bother you?"

He shrugged. "I am here to serve him, and it is my magic. It's what I've known my entire life."

Brenna considered that for a moment. "I think I'd prefer if you weren't biting anyone but me if you can help it."

Smiling, he twisted until he pressed her back into the pillow. "My jealous mate, you want my fangs to be yours alone?" The heat of his breath roamed from her jaw to her throat.

"Maybe." Her whisper was rough. He kissed her again, taking his time thoroughly claiming her. She wove her fingers into his hair and pressed his head down gently. He complied, trailing kisses down her neck and moving to the swell of her breasts. His fangs cut into her and she sucked in a breath, letting it out with a moan. The feel of his mouth on her delicate skin was exquisite. He chuckled, the sound vibrating against her skin. He licked at her and she felt the wound close.

When he pulled away, blood covered her bottom lip. He kissed her again, the metallic taste coating her tongue. Her own blood tasted different from his lips.

Sitting back, he wiped the crimson from her lips and popped his thumb into his mouth to lick it clean. "Beautiful."

She reached for him, but he caught her wrist. "As much as I would love to continue this, my light, we have to attend a dinner with the king and queen," he said, brows furrowing as he lifted her hand and inspected her long fingers. Turning it over, he pressed a kiss to the back of her hand.

"I don't mind. Actually, I'm looking forward to it. I like dressing up pretty."

"You are beautiful in anything and especially in nothing," he growled, wrapping his arms around her hips and dragging her closer. She squawked as he bit down on her ass, not breaking the skin but hard enough to leave a mark. "I haven't *bit* you here yet," he mused.

"Feel free to," she said breathlessly.

"We will never get to dinner if we start that again," he said with a low laugh that sent fire through her blood. As he released her and rose, she considered dragging him back to bed. It would be so easy to seduce him, but she did enjoy wearing a court dress and attending dinners. And she could let him strip her bare afterward.

Sighing, she crawled from the bed and looked for her dress.

"If I'm going to continually be undressing in your rooms, I might need some of my clothes here for afterward," she said.

Emrys didn't answer, but she knew that smirk. He was planning something. She smothered a grin and focused on pulling on her dress from that morning. She had planned to go to the healing ward to practice, but Emrys promised he would help her as long as he was the one making her bleed. Besides, his method of helping was far more enjoyable.

It took a dozen more kisses before she was dressed and walking across the hall to her rooms. Emrys stayed with her, his hands in her hair and tracing her curves. "I thought we had dinner to attend," she teased, turning to seize his face and kiss him on the mouth.

"But we haven't been together in this room yet," he muttered as he lifted her by her thighs and carried her to the bed. Curtains fluttered aside as her back hit the mattress.

She turned her face toward the massive windows that stood open, the sea breeze floating in. In Emrys' rooms, they were in near constant darkness, but here in her suites filled with dreamy sunlight, she could see every detail as he kissed her chest and worked down her stomach, unlacing her dress. As he nipped at her breast, he slipped both hands under her skirts and hauled them up before hooking fingers into her undergarments and tugging them down to her knees.

"We are going to be late," she said, each word strangled as he kissed the sensitive inside of her thigh. "Did you change your mind?"

"Yes," he growled. "I want everyone to know you are mine."

She opened her mouth to protest, but her brain went blank as he licked her center in one languid stroke. Instead, an embarrassing moan escaped her. Her next breath was a gasp.

Emrys hauled one of her legs up over his shoulder and grabbed her hip, holding her still as he worked her with his mouth. A string of nonsense words poured out of her, ending with his name repeating, pleading. Brenna tensed, every muscle feeling as if she would break, as her world shattered and reformed around her.

With a satisfied grin, Emrys laid her skirts back and crawled up her body to kiss her. She parted her lips, tasting herself on his tongue. Sighing, the arm cradling his face flopped back down onto the bed beside her. "You are most beautiful like this." Emrys kissed the tip of her nose and said, "It's time to get dressed, my light, or we will be late for dinner."

"You are truly evil, doing that to me and then expecting me to walk and talk." Her hair stuck up on one side and her legs felt like jelly. Sucking in a deep breath, she shook out her arms to rid herself of the lingering tingles before sliding off the bed.

While brushing out her hair, she looked over her shoulder and grinned at Emrys. "Do you want to select a dress for me to wear? I don't know how formal these dinners are."

"I'd love to," he said, his tone suggestive.

Unable to tame her curls, she brushed them out and twisted them into a chignon, securing it with diamond pins. She selected ear cuffs to match and spent a moment admiring her reflection, the jewels glittering in her ears while her face held a beautiful flush and her lips were swollen.

When she turned, Emrys held a dress of shimmering black. She had never worn it, as black was Meara's preferred color, and she more often wore softer golds and creams. In fact, she did not recognize the dress at all. Frowning, she inspected the gleaming fabric. Gold thread wove throughout the black silk, so the entire dress seemed to glow like embers beneath shadows.

"Did you get this for me?" she asked.

He shrugged. "I had it commissioned for you after I met you."

"Truly? And what if we had not seen each other again?" she said, wrinkling her nose at him.

"Not possible." Emrys smirked at her. "I would not have let that happen. I could have sent my forces to give Cerne his orders. I came to see you."

She slipped her dress off, preparing to don the gifted gown when a thought struck her. "Why?"

"I thought I made that clear, but if you need to hear it again, I am happy to remind you." He stepped closer, his eyes the darkest crimson. "I felt it from the first moment I saw you. And then I tasted your blood and I was sure."

She swallowed, overcome by the intensity of his affection. "I saw you standing by the king," she finally admitted. "I thought you were incredibly handsome, but I never thought you would be interested in me."

"How could I not be?" he said. He leaned back against the dressing table, rolling his onyx shirt sleeves and watching closely as she pulled the dress on and laced up the back. It was loose in the faerie style, dipping low to show her breasts and a vee of her belly.

"I think I'm ready," she said, spinning to show how the dress shimmered when she moved.

Emrys tapped his chin. "Almost." He withdrew a box from his pocket and opened it. A gold necklace sat within, a briolette cut sunstone on the end of a long chain. Her mouth fell open as he lifted and clasped it around her neck. The stone settled between her breasts, and she picked it up to study the swirls of gold glittering from within the blood red gemstone.

Looking up, she had to clear her throat. "Thank you. It's the most beautiful thing I've ever received."

Emrys' smug smile stayed in place as they walked through the passages and entered the dining hall. It was the same vast room as the banquet, but now a massive quartz table stretched the length of the room. Dishes of food and bouquets of white flowers covered the glittering surface. Most of the chairs were occupied, and the attendees looked up as they entered. Voices quieted, dropping into whispers, as Emrys led her to the last few empty seats toward the middle.

King Argyro sat at one end, his charcoal beard threaded with silver beads. Queen Araluen sat opposite her husband with her jeweled hand holding a chalice casually as she spoke with a grizzled fawnling beside her.

"Lord Emrys," Argyro said. "Good of you to join us. I would like to speak to you after our meal."

"Yes, Sire." Emrys held out a chair and Brenna sat, allowing him to push her in. He slid into the chair beside her and set about pouring two goblets of wine. The dark red liquid made her think of the blood she licked from Emrys' chest, bringing a flush to her cheeks.

Emrys leaned close and murmured low in her ear, "Stop blushing like that. It makes me want to throw you on this table and give you a reason to." The heat across her face deepened, the blood tingling in her skin.

Queen Araluen addressed her from further down the table. "Brenna, so glad you could join us again."

She smiled, taking a shaky breath and willing the redness in her face to cool. Emrys' hand rested on her thigh, warm through her thin skirt and not helping matters. Exhaling, she focused on the queen. "Yes, Your Majesty. I am grateful."

"How is your sister?"

Brenna looked to Emrys. He squeezed her leg and answered the queen, "Unfortunately, she chose not to join her in this visit."

"Pity," Araluen said, taking a sip of her drink.

As if her action was the permission, the room relaxed and the two dozen guests began eating and conversing at normal volume.

"Brenna," Emrys said, "this is Herrick."

The fae male was slender and tall, with dusty green scales running up his arms and over his cheekbones. He nodded his head and smiled, showing fangs and a forked tongue. "My lady."

"Lovely to meet you, Herrick," Brenna said, practicing a courtly smile.

"Herrick is the commander of the high king's armies," Emrys explained.

"Oh," Brenna said, "that must be a daunting role in the current circumstances. Thank you for your work."

"It's my honor."

"How goes preparations? Have the forces from Caelia's court arrived?" Emrys asked, taking her hand as he rested his forearm on the table and leaned back, stretching out his lean legs.

Herrick hissed. "No, the Winter Court was unresponsive."

"Are they not loyal?" Brenna asked, her voice pitching high.

Emrys sighed. "Caelia is close friends with Sigmis. And the Court of Shadow and Snow is near to the Court of Darkness and Void. They will not stand against Argyro, but she will surely drag her feet. It is why we sent messengers off to her first."

"We do not need their frigid soldiers," Herrick snapped.

"Right," Emrys said, tipping his chin up and summoning his charming grin.

Herrick turned to speak with the fae female beside him, one with thin horns that spiraled above her head. Emrys took a long drink of his wine and tipped his head toward Brenna.

She ran her thumb over his knuckles. "How long do you think we have?"

"They are still arranging their troops. It will be at least a week," Herrick said.

"But it could be that soon?"

Emrys leaned nearer. "Do not worry. They are no threat to us."

Brenna's stomach flipped. She hadn't been thinking of herself, but of her sister. But it wasn't something to discuss at this dinner.

After dinner, a trio of musicians played, and a few of the fae danced. Emrys twirled her around the room, his hand gripping her waist tightly. She lost herself in the music and the feel of the spins and dips. Her worries would catch up with her shortly, but for now, she could savor being the center of Emrys' attention and all that entailed.

CHAPTER FORTY-SIX

Meara

Her mother forced her to go to bed when the moon was high. Meara could barely stand, but she did not want to quit working. She was addicted to the progress she had earned with sweat and willpower. Every hour, she grew in her control, and in the dying hours of the night, she finally shifted back into her raven form successfully. When she couldn't repeat the success, she burst into tears.

The next few days were much the same. She wove her shadows and then worked to shift into her raven. She was successful again, and then again. Eventually, she honed the magical muscle that triggered her shift until it came at will. That night, she flopped into her mother's bed, so exhausted she could barely keep her eyes open.

Her sleep was so deep, she did not awaken when her mother rose to tend the shop. Only when Rydan came to fetch her, did her mother knock on the door. Meara lurched up, scrambling for a blade.

"Hush, child. Your friendly prince is here." her mother said. Scoffing, Meara dragged herself up and pulled on clothes.

Rydan waited downstairs. "How was your day yesterday?" he asked politely.

Meara smirked. "I made good progress."

"Really?"

"I'll show you when we reach the training yard," she promised. They set out, crossing the street and heading for the gates.

Rydan crossed his arms. "I don't care for the feel of your shadows. Perhaps you can demonstrate on Eladin for once." His demeanor was restrained compared to the days past, and Meara sensed the weight of the upcoming conflict dragging on his soul. Darkness hollowed under his eyes and his appearance was less tidy.

"Meara!" Eladin exclaimed. His hair was tied back into a bun and tendrils fell over his temple. The shaved side of his head was shadowed, as if he was too busy to maintain it. All of the brothers looked worn.

"She has magic to show us," Rydan said, and her heart warmed at the pride in his voice. She had yet to demonstrate her ability, but he had confidence in her. "Who wants to be the victim?"

"I don't need a victim," she protested, laughing.

"Oh, yes, you do. I volunteer Emeric," Rydan said.

Emeric scowled and shoved Rydan's shoulder as he joined them. "I think not."

She smiled at their brotherly tussling, and in the end Eladin stood in the center of the training ring, clutching his staff to his chest. His smile turned wry. "Alright, Shadow Queen, do your worst."

Meara exhaled, reaching for the magic in the air around her. It came willingly. Darkness billowed around her feet and she allowed it to crawl up her calves. It was playful. She drew in more and more until it was no longer sheer, but a thick blanket of blackness. Eladin shivered. She studied him for a moment, feeling a twinge of guilt before she unleashed the shadows on him.

Eladin stiffened as the darkness descended on him. He curled under their mass, hunching in on himself. Meara pressed forward, pouring more and more. The prince let out a low moan as he disappeared into the gloom.

Worried, Meara pulled the magic back and allowed it to dissipate. A sheen of sweat coated her neck, but she felt strong. Eladin did not fare so well. He curled up on the ground with his arms over his head. She rushed forward and dropped to her knees. He moaned again softer and slowly unfurled to blink up at her.

"Brother, you are embarrassing us," Emeric said, nudging a trembling Eladin with his boot.

"That was horrible," he croaked. "Like a waking nightmare I could not escape from."

"Was it painful?" Meara asked.

Shaking his head, Eladin pushed himself up. He stretched out his arms and rolled his shoulders. "Next time it is not my turn! Never again."

Rydan picked up his forgotten staff from the ground. "So that would disable you from fighting?"

"Absolutely!" Eladin rubbed his arms, chasing away the last of the dread her magic had caused.

"I'm sorry," she said.

Eladin laughed, though it was shaky. "No, don't be. This is fantastic. If you use that on those bastards trying to kill us, they will piss themselves."

"You didn't, right?" Rydan asked, frowning at him and

leaning back to check his clothing.

Eladin shoved him. "No, but you would have."

"That was impressive, but I am not keen on you joining the army ranks. Can you cast it from a distance?" Emeric asked, his expression grave. She could see thoughts turning behind his eyes as he strategized how best to use her.

Sighing, Meara turned to face him. "I am working on it. Among other things."

"Other things?"

Tensing, Meara called upon the raven, letting the magic rush over her until she stood on the dirt and ruffled her feathers. The princes stood stiff and silent, staring at her. She tilted her head to peer at them. When they made no move, she shifted back and ran her fingers through her hair to untangle it.

"Did I forget to tell you that I came here as a raven?"

Emeric's eyebrows shot up. "I had wondered how you got through the gates."

"Alright brother, I think we should both experience her shadows so we know what we are dealing with," Rydan said, clapping his hand along Emeric's back.

"I'd rather not," Emeric muttered, but in the end he agreed and she left both princes shaking on the ground.

Over a quick meal, Emeric questioned her on her abilities, and his eyes brightened at her answer. "This will be helpful. But I think it's best we introduce you to our troops so they are not frightened by your shadows."

"I will try to keep it away from them," Meara said.

His shoulders rose and fell. "Battle is unpredictable. I want to be prepared."

"If you are sure."

He brought her to the training yard and took her from unit to unit, sternly telling the men what to expect and instructing them to watch out for her. When the entire army gathered, Emeric addressed them. "You have all met Lady Meara. We are lucky to have her on our side. But other faeries will have magic that is just as terrifying as hers and even worse. Therefore, as you run your drills, Lady Meara will send her shadows among you. I want you to not only withstand them, but adapt to them. She will direct them at our enemies, but you must be prepared to experience the edges of her magic."

"Yes, sir!" The forces shouted as one, and the great chorus constricted Meara's chest.

She couldn't stop them from marching, but she could protect these men. If she was lucky, she could halt both humans and faeries during the battle, and give the leaders a chance to forge peace.

The soldiers moved into their units and began their exercises. Meara watched for a moment, but then shifted to her raven form and took off. She circled, moving higher until she didn't have to work as hard to stay aloft. Her thoughts as a raven were calm and simple, but she knew what she needed to do.

The humans fought below her, and she reached for magic while in this body. It felt strange, clumsy, but she managed it. It streamed from her wings like ribbons of smoke. As she continued, it became easier until she let it fall from her talons. The smoke faded away as it left her.

Her frustration felt distant and muffled. She banked left and circled back, opening her wings to glide lower. A gust of wind blew her upwards and she fanned her tail, slowing her light frame until she could dip lower.

Gathering more magic, she concentrated it into a sphere and directed it downwards. This time, it dropped and began to unravel, but much of the darkness landed on a group of humans. The warriors ducked and shouted, but their leaders corrected them and they recovered quickly.

Again and again, she sent shadows down at the training soldiers. It grew thicker each time, and she gathered it lower and lower until it was no longer dropping but coalescing on the ground to swallow them up. Her keen raven sight moved between men, deciding who to target next, when a familiar man waved his arms at her.

Cocking her head, she swooped down and landed before him, shifting back gracefully. "What?" she asked, blinking as her human mind caught up with what she had done. Brow furrowing, she twisted to look over the crowd. Some soldiers crouched on the ground coaxing up the men she had hit with her most recent shadows. They were pale and shaking.

"I think you've gotten powerful enough you should no longer practice directly on our men," Rydan said. His smile faded into a frown as he looked over the field. "At least now they know what you are capable of."

"I need to get stronger," Meara said. "How long do we have until we march?"

Emeric sheathed his sword with a metallic clunk. "Liosliath forces are on their way. Two days, maybe three."

"I don't want you near their forces," Rydan said, lowering his voice.

Meara propped her hands on her hips. "I have no desire to go near them."

"I will sort out which units will be where, and she can be placed far from them," Emeric said, raising his hand to calm his brother.

"Good," Rydan growled. "If you want to keep practicing, do it somewhere else, please. Preferably over the marshland."

Meara nodded and shifted into her raven, taking flight and coasting over the city and out toward the wilds. She worked until the light faded and her grasp on her magic was slipping.

Soaring to the keep, she transformed back and rejoined the princes. They eyed her shaking hands.

"Come on, you need a solid meal," Emeric said roughly. She followed them into the castle, past the great hall she remembered from the betrothal party. They paused at the meeting room to check in with King Eldric, and then went on to a smaller dining space.

"This is where we eat when it's just our family."

They settled on cushions around a long low table and servants brought a platter with roast lamb and a kettle of thick soup full of root vegetables. Hungry as she was, it tasted delicious, even if the cooks lacked the mastery of delicate flavors and spices she had grown to enjoy among the faerie.

They spoke of family, friends, and the desire to keep their people safe. Meara tore at a thick barley bread and dunked it into her remaining soup. The servants brought jugs of ale and the princes filled tankards and began to drink. She sipped at hers, finding it bitter compared to the fae wine.

Rydan and Emeric became absorbed in a discussion of borders, and Meara found Eladin watching her. She leaned over. "How are you doing?"

"Fine," he said, though the tightness in his jaw betrayed him.

"I'm sorry you are separated from Tayen," she said quietly.

Eladin swallowed, looking away and taking a drink. "I am trying to pretend that is not my situation," he said, his exhale jagged. "But I do not think he will fight. He knows I cannot avoid the battlefield. He is peaceful in his soul and he will work to restore that peace to his people."

Heart aching, Meara smiled, reaching over to squeeze his calloused hand. Eladin's voice grew thick. "I will see him again soon."

"I'm sure you will."

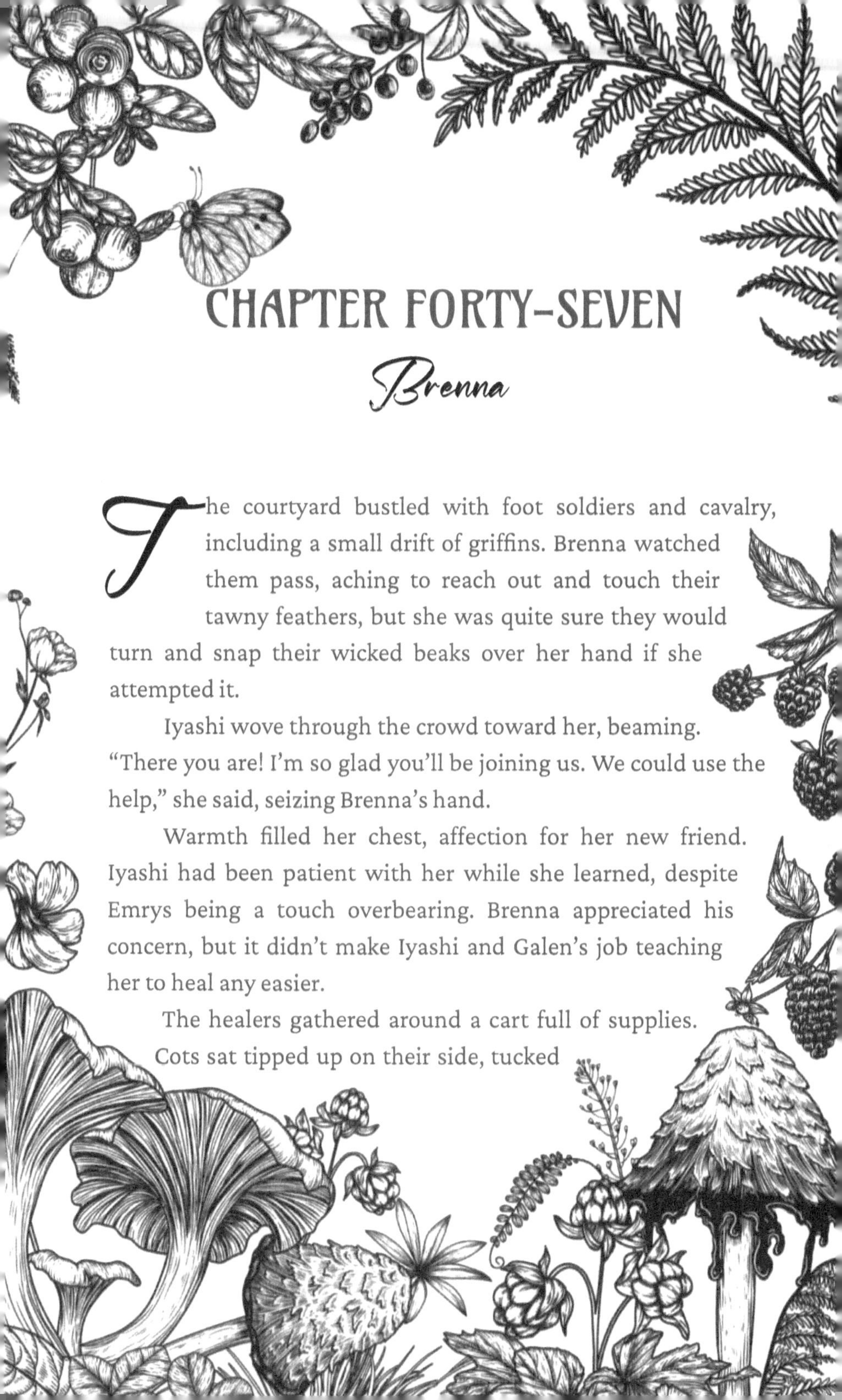

CHAPTER FORTY-SEVEN

Brenna

The courtyard bustled with foot soldiers and cavalry, including a small drift of griffins. Brenna watched them pass, aching to reach out and touch their tawny feathers, but she was quite sure they would turn and snap their wicked beaks over her hand if she attempted it.

Iyashi wove through the crowd toward her, beaming. "There you are! I'm so glad you'll be joining us. We could use the help," she said, seizing Brenna's hand.

Warmth filled her chest, affection for her new friend. Iyashi had been patient with her while she learned, despite Emrys being a touch overbearing. Brenna appreciated his concern, but it didn't make Iyashi and Galen's job teaching her to heal any easier.

The healers gathered around a cart full of supplies. Cots sat tipped up on their side, tucked along jugs of fresh water, boxes of bandages, salves, herbal tonics, and surgery kits. Galen and his adepts were trained both in healing and medical care. Brenna would be restricted to magical healing only, but she hoped to assist them however she could.

"Welcome," Galen said, glancing up from his work for a moment. Iyashi stepped beside him and reached for the remaining supplies, but when Brenna asked to help, she was waved away.

Companies of fae warriors marched through the gates. Brenna spun, searching for Emrys in the crowd. She knew he was busy with his duties, but she missed him and was terrified she wouldn't see him again before the battle. He had left early that morning and she had only woken for a moment as he kissed her shoulder and rolled out of bed.

As she peered through the crowd, he appeared. Familiar dark hair shone in the bright sunlight as he moved toward her. Her heart rose as he swept her up and kissed her firmly. "You look beautiful, my love," he said quietly. Her feet landed back on the ground, though she clung to his arm, grateful for every moment together. Emrys eyed the healers gathered and focused in on Galen, stepping closer to him. "Your team is to stay in the back, as planned."

"Of course. We are apprised of the strategy," Galen said, raising his chin.

Emrys glowered. "I expect Brenna to be far from any danger. If I find out that you let her get near an enemy, you will wish you had fallen during this battle."

"Understood." Galen pronounced each sound crisply, his stare bold.

Brenna swallowed, tugging Emrys back. "You are the one in danger. Please be careful. I could not bear it if you were hurt or worse."

Lowering his head, he kissed her forehead. "You don't need to worry about me. Worry about the humans who block my path." He raised his palm and cradled a small flame.

Her lips parted. "How?"

Emrys grinned, ignoring her question. "I have to go. Stay back with the healers. I won't let any enemies reach you." He kissed her and then held her jaw while he rested their foreheads together. "Brenna, I love you."

Her throat constricted. "I love you too."

His exhale was tortured. Reluctantly, he peeled away and left her. The absence felt cold with fear rising up her throat. She watched him walk to his post beside Herrick.

The crowd parted. A great golden griffin flared its wings as it walked through the courtyard. King Argyro sat upon its back, his silver armor flashing in the sun. She had to raise her arm to shield her eyes.

Tail lashing, his griffin climbed atop a raised platform. Argyro raised his sword high. Diamonds glinted on the hilt. As he began addressing the crowd, a hand rested on her shoulder.

Brenna spun to see familiar antlers rising above a concerned expression. Bronze scalemail covered Cerne's leather armor. Daggers and an axe hung from his belt, though he was a weapon even unarmed. His voice was hoarse. "Brenna, what are you doing here?"

She crossed her arms. "I've been training to heal. I am marching with the healers."

Emotion flashed across his face, but settled into a frown. "Did I see you with Emrys just now?"

Her hackles rose. "Yes, we are mates. It's done, so I do not need your warnings."

Cerne paused, his eyes trailing over her, concern pinching his brows. "After today, I will return to the Autumn Court. You are always welcome. If you need me, send word."

"Thank you, Cerne," she said, softening. "I'll see you soon."

"Brenna," Iyashi called. Cerne nodded, stepping back and releasing her from their goodbyes. Letting out a cleansing breath, Brenna moved to help Iyashi load the last of the bundles of supplies into their cart. They would be the last to leave the courtyard, but it wouldn't be long now.

The troops moved out, grouped together by their courts. The king's forces went first, led by Herrick, with Emrys upon his black stallion staying close.

The Autumn Guard followed Cerne, bronze glinting over dark leather. The Summer Guard was flashes of gold and black behind Luce, his glowing spear strapped to his back. She watched them, entranced.

Galen called for the cart to move and their horse heaved it forward. Brenna walked beside Iyashi, rubbing her arms with her hands anxiously. As they crossed the rivers and entered Sablewood, her anxiety rose.

It was eerily quiet aside from the hushed sounds of hundreds of faeries moving gracefully through the trees. Without her fae hearing, they may have been silent. It was a stark reminder of how inhuman they were.

After a time, they halted. Brenna looked to Galen, brows furrowed. He rubbed at his short beard. "Some units are moving ahead to ambush the approaching human army, but the rest of us must stay back here. Once the fight begins, we can move closer as the others join the battle."

She strained to see further into the trees, but the fae warriors of the front line melted into the brush. Her pulse clambered in her ears as she waited for the chaos of battle.

Galen's eyes caught her, and he gave a reassuring nod. They were like ocean waves, so different from Emrys' bloodstained ones. She smiled, grateful for his steady support. Beside him, Iyashi gripped a staff and chewed on her lip. Brenna was grateful to be with the healers where she could make a difference.

A chilled breeze threaded through the trees. Not even the birds called. Brenna's chest tightened, and she expelled her breath slowly, attempting to steady herself. There was nothing to do but wait.

CHAPTER FORTY-EIGHT

Meara

Winter arrived with the marching of soldiers. A biting wind slapped at them as they crossed the marshland and entered Sablewood.

The trees enveloped them, welcoming them in. The wind twined between trunks but lost its sting when buffered by foliage. The mist of winter rain faded away under the cover of leaves, replaced with a thick fog rolling across the muddy forest floor.

The humans marched steadily, resolve hardening their motions, curling hands into fists and curving mouths into grimaces. Rydan led the front with his battle axe tucked into his belt beside a long, thin sword to give him further reach in battle.

Emeric led the cavalry. The tattooed runes across his throat and over his jaw were smudged with charcoal from a night spent around the fire tending to his troops.

Men's hair was braided back, revealing more runes tattooed across scalps. Meara had replicated their style, asking her mother to braid her hair snug against the center of her skull and down her back. Coal painted her eyes, leaving a dark stripe across her face.

Listlessly, Meara identified the medicinal and edible plants they passed. It was a fruitless attempt to soothe herself. Shadows grew long, and Meara wondered if they would reach Roven before they met with the fae.

All seemed quiet.

Men ahead let out yells of shock and then pain as faerie materialized around them. Dryads emerged from the trees themselves, sylphs appearing from the wind, nymphs from the brush. Foxes, deer, and even a snake shifted into their fae forms and drew weapons against them. Meara watched, horrified as the first line of humans buckled and fell.

The human soldiers backed up, closing ranks to block out the faerie that rushed them. Beside her, Eladin drew his sword. His jaw was set, but his eyes glittered with fear and sadness. "You'd better go," he said, jerking his chin upward.

Nodding fiercely, Meara pulled upon the magic around her, wrapping her shadows until they consumed her and pale flesh was replaced with iridescent black feathers. With a beat of her wings, she launched into the air, climbing until she was above the foliage. The bitter wind picked her up and dragged her higher.

Through the branches, she spied glimpses of the battle.

A human soldier landed a blow on a frost sprite with short, white hair. His blade cut deep, almost severing her arm. Meara screeched, her cry echoing off the treetops and bounding back to her. They had used iron to forge weapons against the faerie. She knew they needed every advantage they could get, but the sudden, unexpected brutality sent shockwaves of horror through her.

Tucking her wings, she dipped into the leaves, desperate to see what was happening. The fae clashed with the human forces, metal ringing over the sounds of grunts and screams. It was impossible to tell where to send her shadows to help and not harm.

A flash of orange drew her attention. Tayen swiped a dagger at a burly human soldier. Her heart shattered seeing him, as if an iron blade had cut into her. Another fighter ran at Tayen from behind, and Meara sent out a spiral of shadows toward him without thinking. He fell back, screaming, and Tayen brought the hilt of his blade down on the man's head to send him into unconsciousness. He paused, looking up as if he recognized her magic and knew she was not a wild bird. Meara darted into the branches of the nearest tree, dodging around the trunk and coming out the other side where he could not see her.

Horses whinnied, and her gaze swept over Emeric as he swung his sword from his mount. The horse's hooves kicked out at the fae warriors before him. Tails whipping, they leapt aside.

Meara tipped her wings, circling a tree and working her way deeper into the worst of the fighting.

A faerie with tan skin, short, blunt horns in his curly hair, and a great mahogany beard stood tall, stretching his arms wide. Around him, the humans slowed, their muscles relaxing. The faeries began to cut them down. Horrified, Meara sent a thin blanket of her darkness over them, jolting them alert and giving them a chance against the enemy that was stronger and faster than they were.

Banking, Meara rounded another tree trunk, and dove lower, looking over the fray. She couldn't help looking for her sister. Brenna should not be here, but something whispered in her mind that she was, and Meara could not ignore the worry any longer.

Below her, a flare of flame lit the haze. Dressed in black from his pauldrons to his greaves, Emrys spun, lifting a dagger high and bringing them down on his human opponent who crumpled into the mist. With his free hand, he called forth a fiery sphere and launched it at another soldier. Meara turned, circling back to get a better look. She could not understand how the male was using fire magic.

Ahead of him, Eldric rose on his great sabino stallion, his axe swinging from his high seat to strike a dryad below him. Emeric rode beside him, his iron sword cutting great arcs. A drake screamed as Emeric cut between his shoulder blades and sent him sprawling into the leaves.

Behind them, Queen Malacia rode a massive black horse. Her court dress was replaced with black leather and a long blood red cloak. An amber diamond glinted in her crown. Beside her, King Barrach rode a cream horse that reared back and kicked at the faerie before him. His black plate armor seemed to absorb the light around him.

The royals cut through the fae, pushing deeper and splitting a line for the human troops to rush in. Blood painted the ground as the violence intensified.

A tall, golden figure pushed through the melee. She could never mistake Luce for another, even with his hair tied back and gold chainmail glittering as he moved. He held a scythe in one hand and his spear in another, swinging the longer weapon to part the masses while the shorter blade handled anyone foolish enough to attack him.

Luce swung his spear at Malacia. Her horse danced back and he pushed forward. Eldric's words came back to her. If Malacia fell at the hands of the fae, he could call for a truce. Luce was going to kill the blood-soaked queen.

Meara gathered up her shadows to attack the woman. They gathered around her, causing her horse to rear up. Luce twisted, looking to the sky. She could feel his eyes land on her, and surely he knew exactly who she was. Whatever his thoughts, Luce tore his focus from her and waded into her darkness.

A tense moment passed. She pulled the shadows back to reveal Luce pulling the scythe from Barrach's prone body. Blood pooled around the king, and Luce's face was a stony mask. He looked around, but Malacia was gone. Meara let out a growl of frustration and banked away, looking for the doomed queen.

Another flash of fire sent fear like ice through her. She flapped her wings and flew deeper into the forest, to the back of the fae army. Healers tended wounded faeries, but a handful of human soldiers advanced on their peaceful group.

A fae female dressed in blood red trousers and a loose black tunic, her shining blonde hair tumbling from a braid at her crown, shot streams of fire at the humans. They held up shields to divert her fire and pushed closer with iron blades ready.

How dare they threaten her sister.

Her darkness flooded the men, crawling up their legs and devouring them until they screamed from the forest floor. When she pulled back, blood dripped from their eyes and noses. Dread pooled in her stomach, but Brenna smiled as she looked up at her.

Meara dove, landing beside her sister and shifting back. She straightened, the muscles along her spine screaming at her. Brenna slammed into her, clutching her tightly and digging her nails into her back.

"Ow, that hurts," she said, though she made no move to pull her away. Instead, she slipped her arms around her sister and squeezed her back. "Are you well?"

"Yes," Brenna said, her voice going thick and weepy.

"I have to go," she said. She wanted to tell Brenna her desire to destroy Malacia and free them from this conflict, but she just killed several men in front of her. She couldn't handle the additional weight now that she had her full emotions tearing into her. It was simpler as a raven.

"Meara! Stop!" Brenna cried, trying to hold on to her as she tore away and shifted. Meara soared upward and dove between branches, running from her sister's calls.

As she searched, she gathered shadows up to slow and disable the faerie warriors as they tore through the humans. The number of human soldiers was dwindling, and the fae gathered into groups. They were losing before she could take action to end it. Her motions grew frantic as she searched the forest, weaving between trunks erratically.

Tayen's orange hair caught the light, and Meara watched as he held shaking hands up to maintain his shield. Sweat ran tracks down his dirt-streaked skin. Eladin huddled against him, staying close so Tayen's shield could envelop both of them. The fighting around them slammed into his shield, and she saw Tayen sway. He wouldn't hold up much longer.

Shouts drew her attention to the leaders once more. Argyro's silver armor flashed as he swung his broad sword in a deadly strike that Emeric blocked. The force of it drove him to his knees.

Meara banked, darting toward the fight. She was exhausted, her wings felt heavy, and drawing up shadows felt like dredging up heavy swamp mud, but she would not fail her friend. She gathered threads of darkness, swirling them around Argyro's chest. They were almost invisible, they were so thin, but it was enough to cause the silver king to hesitate.

Emeric lunged, striking his dagger in a vicious uppercut. Argyro moved to block, but he was too slow, and the blade cut into his wrist. The iron sliced deep, severing his hand from his arm and sending his shield clattering to the ground. Argyro moaned, an agonized, strangled sound that rattled her bones. He doubled over, clutching his wrist to his chest as blood soaked his sleeve and coated his armor. Emeric staggered forward, raising his blade again but hesitating.

Like an ebony wraith, Emrys leapt between the human prince and the faerie king. His vambrace deflected Emeric's blow, allowing him to shove the human prince off balance. Emrys surged closer, his blade slashing up into Emeric's stomach. Fangs bared, Emrys shoved the dagger deeper, watching Emeric fold over it and collapse. When he tumbled onto his back, his chest no longer rose and fell.

The noises of the battle muted, and Meara's vision tunneled until she saw nothing but shadow and blade. Emeric did not want this fight. He did not deserve this death.

Her grip on her magic was weak, and it spiraled out of her control, shadows trailing off her wings and gathering around her claws. For the first time, she felt her magic's terror, and it felt like barbed wire dragging across her heart.

Meara tumbled through the air, plummeting down and opening her wings to glide upwards. Everything hurt. She flapped harder, trying to escape the battle, when she saw the amber of Malacia's crown glinting in the dappled light. The queen marched behind a line of remaining Liosliath soldiers, shouting orders.

Hatred fueled her, and Meara's shadows licked at the queen, but she was too weak to do much. Perhaps she could do more in her fae form.

Diving down, she landed at the base of a massive oak tree and shifted back, drawing a knife from her thigh sheath. Being so close gave her a second wind, and she pulled the threads of magic from the air around her, concentrating them on the queen who began to shake and hunch defensively.

Luce appeared at her side, gripping his weapons with bloody knuckles. He watched the queen for a moment, reading the situation. And then he nodded and charged forward, scythe ready. Meara lurched forward so they ran side by side.

Malacia fell back, her fearful cry rising through the din. "I surrender!"

Luce stopped with his blade raised above her.

"I surrender," Malacia screamed.

Snarling, Meara pushed nearer. She would end the queen the same way she handled the men attacking her sister. The darkness around the queen thickened until she was sobbing.

Luce grabbed her arm. "Stop."

"Why? She should die!" Meara hissed. "She forced the alliance. This blood is on her hands."

"She surrendered," Luce said, giving Meara a shake to break her from her murderous state. She fought against him, gathering her shadows around Malacia. With a growl, Luce extended a hand and poured light over the human woman, clearing the weakened shadows.

Meara fell to her knees, her body giving out as she faced her failure. She felt Luce's arms under her, scooping her up before she lost consciousness.

When her vision swam into focus, Brenna leaned above her, wiping at her forehead gently. Before she could speak to her sister, she slipped away once more.

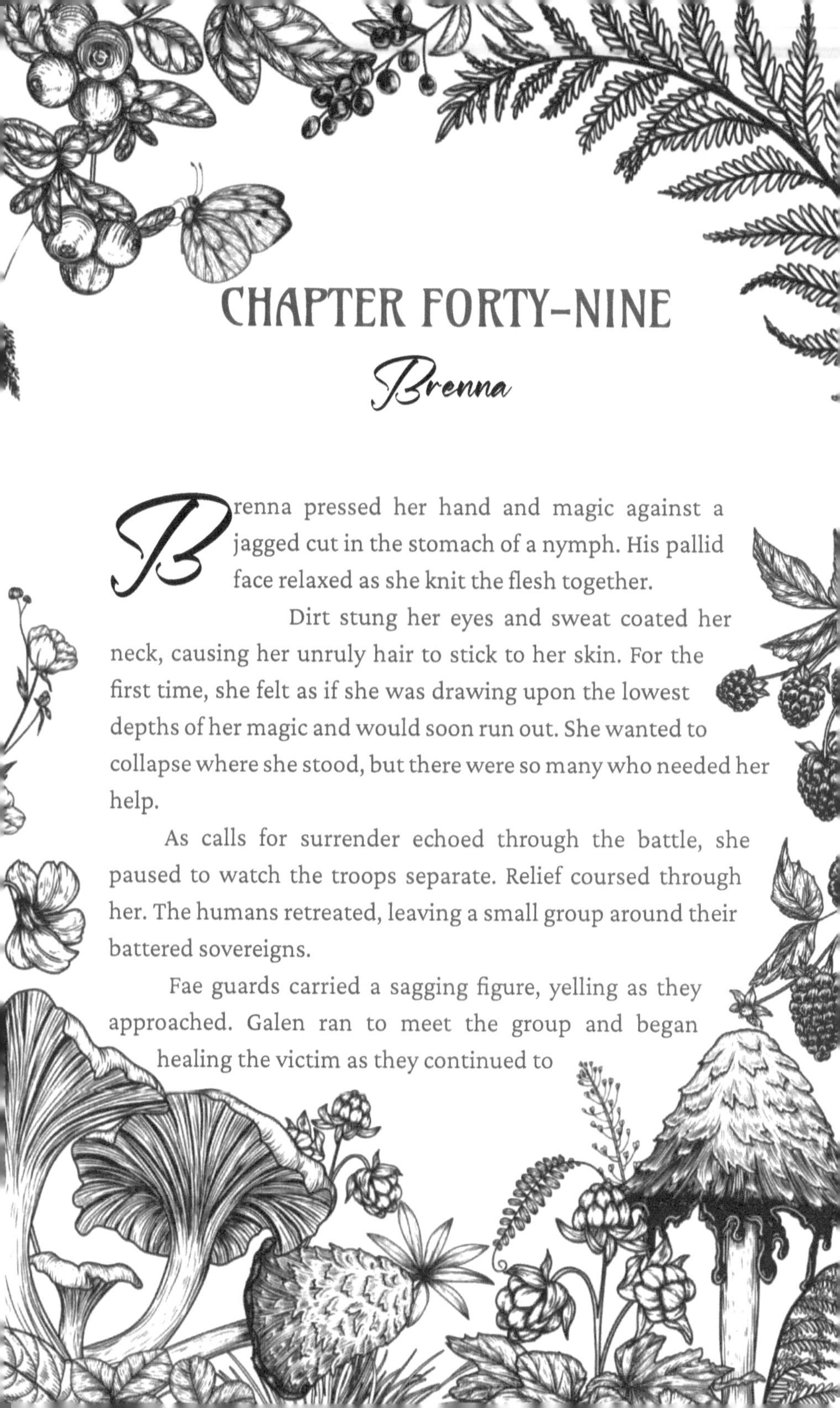

CHAPTER FORTY-NINE
Brenna

renna pressed her hand and magic against a jagged cut in the stomach of a nymph. His pallid face relaxed as she knit the flesh together.

Dirt stung her eyes and sweat coated her neck, causing her unruly hair to stick to her skin. For the first time, she felt as if she was drawing upon the lowest depths of her magic and would soon run out. She wanted to collapse where she stood, but there were so many who needed her help.

As calls for surrender echoed through the battle, she paused to watch the troops separate. Relief coursed through her. The humans retreated, leaving a small group around their battered sovereigns.

Fae guards carried a sagging figure, yelling as they approached. Galen ran to meet the group and began healing the victim as they continued to walk. Silver armor was streaked with blood, and Brenna startled when she saw King Argyro clutching at his wrist. Her stomach churned when she saw his hand was fully severed.

She leapt back to clear space as Iyashi joined Galen in working to stop the profuse bleeding so they could heal him. Iyashi called for rags and Brenna ran to fetch them. Time blurred together as they worked and she assisted. The idea of helping with medical care had lost its charm and Brenna felt a twisted sorrow that turned her stomach.

When the guards transported Argyro and Galen away, she nearly dropped to the ground. It would be ages until they could join them, for many faeries needed healing before they could be transported.

Tayen lay across one of the cots with his eyes closed and Ayala knelt beside him. Brenna pressed her fingers to his forehead as she pushed healing energy into the jagged cut along his hairline. With a gasp, he awoke. "Eladin!"

Ayala gripped his hand. "He is fine."

"They were going to kill him," Tayen argued, his golden eyes wild.

Brenna smoothed his hair. "It's over. He's alive."

"I have to see him," Tayen said, bending and pushing to his feet. Brenna steadied him, supporting some of his weight as he staggered forward. Ayala scowled but took his other side.

The human rulers sat upon their mounts with the reins held by fae guards. Emrys stood before them, directing forces between the human troops and the faeries preparing to travel back to Court Tara. With a slicing gesture of his hand, Emrys ordered the captives forward and swung his own horse around to face Court Tara. In the back of the line, Eladin slumped in his seat, dried tears cutting lines through the dirt and charcoal on his face. Otherwise, he seemed unharmed. Tayen stiffened as he watched his love ride past him.

"Now that you've seen proof, you must rest," Ayala insisted.

A broad, blond faerie strode through the trees holding a female with flowing iridescent black hair in his arms. Brenna gave a startled gasp and rushed forward, leaving Ayala to support her brother as he hobbled back to his cot.

Luce frowned down at Meara in his arms. Her pale skin was ice and her lashes fluttered as she fought for consciousness and lost. Brenna brushed her hair away from her face.

"Brenna, we are leaving for Court Tara!" Iyashi called.

Luce cleared his throat. "I will carry her. She drained her magic, but she is uninjured, I believe."

"Thank you," Brenna said, reluctant to leave her sister. But as Iyashi called for her again, she tore herself away.

Their injured were placed on horses or, for the worst of them, in the cart. The journey back to Court Tara was tedious and painful. Brenna grit her teeth and endured, because many around her were gravely injured and she was simply exhausted and drained. Once they arrived, she stopped long enough to wash the worst of the grime from her face and arms, as well as drink water and eat a slice of thick bread to refuel her magic. Then she resumed working to help the injured.

Meara was placed in a spare alcove in the healing ward. Brenna glanced her way as she worked.

She leapt when a hand touched her shoulder. Iyashi frowned at her and tipped her head toward Meara. "Go to your sister. You will drain yourself and end up by her side anyway if you keep going like this."

"Thank you," she said, allowing Iyashi to take her place. Wiping her hands on her apron, she jogged over to Meara's slender form stretched out on the cot.

Violet eyes blinked up at her. "Brenna?"

"You idiot!" Brenna smacked her arm lightly and brushed away the tears forming. "Don't ever fly off like that again."

"I'm sorry," Meara said. Her voice was raw and dry, as if she had been screaming.

"What were you even doing?"

Her sister bit her lip and looked away, clearly hesitant to share.

Brenna pushed forward. "They said you were staying with Mother. How did you end up in battle?"

Heavy footsteps interrupted them. Herrick loomed in the arched entrance, the lamplight turning his scales a sickly shade of olive. Cerne and Emrys flanked him. Emrys wore a clean black shirt and vest.

Brenna rose, standing in front of her weakened sister as she watched the three fae males approach. Emrys' mouth tightened as he regarded her, and she grit her teeth and gripped the edge of the raised cot Meara lay across. She glanced at Cerne. His expression was shuttered.

"Step aside," Herrick ordered.

Brenna hesitated, but Emrys held out his hand and she took it, allowing him to guide her to his side and curl his arm around her shoulders. His embrace comforted her as she watched the army commander step nearer to Meara.

"Meara, you are under arrest for treason."

Her sister jerked away, trying to sit up, but Herrick grabbed her arm and halted her.

"Stop!" Brenna hissed. Emrys gripped her tighter, preventing her from helping her sister. "Let me go!"

He held firm and made a soothing noise against her hair. "Everything will be well in the end, but you can't stop her arrest."

"What did she supposedly do?" Brenna snapped, glaring at Herrick. The drake commander was unmoved by her anger.

Cerne stepped forward, his hands anxiously tugging at his cuffed shirt. "Meara marched with the human army and used her shadow magic against the fae."

"No," Brenna said, her voice dropping out.

Emrys held her against his chest. "I will take care of it."

She turned her head to watch Herrick and Cerne haul Meara up and walk her out of the healing ward.

Sagging against Emrys, she let him stroke her hair and whisper reassurances. "Come with me, you need rest."

"I should help," she protested.

"You've done enough, and more healers are on their way to help. It's time for you to rest and besides, we need to discuss your sister."

Nodding grimly, Brenna untied her apron and dropped it in the laundry before following Emrys out of the healing ward.

"Where are they taking her?" she asked as he led her down the hall.

"She'll be locked in a spare bedroom for now. I made it clear to Herrick she was not to be jailed."

She pressed her hand to her chest, rubbing at the ache there.

The path between the healing ward and their rooms was familiar enough she barely noticed their progress until Emrys pushed the door to her beautiful suite open. Starlight bathed the space in gray-blue light. Numbly, she followed him inside.

"I have a plan for Meara. She won't be imprisoned for very long. But first, we need to take care of you."

Brenna was too tired to argue or fight for more information. Emrys had never failed her. She tamely followed his gentle prodding as he drew a bath and returned to undress her.

"You were incredible," he murmured, unbuttoning her work dress. She sighed deeply as he pressed a kiss to her neck before tugging the fabric off her shoulders. He stripped her bare and carried her into the bathing room and sat her in the tub. Candles flickered along the window ledge, providing light now that night had fallen.

Steaming water melted her tired muscles and she leaned back against the side of the tub.

Ignoring the water soaking into the edge of his rolled sleeves, Emrys washed her arms, shoulders, and back. She would have loved to have wasted hours soaking, but concern for Meara pushed her to finish washing up and climb out. Emrys held out a plush robe that she slipped on.

"I feel much better now, thank you," she said with a tired smile.

"Eat and we can talk."

A tray of salted meat and fruit waited by the hearth, and Brenna popped a grape in her mouth as she sank into the armchair. She drew her legs up and hugged her knees.

"I can't believe Meara fought against the faerie." She chewed her food, considering. "I understand her wanting to defend the humans. We grew up with them," she mused, sipping the tea Emrys poured for her.

"She made her choices, but we can help shield her from the full weight of those consequences if you wish to," he said solemnly.

"Of course I want to. I can't let my sister be branded a traitor and, what? Exiled? Imprisoned?"

Emrys rubbed his jaw thoughtfully. "It would be Argyro's and Araluen's decision, typically. But considering the circumstances..."

"What?"

"Argyro can no longer rule," he said simply.

Brenna blinked at him for a moment, comprehension slow to form. "Why?"

"Our law states that a king or queen must be whole in body and mind. He cannot rule without his hand. It limits his ability to wield magic."

Her brows furrowed and she sat back in her chair. "So what does that mean? Does he have an heir?"

Emrys folded his hands on his knee. "He does not." His gaze trailed down her body and she cocked her head, waiting for the rest of his thought. "Even if he did, it would not mean the heir would inherit. The high king and queen must always be a wedded pair that can share their magic craft to prove their bond."

"I thought the fae did not often marry," she said, setting her cup down.

"True, though it does happen. More often for political gain, which is why the couple must also magic share to prove their relationship is genuine."

"That makes sense." Her voice trailed off as his intense gaze snagged her. "What?"

"I want you to marry me, we can claim the throne."

Brenna's thoughts sputtered out and she gaped at him. "I can't be a queen," she stammered.

"You can. Together, we are eligible." He leaned forward and took her hand, stroking along the inside of her fingertips. "We can bring peace and pardon Meara for her treason."

"I," she started, the thought dying on her tongue. "Can I think about it?"

"My light, this isn't how I thought to propose, but we do not have time to spare. Discussions of the throne will begin soon."

"Give me a moment," she said, rising and striding to the window. Pulling the robe tight, she stared over the winding river. The moon's reflection rippled as the water moved.

If she married Emrys, she would be secure in his affection. She would have status. If she was crowned queen, she would have a purpose and a role, security, and power.

The idea terrified her, but Emrys had been second to the King for years. He knew how to manage the faerie courts. She would learn and help however she could. If she said no, he would be unable to claim the throne and fulfill this role she felt he was destined for.

Turning back to Emrys where he sat patiently, she asked, "If the throne was not available, would you still want to marry me?"

Rising, he moved with dark grace to her side, tipping her chin up and staring into her eyes. His crimson irises flared with heat. "Yes. I've thought of little else."

"Okay," she breathed. They stayed frozen, his patient gaze waiting for her to elaborate. "I will marry you."

Emrys kissed her, cradling her jaw in his hands, until she was breathless. "I want to take you to bed," he whispered, "but my desires will have to wait."

She smiled, the reality of their betrothal sinking in. "So when would we wed?"

"Immediately. It must happen before we can be crowned," he said. Releasing her, he crossed to the wardrobe and pulled out a dress she didn't recognize.

"Did you order another gown for me?" she said, cocking her head.

"Yes. One fine enough for a wedding."

As he held it up and the lamplight washed over it, gemstones sparkled and gold thread gleamed. Brenna pressed her hands to her lips as tears ran down her cheeks. It was such a silly thing to cry over after all the violence she had seen, but she simply had nothing left.

Sniffling, she ran her fingers over the garment. Flames of ruffled fabric ran up the dress, meeting with jeweled beading over the bust.

Emrys draped the dress across her bed and pulled her against his chest. "My Fire Queen."

Brenna stepped into the throne room on Emrys' arm. Hundreds of eyes were drawn to them. He was a polished obsidian blade, and her a walking inferno. She left her hair flowing down her back in the fae fashion, only tucking it behind her tapered ears, now adorned with gold and diamond cuffs.

Emrys leaned close and whispered, "Looks like we are here in time." His smirk sent prickles of heat through her. This male was to be her husband, and they would rule side by side.

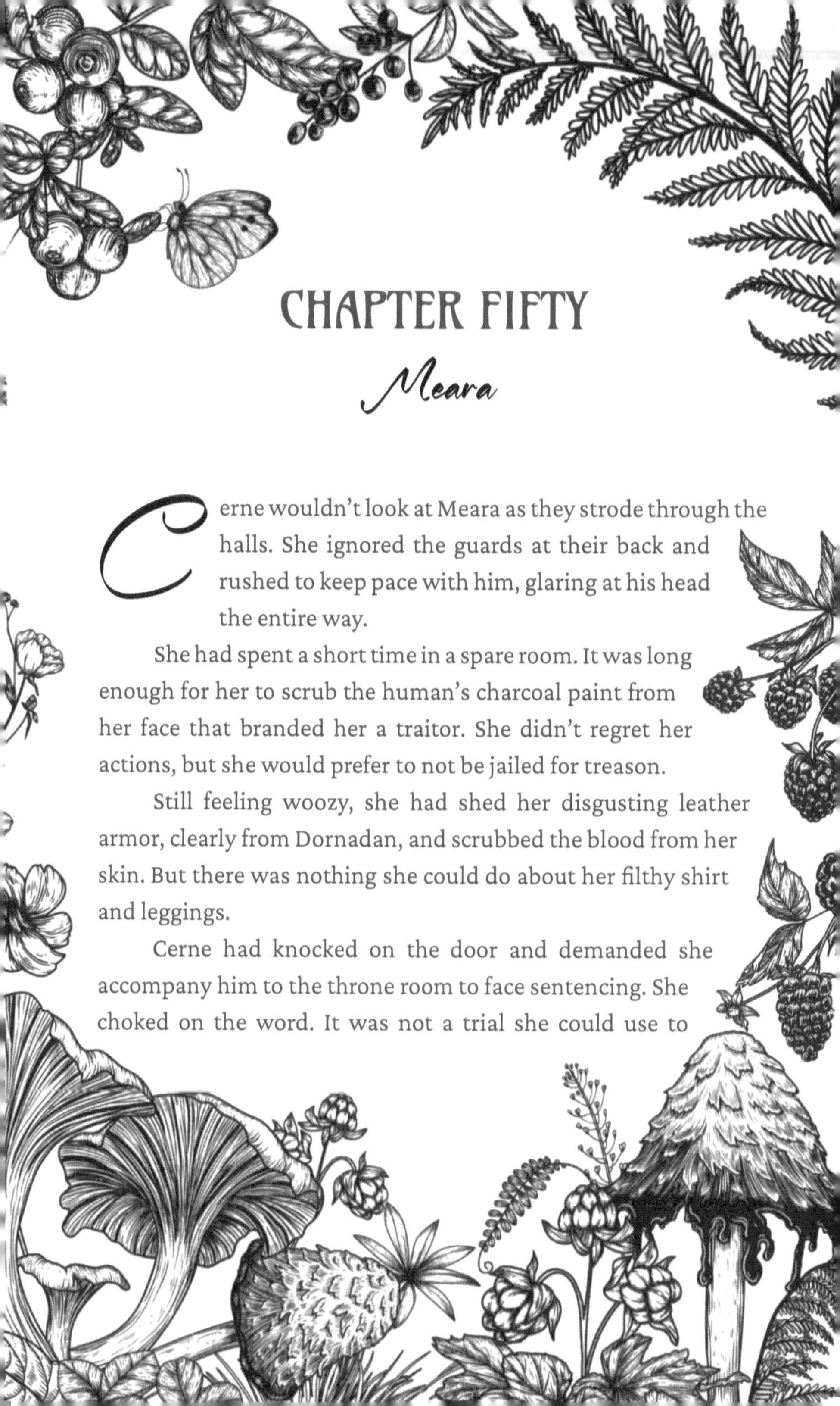

CHAPTER FIFTY
Meara

Cerne wouldn't look at Meara as they strode through the halls. She ignored the guards at their back and rushed to keep pace with him, glaring at his head the entire way.

She had spent a short time in a spare room. It was long enough for her to scrub the human's charcoal paint from her face that branded her a traitor. She didn't regret her actions, but she would prefer to not be jailed for treason.

Still feeling woozy, she had shed her disgusting leather armor, clearly from Dornadan, and scrubbed the blood from her skin. But there was nothing she could do about her filthy shirt and leggings.

Cerne had knocked on the door and demanded she accompany him to the throne room to face sentencing. She choked on the word. It was not a trial she could use to defend herself, but simply a decision made for her by rulers she hardly knew.

Cerne's jaw clenched as he continued to ignore her. He was being childish.

"Cerne," she said. "I would think you'd understand. I wasn't trying to hurt you."

He stopped so suddenly she had to skid to a halt and step back to face him. His mossy eyes burned with anger. "You did not hurt me. You killed my people."

She couldn't deny it, but that didn't stop her own anger from flaring. "I was trying to keep innocents safe. Slow down the massacre of humans that I could not stop. They never stood a chance and you know it. Those were your friends and allies."

"They were no longer friends when they declared war and moved against us." His mossy eyes were hard.

"Emeric and Eldric didn't want to do that," Meara said, throwing up her hands. "They were forced into it because of their treaty with Liosliath. Eldric wanted peace."

Cerne huffed and turned away, resuming his walk, but Meara wasn't done. Hurrying after him, she spat, "If the faerie hadn't stolen away a human girl, none of this would have happened." No response.

They reached the throne room. The doors stood wide open and voices poured out, echoing into the entrance hall. He paused, narrowing his eyes on her. "Don't make me regret not placing iron chains on you."

She clamped her teeth shut. He grabbed her elbow and dragged her inside. They stood toward the back.

In front of the vacant thrones, King Eldric and Queen Malacia stood with faerie guards around them instead of their own people. Documents sat upon a marble pedestal. Malacia lowered a fountain pen to the papers and signed. Eldric must have done so already because he watched, his eyes dull.

A memory of Emeric lying in his own blood forced its way into her mind and she cringed. The human king must be grieving deeply. She looked for Eladin, but her eyes caught on a glittering figure standing near the front.

Brenna stood tall and graceful, golden hair streaming down her back in loose, wild curls. She was unrecognizable in a dress that reflected the flickering flames around them. Jewels glinted on her pointed ears. Her hand rested on Emrys' forearm, and Meara's stomach clenched.

The humans filed out. Malacia sneered at the faerie around her, and Meara clenched her fists. If Luce had not stopped her, the queen would not have lived to threaten both Dornadan and the fae again. And Meara had no doubt that she would.

Someone slammed a staff down on the dais. Aletris stepped up and addressed the crowd. With her ivory dress and sunburst crown, she reminded Meara of a priestess.

"Our dear high king can no longer fulfill his duties, per our traditions. We must deliberate on who will step up into this arduous role."

The low voices of the faerie nobles gathered rose into a dull roar.

Aletris took the golden staff in her hand and struck the stone floor once more. "Who is eligible and willing?"

"Why can't Argyro rule?" she asked Cerne quietly.

His mouth was a grim line. "He was injured severely."

"Won't he recover? What about Queen Araluen?" she said, her voice rising.

There was a harshness to his expression she had never seen on his face before. It was as if his playful confidence had burned away to leave nothing but tightly reigned anger.

"The high king and queen are no longer eligible to rule. Another wedded pair must be selected." He stiffened. She turned to follow his gaze.

Emrys stepped onto the platform with Brenna at his side, her eyes staring straight ahead. Meara's stomach dropped.

"I, Emrys, son of Baelor, brother of Elio, son of Azar, am eligible for the crown. My partner and I are to be wed within the day. We magic share." Emrys raised a hand and conjured a flame that faded into light. Horror filled Meara's chest, churning her stomach.

"But your partner is not of royal lineage," Aletris argued.

"She is." Emrys stated calmly. "She is the daughter of Lord Daryan and Lady Lakiya, and an heir of the Court of Spring Renewal."

Meara watched her sister's body tense, mirroring her own shock. Daughter of Daryan, the Spring Lord who lost twin daughters. Over twenty years ago. Killed because of a prophecy. That could not be possible.

Silence followed his declaration, before furious whispers broke out throughout those gathered.

Aletris had to knock her staff against the ground once more. "We shall have to confirm this." Her voice was hard, but Meara heard the shock underneath her words.

"Absolutely," Emrys said, his smile feline.

"Very well." Aletris said. "The court rulers shall deliberate to confirm your claim. Are there any others that wish to rise?" She looked over the room. No one addressed her.

Emrys ducked into a shallow bow. "We await your word. I do have one request. Please delay ruling upon the charges against Lady Meara until tomorrow."

Aletris looked to the lords and ladies around her and then nodded. "Very well."

"Thank you," Brenna said, smiling graciously. She dipped into a graceful curtsey, though she kept her chin high.

Meara looked to Cerne, her frown deepening. His eyes flicked to her and away. "Did you know?" she hissed.

Cerne's lip curled and he refused to answer her.

Emrys took Brenna's hand and ushered her down the walkway. She walked with her head high and shoulders back. Meara stared, her shock ebbing into anguish at the thought her sister was to wed a faerie she barely knew. The crowd began to disperse, and Cerne finally turned toward her. She glared at him. "Did you know who we were?"

He crossed his arms. "If I had any evidence that you were my friend's deceased daughters, I never would have brought you here."

She stared at him and the way his face hardened. "Did you suspect?"

Cerne scoffed, but did not answer her question. "You must return to your assigned rooms until tomorrow." He nodded to two uniformed guards who seized her arms. "This is for your safety. Others would not wait until your sentencing to exact revenge. I cannot protect you any longer."

"I can walk!" she said, struggling against them. "Cerne, I am not done with this." He turned away from her, leaving her almost feral, growling as the guards pulled her out of the throne room.

Meara planted her feet until the guards were practically carrying her. She snarled at them, when they were intercepted. Luce crossed his arms, biceps bulging in a subtle threat. "Sirs, I will take her to her room."

"My lord, we have orders," one protested.

Luce held up a hand glowing with light. "I am the one with light magic that can control her. Do you really want to risk her nightmares swallowing you up?"

Meara grit her teeth. She did not control nightmares. Though she felt as if she was in one. She fought the fog of panic overtaking her brain, trying to recall what was stated of the prophecy and Daryan's daughters. All she could remember was that some faerie wanted them killed to eliminate the threat they would become. And that the Lord of the Summer was responsible for their supposed death. Her breath wavered as she looked up at Luce. The guards stepped back and he held out a hand to usher her forward. She shouldn't go with him, but she had no choice.

They navigated halls she did not recognize in uneasy silence. She couldn't help but feel she was walking to her death. "Are you going to finish the job your father started?" she finally asked. The least he could do was be honest about his intentions.

Luce's jaw ticked as he ground his teeth together. She waited for an answer that did not come until he pushed open a sunburst door and brought her into the summer court apartments.

Before she could take in the room, Luce turned and slammed his hand into the wall, penning her between the closed door and his bulky frame. She swallowed, noticing how much broader he was than Cerne. He could crush her with his bare hands, no need for his magic.

"Meara." Her name was a plea on his lips. "If I wanted you dead, it would be so easy. But I am not my father."

She raised her chin. "I'm the reason your father is dead."

"He was cruel. I hold no anger toward Daryan."

Flinching, she looked up into Luce's mismatched eyes. "Then why the feud?"

He laughed. "I simply do not like Cerne."

Her world was falling apart around her and she was backed up against a wall with someone who should be her enemy leaning over her. A hysterical laugh worked its way out of her throat.

"Meara," he said again, silencing her. "You need to leave."

"I can't."

"You must," he reiterated.

Meara frowned, crossing her arms. "I have to protect Brenna."

"How are you going to do that from the prison built under this castle?"

"My sister is becoming queen. She won't let that happen."

His laughter was short and humorless. "Emrys will not allow that. She may pardon you, but Emrys will keep you far from Brenna. Whether it be exile or imprisonment in another form, he will not allow you to stay here, nor will he let you go free."

"All the more reason that I have to protect my sister, no matter the consequence."

"You are going to have to trust me to watch out for her, because you cannot, no matter how determined you are otherwise." His tone left no room for argument.

"If I refuse?"

He paused, running his hand through his hair. "Meara, I am asking you to let me help. You can write to Brenna, and if I am wrong, I can bring you back once things are cleared up."

She exhaled sharply, and Luce took it as acceptance.

"I've spoken to Sigmis. He can shelter you in his court. He wields shadows as well, so it's a good opportunity for you to gain better control and learn the extent of your abilities."

"The Court of Darkness?" she asked, shocked he would suggest such a thing. "They are the reason this war happened!"

"You don't believe that," Luce said, tilting his head. "And perhaps you can speak with Elysia and Kyrell and learn the truth of their situation."

"Unlikely," she said with a growl.

"Meara, you must trust me," Luce growled, deeper and rougher.

Hands clenched into fists, Meara huffed. "I suppose I have no choice."

"We must get you out of here before the nobles such as my mother begin to travel home after the coronation tomorrow morning."

"Coronation," she repeated, her expression crumpling into bitter defeat. "She's going to marry him."

"We cannot stop it," Luce said, pausing. "I'm sorry."

Meara dragged her hand over her face. "I wish I could talk to her. But it probably wouldn't do any good."

Luce nodded silently.

"So what's the plan?"

Harin of the Summer Court arrived an hour later, his horse ready to ride. The fae spoke quietly for a few minutes, and then Luce boosted her to sit on the horse's haunches with her arms looped around Harin's waist.

"Are you ready?" the illusionist asked.

"No, but I have no choice," Meara said, her voice hollow.

"Be safe and swift," Luce said, patting the horse's shoulder. Harin nodded. He rested a hand on Meara's thigh, and she felt a shimmer of his magic as he cast an illusion to hide her.

She leaned against his back as they rode out of Court Tara and turned north, toward the Summer Court. It felt as if her heart was being ripped out and left behind in the white stone palace, and she vowed she would return for Brenna when she was strong enough.

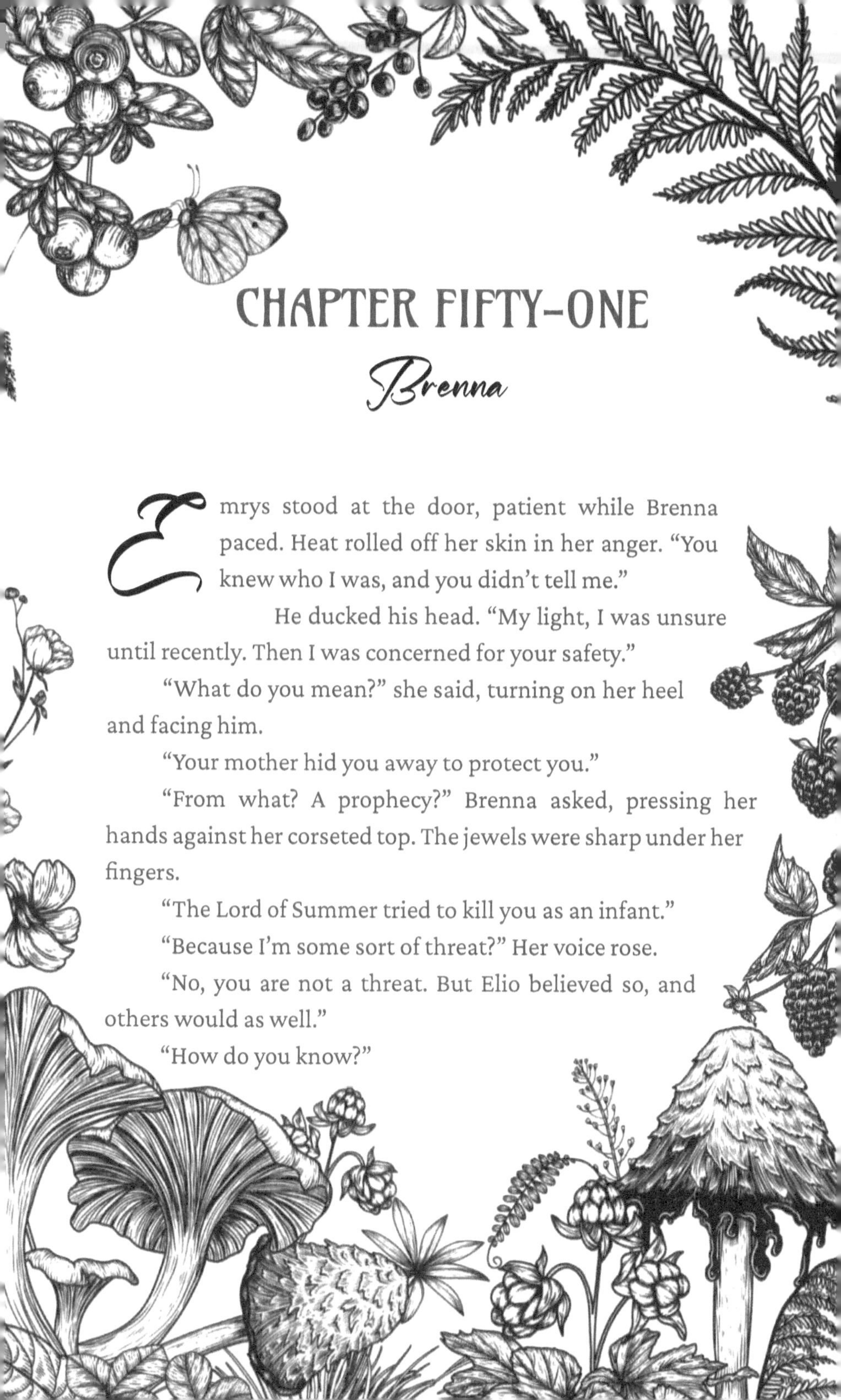

CHAPTER FIFTY-ONE

Brenna

Emrys stood at the door, patient while Brenna paced. Heat rolled off her skin in her anger. "You knew who I was, and you didn't tell me."

He ducked his head. "My light, I was unsure until recently. Then I was concerned for your safety."

"What do you mean?" she said, turning on her heel and facing him.

"Your mother hid you away to protect you."

"From what? A prophecy?" Brenna asked, pressing her hands against her corseted top. The jewels were sharp under her fingers.

"The Lord of Summer tried to kill you as an infant."

"Because I'm some sort of threat?" Her voice rose.

"No, you are not a threat. But Elio believed so, and others would as well."

"How do you know?"

"We can review the prophecy, but I know you are not a threat to the fae. Being powerful does not make you dangerous. You are their new queen." Emrys tucked her hair behind her ear, trailing his finger over the gold cuffs. "We have a seer ready to marry us under the moon in under two hours."

"Two hours," she echoed. "My father is Daryan, Cerne's exiled friend." The stories she had heard began to click together in her mind. "He is here."

Frowning, Emrys ran his hand down her arm and took her hand. "I'm sorry, Daryan left immediately after the battle. I had to compel him to come and help, and once the task was complete, he departed."

"Compel?"

"With my blood magic. It was a combination of crafts that exiled him, tied to his blood through me."

"Did he know about us?" she asked, her eyes falling to the carpeted floor.

"No." Emrys ran his thumb over her knuckles. "But we can contact him if you wish. But not before our wedding and coronation. Right now, we must prepare."

"I don't know what to do," she said. "What is expected of me?"

Exhaustion and desperation fought to overwhelm her, until only his touch anchored her.

He kissed her forehead. "Attendants will get you ready. And then we will recite vows and seal it with a kiss. It is nothing to worry about."

Her teeth sank into her bottom lip. Sighing, Emrys rubbed his hands down her arms. His voice was low and warm. "It will be fine. Try to relax. I have to go. The court rulers should have decided by now if we are to be the next high king and queen. Servants will be here soon to help you."

"I have to talk to my sister," she said. "She is probably worried sick right now."

Emrys sighed. "There is no time to go to her, but if you write her a letter, I will have it delivered."

"Thank you," she said faintly.

"You'll find supplies in the desk. I'll have someone fetch you in a bit." He buried his fingers in her hair and kissed her soundly. When his mouth was on hers, it felt as if everything would be alright. And then he was gone.

Brenna brushed the delicate petals of the flowers crowning her brow. Spiky dahlias, delicate cannas, and ruffled ranunculus woven together with more flowers she couldn't identify, all of them a deep crimson.

Her hair spiraled over her shoulders, but the attendants had intertwined small braids with golden beads, so her hair sparkled when she moved. She was exhausted, but they had to wed tonight if they were to be crowned in the morning's light.

"Are you ready, my lady?" A petite nymph addressed her. His hair was moss and his skin a soft green to match. He smiled up at her politely. She wondered if he had served Queen Araluen, and guilt prickled at her. She didn't mean to replace the elegant high queen, but it was what was necessary.

"Yes, I think so," Brenna said. Her fingers tangled as she tried to keep from messing up the beautiful makeup and finery the attendants had created.

"Right this way," he said, opening the door for her.

Tayen waited in the hall. His injuries were healed, but dark circles shadowed his eyes. "You look lovely, Brenna," he said softly.

She rushed forward and threw her arms around him. "I'm so glad you're here."

"Of course," he murmured. "Cerne and Ayala are waiting outside already, but I hoped to walk you." She linked her arm through his, and it felt familiar and reassuring. He leaned close enough that the servants trailing them would not overhear. "Are you sure I can't talk you out of this?" It sounded like a jest, but his eyes were deadly serious.

"No, I have to do this," she said, resolute. "And I want to."

Tayen was quiet for a moment as they walked. "I truly hope he makes you happy and doesn't hurt you. But if he does, I will be here."

"Tayen," she said, her stomach feeling hollow at his declaration. "I love you. Thank you for being my friend."

He smiled, but it faded. Frowning, Brenna tugged on his arm. "What's wrong?"

"Nothing." His smile was back, brighter.

"Tayen."

Exhaling, he ran his fingers through his curls. "I do not want to share my troubles at your wedding."

"We aren't there yet, and it's not normal circumstances. So please tell me."

Tayen swallowed and glanced down at her. "I spoke with Eladin before he left, and he no longer wishes to see me."

"What?" she yelped. "Why?"

"He is the crown prince now, and that comes with certain expectations."

"Tayen, I am so sorry." She slowed, placing her other hand on his shoulder. "I am sure he regrets that already. And perhaps things will work out after all." The pain in his eyes stopped her words.

"I'm afraid you have bigger concerns." Tayen cleared his throat, resuming their walk. Servants waited in the entry hall to open the looming doors for them. "What about your sister?"

Brenna held her breath for a moment. "I'm doing this for her. As queen, I can pardon her."

Tayen's voice was soft, just for her. "We can find another way. Do not marry him if that is your reason."

"It's not. But the urgency is to do with that."

He nodded, accepting her answer.

A million stars glimmered overhead as they descended the stairs. Emrys waited upon a stallion draped in lace, garnet fabric over a coat of night. He lifted her up to sit before him, his arm snaking around her waist securely. As they rode through Court Tara, he whispered praise and promises of their life together with his lips to her neck.

Nobles waited along the ramparts and bridges to witness their marriage ceremony. Brenna's heart raced, not knowing what to expect. The night air nipped at her bare feet, making her feel like a child.

At the edge of the river, Emrys dismounted. She slid off the horse into his arms, closing her eyes in a moment of comfort before facing the expanse of flowing water and the wide arc of fae witnessing.

Hand in hand, they walked into the water to the point the two rivers converged once more before branching out as they reached for the sea. The icy current rippled over her toes and tugged at her dress. She shivered from the cold.

Emrys leaned close and ran his hands over her arms, using her own magic to warm her skin. His palms skimmed down her forearms until he captured her hands. He was so handsome with crimson flowers matching the shade of his eyes, his skin a milky tone in the moonlight. The way he looked at her, she felt treasured.

She glanced at Tayen, standing with Ayala and Cerne along the bridge. The only thing that would make it better was if Meara was there too. But that was not allowed. Tomorrow she could pardon her sister and free her. Surely Meara could forgive the rushed wedding when it meant her freedom. Brenna took a slow, calming breath as she reminded herself of that. Meara had never failed her, and now that she had the chance to save her, she would not fall short.

Emrys squeezed her hand, and she smiled up at him. His expression was soft, but somber, as the seer approached. The sylph wore long, flowing robes that trailed in the water. Moonstone adorned her neck and hair.

She led them in repeating vows, and Brenna echoed Emrys, each word sending her pulse pounding in her ears and drowning out the river.

"By moonlight and sunfire,
I pledge my soul to yours.
As constant as the river's flow,
I bind my heart to you.
May our bond be as ancient as the star's song
and as enduring as the mountain's stone."

Emrys grinned, lifting her hands to show that her palms were glowing. Brenna's anxiety fell away and she smiled back, letting Emrys tug her forward by their joined hands. He dipped her sideways and kissed her.

Clapping resonated around them, but Brenna could think of nothing but his lips on hers. Her flower crown began to slip, and she grabbed it. Emrys lifted her back onto her feet, leaning down to kiss her once more.

"My wife," he growled, "and my queen."

All she could do was reach up and pull his face down to meet hers again. The seer officiating walked away, leaving them standing with the shallow river rippling around them as they pressed closer, his hand firm on the small of her back as she clung to his jacket.

"Come, we should celebrate," Emrys said. He swept her up, sending a spray of water into the air from the hem of her dress. With haste, he carried her to his horse. They rode the ways up the hill to the castle, to the king's palace that would soon be theirs.

She leaned against him, relieved the ceremony was over. Emrys placed brief kisses along the shell of her ear before pulling her hair to the side and kissing the nape of her neck. She sighed as his teeth scraped the sensitive skin there.

"I can't wait to get you back to our rooms," he murmured.

She rested her head back against his shoulder. "I believe there is a feast in our honor. Our attendance is expected."

"I don't care."

"I'd like to go," she said gently.

Emrys sighed. "For you."

"Thank you, husband," she said, testing out the word. His grip across her stomach tightened, clearly liking the word.

"By the way, I sent a summons to your brother. I thought you'd like to meet him," he said.

"My brother?" She blinked.

"Yes, you are the younger sister of Amadi, the Lord of Spring. He is a kind faerie, and I think you will like him."

"Thank you," she stammered, still reeling from the revelation.

The banquet hall was bursting with nobles, far more than the night they had met. It felt much the same, but there was a nervous energy among the people who stood when they entered.

Emrys raised his hand in greeting, and cheers broke out. Her cheeks tingled with a blush at all the attention. Her new husband led her to a raised table at the end of the hall.

Musicians played soft music as they were served a fine dinner, despite the late hour. She ate venison glazed with berries and roasted mushrooms, along a pudding of roasted, sugared hazelnuts. Emrys distracted her from her meal frequently as he kissed her any time a guest was not visiting their table to wish them well. And most nobles in attendance made sure to pay their respects, no doubt trying to earn good standing with the future rulers.

The army commander, Herrick, wished them well and presented her with a jeweled dagger. It was lovely, but she was relieved when an attendant whisked it away.

Aletris approached, a courtly smile in place. She expressed her joy at their union and offered Emrys a sun charm with a bit of sunlight trapped inside of it. The carved crystal gleamed at his neck, showing the favor of the Summer Court.

Galen visited long enough to thank her for healing. Emrys dismissed him quickly, and Brenna squeezed his hand in reprimand. He took the opportunity to pull her closer and nibble on her neck.

With a goblet of sparkling elderberry wine, Brenna strolled the room with Emrys beside her. She knew her sister was not in attendance, but she couldn't help but look for her. Emrys leaned in close, his voice smooth. "Will you dance with me?"

Exhaustion pressed upon her, so she was grateful for the gentle music. Emrys's grip never faltered, and he turned her gently, mostly holding her tight against him. She could fall asleep standing, tucked into his arms.

When she yawned for the third time, he insisted they retire to their rooms. They left the room to continue dancing and eating, and he led her down the hall to his chambers. She would keep her own rooms for now, but she had no intention of sleeping in them ever again.

There was a cozy familiarity to slipping her dress off while her new husband shrugged his jacket off and unfastened the jewels at his cuffs. She bit her lip while selecting a small wisp of night dress in dark red, his favorite color. They only had a few hours before the coronation, but it was their wedding night. Excited heat fluttered in her stomach as she turned to face him, but the worried line of his mouth changed her mood in a split second.

"What?"

He dropped his head, dragging his hand through his hair. "I got word during our dinner. Your sister has fled."

She had ignored her worries all evening, reassuring herself that Meara was safely locked in the palace and away from any harm until Brenna could sort out the mess she landed herself in. But that wasn't the case. And she should have known Meara wouldn't tolerate being locked in a cage, no matter how short the time was or how comfortable the cage. She swore, clutching her middle, trying to breathe through the panic.

"How?" she spluttered.

"They don't know. No one seems to know anything." He shook his head, his expression pained. "I'm sorry, my love."

"Are you sure she left on her own? Or would someone have taken her to hurt her? Or hurt us?" Her fingers pressed to her lips.

"There is no reason to think anyone forced her to leave. There would have been signs of a struggle, and she has her shadow craft."

She stared at the window, where the curtains were pulled back to reveal the night sky. Emrys stepped closer, placed an arm over her shoulders and pulled her against him.

"Did you give her my letter explaining?"

Emrys nodded. "It was placed in her room. I do not know if she chose to read it." Brenna exhaled harshly, resting her head back against him. "We will find her. But first, we must gain the power we need to protect her." He kissed her hair. "Besides, this isn't the first time she's run off."

Irritation sent warmth through her body, but he was right, Brenna realized. This was becoming a habit for Meara. She chose to run instead of trusting her. Turning in his arms, she nestled against Emrys' chest. His hands stroked her hair and down her back, soothing her.

"It will be okay," he said softly. "I love you, and I know she is important to you, so she is important to me."

"Thank you," she whispered as he pinched her jaw in his fingers and raised her mouth to meet his. There was a solemness to their movements. This bond was no longer simple passion.

Partnership and a responsibility to their people had deepened the significance behind their relationship. Bound by magic and now by vows, she felt the deep meaning in each touch of his fingers on her skin, each time he pressed his lips to her body. She let her devotion show in how she returned his affection.

The sunrise rose from a blood red to a pale daffodil as Brenna waited in the throne room. She stood tall, putting forth a confidence she did not feel. The corset built into her dress kept her back straight, and she was grateful for its snug embrace.

She wore the same dress as the first time they were presented at court, not so long ago - when she had met Emrys. It was her favorite, with a multitude of fabric wildflowers cascading down her body. It looked regal, and she felt like a princess. Soon to be a queen.

Emrys held her hand, though it was the only place they touched. He wore a burgundy doublet stitched with gold. Matching gold rings glinted in his ears. They made a stunning pair.

The throne room was full to bursting with nobles and citizens of the high king's court, all anxious to see a new king crowned. The seer was present, her hair braided and pinned back now.

"Come forward and present yourself," the seer said. Emrys took a step, and Brenna followed his lead. They stopped before her, their backs to the crowd of witnesses.

As she raised her hands, those gathered hushed.

"Do you swear to uphold the law of our lands, provide counsel to the rulers of each court, keep the peace between them, and care for all of the faeries that will be your subjects?"

"I do," Emrys said.

Brenna drew in breath and raised her chin. "I do, as well."

"Very well."

An attendant provided the seer with a thick cord made of many strands of different colors: solid black, pale pink, intense orange, metallic gold, solid white, stone gray. The seer raised the cord high for all to see.

"With this, I bind you to all of the fae courts, for you will lead and serve all of them equally."

Emrys raised their intertwined hands and the seer wrapped the cord around their wrists, tying them together with a complex knot. She took a vessel and dabbed a sweet smelling liquid to their foreheads, between their brows and at their temples.

"I anoint you as the chosen leaders of this realm, per the loyalty of the courts and the magic of the land."

Anticipation tensed in Brenna's chest, leaving her breaths shallow and uneven. The moment had come, and she wasn't sure that she had truly believed it would happen.

The seer held up a crown of delicate gold filigree studded with rubies. Brenna ducked her head and allowed it to be placed over her curls. Its weight was strange.

Emrys was next. A crown of gold stained with black. The carved details stood out in gilded relief, surrounded by shadow. He smiled as it was placed upon his black hair.

The seer raised both of her hands, and Brenna jolted as her eyes went white. The voice that poured from her lips was both high and deep, like a chorus speaking in perfect harmony.

"Blood weds flame, two rival lines entwined,

Fire to heal and fire to consume,
As the blood of the people feeds the land,
Shadows rise and darkness looms.
One sister destined to rule, the other to shatter the throne,
Bound by blood, by choice, and by fate."

She came out of her trance with a small gasp. She turned, raising her hands, and declared, "I give you the Fire Queen and her Blood King."

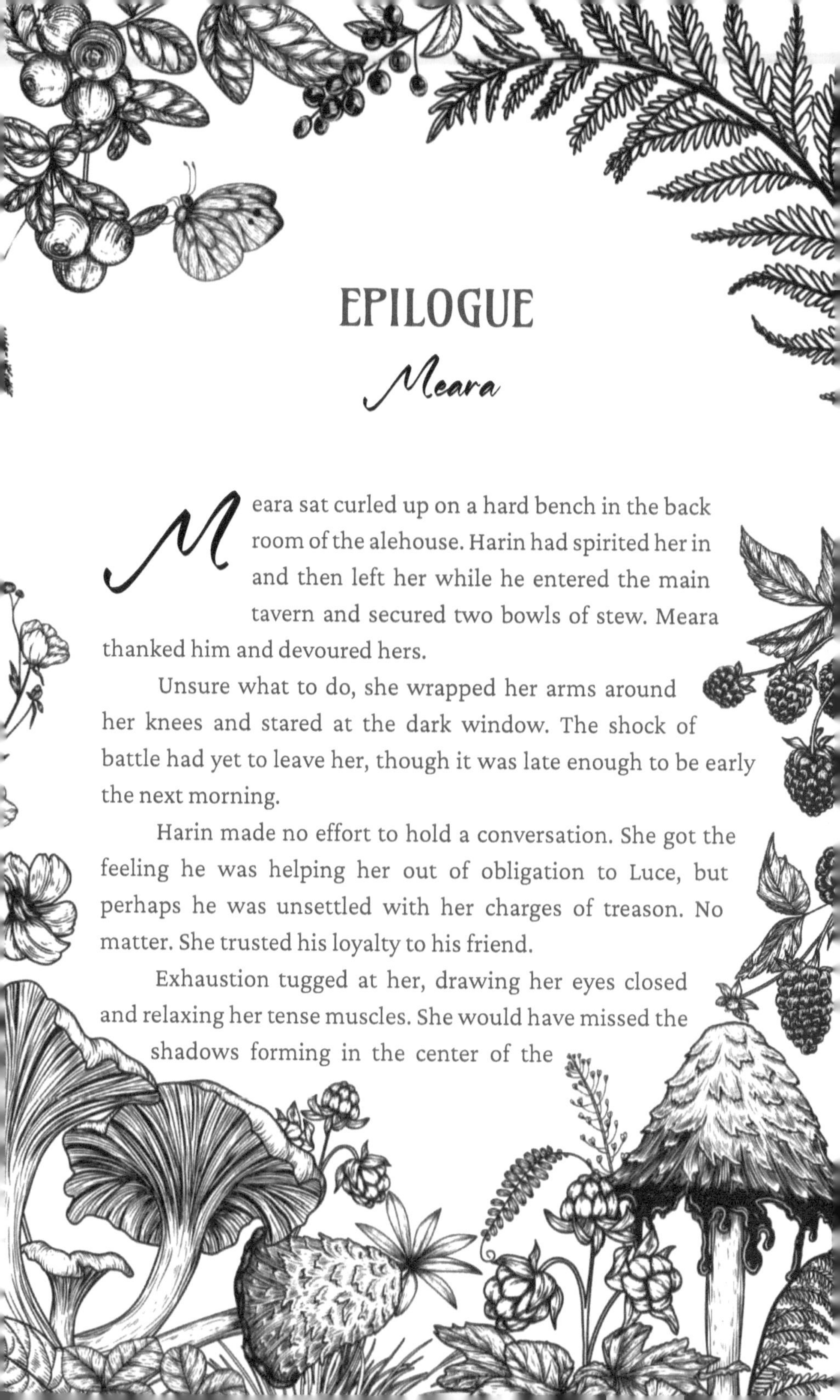

EPILOGUE
Meara

Meara sat curled up on a hard bench in the back room of the alehouse. Harin had spirited her in and then left her while he entered the main tavern and secured two bowls of stew. Meara thanked him and devoured hers.

Unsure what to do, she wrapped her arms around her knees and stared at the dark window. The shock of battle had yet to leave her, though it was late enough to be early the next morning.

Harin made no effort to hold a conversation. She got the feeling he was helping her out of obligation to Luce, but perhaps he was unsettled with her charges of treason. No matter. She trusted his loyalty to his friend.

Exhaustion tugged at her, drawing her eyes closed and relaxing her tense muscles. She would have missed the shadows forming in the center of the room, if it wasn't for the distinct feel of magic building. She sat up, hands going to her belt where a weapon should have waited. Gritting her teeth, she watched the darkness grow until a fae male stepped through it.

His tan skin was darker in the dim, his black hair an indistinct mass. While her hair looked like a raven's feather, his looked like the abyss. Eyes like onyx jewels regarded her.

"You must be the girl that needs my help," he said with a sly smile.

"Lord Sigmis," she said in greeting. He dipped into a shallow bow in reply. "Thank you for your help."

She wanted to jump back and run, but she also felt in her bones that Luce was trustworthy, and if he called Sigmis his friend and wanted her to go with him, then she should.

She had few other options: imprisonment, fleeing to the human lands, looking for another fae court to give her sanctuary. Trusting Luce seemed like the best choice. Nodding, she stepped forward and accepted Sigmis' outstretched hand.

His shadows felt different than hers. Hers buzzed with energy, and his felt like that would steal energy from her. They felt hungry. She tensed as he drew her forward and into darkness. Cold washed over her.

When the darkness lifted, she stood in a wide space. It could have been a throne room if there was a throne, but it was simply empty. The floor was black stone with glass set into it. Her eyes widened. Beneath the glass, something moved. It was fiery and bright, and she realized it was molten lava.

Her gaze shot to the window. Black rock stretched out from his home before the landscape melted into snowy hills and forest. They were within a mountain filled with lava.

"Is your home on a volcano?" she blurted, shock overriding her good manners.

Sigmis shrugged. "It keeps us warm." She gaped at him. He strode across the floor away from her without another word.

"Wait, what do I do?" she asked, jogging to keep up with his fluid gait. He ignored her, and she bristled.

When he opened the dark wood door, it revealed two people standing on the other side. One was a younger version of Sigmis, with a charming boyish quality to his face. He grinned at her. Beside him, a young woman clung to his arm. Innocent eyes framed in dark lashes looked up at her from a pale complexion. Blood red hair hung around her shoulders in loose waves. Princess Elysia.

Meara stopped mid stride and stood frozen, staring at the pair. Elysia did not look like a prisoner. A healthy flush filled her cheeks, her eyes sparkling. It was nothing like the withdrawn princess she had seen those weeks ago in Dornadan.

"Princess," she croaked.

"Oh, you know who I am!" she exclaimed sweetly.

A dozen questions rushed through Meara's head, and she struggled to sort through the conflicting thoughts. Beneath it, anger swirled, growing.

Kyrell pushed past his older brother. "Come along, you must be exhausted. You should rest."

At his side, Elysia reached out and took her hand. "I heard what you did for my people. Thank you for trying to protect them."

Meara flinched. She had failed in that goal, and it was the last thing she wanted to discuss. Instead, she asked, "Why are you here?"

Elysia's brows furrowed as her head tilted. Intervening, Kyrell waved his hands to move them forward. "Come along, there will be plenty of time later to talk. It's past time for bed."

Numbly, Meara followed his instructions and began walking. Elysia walked beside her, stunning with a delicate slope to her nose and dark lips that curved in a cupid's bow even when she smiled.

From the glances Elysia exchanged with Kyrell, it was clear they were in love, and Meara's stomach clenched at the revelation. How could their love possibly be worth the war they caused? Her jaw clenched, keeping those thoughts inside her head.

They led her to a small bedroom, and Elysia drew the curtains to shut out the stars. "You should sleep as long as you can. We have plenty of time to sort things out."

"Yes, thank you," Meara said.

Kyrell bowed slightly. "Until then."

Once the door was closed, Meara sank onto the bed. Despite her spinning thoughts and worries over her sister. Exhaustion dragged her down, muffling her anxieties until she lay on the bed and let sleep drag her under.

CHARACTER GLOSSARY

Queendom of Liosliath

Meara Aldridge *(Mee-ra)* - Sister of Brenna and daughter of Aisling, apothecary assistant

Brenna Aldridge *(Breh-nuh)* - Sister of Meara, daughter of Aisling

Aisling Aldridge *(Ash-ling)* - Apothecary of Liosliath, adoptive mother of Meara and Brenna

Luella *(Loo-eh-lah)* - Works at her family's bakery, courting Sandon

Orla *(Or-lah)* - Younger sister of Luella, works at her family's bakery

Mrs. Fisher *(Fish-er)* - Housekeeper at the Lyndhurst estate

Herman "Hermie" Lyndhurst *(Her-man)* - Oldest son

Lottie Lyndhurst *(Lah-tee)* - Middle child of Johnathon

Clarence Lyndhurst *(Clair-ence)* - Youngest son of Johnathon

Johnathon Lyndhurst *(John-uh-thon)* - Master of the Lyndhurst estate, minor nobility, employer of Mrs. Fisher and Brenna

Sandon *(San-dun)* - Son of a farmer, courting Luella

Kipp *(Kip)* - the butcher's son, friend of Sandon

Queen Malacia *(Muh-lay-shuh)* - Queen of Liosliath, married King Barrach of Tuar

King Barrach *(Bah-rahk)* - King of Tuar, married Queen Malacia of Liosliath and merged their kingdoms

Princess Elysia *(Eh-lih-see-uh)* - Daughter of King Barrach and his first wife, betrothed to King Eldric of Dornadan

The Court of Autumn Harvest

Cerne *(Sern)* - Lord of Autumn, shifts into a stag

Tayen *(Tay-en)* - Ambassador for the Autumn Court

Ryles *(Riles)* – Steward for the Autumn Court, Dryad

Kirrily *(Keer-uh-lee)* -Attendant, Daughter of Ryles, Dryad

Seda *(Say-duh)* - Master of the Autumn Guard

Ayala *(Eye-yah-la)* - Sister to Tayen, spymaster, Sylph

Dyani (*Dy-yahn-nee*) – Dressmaker, Fawnling

Perran (*Peh-run*) – Healer, Brownie

The Court of Learning

Xurey *(Zur-ree)* - A traveler, shifts into a horse, Puca

The Rangers

Farran (*Fair-an*) - Leader of the Rangers, rides Tavora

Lorand (*Lohr-and*) - Second in command of the Rangers, rides Runa

Cahira (*Kuh-herr-uh*) - Member of the Rangers, rides Baran

Melisande (*Mel-ih-sahnd*) - Nobility, betrothed to Farran

The Court of Summer Harvest

Aletris (*Ah-lee-trus*) - Lady of the Summer Court, Nymph

Luce (*Loose*) - Heir of the Summer Court, son of Aletris and Elio

Vasara (*Vah-s-ar-uh*) - Friend of Luce, Ice Sprite

Harin (*Har-in*) - Friend of Luce, spy for the Summer Court

High Court Tara

Argyro (*Ar-jeer-ro*) - High King, spouse of Araluen, the Silver King

Araluen (*Ah-ruh-loo-en*) - High Queen, the River Queen

Emrys (*Em-ris*) - Advisor to Argyro, son of Baelor, cousin of Luce

Iyashi (*Eye-yash-i*) - Adept healer, Naiad

Galen (*Gay-len*) - Master healer, Ramsling

Herrick (*Hair-ric*) - High Army Commander, Drake

The Court of Spring Renewal

Amadi (*Ah-mah-dee*) - Lord of the Spring Court

Daryan (*Dair-ee-an*) - Exiled former Lord of Spring, wedded to Lakiya, father of Amadi and unnamed twin girls

Lakiya (*Lah-kai-yuh*) - Former Lady of Spring, wedded to Lord Daryan

The Court of Snow and Shadow

Caelia (*Say-lee-uh*) – Lady of the Court of Snow and Shadow

Seren (*Seh-ren*) – Seer, Sylph

The Court of Void and Darkness

Sigmis (*Sig-miss*) - Lord of Darkness, Shadow Sprite

Kyrell (*Kye-rell*) - Heir of the Court of Darkness

Kingdom of Dornadan

King Eldric (*El-drik*) - Widowed King of Dornadan, father of Emeric, Eladin, and adoptive father of Rydan

Prince Emeric (*Em-muh-rik*) - Heir to the throne

Prince Eladin (*Eh-luh-din*) - Second son of King Eldric

Prince Rydan (*Rye-dan*) - Warrior, adopted son of Eldric

Creatures

Airgid *(Arr-gid)* - Silver dappled stallion, Ayala's mount

Eirlys *(Eye-rliss)* – Feisty white mare, Tayen's mount

Bran (*Br-an*) - Black gelding of the Autumn Court

Clover (*Cl-o-v-er*) - Buckskin mare of the Autumn Court

Harkin (*Har-kin*) - Bay stallion, Cerne's mount

Kemuri (*Keh-moo-ree*) – Blue roan mare, Rydan's mount

Sorin (*Soah-rin*) - Hunting hound loyal to Luce

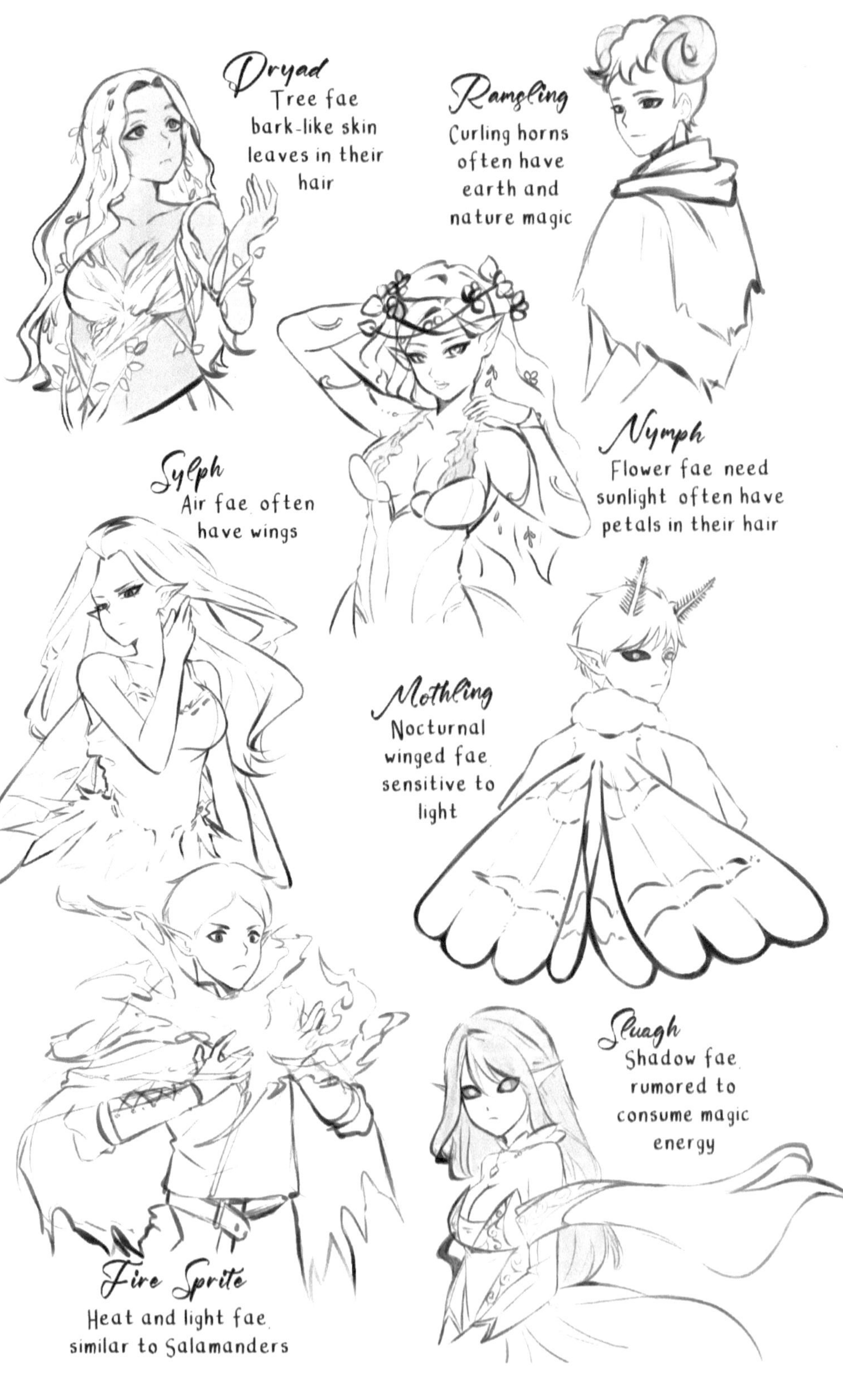

Dryad
Tree fae bark-like skin leaves in their hair
Ramsling
Curling horns often have earth and nature magic
Sylph
Air fae often have wings
Nymph
Flower fae need sunlight often have petals in their hair
Mothling
Nocturnal winged fae sensitive to light
Sluagh
Shadow fae rumored to consume magic energy
Fire Sprite
Heat and light fae similar to Salamanders

Guide to Common Fae

Dearg Due
Blood-drinking fae have fangs prefer darkness

Frost Sprite
Ice fae prefer colder places

Fawnling
Fae with deer ears some have antlers or tails

Brownie
Earth fae often live in burrows commonly have healing magic

Huldra
Fae with fox ears some with tails prefer to live along rivers

Drake
Scaled fae may have horns often have fire magic

Naiad
River fae may be aquatic see also Merrows and Nixies

ACKNOWLEDGEMENTS

Thank you to my husband for holding down the fort while I'm writing. And to my mother for always cheering me on and fixing my spelling.

Thank you to Ilea, Karina, and Anandi for your editing and encouragement. I can't imagine where this story would be without you (probably half written and abandoned on a hard drive).

Thank you to my author crew for afternoon writing sprints and late nights brainstorming plot points. Especially Tereza Kane and Harlowe Savage as we lift each other up in this insane process called publishing.

Thank you to my wonderful artists, Bamboo, Olesia Bezuhla, Yuma Yukino, Art by Tori, and Hannah Sternjakob, and Bronwynn Gooch.

Thank you to my wonderful audiobook narrator Sarah Ruth Thomas for bringing my story to life in a brand new way and for your endless patience.

Thank you to authors K.M. Davidson and Katherine E.N., and also Dakota for beta reading this book and giving me invaluable feedback. And thank you to Kristina for your endless encouragement.

Lastly, thank you to Laura, the owner of Literally, a Bookshop, for helping to bring my books to the world.

BOOKS BY ALY HOLLIS

Bracken Creek Wolves

Campfires and Canines
Moonlight and Mischief
Secrets and S'mores
Wolves and Watercolors
Soulmates and Snow Drifts

Flipped Fairytales

Wish Me Freely
as a part of a multi-author collection

Sablewood Trilogy

Raven Rebel
Ember Queen
TBA

ABOUT THE AUTHOR

Aly Hollis lives in the sunny southwest with her husband and two preteens. She loves writing cozy fantasy and angsty paranormal romance. Raven Rebel is her epic high fantasy debut.

Aside from writing, Aly likes to bake, paint, and debate book tropes with her friends.

Aly is currently writing the sequel to Raven Rebel, which will be called Ember Queen and is expected to release in 2026.

For updates, follow along on social media or join her email list!